AN AWAKENING HEART

AN AWAKENING HEART

A NOVEL OF THE MORAVIANS
IN EARLY AMERICA

BARBARA DOWD WRIGHT

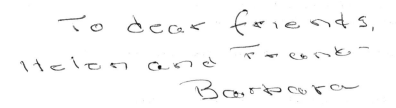

To dear friends,
Helen and Frank-
Barbara

Moon Trail Books · Bethlehem, Pennsylvania

Moon Trail Books, LLC
24 West Fourth Street
Bethlehem, Pennsylvania 18015
Printing by Valley Graphic Services, Inc.
Bethlehem, Pennsylvania

To my family, past and present,
but especially to George

In essentials, unity
in non-essentials, liberty
and in all things, love.

MORAVIAN MOTTO

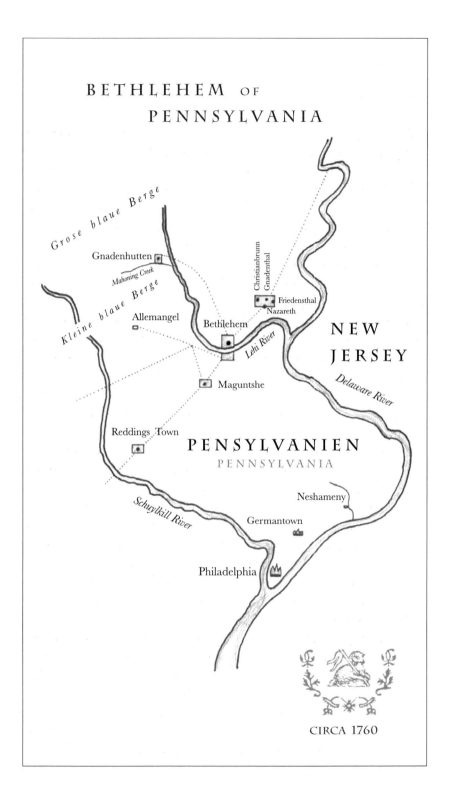

BETHLEHEM OF PENNSYLVANIA

Grose blaue Berge

Gnadenhutten

Mahoning Creek

Kleine blaue Berge

Allemangel

Christianbrunn
Gnadenthal

Friedensthal
Nazareth

Bethlehem

Lehi River

NEW JERSEY

Delaware River

Maguntshe

Reddings Town

PENSYLVANIEN
PENNSYLVANIA

Neshameny

Schuylkill River

Germantown

Philadelphia

CIRCA 1760

AUTHOR'S PREFACE

Perhaps the small, frame house no longer stands in the New England village, but I can remember climbing the hill to the hen house at the edge of the deep woods, or walking the uneven ground of the orchard in search of apples ripe enough to eat in August. I can smell the phlox, then taller than I, see the dark pines and feel the morning sun on my back and the wet grass on my bare feet. The twin mysteries of seeing oneself and being oneself in memory can take me back to that house, where old highboys and low trunks rendered their contents only when Great-Aunt Winnie proclaimed their freedom on a rainy day. As lightning flashed and thunder rumbled, she became a magician and my brother and I wide-eyed participants. She bent over the open lid while we waited to discover the wonders she had rescued from obscurity. On those wet afternoons, she became a merchant in a Middle Eastern bazaar, a Chinese trader from Canton, or a haughty dressmaker. She held shimmering silks and heavy satins; she draped embroidered flower designs on my shoulders and counted into my brother's hands small green scarabs.

Less sensuous, less intriguing at the time, were the contents of the cardboard boxes stacked helter-skelter in one of her upstairs bedrooms. There Great-Aunt Winnie, a prolific diarist herself, showed us the letters and diaries of my mother's family that she had collected and saved. But even the scratches of a quill pen were not nearly as fascinating to me as the silken fabrics my great-uncles had collected in the Far East. At age seven I was not interested in the recorded fragments of lives my great-aunt had collected. I only wondered if she would let me take one green scarab home to the Midwest where I could wrap it carefully to secrete in a dresser drawer.

Many years after Great-Aunt Winnie's death, the boxes came to rest in the attic of my own house. Their contents seemed to push at the cardboard flaps as though daring me to delve in. Hesitantly at first, because I did not know where to start, I began to read at random: pre-Revolutionary War sermons printed written by Puritan ancestors on soft rag paper warning of fire and brimstone; a note of longing my great-grandmother wrote to her husband fighting during the Civil War; letters telling of a great-uncle's rapture while he listened to the soaring strains of Sarasate's violin and marveled at Clara Schuman's skill. What stories previously unknown to me I held in my hands! I kept digging. Then I found a treasure as magical as any of Aunt Winnie's silks and scarabs, starting me on a journey whose end I could not imagine.

These were the diaries of my great-great-grandmother, Sophia Louisa Krause Blech. Born in 1811 in Bethlehem, Pennsylvania, she lived only thirty-five years, but what she called "the receptacle of my feelings" gave me my first glimpse of the lives of her Moravian family. These were pious people whose ancestors had built sturdy stone structures, who educated boys and girls equally, whose trombones echoed throughout the Lehigh Valley. Sophia's ancestors were members of the Church of The United Brethren – later to be called Moravians. They came to the New World in the eighteenth century to build a self-sufficient religious community that encompassed the age-old concepts of their forebears. They held that all people were loved by God. As messengers of faith, they would be "leaven in the bread of Christ" and, by their lived example, bring hope to the world. They brought with them copies of the most sophisticated music of their homelands to play in the valleys of Pennsylvania and hills of North Carolina. Their meticulous records gave me more than a glimpse into the communities they fashioned in the far reaches of the globe. But the individual memoirs of my ancestors spoke to me only in whispers too faint to discern until I traveled to the lands where their personal pilgrimages began. Reading young Sophia's words, I knew I had to take a pilgrimage of my own. I had to know how it all began, not only by reading but by seeing with my eyes and hearing with my ears.

The strains of *Gaudeamus Igitur* filled the narrow street that led to Bethlehem Chapel in the beautiful city of Prague. It was late in the 1990s when I stood in front of that ancient building and remembered the peasant priest, John Hus, whose words ripped the hierarchal fabric of the powerful Roman Catholic Church when he opposed the selling of indulgences and proclaimed that Scripture rather than the Church was the guide for all Christians. He was burned at the stake as a heretic in 1415. But the flames that consumed the life of John Hus burned his idea into the consciousness of a diverse group established in 1457, who called themselves the United Brethren.

At times accepted, at other times persecuted, the United Brethren subsequently established many churches in Moravia, Bohemia and

Poland. Nearly wiped out in the seventeenth century, beginning in 1722, a small remnant found refuge on the estate of a young Saxon count who had possessed a dream from childhood that he would somehow found a new kind of community. Was Count Zinzendorf's dream clear before the refugees asked to settle on his land? Or was it his reading a treatise of the brilliant seventeenth-century Moravian scholar John Amos Comenius that inspired his dream? Caught in the crossfire of Europe's religious wars and exiled from his homeland, Comenius escaped into Poland. Legend says that he knelt at the crest of the Giant Mountains and prayed that God would leave a "Hidden Seed" in the Czech lands that would blossom into a renewed faith and church. Then the martyrdom of Hus would not be in vain.

Comenius' treatise gave reality to Count Zinzendorf's vision that men and women could fashion their lives in imitation of the early Christian communities where the "word became flesh and dwelt among us." They reached out to help those who hungered, taught those who yearned to read the written word, brought solace to those who suffered, and hope to those who dreamed.

I stood on the balcony of the wooden tower that looks out over miles of land. Green in summer, the hills rise gently to meet the sky and a sense of peace and tranquility settles on the well-tended fields and small, neat woodlands in the distance. I could well imagine the first travelers who called themselves the United Brethren arriving from Eastern Europe to find refuge here at Zinzendorf's estate over 200 years ago. Wrenched from their homelands, weary of war, they must have been filled with the zeal of creating a new beginning. On June 17, 1722 the first tree felt the bite of an ax and fell crashing to the ground. The settlement of Herrnhut was born. Within five years, on an August day, the swelling number of souls in Herrnhut pledged loyalty to each other and to the values of their fifteenth-century ideals of faith, love and hope under the guidance of Zinzendorf. The United Brethren were ready to spread their message.

But the felling of the first tree and the songs of praise on that August day could not have been heard by my foremothers. Christina Böhner would have been asleep in her mother's arms in the tiny village of Gelzhausen many miles from Herrnhut. Susannah Eller lay in her cradle in the village of Büdingen, too young to mourn the death of her father. Neither child knew she would travel a lonely road to Herrnhaag in Germany's Wetteravia, to come together with other traveling pilgrims, or that she would be joined by lot to husbands they barely knew and travel later across rough November seas to America.

My excitement mounted as I traveled west from the golden spires of Prague and the tranquil hills of the count's estate. I wanted to imagine the pilgrims' fervor as they approached the place where their journey would begin. I wanted to feel what it was like for them and to breathe the summer air, to hear their hymns that echoed from gentle hills throughout the valley. Most of all I wanted to share the story of their eager innocence as they caught the corner of a vision that would grow as they traveled the rough roads of an eighteenth-century wilderness.

I drove past the medieval town of Büdingen, its stone towers touched pink by the sun and its surrounding moat now dry. Driving so quickly, I thought of my forebears' slow journey as they walked the many miles from Switzerland, Swabia and Silesia. A few miles past Büdingen a sign announced Ronneberg. I knew I was close, but when I asked for directions to Herrnhaag, I was met with a questioning stare. A bit farther down the road, I saw a small, wooden sign. It said Herrnhaag.

I left the car to walk toward a massive stone building, its dormered windows dark and unwelcoming. My feet flattened the high grass, trampling the Queen Anne's lace that lay like a dusting of snow on summer's green and gold. There were poppies, too, their redness sprinkled as though some Titan had pricked his finger and, at the first sharp pain, shaken his hand above the landscape. What happened there so long ago when my ancestors gathered before they left for faraway places? I have no photographs or paintings to let me trace the shape of their mouths, the color of their hair. Did Christina Böhner love young Matthew Krause before their future was sealed by lot? And when did Susannah Eller learn to trust George Partsch? Did the sound of their own sweet voices raised in song give them the courage to take a large leap into the unknown?

I have written their stories not only from the words of their memoirs and the church diaries that record their lives, but from the spaces between the words where I can hear the sound of their hearts, passed on to me by an endless Möbius ring of DNA that lives through the centuries. Their courage and struggle to live, joyfully and kindly, in a peaceful community during America's birthing, often overwhelms me and still astonishes me. And although the nature of another's faith is always uncertain, I know I have translated their passion if not with perfect accuracy, at least with love.

HISTORICAL NOTE

The Moravians, formerly called The Unitas Fratrum, have been referred to by some as The Happy People. How can this be so? Their spiritual ancestor, the Bohemian priest and teacher Jan Hus, was burned at the stake in 1415; their seventeenth-century Bishop, John Amos Comenius, called the Father of Modern Education, was exiled from his native Moravia into Poland. Persecuted, tortured for their faith, and almost annihilated, these early pilgrims nevertheless carried within them the persistent belief that God was present in each human being's awakened heart, and their faith gratefully acknowledged God's ongoing attendance in human history.

In the year 1720, a small number of weary travelers from Bohemia and Moravia found refuge on the estate of the German Count Nicholas von Zinzendorf. It was under his guidance that the far-reaching missionary work began, ultimately covering the globe from Greenland to South Africa. Although sharing many of the theological concerns of other Protestant groups, the Moravians fashioned distinctive practices. A so-called Choir system was developed in which men and women were divided according to age and marital status. Women's dress reflected this; little girls wore red or green ribbons on their white caps; adolescent girls, pink; married women, blue; and widows, white. There were also Choirs for each group who carried out the work of the community, replete with parties and singing fests. Worship for the Moravians was never separate from everyday work and leisure. They believed that doctrinal principles were not as important as understanding the ways in which God guided and shaped their communities. The cohesive nature of these communities provided the psychological strength to live civilized lives in often violent parts of the world.

This book is the story of one group of Moravians who settled Bethlehem, and Nazareth, Pennsylvania, as well as Bethabara, North Carolina. Sharing work, as one household, these communities formed an organic whole, but did not reject ownership of private property or the fruits of personal endeavor. In the early settling of America, the Moravians' mode of living was organized, efficient, and an oasis amid the turbulence surrounding the French and Indian wars.

Christina and Matthew Krause were actual people, as were Susannah and George Partsch, and many others portrayed here. Some of the dates have been slightly altered to compress time, and the thoughts and words of the personæ are the author's.

CHRISTINA BARBARA BÖHNER FAMILY TREE

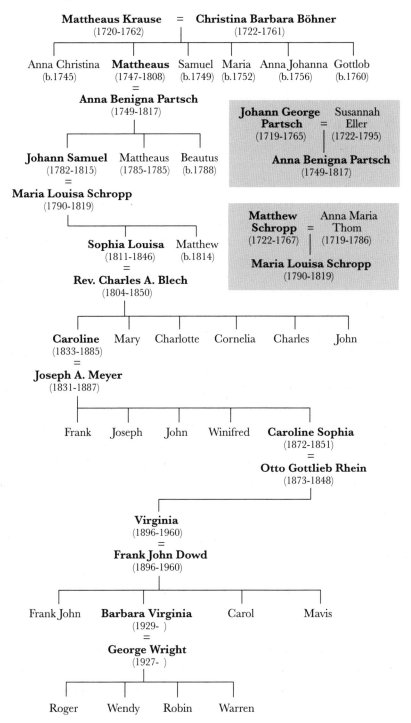

Mattheaus Krause = **Christina Barbara Böhner**
(1720-1762)   (1722-1761)

Anna Christina   **Mattheaus**   Samuel   Maria   Anna Johanna   Gottlob
(b.1745)   (1747-1808)   (b.1749)   (b.1752)   (b.1756)   (b.1760)
                    =
            Anna Benigna Partsch
                (1749-1817)

Johann George   Susannah
Partsch   =   Eller
(1719-1765)   (1722-1795)

Anna Benigna Partsch
(1749-1817)

Johann Samuel   Mattheaus   Beautus
(1782-1815)   (1785-1785)   (b.1788)
      =
Maria Louisa Schropp
(1790-1819)

Matthew   Anna Maria
Schropp   =   Thom
(1722-1767)   (1719-1786)

Maria Louisa Schropp
(1790-1819)

Sophia Louisa   Matthew
(1811-1846)   (b.1814)
      =
Rev. Charles A. Blech
(1804-1850)

Caroline   Mary   Charlotte   Cornelia   Charles   John
(1833-1885)
      =
Joseph A. Meyer
(1831-1887)

Frank   Joseph   John   Winifred   **Caroline Sophia**
                              (1872-1851)
                                  =
                        Otto Gottlieb Rhein
                            (1873-1848)

Virginia
(1896-1960)
      =
Frank John Dowd
(1896-1960)

Frank John   **Barbara Virginia**   Carol   Mavis
          (1929-)
              =
      George Wright
        (1927-)

Roger   Wendy   Robin   Warren

CHAPTER ONE

Christina Barbara Böhner Krause
Bethabara, North Carolina   September, 1761

I remember it was sowing time. I had cast my portion in one last toss of that March day, but one seed remained nestled in the hollow of my palm. Although the buds had not yet burst into green, the willow drooped yellow over the river and in the warm, wet North Carolina spring I knew I was again with child. Once more my body would change; slowly at first and then, as time passed, my breasts would be heavy, my nipples darkening. The little one confined in my spare frame would stretch and kick its legs in the effort to expand its dark red chamber. I would smile to feel it.

That spring day, I looked up to see my husband's tall figure moving in cadenced rhythm as he bent and stretched, his long arm making a perfect arc as he scattered seed. My Matthew. My love. He was so sure when I was not; so steady on the path. Always his thin fingers could find the mistake, the knot, the part that did not work. He could fix it. And his hands did comfort me. Sometimes I thought that the reason I turned to him so often in the night's stillness was to fill the empty place within me; for in the secret recess of my heart was a dark void. . . .

It is early September now, and the air has cooled somewhat. What we sowed then has become our harvest of golden flax and pungent herbs. I am very heavy. A swelling has begun in my hands and feet and this saps something from me. I am of little use to the others as they harvest and spin, praising our Saviour with their good work. In my enforced idleness, memories fill my days, and as if from a far distance, I see myself as I was.

It is hard to believe so many years have passed since I first stepped from the swaying ship that had been my home for months and began my journey over America's rough paths. What joy we carried with us! What innocence. With such girlish determination I wanted to become part of our great mission. I was so eager. I was so hopeful. But today, close to a birth and, perhaps, to death, I feel an urgent need to search my heart before recording my earthly pilgrimage so as to weed out the doubts and, yes, sometimes the anger, in order to greet our God with purity of spirit and fullness of faith.

My beloved Brethren and Sisters walk their pilgrimages and reflect the light of their faith with easy grace, while I have walked too often in my own shadow. Belief, a constant brightness for them, has been for me but flutterings of light too easily extinguished. Am I somehow deficient that I cannot hear and believe; or has it been my stubborn will that resists their teachings?

Joyous trumpets still herald friend and stranger to our midst, and deep-throated trombones signal the journey to our Saviour; but that mournful sound may not yet tremble over these red hills for me. Perhaps I will have time to sing my memories alone and listen for the echo of His will in my heart before my journey is done and I rest in His arms.

O Holy Mother. Oh, Holy Mother. Do something. Please do this for me now."

I knelt in my childhood church in Gelzhausen, Germany; my back rigid, my hands clasped so hard together they hurt. Though it was warm summer of 1732, the little church was damp and cool. I shivered but did not unclasp my hands to warm myself with my arms. No candles flickered at the wooden altar and Sunday's field flowers were long thrown away. Little light came from the high, plain glass windows, but as I looked up to the statue of the Divine Mother before me, I wished for her lips to move, her hand to beckon; a sign, any sign. I never bothered to wipe the tears from my face. Why should I? There was no one to see me.

"Please, Our Lady. Make her well. Make her well."

I would have said the words of my childish prayer aloud had I been more bold; but no. That was not the way I was. That is not the way I am. I stared at the face of the wooden statue and saw, for the first time, that the Madonna's tears had been painted.

When I scrambled to my feet, my knees were sore, and easing myself from the wooden pew, I caught the heel of my shoe in the hem of my dress. Who will hem my dress? Who will stop the hurting? A memory then, fleeting but clear. As a small child dizzy with the spring smell of new meadow grass, I ran barefoot near my father's forge and stepped on a sharp metal scrap. My cry brought my mother and she wrapped my little foot in a clean rag and held the wound with her thumb until the blood stopped seeping and the pain diminished, leaving only the regular beat of my pulse—or was it hers?

"O, Holy Mother." I turned to plead with the statue again, this time on my feet. "Make the sickness go away. Do not let it take my mother too."

I left the chill of the little church then and stumbled down the lane to my father's forge and the small, attached rooms behind. "Water," I thought. "Water. I will get water for my mother. I will wash the fever away."

A small brook ran behind our little dwelling, and my mother said she carried me there before I could walk. She told me I held out my arms to the water though I cannot remember doing so. I only know that rushing water remains in my memory even now, its splash and gurgle the most comforting sound I can recall. In the summer, when our little hamlet of Gelzhausen was quiet in the noonday sun and my father rested, my mother, basket on her hip, took our few clothes to wash.

I see my mother forever young, walking swiftly over the sweet clover before me while I ran to keep up. She was tall, taller than I am now, but we share the spare bodies of her people. I loved to watch her. There was such a sureness about her as she poured from the steaming kettle or shook the blankets against a morning's sky. She seldom walked a path but moved through the meadow as though on some errand of her own, her head up, her brown hair parted in the middle and wound into a thick knot. She spoke very little and I cannot remember her laughing, but I can recall her smile.

When I stopped to pick up a yellow weed she never said I must not. And if I ran to show her my treasure, she said nothing but took its poor drooping stem, and straightening it with her finger, she smiled at me and ran the blossom across my cheek. I felt the tickle and ran away laughing for her to follow, but she did not. She always bent in the same way to lift my father's nightshirt from her basket and shook it out before she dipped it into the cold water. The sameness of these acts was a comfort; I felt safe. There is no safety except in our Saviour, my Brethren say. That is what they truly believe.

IT WAS ON SUCH A DAY a few weeks earlier that my life was destined to change. As I waded into the brook between the grasses and felt my toes sink into the cool mud the sun shone on the water as it always had. I cupped my hands and bent to drink. The brook was spring fed and cold even on the hottest day. In the winter it never froze because it moved so swiftly amongst the rocks. Perhaps that is why I loved it—the movement and the rushing to somewhere, though even now I do not know where it went except that it must have been to a sea. That is where I went—to the sea. But as mud squished up between my toes and I held my dress up around my waist, it was just wash day, and summer, and my mother would soon call to tell me not to wade too far.

"Mother Böhner. Mother Böhner, come quick." It was my sister-in-law, Greta, calling. I could hear fear in her voice.

My mother dropped a wet piece of clothing in her basket and turned to run up the slight hill to our house. I ran ahead, sure-footed, over the heavy grasses. When we reached the back entrance I could see Otto, the elder of my brothers, leaning heavily on the kitchen table. His face was very flushed. Greta, a large woman, seemed to have diminished in size as she plucked at his sleeve. Otto did not notice. When my mother walked through the door behind me, he took a step toward her but had to stop and steady himself. He was a squarely built man, not tall but broad. He tried to smile. "I have not had too much beer, Mama."

"Mama Böhner, he is so hot. There is sickness in Heilbrunn. So close, so close." Greta squinted, looking at Otto, and plucked again at his shirt.

My mother's calm face changed little but I knew her well and, seeing the small wrinkle between her eyebrows deepen, I could feel her worry though her voice was cheerful as she spoke to my brother.

"Rest here for a while. Greta has enough to do with the babies you have given her and does not need a husband who pretends to be dizzy." She reached out to touch his cheek. "Christina Barbara, run to the brook for water."

She handed me the wooden bucket and I ran out the door, the rope handle scratchy on my arm. My legs were long and I felt I could fly. My bucket swinging madly, I ran down the slight hill behind our house to the brook. So many memories about that time have left me, but I clearly can recall the sunlight bright on the brook and feel the cool water as I dipped the bucket. Water wet my petticoats as I knelt and I cried out when a small stone dug into my knee. I have yet the scar for the cut was deep; but all I could think on that hot August day was to hurry. My heart beat in my neck and even the short time it took to fill the bucket seemed so long.

My mother ordered Greta out of our small house, and, though her voice was quiet as it always was, there was no way in which Greta would disobey. Mother said she would nurse my brother back to health and, for the sake of her little ones, Greta left the house, turning back only once; but I do not know if my brother saw her.

I can yet see in memory my dear brothers, Otto and Heinrich. Born close to one another, many saw them as twins because they were so much alike in their pale coloring, their features and movements. Both looked like my father. Thick-set men, already half-grown when I was born, they treated me with warmth and affection though my quiet nature, so different from theirs, caused them to shake their heads in unison when their teasing made me stamp my foot and turn away. Had I been like them, I would have flung myself against their burly chests and beat them with my fists while they roared with laughter. But I would not have done that.

Cool, wet cloths never soaked up Otto's fever when we placed them on his body, and finally his unblinking eyes wild and unseeing, he stopped breathing. My mother held on to Greta's arm when she pushed aside the curtain. I heard Greta shriek. I heard it all the way down our road. It hit the small houses and shops on one side and then another, and when it stopped it felt to me as though the earth, too, had stopped breathing, it was so quiet.

I had prayed when I brought each bucket of water from the brook. I prayed when I lifted the kettle from the hook and knelt down every night by my bed to pray again. What good did it do? Who heard my whisper, my inner scream? We waited. It did not rain and I watched from our doorway as people moved in and out of their houses, nodding but saying nothing. I knew they were afraid. When Heinrich fell as he helped my father at the forge, I, too, was very afraid. I sat in the grass at the back of our house and held my rag doll to me. I rocked her and kissed her faceless head. I told her my brother would be well. But this never happened. Both my big older brothers sleep forever in wooden beds and I never heard their boisterous laughter again.

I OFTEN SAT on the front stoop of our small house to watch the people go by on the main road where we lived. I held my doll and when some travelers stopped to speak, I would nod and smile. But I said nothing. Some travelers' words did not say what their faces did. Or what their bodies told me. "It is a bright and good day," the Miller said when he greeted my father. But his shoulders were bent, and the scowl that covered his face told me he did not think it was a bright and good day. Once, a woman danced before me on the road. Her black dress was tattered and even torn at the skirt. She danced in circles and sang words I could not hear. The tune was merry. When she was close enough, I saw that her face was old and lined and very sad and her words about singing rain made no sense.

I wondered about words before I learned to form their shapes on my worn slate. I looked at the curves and slanting lines. And when I heard a word spoken, I saw its shape in the air and watched as it floated there.

"Little solemn face, do you hear me?"

That is what my father often said as he swooped down to take me on his lap. I could smell his smoky clothes and his salty sweat. I reached up to trace the lines in his neck above his open, collarless shirt. Holding me on his knees, my father would take a small piece of metal and bend it to his imagination in shapes that made me laugh. He would ask me what the shapes were, a cow, a dog, or even the shape of our little clockmaker who limped his small way down our road. He had strong, square hands and thick fingers and his hands were always warm.

My father was the son of a farmer who died before I was born but I heard that my grandfather had grown old and discouraged waiting for seedlings to come green. When my father was but eighteen, he walked a short distance to our small village of Gelzhausen, where he apprenticed to the Smithy. He had worked with tools all his life and knew how parts fit together, how to twist thin metal to his will, so it did not take many years before he began a small business on the main road in Gelzhausen. We lived behind the shop and I often think I hear the sound of metal on metal ringing in my ears when I awaken, though I am now so far away from my early home.

I was born in 1722, when my father was in middle age, and if my coming was a surprise to my mother and father, they never let me know. My father said I was his treasure. When he said this, I felt dressed in precious gems though I had never seen any. I thought they must glow like the one stained-glass window in our little stone church. When father gathered me to his sturdy body I felt not only the heat of the metal he had tamed, but his own energy that filled our small house with bursts of his laughter and snatches of song. Such a strange matched pair, my mother and father. Yet I knew they fit together. Sometimes my mother put her hands over her ears when my father pounded the table and threw back his blond head to laugh until the sound startled the horse tethered by the forge. But I saw her smile. Then she would place her hand on his thick shoulder and he would lean against her breast.

Our house had echoed deeply when the men all spoke at once, none seeming to hear the other as they argued about the quality of the latest brew, pushing each other's shoulders. They were so big to me, the three of them; not tall but wide. My mother moved between their solidness, wordlessly putting a plate on the table, pouring water into a mug. I still cling to those memories of laughter and merry sound. To the time when my father warmed me with his vigor and my mother surrounded me with her protective and enduring love.

How did this sickness come to our house? Did it ride in on a horse and leap to my brother's shoulder as he held the animal's hoof? Did it slide down my father's throat when he laughed aloud with a traveler? Flushed now as my brothers had been, he told my mother to stay away. But how could any of us stay away in that tiny house? I ran to the brook and back so many times. My mother laid the wet cloths on Father's face, his chest, his arms. Once I saw her bend to his bare chest and kiss him.

I was very afraid. More afraid than when a mad dog ran into our town and in its madness sniffed and howled its way from doorway to doorway. Its hair was matted and I could see bare skin in sore patches. When it came to the front of our house where my father worked at his forge I was close enough to see foam at the corner of its mouth and its pointed fangs. I was struck with fright and could not move. Worse than the frenzied madness of the creature was seeing my father take his burning tongs to swipe at its head with a roar and to see the creature fall. Blood ran from its mouth but did not soak in and lay sticky on the hard earth as I stared. Later, much later, while I wept anguished tears, I would hear how the blood of our beloved Brethren and Sisters had stained the white snows of the Pennsylvania forests.

The sickness came more slowly to my mother or, perhaps, she did not let me know when she stumbled or the film came to her eyes. But one morning she did not rise from her bed. I tried to spoon broth into her mouth; I told her I was big and strong and grown-up enough to help them both; for my father, no longer powerful, was now just a large form that struggled with death in a narrow bed. Why do I not get this fever? Why do I dip the cloths in water to wash my parents' bodies and lean close to hear their voices, but it does not come to me? I wanted it to come to me. I breathed in my mother's breath to take in its fetid, sour smell and make it part of my strong self. I thought that if I could not make them well, I would will them to make me ill. But it did not happen.

Her face was pasty and yellow. Her long brown hair spread out in strings on her pillow. How could this happen so quickly? How could my mother be sick? My mother was never sick. It was she who took care of me. I dipped the clean rag in water and tried to wash her face. I could feel her nose, her lips, the rise of her cheekbone beneath my fingers. I did not want to wash her eyes. I wanted her to open them and tell me she would get better. I wanted her to get up and help me get soup for my father. He was wrapped in a blanket that had once covered my poor brothers. My brothers who would never chase me, laughing, into my mother's arms?

"Listen Christina Barbara . . ." She stopped and took a breath, such a little breath. It did not even make her chest rise but seemed to get stuck in her throat. I tried to stop my sobs. I could not see her clearly because of my tears, and took my hand that was free of hers to wipe them away.

"Christina. Your father will not have strength. He cannot . . ." Her voice was faint and sometimes she said things I did not understand. Things about people I did not know. What had she wanted to say to me? That my prayers would not be answered? That she would die and leave me with my father, who would live but never laugh again?

One day I found a bunch of flowers on the stone stoop. They were wilting in the heat. Cut flowers were bad luck. They died. No one told me this but I knew it was true. When I saw them there, the petals all curled and the leaves drying, I threw them as far as I could. They scattered orange and yellow in the air. At my mother's side I dipped the cloth once again in the water and wrung it out, the splash of the brook then in the wooden pail.

All that merry noise gone. All that laughter. No more ringing of metal on metal. Now, only nails hammered into wood. First the sides, so strangely shaped to hold my mother's wasted body, and then the final hammer blows to secure the top. My father sat watching. He said nothing. For so long he said nothing. Even after our townspeople had come to our house with food and drink; even when his friends put their arms around his broad shoulders or shyly patted his back, he said nothing but only looked at them as if he saw them not. Finally summer turned to fall and the wind kicked up the dry dust of our road. I walked into our shop and when I saw a thin piece of metal lying on the dirt floor, I picked it up. It was cold and hard in my hand, but bendable. Even I was strong enough to curve it on one end. I pushed back the curtain between the shop and our living place and put the piece before my father who sat, still silent, at our table.

"Can you bend this? Can you see what it might make?" I said. He did not look up at me but reached his fingers to touch the metal. His thick fingers were once so strong! He took it in his left hand and with his right he bent and twisted and curved. Then, finished, he held it in his hand and stared.

"What is it? Should I guess?"

I tried to make my voice light. He said nothing. I looked again at the twisted metal and took it from his unresisting hand. I turned it this way and that. I held it up and turned it slowly in my hand. What could it be? The curved pieces might have shaped an "S" or a "Z" perhaps, but I knew they didn't. I hoped for a sheep, a cow, or even a cloud. But it was the shape of nothing.

Not long after that, I awoke one morning to see his empty bed. His blanket was not crumpled nor could I see the dent of his wide body pressed into the narrow pallet. It was bitter cold for no fire had been set. I stepped through the three rooms of our house and into the main work area. There was the feeling of emptiness. Not just the quiet, not just the cold. There was no swirling life and even the dank smell of death that had clung to the blankets had faded and left a void. I stood in the middle of that space where I had once felt warm fire and heard the sharp sound of metal on metal and I knew I would not see my father again. I should have moved, I should have taken my cape and gone into the street to look. But I could not move. My feet were cold on the black, earthen floor.

No one in my town had noticed his lone figure leaving in the dark. No one had heard his shuffle on the dusty road and opened a door in the night to call out; or, perhaps feeling the aloneness of the now-bent figure, had watched, but said nothing. A small knot of men met in front of our shop to discuss searching. Hands in their pockets, their shoulders touched as though to get solace from nearness. When they turned to speak to me they averted their faces. "The brook. We will look at the brook," one said. Another said he would walk to the next town to see if anyone had seen my father; another said he would write to the authorities in Heilbrunn. It was not what they said but what they didn't say that confirmed my certainty that he had disappeared and would not return.

It was not only our small house that sheltered emptiness; the dusty road in front of the shop, the short side roads, and even the setting sun that slanted on stone held for me a vacancy. There had been some talk of my living with a childless couple in Heilbrunn, but Greta, perhaps finding some comfort in the surroundings where her husband had lived as a boy, came, bringing her little ones to stay with me shortly after my father disappeared. Although she sometimes looked out our window as though she expected Otto to stand as he always had at the forge, she never let her sorrow show in tears or dejection. There was a vigor about Greta, a way in which she moved her large body almost gracefully from hearth to pump, stopping to push a wisp of light hair away from her face. She had a way of knowing when I felt the emptiness of any orphan and she would stop her sewing to hold me close to her, the rounded curve of her breast a comfort. Greta's thick fingers sewed a neat seam but her work was a silent task and even the cries and laughter of her little ones did not fill my heart when I awoke in the early morning, waiting to hear the familiar clanging where there was none. Sometimes I heard Greta's sigh as she settled her heavy body under the blanket, and knew she, too, was lonely.

Dear Hans had loved Greta since our two families sat close together in our small church. As yet unmarried, he came soon to our door, his wide face unable to contain his happy anticipation. Many of the townsfolk watched unashamedly as he made his way, not quite running but with a purposeful step, often holding a long loaf of bread or a wrapped sweet in his large palm. Everyone had known of his disappointment when Greta had married my brother Otto years ago, but Hans was not a man who harbored grudges and though he often was here to help my father at the forge, he had kept his eyes on the flames.

One early evening I watched as he slipped an arm around Greta's ample waist to pull her close, his other hand on the cold forge. Then I knew the fire would burst forth again; I would smell the smoke in my bedclothes and stand as I always had to see the glowing iron, sparks flashing, change under a strong hand.

Greta and Hans wed in our small church, her children strewing flowers before them, our Holy Mother bent to watch as Greta placed a bouquet at her feet, for she was a dutiful Catholic and knew to ask for Her blessing. And so, the sound of ringing metal began again.

FRAU SCHLUMBERGER WAS VERY FAT. She swayed from side to side as she walked, and when I first saw her, the thought came to me that if I could but turn her once, like a top, she would twirl forever down the crooked side streets of Gelzhausen and out into the rolling countryside until she toppled over the edge of the earth. Herr Schlumberger was very thin. He was also tall, his breeches unable to contain his blouse; first it slipped out one side and then another so that the poor man was always tucking it in with nervous fingers. I later heard that those fingers touched violin strings with such skill that those who listened were transported from a drawing room in Heilbrunn or a simple kitchen in Gelzhausen to the very gates of Paradise. But at the time I knew nothing of his talent, and barely listened to the talk between the Schlumbergers, Hans and Greta.

I sometimes wonder now if Greta was worried about me. Or, perhaps, as I reached twelve years of age, she did not know what to do about me. Her children were very young and she had no experience with raising a girl about to become a woman. Though I shared few of my thoughts, she must have seen a particular sadness in me after my father's disappearance. She often tempted me with sweets, and Hans even tried to make toys from metal, as my father had done. Perhaps they thought a trip to Heilbrunn would lighten my mood. At any rate when the Schlumbergers arrived at our door, it was only for Hans to check their horse's shoe. However, there was no particular reason for them to take an interest in me.

Our God moves in very strange ways.

I have no memory of any conversation between the Schlumbergers and my brother-in-law, but I can recall clearly the scent of rosewater and not-quite-clean clothes as Frau Schlumberger enveloped me in a rush of pity and concern. Even in my surprise I noticed her eyes were shrewd, knowing and kindly when she drew back to look into my face. I like to think now that she saw something unique in me, but more probably she saw an opportunity to perform a kind act for an orphan girl when she suggested to Hans and Greta that I might like to see Heilbrunn and even visit a Protestant church there. Herr Schlumberger explained that they were traveling to Heilbrunn to hear the preaching of the Count of Zinzendorf, whose piety had been noted in certain religious circles.

I had no interest in hearing this man, but the idea that I might sit in a carriage and travel all the way to Heilbrunn fired my dreams. Their carriage was enclosed, and even if it rained, I would not be wet. Perhaps I would wave to the village girls in Gelzhausen as I drove by—just a slight wave as the carriage bumped over the ruts of our main road. They would stare, too impressed to return my wave.

If my dear parents had been alive, they might have had objections to my going to a church other than our Holy Catholic one, and even Greta and Hans, who were less strict with me, had some misgivings. After the

Schlumbergers' invitation had been made, they left their one horse with Hans and prepared to stay with friends in Gelzhausen until at least the next day.

From my bed I could hear Greta's whisper. "It will be a very long day, Hans. And she has not yet ridden in a carriage."

"Ah, Greta, she is twelve years old and Heilbrunn is not so far. Johann the Weaver has been friendly with Herr Schlumberger for some years. I think she will be safe." Hans always spoke slowly and was easier to hear than Greta. There was silence for a moment and then Greta said, "She is such a strange little girl sometimes. Though she says little, I think she may dream of removing herself to a higher station in life. Seeing a real Count could give her ideas that might hurt her, Hans."

Hans grunted, "She might be more helpful in the garden—dreaming all the time."

I stretched on my back and did not move. I did not even pull my cover closer to my chin for fear of letting them know I was awake and listening. I did love Greta, but sometimes she seemed very dull. And what was wrong with a dream or two? Why not a carriage for me? It was high time for me to see the world. I simply must go with that funny couple, I decided. I had never seen shops with large glass windows, and there might even be one filled with sweets. My mouth watered and I squeezed my eyes shut as my excitement grew. I imagined Count Nikolaus Zinzendorf popping a sweet right into my mouth. I imagined he had jewels on his fingers.

Hans' voice broke my reverie. "Well, I suppose we can let her go. Someone told me that one of Count Zinzendorf's close friends is a Cardinal. And I see no problem with letting her see the inside of a large church, even if it is Lutheran."

I heard Greta sigh then and the rustle of bedclothes. Hans belched and Greta giggled. I snuggled into my pillow.

I remember the day was very misty, and the inside of that carriage quite cold and damp. Herr Schlumberger sat on a small seat outside with the reins in his thin fingers. After a while, the flat fields rolling past me slowly, I think I dropped off to sleep, my head on the wide, padded shoulder of my traveling hostess. I awoke when the carriage wheel hit a rock in the road and the horse pulled to one side. I saw small shops, some two-storied with timbered decoration and open casement windows. I was wide awake then and peered further out the small carriage window to find the famous old stone tower built over the holy spring. Frau Schlumberger patted my knee. "I see you are awake. Look." She pointed. "You can see the church and old tower from here. There, across the river."

I followed her gloved hand and looked over the red and brown rooftops. How crowded they were, slanted, pushing into one another. I could not tell where one ended and another began. In Gelzhausen there was space between the roofs, and they were never so high. I felt a jolt of discomfort, for suddenly I was far from home. Quickly, to ground myself, I imagined the main room of our house, the hearth on one wall, the curtains drawn to separate our beds. Were all the small shops still in place, I wondered? And the houses of those I had always known? My mouth was dry.

The wheels clattered over uneven wooden planks, and when I looked through a flimsy two-railed bridge, I saw churning gray water below. I shrank back from the window. My heavy companion put her arm around my shoulder, but I held my breath anyway, until I could feel the wheels crunching stones on the other side of the river.

Suddenly the road was crowded with other carriages, some of them very large and ornate. I saw gold on the door of one, and another even had a coat of arms on the door in the shape of an animal I had never seen, with two tails and an open mouth. I tried to see the passengers inside. Surely they would have lots of silken petticoats! My friend Magda had told me about that. And the men, too, would redden their lips and wear beauty marks on their cheeks.

I could not wait to leap from the confines of our small vehicle. It took forever for Herr Schlumberger to ease his horse into a space and jump down, like a grasshopper, to fasten the reins to a hitching post. He stepped up and opened the door from the outside and I sprang down, missing the one step on purpose. Frau Schlumberger, breathing heavily, took hold of a handle at the side and lumbered to the ground. The couple arranged themselves on either side of me, and we walked rather quickly toward the double center doors of the large gray stone church. Frau Schlumberger waved as she walked, and greeted others nodding and smiling.

I had never seen so many people at one time. I tried to peer into each face, and though they blurred together, I could easily distinguish different modes of dress. Some were very fashionable—or what I thought was fashionable—and others were very plain, the men in dark colors and the women with peculiar caps tied with dark blue or black ribbons. Frau Schlumberger whispered to me that they were called Moravians and that some even lived on the Count's huge estate. She continued as we walked in the crowd but I could not listen to her. What if I got lost among all these strangers? What if I never got back to Gelzhausen? Herr Schlumberger's hand under my elbow urged me forward. Right in front of me, staring at me, was a terrible beast coming from the stone wall of the church. It had a human face but its mouth was huge and hideous. I stopped, horrified.

"It's a gargoyle, my dear. The stonemason carved them so many years ago to carry rain water and spit it out, you know. She urged me into the crowd that was squeezing through the door before us. I was not sure I should have begged Greta to let me come on this trip.

The huge sanctuary was filled, and people crowded together, the women crushing their skirts and the men crossing their legs to better make room as more and more people entered the double back doors. I could see a wooden balcony that circled around the sides of the building, and the organ pipes, exposed at the front, seemed to me to be spires reaching to Heaven.

Though the weather was damp and cold, inside the church it was warmer and I smelled the wet wool of capes and the oil used to polish the carved wooden pews. I felt shy and hesitated to follow Herr Schlumberger when he strode up to the front of the church, but because I knew no one there I was afraid I might be lost if I did not stay close. Herr Schlumberger edged his way into a pew close to the pulpit and motioned me to follow. Frau Schlumberger settled her heavy self next to me. I was hemmed in. Frau Schlumberger took out her handkerchief and gave her nose a large blow. I felt laughter well up. Around me the faces of the congregation were turned toward the pulpit. Some were smiling, some very solemn, but all seemed to be impatient. Where was this speaker the Schlumbergers had been chattering about as we bounced the bumpy road to Heilbrunn? This great Count Zinzendorf? They said he had large estates in the eastern part of Germany as well as in the south. I thought he must be very rich. I wanted to see what kind of a powdered wig he would wear and the color of his satin vest. Would he wear lace at his neck and wrists? A scuffle of feet, a cough. We waited.

A man quickly climbed the steps to the pulpit, and for such a large person he was very light on his feet. No lace; no satin, no white powdered wig. I was disappointed. His brown hair was drawn back with a black ribbon and he wore the suit of any well-to-do-tradesman. His face was long; there was a sweetness about his full lips, curved in a slight smile. He said nothing but looked out over the assembly. I wiggled once for space, and Frau Schlumberger placed her gloved hand on my knee.

"Dear hearts." His voice was very deep. He said this, and waited. So did we. Then he scanned the gathering of people and I am sure his eyes lingered on my face. It was only for a moment, but the moment was suddenly precious. I scarcely blinked. As his voice poured over the wooden pews, he spoke of the love of our Saviour and how this love is always with us. Always.

I wished he would speak on and on and I would be taken up in that cloud of words to float above myself, out of myself. Then he told about our Saviour's loneliness, and my tears came. They did not drop to my cheeks. It was more as if they filled my chest. The tightness remained when he walked down the winding steps, more slowly now. It remained as the congregation began to sing, their lusty voices full of hope and promise.

We did not rise from our seats at the end of the service, but sat to wait for those in the rear of the church to greet the Count. I felt very warm and slightly sick to my stomach. The odor of Frau Schlumberger's rosewater intermixed with those bodies packed in beside us, and I longed to be outdoors, misty and cool as it was that day. Finally we rose. Again my stomach seemed to lurch, not nauseous now but a dull ache. The crowd shuffled. It moved too slowly, the women stopping to bob quickly in front of the Count, some tittering softly. Men bent slightly from the waist, a few reached out to touch his sleeve. Zinzendorf was taller than most in the crowd, I saw as I drew closer. I could feel my heart beating harder. What if the Count could see the thumping under my jacket? What if I curtsied and fell? Would I find myself gazing up from the floor or would he reach out his arms to catch me? Would he look again into my eyes and say, "Dear hearts," looking only at me?

"And this is Christina Barbara Böhner, sir." Herr Schlumberger's tenor voice broke into my thoughts. I dipped my knee, afraid at first to look into Count Zinzendorf's face.

"Christina—what a lovely name." His deep voice seemed to vibrate in my breast. I felt my face flame with embarrassment, but I felt compelled to look directly at him. He was smiling at me—such a loving smile. I was enveloped by him, though he did not raise his arms; surrounded by him, though he stood quietly in one space. Then the bodies behind us began to push; I felt the cool air on my face, but my body remained warm for some time.

"Oh, my dear, we must eat a little something. Wasn't he magnificent— such a good and simple man. We must have a pastry." Frau Schlumberger spoke to the air in front of her, moving very quickly as she waddled forward, toppling from side to side. Herr Schlumberger almost ran to keep up and I began to skip. We stopped in a shop that smelled of sugared icing and cherry tarts and sat at a small, round table with a dark wooden top. A young man scarcely older than I brought steaming black coffee and a plate of pastries the like of which I had never seen, or smelled or tasted. The Schlumbergers urged me to take as much as I wanted. The food and coffee helped the ache in my belly, but, listening to their chatting at our small table, a wave of homesickness come over me. I thought of my quiet mother.

"Tina, you must be a bit weary. All this is new to you." Frau Schlumberger, despite her affectionate patter, had knowing eyes. She searched my face.

"You must remember, my dear, your parents are in a holy place and rest with our Saviour." She said this with conviction. "We have learned much in the past few years." She nodded to her husband who nodded in return. He swallowed a bit of tart, and wiping the cream from one side of his mouth with a napkin, he said, "It was the great Count Zinzendorf himself who convinced us to search our hearts and to look to our Saviour for all our concerns."

I felt very full and could not finish the piece of flaky pastry that remained on my plate. Old people like the Schlumbergers might want to search their hearts, but the subject was of little interest to me—unless the Count asked me. Would he take my hand again?

Perhaps I dropped off to sleep on the journey home. I cannot remember the road, or any talk. But the sound of the Count's deep voice echoed in my breast and I felt safe, perhaps as safe as I had felt as a little girl when the sound of my parents' voices rose and fell in comforting waves before I slept. We finally arrived very late at night at our small house in Gelzhausen. I do remember that Greta and Hans asked little about the church or the service. They were somewhat interested in what the Count wore, but other than that, asked no questions. I was relieved, for I had no words to sort out the feelings I had.

Greta had put water in my pitcher so I would not have to pump after my journey. When I now recall her round, plain face it is with great feelings of affection. She was so good to me. I washed quickly for the room was very cold. The dull ache in my belly seemed to be stronger and I wanted to get warm under my blanket. When I undressed I saw blood on my shift.

And that was the beginning: I was just twelve, but the few drops of red signaled that I had become a woman. The flow now ceases as the child within me grows until it will finally gain its freedom. I may return then to the measured rhythm and with its ebb and flow, the yearning that brings new life. O, my Saviour, would that my passion for you could flow as freely as your blood did for me!

EIGHT YEARS PASSED, but Gelzhausen remained the same as it had throughout my childhood. Its main road still was muddy in spring and dusty in autumn. Our small house and shop, now with two new rooms added, was nevertheless much the same. But I was changing. A quiet young woman at twenty, I anticipated, as always, the change of seasons within the small circle of our town and the fields beyond; but when I swept flurried snow from our door, the flakes were suddenly like cool kisses on my cheeks. And full summer's sun did not warm my face as much as admiring glances of some who passed our door.

I was close to the familiar townspeople I had known all my life; the Brewer who smelled of yeast, the Shoemaker who sang, the Tailor who talked without ceasing though his mouth was full of pins; my mother's friend who taught me to sew, and my dear friend Magda, who had married early. She could dance with a partner or alone, with music or not, and as little girls we had walked arm in arm down our road to the church where the old priest taught us to read and do some sums on a slate. The scratch of chalk, the musty smell of his robe and of candles just extinguished, come easily to my memory.

What is more difficult to catch and hold is that sense of wonder I felt on the misty day in Heilbrunn when I first was awakened to the ideas of those people I know now as Moravians, and heard the charismatic man who was to change my life. I could imagine his face. I could even hear the timbre of his voice and though the alchemy of his words held the power to transform me, I was but a young girl and could only measure change with the curving of my body and a restlessness that awoke me in the night to gaze at the moon from my tiny window. Sometimes it was round and full and sometimes a sliver. I tossed beneath my quilt and pressed my body full-length to my mattress.

On Sundays we walked to our church. I went before Hans and Greta, a small child holding my hands on either side, slipping away, running ahead and then back, little faces ruddy, hair flying. At the large door I reached to the font and dipped my finger in the holy water. We knelt on the hard wooden kneelers and I looked up toward the altar. The priest reached to light the candles and I knew he would soon begin the words of the Mass in a language I didn't really know. The wooden benches creaked with the weight of the assembled townspeople as many, grown tired from kneeling, leaned back and crumpled their bodies against the hard edges. Field flowers in crude vases sent a sweet scent from the altar. The priest, his back to us, droned until an altar boy beside him, dressed in red and lace, rang a little bell.

A strange sadness came over me because I felt myself to be an observer of my figure there in the old church: a young woman, kneeling. I held my narrow back very straight, my brown hair wound into a chaste knot, my eyes ahead and full mouth unsmiling. I wore no hat but had placed a small square of lace on my head. It had belonged to my mother; my still, silent mother who would never again nod and smile at me.

I said the words, "Hail Mary, full of grace, the Lord is with thee; blessed art thou among women, and blessed is the fruit of thy womb, Jesus," as I had always done. But the words that had been so bountiful gave me no gratification. I could not look at the priest. I had no wish to search the face of our Holy Mother for help. She had not helped us before. She never winged my prayers to God so he could breathe fresh life into my mother's hot, sweating body. Where do I find the comfort of my mother's deep and encircling silence now that she is gone? How do I fill the emptiness that comes to me every morning as I swim into wakefulness? I looked to Our Lady. The blue paint on her headdress was chipped.

GRETA'S AMPLE FIGURE stretched and rounded with yet another child. She took my hand to place it on her belly with an unsaid question in her eyes. And when Magda's babe would try to suckle my breast, my answering need let me know it was time for me to wed. For there was a loneliness in me, and I knew with certainty that I must fill it in some way. I thought it would be to join with another.

I knew that Greta's brother Friedrich was going to court me. I had resisted the fumblings of the town boys, but had allowed some to kiss me when I caught their eagerness. One young fellow, his face as smooth as mine, had sworn he loved me, but I missed the roughness I had known in my brothers' faces when they teased and ran, and knew, young as I was, that I wanted someone different from those sweet boys who picked me flowers in summer.

Friedrich was very blond and very large and when he came to work for Hans his voice boomed throughout our house. I watched from the doorway as he held the hammer up to strike metal. I wanted to run my fingers down his arm and then suck them one by one to taste the salt of his skin. After some time, as I knew he would, he arrived at our door on a Sunday while Greta and Hans were hovering by the stove. He held a hat in his hands—I had never seen him wear a hat—and I noticed that his dark jacket strained at the seams while his breeches flapped unbuckled at his knees.

He asked me to walk with him. He asked me to sit close to him before our fire. He brought bread and meat and sweet cake and we ate it on the grassy hill just outside our town; once he asked to kiss me. Finally, he asked me to wed.

IT MUST HAVE BEEN in January or February, 1743—I was almost twenty-one years old and it was still winter. Hans lit the fire in the forge outside, and called me to his side. I left the wooden spoon in the large pot where soup was cooking over the fire and hurried to see what he wanted. He pointed to two figures walking toward us. We had our share of travelers who walked through our town on the way to Frankfurt or Heilbrunn. Sometimes a pair of young boys would stop to speak to Hans as he worked outside our house. I supposed they were looking for work or adventure. How would it feel, I wondered, to walk toward adventure with such a free and easy gait? I used to watch as they turned to leave, with a wave to Hans, kicking at stones or stopping to pick one up to throw at a tree as boys seemed to do. But on that winter day I stood next to Hans and squinted but could only make out two women. One was taller than the other; walking stiffly, she held to her companion's arm and picked her way carefully over the stones. They were dressed alike in dark capes and each had her hair covered by a white cap, as the style of our day dictated. But as they came closer and I could make out the details of their costume, I saw that their identical caps were somewhat unique, coming to a point over their foreheads, and tied with dark blue ribbons. I did not need to wonder where I had seen head coverings like this, for many times I had recalled the bowed heads, bent in prayer in the church in Heilbrunn when I was twelve. I stood transfixed as the women came closer and would not have moved had not my soup's bubbling called me inside to the fire. I could smell the onions I had gathered from the root cellar. I stirred and stopped, looking at nothing as I again recreated my trip to Heilbrunn those years ago. "Dear hearts" were the words the Count had used as he looked at us—at me. Could it be that the two on our road were coming to deliver something only to me? I imagined myself being beckoned to Count Zinzendorf's large estate, where I would bend my knees deeply and he would take my hand. He would hold it for a moment. I could almost feel his warm fingers. He would tell me I had been chosen . . . An annoying cluck told me our hen had again wandered into the room. I shook my skirt at her and looked up to see a figure in our doorway; a stranger, yet not a stranger, for although her face was as yet unknown to me, her costume was indeed the same as the Moravian women in the large church in Heilbrunn.

"I beg your pardon, but perhaps you might give us some direction." Such a musical voice. It had a lilt, and although the woman spoke familiar German, it was easy to hear that she was no peasant. I motioned the women to come inside. They stood before me in their brown dresses and dark capes. I could see that their white aprons were spotless and even their shoes seemed too clean to have walked far. My apron was stained with berry juice and I placed my hand over the stain. The woman who had spoken to me held out her hand and, without bending my knee properly, I took it. She looked directly at me. "I am Sister Schmidt and my companion is Sister Happold. We are members of the Moravian *Pilgergemeine* returning to Herrnhaag and it is farther than we had thought it would be," she said. I saw she was weary; there were dark circles under her gray eyes.

"Perhaps you would like to sit a while," I said. "I can get you a drink of water."

She almost sank into the chair. At that moment, Greta arrived from washing at the brook, her arms circled around a basket as my mother's had; her small daughter stopped mid-skip when she saw the two women. Her son, little Johann, reached out to hold my petticoat. I could feel the pull of his hands as he bunched the material to his face to hide. The baby began sucking noises from her cradle and Hans' large figure blocked the light as he stepped into the doorway.

The soup was bubbling and the smell made my mouth water. I ladled it into large dishes. The younger woman said, "O, may our Saviour bless your sweetness," and sat at the table. The older woman said, "We are grateful for your food, but is it possible to wash? We have been on the road for some time and . . . " I reached for the cloth we kept on a nail and dipped it into the bucket of clean water.

As the faces of those two appear again in my mind, I can see that our actions that day, so ordinary, were all part of a great plan. Washing, sipping soup, eating bread, I could not take my eyes from their faces. No sudden brightness filled that rustic room, no whirlwind gusted in the door to swirl the table and chairs and set us all in motion. Our Lady did not appear in a blue mist before our fire and the candles on the mantle remained unlit. But the two women touched my heart as they bowed their heads to sing a Grace, and Time was measured not by the tick of our town clock but with their phrases.

Sister Schmidt was the first to rise from her chair. "Although we had planned to travel on tomorrow," she said, "it may be that there was some reason for us to come to Gelzhausen." She turned to her younger friend, "When our husbands arrive, I am going to suggest that we stay here a few days. I am sure we can be of service in this small village before we move on."

Perhaps I should have begun to nest one bowl in another, to wash the spoons before bits of food hardened, but I could not move. All I could do was look intently at Sister Happold. She was quite young, with full cheeks and a pointed small chin giving balance to the point of her white cap that dipped into the center of her forehead. In answer to my stare she reached to the ribbon tied under her chin to untie it and remove her cap so she could show it to me. Her hair was red and curly and sprang out in all directions once free. I could not restrain an exclamation as I looked at her, and she laughed.

"I try to keep it tucked away," she said, tucking one curl behind her ear. "See if it fits."

I wanted to put it on but I was too shy to do such a thing and gave it back to her. Questions crowded my mind but I did not know if I should ask. I felt almost hungry to hear why they were traveling; and, above all, what did they mean when they said they might be of service in Gelzhausen? I had no words for what I wanted to know.

Greta put her basket down on the floor and lifted her small babe from its cradle. As she opened her shift and jacket to nurse, she said, "I think the Weaver and his wife might put you up for the night." Hans shuffled his feet and said, "I left the fire unattended—I must take care . . . " So saying, he left the room with his daughter trailing after him. Little Johann, shy as he was, stood right in front of Sister Happold and gazed at her without one word.

Sister Happold stepped to the door. "I believe we should walk down the road to see if we can secure lodging." Putting her hand on my arm, she continued, "If you are willing, we would like to see you again, for I feel you have an awakening heart." With those strange words she gathered her petticoat and walked through the door.

"Wait," I whispered, "wait for a moment." But my voice was too quiet and the women had already gone, leaving the sharp scent of rosemary.

That night I dreamed of music, and when I awoke the tune of the Sisters' Grace surrounded me, although the ringing of Hans' hammer kept a different pace.

Such a short time it took for so much to change! My twenty-first birthday was coming at the end of March, and I knew that the sun would again slant on the rooftops longer each day and the loamy smell of rain and mud would call me from the kitchen to stand and breathe in the coming of spring long before it danced on green sandals into Gelzhausen. As I loosened dirt around the lacy carrot tops from the root cellar, or waited at twilight to see the large figure of my suitor making his way down the road, my mind would wander to the Moravian women who had graced our table for those brief minutes.

Late one afternoon I threw the wash water from our bucket and watched the half circle of droplets catch the pale sunlight before disappearing into the earth. Will I someday vanish like those droplets, to mix with the roots of growing things that struggle to push through the surface? Or would my Soul, freed at last, float as vapor all the way to our Heavenly Father where I will swirl around His feet? I never had asked our priest these questions, though when my dear mother was taken, I often asked them of myself. Perhaps the Moravian women would have answers for my persistent questions. Perhaps Sister Schmidt might tell me something I could keep forever in my mind; something that would not sink like those shining droplets that were forever gone.

Over the next weeks it was the elder Moravian Sister whose gentle ways urged me to ponder, to speak, to ask. She had fine wrinkles on her cheeks, their intersections like roads to somewhere. I knew little of roads other than those near Gelzhausen. How was it for her to journey unknown roads, I wondered? I listened to her long, even sentences that rose and fell as though she were singing in the measured tone of a hymn, though of course there were no notes; but the sound mesmerized me. When she spoke of our Saviour it was in such a way that I could feel His presence. His lowly birthplace was as familiar as the stables in our own town—the smell of straw, the low grunting of cows and cluck of hens. And His light must have filled the crude little place and spilled out onto the fields seeking the dark places there and in our hearts.

In that late winter of 1743, I welcomed the dark and quiet when I sat alone before the fire with my own thoughts. The night was very dark, in the fireplace a log hissed. Then a rustle and little Johann came from behind a curtain. His face was flushed with sleep and he rubbed his eyes with his fists. Without a word he climbed into my lap and I began to rock him and hum very quietly. I buried my face in his curly copper hair and thought of the traveling Moravians. Would I, like His disciples, simply follow Him when he asked? Would I become lost if I strayed too far from the stone houses of Gelzhausen, no longer holding the memory of my mother if I could not walk to her resting place?

I tried in vain not to remember the whispered gossip and salacious stories that slithered from house to house. It was only a day ago that I had entered the butcher shop. A cluster of my neighbors, baskets on their arms, stood in silence as the Baker's widow passed her poison from face to face, her lips pursed behind her curved hand as she leaned close.

The Shoemaker's young wife looked very concerned. "It is said by many that these so-called Brethren ask one to cut all ties with their families if one becomes a member. They say their brothers and sisters are only those who live in their community."

Another continued, "People who marry do not even know one another. They marry by the use of the Lot."

"Marry? I doubt they are fit for marriage once that Count takes his advantage!" The Baker's widow knew she had the attention of the women. They clustered closer to hear her as she whispered, each word accompanied with a sort of a hiss. "Well, you do know he surrounds himself with all those young girls—ignorant girls from the sound of it. And who knows what goes on behind closed doors in the manor house in Berthelsdorf." Her words had the desired effect, for there was a collective catch of breath as the women leaned closer.

"Working girls are always the victims. We know that. Those privileged ones take what they want and leave the poor in the muck." A newcomer to our village drew her dark eyebrows together, her voice heard by everyone in the shop.

"I have found Sisters Schmidt and Happold to be good people, Frau Heldon," another answered. "The women are very accomplished at handiwork and I have been told some even play musical instruments."

A woman who lived outside of our town moved closer to the groups as she spoke up in a loud voice with the shocking words, "From what I heard, the church elders watch when couples come together in bed. Can you believe that?" To her satisfaction, the others answered with exclamations of horror.

Not to be outdone, the Baker's widow spoke again. "The Moravian women leave their children to follow their husbands to far away lands." She thrust her head forward. "Women do not follow men from place to place." Unless, unless, of course, they are sluts who follow soldiers from camp to camp. Her smile did not reach her glittering eyes.

The Married Sisters did leave their children and accompany their husbands all over the world. They taught in places I had barely heard about, like southern islands where it is very hot and Greenland where they say the snow never melts. But the whispers around our town were not all against these people who said they were a part of a very old church. I could not help but feel admiration for the missionaries who learned the languages of strangers wherever they went, so as to tell them of Jesus. In that dark night, as I sat by the dying fire, I tightened my arms around my little nephew. If I were truly awakened to my Saviour, my heart would be so full that I could go anywhere, leave anyone. But could I do this? Could I be so filled with a love for Him that I would leave everyone I had known?

Doubt arrives in the dark but disappears at the sound of cock crow, and so it was that winter night. In my waking dream I had seen myself standing alone before a great brightness and, although my clothes were rags, I was not cold. I awoke and slid from my bed. Not bothering with a cape against the early morning chill, I hurried outside to stand and watch the pale yellow sun peep over the ridge of our unfurrowed wheat field. Today, oh, today I shall hasten down the wet road to Sister Schmidt, to tell her I would follow the blessed Count. Barefoot and hungry even I would follow him to my Saviour! Sister Schmidt will ask me then to go with her to Herrnhaag. It was not far away. I could walk in a few days, perhaps. The other Sisters would all come out to greet me and the blessed Count would take my hand again.

I was so lost in reverie I did not at first see my intended walking toward me until I heard him call, his voice loud against the shuttered windows. He strode through mud and puddles unmindful of the splashing. He called again. As his large figure drew nearer I no longer felt the eagerness to have his lips pressing my palm. He called again with a demanding urgency and

I ran to the doorway to hide.

The snow still remained in uneven patches; the north side of our stone church, the bank of the river that saw no sun and even on the side roads little used by townspeople. The main road was so muddy I had to gather my petticoats to my knees as I walked to meet with Sister Schmidt. I found her at the Weaver's loom, and though she did not rise when I entered the low door to his house, she smiled and beckoned. Then she rose to greet me.

"I did want to speak to you again. Before you leave for Herrnhaag. You see . . . " I hesitated, for the words were difficult to form. "You see," my mouth was dry as I uttered the last of my sentence, "I feel I want to travel also to Herrnhaag."

Sister Schmidt stood directly in front of me. "Your intended shares this idea with you?"

"No. We have not spoken of this."

She was silent.

"I am not sure I should marry. Greta says it is the right thing to do. I am not sure . . . I do not know."

"Christina, listen to my question. Do you know your own heart?"

I did not know how to answer. I told her Hans and Greta thought I should marry.

Sister Schmidt placed her hand on my arm and led me to a wooden bench. She gently pulled me down next to her, saying, "You are speaking of obligation. I am asking if you have looked into your heart?"

What did she know of my heart? I knew I had the Saviour in my heart and with His strength could leave behind whatever worldly things I had pursued.

"Sister Schmidt, I am ready to work out my own salvation because the Saviour has touched my heart." I touched my breast with my open palm.

"Tell me, my dear, what has our Saviour asked you to do?" Her voice was quiet. She did not make any attempt to touch me. Her deep-set eyes looked intently at my face. I rose and began to walk from one end of the small room to another. The wooden floor creaked under my steps.

"I am confused. I am just confused."

"No, my dear child. You do not want to look into your heart. You want to listen to your own voice."

"That is not true," I cried out. Tears stung my eyes. "That is not true! I want His will to be mine. If I follow Him, then I will know what He asks of me. I love Him!"

Embarrassed at the sound of my own voice, I put my hands over my face. The old Moravian woman rose from her chair and gently pulled my hands away from my face. Deep wrinkles scored her forehead.

"Christina Barbara. You are in love with an idea. You clasp it to your breast and dance in a dizzying circle." Her gray eyes were calm and she did not smile. "Come," she said. "Sit here with me." She led me back to the bench. "Do you recall that we spoke about how Brother Ludwig— Count Zinzendorf—gathered with those who had come to his estates in Berthelsdorf? It was in August. You would have been but an infant. There was such an outpouring of love. Those who were there could barely describe how close our Saviour was. How He had entered our hearts."

She held my hands gently and her eyes were so kind. "Christina, my dear. The love and dedication of those of us who are members of the Unitas Fratrum comes from our earnest prayers to open our hearts to the dearest Lamb who sacrificed all for us. You see, our love, our faith and our hope binds us together with something that cannot be broken."

Sister Schmidt rose with some difficulty but stood close to me, placing her hand on my shoulder as she continued. "I feel we would welcome you at Herrnhaag." I held my breath, waiting to hear her say I could travel with her and Sister Happold and their husbands. But she did not say this. She bid me first not to marry until I had prayerfully considered my decision to spend the rest of my life with Friedrich. Then she cupped her hands around my face. "You are very young. I think you are very close to understanding our dedication to Him who gave His all for us; but you must know you may travel far—very far—in your lifetime, and you must carry the image of the blessed Lamb before you, for you will need that courage. Listen, Christina. Listen for His words before you make a rash decision."

I walked slowly back to our house, stepping over the muddy ruts left in the main road. I felt heated anger, and with this a resolve grew weed-like in my mind. Perhaps the Saviour's voice was yet mute, but I would will Him to give me a sign. Though lightning might strike all around me, I would stand steadfast with outstretched palms and He would know my resolve to follow Him as did the woman Mary Magdalene.

Of course Greta was heartbroken and Hans was very angry when I swallowed my tears and told them I could not marry.

"You have led Friedrich to believe you will marry him." Hans' voice was like distant thunder. "He and I plan to work together—we were adding rooms—we have a good location here . . . "

"Hush, hush, the child does not know what is good for her." Greta put her hand on Hans' arm. "Listen, Christina. Gelzhausen is where you belong. This is where you were born." Tears spilled from her blue eyes. "This is where your mother rests—and Otto and Heinrich—all of them."

I would not hear her words. I took a deep breath and stood very tall. I was taller than Greta. I raised my chin. "I am led by the Saviour. It is He who leads me by the still waters to join those who believe as I do."

Greta plucked at Hans' sleeve as she had plucked at my brother's so long ago, when he stood unsteadily in this same room. The swift memory caused me to falter and I felt a weakness in both knees.

"Wait, Hans. Perhaps the child is going to join the nuns. Perhaps our God has chosen her for the Habit and for prayer."

Hans hesitated, his broad face perplexed as he wrinkled his forehead. I noticed for the first time that Hans was losing his hair.

"Is that it, Christina? Is that what you want? To join the nuns and spend your days in prayer?" As he said the last words he shook his head in a kind of disbelief.

"No, Hans. It has been Sister Schmidt who has taught me of the true path. She . . . "

"Nuns, Sisters, what is the difference? Either way you will travel far from all who have taken care of you." He spoke the next words in anger. "There will be little dreaming in Herrnhaag, my girl. Pigs still need to be slaughtered."

There was silence in the small room as each of us waited, not daring to look at one another. I thought cups would rattle on their shelves, that an ugly wind would twist the table and topple the chairs, even that the roof might loosen with a giant creak. I stood taller, my hands at my sides. I must be strong. I would be brave. How could I explain my feelings to these two I loved? They had no idea of the depth of my passion; for it must be passion that was leading me to follow an unknown path to discover truth for myself.

Finally, Hans spoke, his voice weary. "You must tell Friedrich as soon as possible. It is not fair . . . wherever you go, you will still have to spin and wash, make no mistake."

"Oh, Christina, I have tried to make you happy." Greta hung her head.

I had to swallow several times before I could trust myself to speak even a few words. "Greta, Hans, this is a journey I must take. I know this in my heart."

"Aunt Tina, Aunt Tina, we found a frog at the creek and it is hopping—it is hopping. Come see." Johann flew into the room.

AN AWAKENING HEART   41

It was then I began to weep. I sat by the table and cried and cried. Johann's little face puckered. Hans put his heavy hand on my shoulder and patted me while Greta wiped my tears with the corner of her apron.

"There, there," they said at once. "There, there."

I thought then that the matter was settled; but it was not. Just the next morning our large kettle crashed to the floor. Greta turned from the fire, her eyes narrowed. "Christina, I have told you over and over to leave the kettle on the hook. Why do you put it on the shelf where it falls so easily?"

An angry retort came to my lips, but at the same time I remembered our Saviour's meek nature. "I am sorry, Greta. I will try to remember." My answer seemed to inflame her more and she swung her bulk around to face me.

"You have not learned how to keep a proper kitchen. Perhaps it is well that Friedrich finds another woman for a wife."

She turned away and I had no answer to bounce off her broad back. I knew I would have to tell Friedrich very soon, but he had taken his hammer to Heilbrunn for repairs and we did not expect him for a few days.

"I know that I have disappointed you, Greta . . . "

"Disappointed me? Disappointed me? It is much more than that, Christina. I don't care who you marry—you can stay here until you are bent over for all it matters. But to leave like this—to go off without a thought of who you are leaving behind." Spoons rattled as she threw them onto the table.

Our supper that evening was a silent one. Hans reached his finger into his mouth to loosen a piece of pork; Greta did not look at me, and even the children had chewed their bread and looked from one to the other of us, waiting for words that never came. I went about my tasks now in a house filled with discomfort. Hans and Greta spoke to me when they needed to, but there was no idle talk and no bursts of laughter over Johann's childish attempts to be amusing.

Sunday of that week was rather warm for February. I knew Friedrich would probably arrive back in Gelzhausen that afternoon. The thought of my telling him of my decision made it difficult for me to stay with one task. I walked to the spring without taking a bucket; I put the kettle on the hearth with no water. As always, Greta made ready for Mass but there was none of the calling back and forth, no offering of a ribbon to tie back my hair.

I heard Friedrich's shout before he entered our door. I knew he would do just that—shout and bump into the chair and then look at me with a sheepish grin. Before he reached to put his thick arms around me, I began to speak. Telling Friedrich was not as difficult as I had thought it might be, for I knew he would soon find another strong girl to lie beside him in the darkness, to mend his clothes and, perhaps, to laugh with Greta as they pared apples. My heart faltered at the thought of their laughter in this house; but I drew strength from my resolve to walk the stormy but elevated path I had chosen. Nothing would dissuade me. Not even Friedrich's heavy face, his eyes watering.

And the telling somehow made my choice more clear. Everywhere I looked, everything I did was changed. The world, gray in late winter, now reflected bright color. I lit the morning fire and saw my Saviour's face in the bright flames; I looked to the lightening sky and saw Him again. The rude and empty metal cross that hung by our front door held in my mind the figure of agony, and tears filled my being so I could not breathe. I would follow my Saviour. No price I would have to pay on leaving could dim this fervent desire to serve Him. The rains swept into our valley and I stood without a cape or shawl, my mouth open to feel the cold drops of my Saviour's tears. When I measured Time by my monthly flow, I thought of His blood spilled for us.

The wind was blowing very hard, as it sometimes does in early spring before the large trees bud. Only the pussy willows by our creek had opened their soft sprouts and I gathered them that morning, rubbing the fur on my cheek before standing the long branches in a corner of the kitchen that caught the morning sun. I looked out to see the new priest of our church walking toward our house, his cassock billowing behind him. He was much younger than our former priest, and was better educated they said. But he was difficult to look at, because one eye not only darted off to the side but teared and the poor man was constantly wiping and dabbing.

I did not answer his knock right away, because I hoped Greta might greet him herself, as she knotted sheets on a line to dry. I was sure she had spoken to him earlier. Finally, when Greta refused to be interrupted, I reached for the metal latch.

"May I come in, Christina?" I bent my head in assent and the wind blew into the house as he entered.

"Hans has gone for the day, I see," he said as an opening. I bowed my head again in a silent assent.

"And your sister-in-law is hanging wash, I see." I said nothing and motioned him to sit by the fire that had blazed up as the wind swirled a flame.

"Christina, I have heard you are acquainted with the Moravian Pastors Schmidt and Happold."

"I am better acquainted with their wives who work alongside them."

The priest reached into his pocket for his handkerchief and dabbed at his eye. "I, too, have spoken with these people and they assure me their purpose is to encourage any who want to listen, to take Jesus Christ into their hearts." When he said the words "Jesus Christ," he bowed his head a little and a tear dropped from his cheek. Then he continued, "The Pastors have told me that they have no wish to change a Christian's heart—only to encourage one to be more faithful in one's own tradition."

I saw no reason to say anything, so I was silent.

"Christina Barbara, do you understand what I am saying?" And without waiting for an answer he said, "One can remain a faithful Catholic, a member of the true Church, and still take the advice of these good people. One need not follow them to their gathering place at Herrnhaag to be a good and true Christian."

I wanted to be respectful but I was impatient. How could I make this young man understand that I had been called to follow our Saviour? He, too, must have been called, yet he would never understand that a mere woman—one with little education or station in life—could also hear the voice of the Almighty.

"Father Peter. I have come to know of my own inadequacies. I have asked Our Lord to help me and He has shown me a way."

His face became a mask of kind solicitation. "Now, now. Of course, you know your own mind. Our nuns are strong women who obey God and their superiors, as I am sure you want to do. Perhaps your true calling is to enter a convent."

The man dabbed his eye and smiled with one corner of his mouth. I did not like his smile. "Christina," he continued, "you must remember it is not for you to judge your condition or the path you must follow. Only one who is trained in the ways of God can do that for you, my child."

I felt my face turn hot and wished for a moment I had not such fair skin that betrayed my emotions. "I am NOT a child." And becoming more bold I continued, "I am as old as you are and as able to decide for myself the condition of my heart." I felt the strength of my Saviour, raised my chin and moved closer to the young man who stared, his one eye streaming now. "I am traveling to Herrnhaag at the first possible moment." Saying these words made my throat close, for I had not known until then I was ready to go.

"You are going to Hell."

"Father, I have no more to say." I motioned him to the door. If I hesitated, I might enter a path where brambles of doubt reached out to hold me fast to this life of tea kettles and wooden saints.

He walked out our doorway without a word. The wind caught at my petticoat and our Lord's cross hanging above the table seemed to move ever so slightly. Surely this was a good sign.

Greta did not need to ask what had transpired when she pushed open the rear door, her arms full of sheets. The baby began to cry in her cradle. Greta dropped the sheets onto the table and went to pick up her child. I said nothing nor did she. When finally Greta sat to nurse the little one, I picked up a sheet to fold it, saying, "Greta, you know I must do this thing."

Greta sighed, her round face sad. There was no anger in her voice. "I have prayed to our Holy Mother—I do not understand why you are leaving the true Church. I fear so for you—I fear so . . . we cannot meet in Heaven, Christina. Not if you leave our Church."

I stepped to her side and knelt beside her. "Oh, Greta. I do feel I have been called to serve Him in a different way. Can you believe it is love that drives me? Can you?"

Greta reached out her hand and cupped my face. "I promised when your mother died—when your father left—I said to myself I would take care of you. I have tried . . . "

"You have been more than a sister to me." I could trust myself to say no more.

Hans stood in the doorway, and, without looking, up Greta said very quietly, "She is going, Hans. She is going with those Moravians."

Hans said nothing but sat down heavily on the bench by the open door, then kicked it closed with one foot.

"Christina, we cannot stop you, but do you know how far this journey is—do you know what awaits you at the end?"

"I only know that love awaits me, Hans."

He shook his head slowly, as one who is very tired. "You must not go alone. I want you to wait until Pastors Schmidt and Happold leave, and then, if you feel the same way you do now, well . . . perhaps I can find someone who is traveling in that direction."

"But why wait, Hans? Why?"

"When those people have left here, you might . . . you might think different." Hans rubbed his forehead with his short fingers.

This was better than I had hoped because I knew that Sister Schmidt had asked me to wait. This way, I would go with the blessing of dear Greta and Hans as well as obeying the Moravian woman's suggestion.

There were small buds on the bushes, but the air remained cold. I waited. Then, the thought came to me I would wait until the cock crowed three more mornings at the rise of the pale sun. I walked the muddy road to the small square where a few crocuses peeped through the earth next to the well. There, a small carriage stood, a few townspeople had gathered. The Schmidts and Happolds pressed the hands of those who had come to bid them goodbye and, stepping forward to say farewell, I put my hand in Sister Schmidt's. Her skin was warm and very dry and her thin bones were suddenly frail to me. "Perhaps" was the word she uttered very quietly. I doubt anyone heard but me.

I watched her take her husband's arm, and turn once to wave. But I could no wait longer. I would not wait. I knew with certainty that I would be truly filled with His presence if I made the journey to Herrnhaag. And soon. There the Moravian Sisters would gather me into their midst and the great Count would again take my hand.

The sun seemed to move more slowly across the sky to lengthen the day, and the nights were filled with whispers of wind. I awoke to see Greta standing over me, candle in her hand. "Christina Barbara, you called out in your sleep and awakened me." Her voice was kind, her forehead wrinkled in worry. I looked into her plain face.

I sat up and patted the side of my narrow bed for Greta to sit near me. "Greta," I began; "Greta, I think the time is coming." She started to speak but I put my finger to her lips. "No, wait. Do not speak until I tell you." And without wasting words, I said, "Greta, I must make plans to leave for Herrnhaag soon."

"You have not spoken of this for a week or so. I had hoped . . . I thought you may have decided to stay."

"You must help me, Greta. You must help me with Hans—to find a way to get there."

"How can you ask this? To speak to Hans when it is against the Holy Church? When it may lead you into sin?"

"Oh, my dear sister. We have had so many words about this. You must know that the Lutherans are good people—I feel the Moravians are, too." My voice rose in the darkness.

Greta pushed my shoulder slightly and the candle flickered. "There are those who go to churches other than ours who are good people." She hesitated and looked into the darkness beyond the candle glow." But our Church is the true and holy one. Only we will see God in Heaven."

Hans' large figure pushed aside the curtain that sectioned my small space. His face was heavy with sleep and his voice rumbled. "What are you doing up at this hour? What is this about?"

Greta stood. "Christina thinks she is going to Herrnhaag and she does not even know the way . . . she does not know . . . " She burst into noisy tears.

"Oh, those Moravian Sisters, they are the ones who have put these thoughts in your mind." She put her face in her hands, "It is my fault. I never should have let you speak with them."

"Hush, hush, Greta. It is not the Moravian women who have put these thoughts in my mind. It is the Jesus the Saviour . . . "

"Stop this! Stop this."

Greta reached to put her hand over my mouth. "You are not to say this kind of thing." She looked around as though to see some dark angel, then turned to lean her heavy body against her husband's.

How I loved them both! I love them still. They had been mother and father to me. But I had no words to explain to them of my decision, I had only my strong resolve and it was this alone that gave me the strength to pack my few belongings in a small carrying case, to bid my friends goodbye and to swallow my fear of making the journey.

It was at the beginning of a wet March that I started off. It was early morning. A jay called his piercing song and, with a flash of blue, settled on the wooden fencepost, cocking his head from side to side. We stood outside the shop to say farewell. Jacob the Herdsman sat on the seat of his open cart, the large milk containers rattling against one another when his horse stomped. He wore his wide-brimmed black hat low on his forehead and seemed deaf and blind to our presence.

Hans and Greta held to one another in front of me, and I could not speak, for I felt such a rush of unexpected tears as I looked at their dear faces. Little Johann reached for my hand with a shrill, "You must not go,

Aunt Tina. I will not let you." Saying this, he reached up to wrap his arms around my waist.

We all stood for some minutes. Little Trudy burrowed in my petticoat. Hans looked at his feet. "Well now, Christina, the trip to Herrnhaag is not very long." And then, trying to smile, he wiped his cheeks with the back of his large hand, and said, "You will not even be that far away. There is no reason for you womenfolk to be so sad."

Greta started to speak, hesitated, and then said, "Those people . . . those Moravians, they travel, they . . . " And, of course, I knew why we were crying. I knew why I felt such heaviness in my chest. It was not that I was walking to Herrnhaag, but that I might go still further; that I might be called to America or some other faraway place and never see them again. No, I thought. No, I will not think of that now. I will see them somehow, while also staying with the Moravians for my Saviour's sake.

I looked up to the fencepost and saw that the bird had flown and I had not heard its parting cry.

CHAPTER TWO

The road was sometimes straight and sometimes twisting and, as the horse and carriage jogged along, it occurred to me that my thoughts were like the road stretching out before us. I could imagine my life in a straight line, my footsteps steady and sure as events appeared before me in an ordered progression and I nodded yes or no, making choices that would bring me closer to my Saviour. Suddenly, as the cart swung to one side and I pressed my hands onto the wooden bench, I looked up to see that the curve in the road was right-angled and there was no seeing beyond. Then I knew with certainty that my life was full of surprise and even mystery, and though I might nod yes or no, a great plan was unfolding and I was being swept along, a small mite in the hand of Him whose mighty breath blows through our world. I do not remember that these thoughts frightened me as Jacob sat silently beside me, the reins resting in his work-worn hands.

Our road wound through a valley, and there were few woods, just an occasional stand of trees that stood bare against the daylight. The gurgle of water followed us, the creek sometimes spilling over the banks of tangled weeds. We had had much rain that spring but the clouds above us seemed transparent now, unable to hold water. I thanked my Saviour for the day's dry weather for our cart was open and I did not want to arrive at Herrnhaag looking bedraggled and forlorn. The thought of actually being at Herrnhaag made me uneasy. Jacob had told me he would drop me off just after the town of Grundau and I would have to walk the last miles alone. What if I took the wrong road and became lost? Would doors open to my knock only to be shut again with the owner's curled lip of anger? And what of nightfall on a lonely road with only the wind to whip at my cloak? Or worse, the sound of a heavy tread behind me. No one would hear my screams. I swallowed once trying to dissolve the lump in my throat. Oh my God, I would be so alone. I coughed to summon some moisture and glanced over at Jacob without turning much. The Herdsman looked straight ahead and then, as though speaking to some unseen person in front of us, he said, "I know an inn on the road. We will stop there for the night."

Stop for the night? I had not thought about this. Where would I sleep? Where would he sleep? I took a breath. "Jacob, will a room for the night cost very dear?" I thought that if I asked about money he would need to give me some explanation of the inn's accommodations.

"Not much."

I felt in my pocket for my small money purse. Hans had given me coins, pressing them into my hand. They had been warm from his. I felt tears suddenly and looked off to one cart wheel where a blackened slash was visible with every revolution. Three times it came into view before I could speak.

"I suppose you have stopped there many times on your trips to Grundau?"

"Yes."

It was useless to ask this man any more questions. I decided to stay in the cart if the place was unclean. Or, if some pleasant woman ran the place, I would tell her I was on my way to Herrnhaag to join the Moravians and she would give me a small, clean room. But then I remembered many people did not like the Moravians; in fact, it seemed quite a few thought they were very odd in the way many lived as traveling pilgrims, starting small churches wherever townspeople would listen. But I had made my decision to follow my Saviour and would not swerve from my course. I clutched the small purse in my pocket.

The road entered a small wooded area and, as the bare trees closed behind us, I felt Jacob pull on the reins and the horse came to a full stop. He turned and looked at me. His black hat covered his forehead and seemed to rest on his heavy eyebrows. His eyes were deep-set, his nose crooked. He looked away from me and spoke.

"You might want to go into the woods and . . . " He stopped. Whatever was he talking about? He jumped down from his seat, saying, "I am going off there . . . "

Thank goodness. He was going to relieve himself. I had wondered for at least an hour how to approach this matter, as my bladder rapidly filled enough to burst. I hastily jumped from the cart and walked into the woods to raise my petticoat slightly, my feet apart. A bird chirped and then flapped by close to my head, its wings so near I could just about feel wind in its wake. It chirped again and I felt comfort in the cheery sound of God's creature.

After jogging along for an hour or two we came to an area of small dwellings, mostly half-timbered. They clustered together much like the shops and houses in my dear Gelzhausen. I looked into the faces of men and women who walked on the road beside us, hoping that one would be familiar, but although they smiled and some greeted us, there was no one I knew. Jacob pulled on the reins and we came to a jolting stop in front of a two-storied building of evenly cut stone. A porch in front seemed stuck on and tilted slightly to one side, its wooden steps missing one riser. Surely this was not the inn Jacob had in mind. He turned to me, "Doesn't look much on the outside but I know the owner and she is a respectable woman." He jumped stiffly from the cart. Should I follow the Herdsman or was I supposed to sit and wait for him to tell me what to do? I began to feel acute discomfort and played with the strings of my hat, pretending to concentrate on undoing a knot.

"Come, come, girl. Get down and come inside."

I looked up to see a short, rather stout woman. Her voice was friendly enough, her cap sat precariously on one side of her head, her graying hair uncombed. Would her rooms be as untidy as her hair?

"Come now, girl. I have a light supper for you and Jacob."

I drew up my skirt and climbed down carefully. The woman had already turned her back and was hurrying into the inn. I followed her into a large room, the ceiling very low with exposed beams that would have caused a tall man to stoop. There were four or five rough-hewn tables and chairs at various angles. Through the smoky air, I could see three men eating and drinking. One raised his stein as I entered the room, another licked his fingers. I could make out the figure of a man slouching in one darkened corner. He stuck out his tongue and licked his fat lips slowly while motioning to me with a crooked finger. I could not turn away and it was as if his face, almost hidden in the semi-light, held me and made me watch his motion. I backed up, my eyes still holding the man's figure as though I had framed him.

"Hey, girl, that's m' foot." Jacob placed his hand under my elbow with a chuckle. I was terribly embarrassed and turned to apologize. When my eye sought out the terrifying corner it was empty. Jacob guided me to a table and pulled out a wooden chair that scraped against the floor. He motioned me to sit opposite him. I was very thirsty and the smoke from the men's pipes scratched against my throat.

"Here, girl. You must need a good swig to wash the dust from your mouth." With a thud the Innkeeper put two steins of beer on the table.

The beer was surprisingly good, thick with foam and heavy with hops. Our supper arrived, a large chunk of cheese, which calmed the increasing flutterings of my stomach, and a plate of cabbage, overcooked but warm and spicy with pepper.

I had gulped the beer rather quickly in my thirst and the effect was to render me not really dizzy, but rather relaxed and sleepy. I had such a need to stretch out at that moment on a clean bed in a quiet room but I was not sure what I was to do. Perhaps this is all part of my Saviour's plan for me; to compose myself in strange places and to sleep wherever I found myself. I bowed my head and closed my eyes to try to picture His dear face.

"Looks as though you are ready to sleep." Jacob's voice broke into my attempts at prayer. "Bettina," he called. "Bettina—we are ready for sleep."

We, I thought? We? Was Jacob to share a room with me?

Our Innkeeper turned to Jacob, saying, "I think you will want your room downstairs." She smiled ever so slightly, and when I looked to Jacob's face, I could not read his expression.

"Here, girl, follow me." She led me to a narrow stairway and down a long hall. I could smell cabbage, not unpleasant, and another much older smell of wood fires and pipe smoke that had curled around the daub and wattle walls.

"There are not many traveling tonight, so you can have a room to yourself."

"Oh, thank you." And thank God, I thought. I did not relish the thought of having to sleep with a stranger nor hear the snores of the Herdsman, even if across the room.

We walked down a hallway with three or four doors on either side and at the end she opened one. I could see but little, for the hall was lit by only one lamp and I peered into the darkness of the room. Bettina lit a candle and in the partial light I could see that the room was very small, containing one bed, one chair and a tiny table that held a pitcher. My bag was on the floor next to the bed.

"The chamber pot is under the bed. I think you will find the room clean." She moved to open a tiny window. "The night air will not hurt you here."

Suddenly, I was very tired. The cabbage weighed comfortably in my stomach, the bit of apple dessert left a clean taste, and the beer made me want to lie down without even washing. I would dream of the Count receiving me at Herrnhaag, his jeweled hands tying the ribbons of the Single Sisters under my chin.

The Innkeeper cleared her throat and I remembered my manners. "Thank you very much. Will you take payment now?"

"No, Jacob has taken care of that." She smiled and I could see the dark places where her teeth were missing. She turned and left, closing the door quietly.

I removed my hat and put it over the short bedpost. When I slid from my shift and petticoats, I could feel cool air and the candle flickered uncertainly. Not allowing myself to give in to fear, I nevertheless drew the metal latch across the door. I reached for the pitcher and the water was quite cold, but I washed my face, hands and upper body. Finding no towel, I dabbed myself with a corner of the sheet. Colder now, I climbed under the blanket and curled into a ball to keep warm. Could I pray to God without getting out of bed and kneeling? Surely it does not matter. I blew out the candle.

I fell asleep immediately but it was still dark when I started, fully awake. The room was quiet. What had wakened me? Then I heard a thumping noise, regular it was. Was some one knocking at the inn door? Then a dog barked. The darkness in my room took on a sinister feeling as the dog began to snarl deep in its throat. It was a wild and frightening sound, as if the animal was full of fear and hatred and was helpless to utter any sound but this one of anguish that scratched my breast. I thought of the mad dog that had loped into Gelzhausen and had died in its blood when my father swung at it with his muscled arm. I curled into myself. Voices then, whispers—a door opening and shutting and then quiet. I suddenly longed for my narrow bed at home, the curtain making it private and safe, the sound of Hans snoring and of Greta when she turned in her sleep and murmured. What if the Moravian Sisters turn me away? Perhaps I am not yet ready—Sister Schmidt had urged me to wait for a sign.

Please, O please, my Lord, I prayed. Show me something. Let me hear your dearest voice.

I heard laughter then, it seemed musical—a beautiful sound that floated to my window in a crescendo. It was a woman's laugh, deep and husky at first and then high and sweet as though the bearer had just given a gift and was pleased with the giving. Could this be a sign? How strange to hear a woman's laughter in the middle of a dark night in early spring. How very strange that such an unlikely sound as a woman's laughter filled me with a kind of peace. But when the sound ceased, I was no longer afraid. I was no longer lonely.

After a brief breakfast, Jacob and I again sat side by side in his cart as the horse pulled forward. The weather was warmer that morning, with blue breaking through the wispy clouds as the sun rose, and I felt somehow safer than I had the day before. Jacob smacked the reins to hurry the horses and the loping of the rhythm changed. He spoke for the first time since we had begun that morning.

"The road from Grundau to Herrnhaag is safe and you will not have long to walk."

"Will I know Herrnhaag when I get there?"

Jacob turned to look at me. "You cannot miss it. I do not know anyplace hereabouts that has such big houses. They sit in a square." This was the longest sentence I had heard him utter and I wished I could ask another question that would bring forth so much information. I tried again. "Will I know which of the houses is for the Moravian Sisters? Will I be able to tell?"

Jacob shrugged. "Don't know about that." He slapped the reins and the horse picked up more speed.

It seemed to me that we approached Grundau very quickly. The houses were close to the street the way they were in Gelzhausen, but the road was so narrow we had to stop and wait for oncoming horses. Jacob sat contentedly with his reins in his hands, and I wished for one quick moment that we could just sit there and not move forward. But with a jolt we began again, not stopping until the small houses sat on larger spaces finally giving way to fields, some newly ploughed. I felt comfortable that morning, the fields stretching before us, the sun warming my back. The jog of horses' hooves was familiar to me this day, as though I had been on the road for some time. Surely this journey was one I was destined to take. I did not feel the horses slowing, but suddenly Jacob drew on the reins and we came to a full stop.

"This is as far as I can take you—have to go off to the dairy farm now and do some business."

I could not move from the cart. "How far did you say?"

"Not far—few hours maybe."

The time had gone too fast. I was so content only a few moments ago. I had the wish to cross myself to make myself braver, but instead I climbed down, holding my small bag. Surprising me, Jacob also alighted and put one hand on my shoulder.

"I think you will easily find your way. I hear the Moravians are a good people." This sudden kindness on his part brought tears and all I could do was to nod and try to smile. He got up into his cart then, turned it around, waved once, and retraced his trip on the dirt road.

The road was straight at first. I could see ahead to a small rise. The only sound was the gurgle of water, the call of a crow. The wispy clouds blew quickly across the sky but I could feel no breeze. I began my journey with quick steps, my shabby bag bumping against my leg, my shoes sounding a regular beat on the road. When I came to the rise in the land, the road dipped again into a stand of trees. I could hear the call of small birds and see their fluttering flight as they darted across the road to hide themselves in the bushes on either side. Their song was full of promise and I knew that spring would come in a few weeks.

My thoughts flew back to Gelzhausen. It was lovely in spring. I remembered budding trees on either side of our main road, the smell of cow manure as the women mixed it with the black dirt of their window boxes so that the tiny greens would become flowers cascading pink to the ground. I told myself I was in the right place, but I felt as though my heart pounded to escape me and would fly back to Gelzhausen with the familiar sights and sounds of my childhood. I felt a rush of cool wind and noticed that there were darkening clouds gathering behind me. I knew I must hasten but I had to stop there on the road to call up my dream, my mission, my task given by my loving Saviour. I wished to be as certain as the fishermen who left their nets on the sands of Galilee's Sea. I stood on the road to Herrnhaag and could not summon the certainty I needed. How would I push my footsteps on the dirt road that led to the place of the Moravians? Wavering at first, I began to sing the hymn I had heard sung by Sister Happold. My notes, reedy and weak, became stronger with each breath. *"Jesus, still lead on till our rest be won. And although the way be cheerless, we will follow calm and clear."* I sang to the still brown fields and to the clouds that moved closer by an unseen wind. *"We will follow calm and fearless; guide us by thy hand to our Fatherland."* I sang to keep time with my steady pace and for courage that I tried to wrap around my spare frame.

I could tell it was middle afternoon when I stopped to rest and, as I sat down under a large oak to unwrap the cheese and dried apples the good Innkeeper had given me, my mind wandered in a kind of fancy, half-hoping my Saviour would show me a sign of His presence. Might I see a blood-red berry at my feet or—with a catch in my throat—would that He would call my name! I imagined Count Zinzendorf stopping his grand carriage and offering me a ride to Herrnhaag. Oh, I knew this was a childish fancy, for I was a woman now; but I could not help but wish he would teach me as he had the poor gypsies who had pitched their tattered tents only a few short years ago. Then, learning from the Count, I could teach the poor wretches how to plant and pray to our dear Lord. All those long years ago the Schlumbergers had told me about the Count making schools and helping the ragged children. I remembered those flaky pastries I had shared with the Schlumbergers; how fresh, thick cream coated the roof of my mouth. I chewed my dried apple and leaned against a tree.

The road curving ahead was empty. Indeed, I had seen few carts and only two or three travelers who had smiled or greeted me, but did not stop to speak more. I was alone. I was traveling a road that must lead to my heart's wish but I was so alone. There was no one person to lean close and tell me where my footsteps, so eager at first, would take me. No mother to tuck my hair behind my ears and look into my face; no father to hold me close in the smoky comfort of his shirt. If only I could hear for one minute the sound of Hans and Otto shouting and scuffling before the lighted forge. My sigh startled me and was taken by the afternoon's wind. I stood and brushed the crumbs from my petticoat. Greta would say to me, "Christina, I just swept that floor and now you have scattered crumbs." The thought made me smile. Greta's face swam into my mind, her broad brow, her comfortable bulk. I thought of her tears and the fear that I would not ever see her again in Heaven if I left the Holy Catholic Church. Poor dear Greta. Would she ever understand my passion to serve my Saviour? And old Hans. All he ever thought about was how to make a penny. I will write to tell them of my glorious work. Then they will understand and not worry. I tried to erase from my mind the picture of Greta in tears, and instead think of her mashing berries for jam, her thick fingers sweet and purple.

The day was fast becoming dark now and I could smell rain. I tried to put away any doubts and hastened my steps. The road took a sharp curve and rather than take what seemed the long way around, I cut across and entered a small woods; this was a mistake, I found, for the ground was damp and my shoes stuck in the mud as I walked. I picked up speed, starting to run, but stopped suddenly when the buildings came into view. They were enormous. But situated as they were, I had not seen them even a few yards back. I could feel my heartbeat quicken—probably due to my haste, I told myself. But, of course, that was not the true reason. The brownish-red stone structures were most probably the Brothers' and Sisters' houses. I could see yet another large stone building and these three were situated around a kind of square made of grass and pebbles. To one side, small fruit trees were planted in ordered rows. Unleafed, they looked spindly and fragile.

I saw no sign of human life. I started across a field, the new grass clumped together on molehills making the walking difficult, though I hardly noticed. The red stone buildings were two-storied, the third house showing dormer windows jutting from the roof. If only I had asked which one was the Sisters' House. How embarrassed I would feel if I knocked on the wrong door. What if the Count himself stood in front of me before I was ready? The palms of my hands were wet. I was near enough to see that although the top windows were dark, candles glowed in the lower windows. I changed my small bag from one slippery hand to the other as I stopped to look more closely, for I thought I had heard a voice.

A young woman stepped briskly out, kicking the door behind her. She carried a bucket and seemed headed for a well that was placed in the center of the open space. I stopped walking, hesitating to speak, but she must have seen me because she raised her hand in greeting and called out *"Gruss Gott,"* motioning me to join her.

She was taller than me by about only an inch but her frame was larger, her shoulders broad and her breasts straining under her jacket. I could not see her hair, covered as it was by her cap, but as I drew nearer I saw that her eyes were blue, with pale lashes. Her mouth was her most striking feature, wide and generous, and when she began to speak to me her smile pushed at her round cheeks. She looked at me with a frank, open stare and, noticing my dusty dress, said, "You have been walking for a while, *ja?* Now you have found us." She motioned me yet nearer. She lowered the bucket into the stone well. Easily cranking it upward, she said, "I suppose you are here to join the *Schwestern*—the Sisters—that is what most traveling women come for. I have been here for some months already. It is *sehr gut.*" She shrugged her shoulders after setting the bucket on the ground and continued, "It did not take them long to find I could cook. I have been cooking most of my life." With a laugh she picked up the bucket. She began to walk toward one large house and inclined her head for me to follow.

I wanted to speak to this woman who seemed friendly enough but the words would not come. She must think me completely dumb. She turned sideways to look at me and said in a matter-of-fact tone, "My name is Susannah Eller. I was born near here, in Büdingen."

By this time we had come to the front door. But before I moved to open it, I said, "My name is Christina Barbara Böhner and I have come from Gelzhausen." Susannah nodded toward the door and, when I pulled on the heavy latch, I heard the sound of women's voices but saw no one. My gaze moved to the tall windows and the lovely staircase that curved toward the second floor. My initial impression was one of light and space and a kind of elegance I had never seen before. Susannah and I stepped inside and I heard the thud of the door as it shut behind us. It seems now that my decision to join the Brethren was confirmed at that moment by the clang of the heavy latch as it fell into place.

How could I have felt loneliness when I was surrounded by the Moravian Sisters? Yet, despite the swish of another petticoat, the tap of another shoe and a voice rising in song next to me, I burrowed deep into myself that yet held an empty place. And how to account for my longing for the familiar, hard bed tucked in the room behind the forge, when I lay in the large dormitory room on the top floor of the Sisters' House, listening to the breathing of those women on each side of me? Yet I needed to comfort myself by recalling that small bed at home. And sweet as the singing of the Sisters was on awakening, I longed for the clang of metal on metal and the hiss of cold water on red-hot iron.

It must have been the sound of Sister Schmidt's voice that lifted me out of the dark well of longing for home. Was it only a few short months ago that she had entered our small dwelling in Gelzhausen, bringing with her the sweetness of my Saviour's love? She arrived in Herrnhaag shortly after I had entered the Sisters' House. I was working in the immense kitchen and heard her speaking. I must admit to a sense of unease, for I was not sure how she would greet me. Would she tell me I had come too soon? That my impulse was childish? I stood tall and sucked in my breath. After all, I reasoned, had I not worked to transform my heart to receive tranquility and certainty? But I should have known. Her face was warm and welcoming as she came forward and embraced me.

"Christina Barbara. I see you have been moved by His spirit. Welcome, my dear. Welcome."

My heart warmed to her voice. A glow enveloped my whole body as I answered her. Though she and her husband stayed but a short time at Herrnhaag, her coming seemed a signal that my decision to be here was correct and my heaviness lifted a little.

Was the Saviour working His miracle or did I so want Him to that I felt the stirrings of change when there were none? Pouring hot wax into the candle molds, my hands were as steady as they had always been, yet an extra beat of my heart would let me know before I knew that something was changing. The routine of the day remained the same. I awoke to the high, sweet voices of the Sisters who sang every morning, and to the clang of the great bell that divided the hours. I felt the warmth of a Sister's shoulder as we sat in prayer and the slip of wool across my hand as I fed it to the whirring wheel. But as the Night Watch called the hour, and I leaned far out the high dormer of our common bedroom to better hear his song, I knew that living at Herrnhaag was as I had hoped, and at the same time so different from what I had imagined.

My childish daydreams had faded. There were no rubies sparkling on the Count's fingers when he used his hands to describe the beauty of our Lord's bounty. He had never bent to place his arm around my shoulder nor asked me to read a passage from the Lord's book. But my awareness of him followed me as I climbed the graceful staircase of the Sisters' House or drew water from the well, and I must admit he was often in my dreams. The grand title I had rolled so deliciously around my mouth—Nikolaus Ludwig Count von Zinzendorf and Pottendorf—when I wound my way down to the brook behind our small house, became for me, simply Brother Ludwig. So gentle, so persuasive, he spoke to the Single Sisters as a father and friend. He looked closely at the women when he told us that the Saviour had been brought into the world by a woman, and that because of this, women should be honored and respected. He even reminded us that Jesus, our dear Lamb, had appeared first to Mary Magdalene, which showed that a woman's heart is a true heart. When his eyes scanned our faces as we sat listening to his words, I held my breath until my turn came as for one fleeting moment he looked only at me. It was at those rare times that I renewed my vow to blend myself into the Moravian Sisters' bustling midst, to move as a living force for the sake of our Saviour whose blood had bought our freedom. I began to know that God's love must be translated into life here; to become part of every small task. For what was the point of planting a seed or gathering harvest unless the seal of His love touched each fruit with a blush?

As for my new friend, Susannah, I began to learn more about her every day. With her wide smile and blunt speech it seemed to me she spoke what was on her mind, and if I saw a pensive look cross her rounded face from time to time, I paid little heed. I should have been more observant. I should have seen more in her face than I did. But, Lord forgive me, I was so self-absorbed, so mystified with the burgeoning awakening in my own heart, that I could not look into hers.

April in Herrnhaag brought more rain, but it was not as gray as it had been in March, nor as cold. And every morning, as a weak sun sent but little warmth yet, Susannah and I ran to the field we had planted to look for signs of life from the small mounds of dirt where somewhere a tiny seed was sending sprouts up toward the sun. We laughed aloud as we ran, holding up our petticoats and racing past the tall walls of the Sisters' House, across the dirt road and past the orchard of fragile trees just as tall as we were.

Breathless, Susannah said, "You got here before me this time, Christina. Next time I shall start before you." Her face was pink from our exertion and, when I looked closely at her, I saw that she had placed her hand upon her breast with a quick intake of breath. It was not our short run, I was certain, but one of those rare moments I had previously observed in her when, it seemed, a stray thought had assailed her.

"Christina, before we help to carry our Saviour's word to the unknowing people of another land, do you know we have to marry? At least to leave for America on the ship the *Little Strength*. That's what one Sister told me."

I had bent over to catch my breath and, straightening, I said, "If a man has made a choice among us, I understand the question of marriage will be submitted to the Lot to learn our Saviour's will. How else would we be sure, Susannah?"

She looked away from me. "It is the Brothers who ask for a woman. Or about a woman. Then the Elders use the box with the papers in it. You know, the papers that say *Ja* or *Nein* or to wait. If the Saviour approves, then the Elder sends a note to the woman."

I could see that Susannah was increasingly concerned as she bit her lower lip and looked directly into my face.

"But if a man proposes our name to the Elders, we can refuse," I answered. "We can always refuse." I did not know what had caused Susannah's face to take on such a worried countenance. I tried again, "Sometimes we might see a Brother and wonder if he sees us . . . Perhaps sometimes a woman chooses a man as well." I felt my cheeks flaming.

"Christina, we have been here for a little time only. Nothing of the brothers do I know—whether they are kind or cruel."

"Oh, no. Never cruel, Susannah. Never cruel. Our Saviour would never choose the wrong man for any of us." As I said these words I tossed my head as though I was very certain, but my mouth was dry.

"I am afraid, Christina."

I was silent. I did not know what to say. Perhaps I, too, was a bit frightened? But I think I felt more a kind of anticipation. "Surely our Saviour would not choose wrongly for us. Susannah, we cannot be afraid. We should try to pray to be helpful—to do His work . . ." I said these words, but at the same time reproached myself. I had not helped Susannah.

She picked up her petticoat. "I will race you back to the house, *ja*? And this time I will run faster."

Susannah Eller Partsch
Bethlehem, Pennsylvania 1760

So. The bread is rising under the clean towel and I don't have to watch it now. It rises by itself like it always did, warm and smelling *sehr gut*. My arms are sore from kneading, but this is a good thing. It keeps me from my worry. *Ach*, if only we would hear a word from Bethabara. It has been too long and I know they suffer from fever. So long it takes for a message to reach us here in Bethlehem, even though the year is 1760 and the roads should be better. There, now. I will sit and rock for a while and think about something else. I will put my mind back to Herrnhaag in 1743, when I first knew Christina. I will think hard about that and make myself be there. . . .

I CAN RUN FAST. But no one knows. *Ach*, I was such a little girl when

I learned to run this way. Now with my new friend I am walking. Our steps match. Christina Barbara does not say many words. She smiles at me, though, and looks right into my face. Her eyes in the candlelight are brown, but in the sunshine they look green like the still water in the moat around Büdingen. That afternoon when I saw her coming toward me at the well, I thought she was not strong, for her body is slight. But she can carry two heavy pails just the way I do. When we plant together, with care she pushes the tiny roots into the ground.

I think I might tell her things. About my life and where I lived. *Ach*, the smell of hay drying in the fields, the cobblestones, the small house, ice on the old moat. I could tell her about Frau Schubert's where I was sent as a little girl; the winding stairs to the attic room, so dark in winter. How I made myself small in the room where Frau Schubert played the harpsichord so she would not see me; and how Herr Schubert's gardener showed me how to pick peaches just when they were ready. I could tell her already how I loved to cook for Councilor Schmidt, where I got a job when I was seventeen.

Christina and I are silent now. She reaches out to squeeze my shoulder and opens the door to the main house. We part in the large front room. She climbs the first steps of the curving stairway and, at the corner landing, she turns.

Could I tell my new friend how lonely I was? Could I say how I used to watch the girls laughing and trading ribbons? I pretended not to care, and counted the leaves on one tree branch or played with the smooth stones I gathered in my hand. I sat alone, trying to write on my slate. I never learned to write much. *Ach nein*, or to read. Many of the women here read. Anna Maria Thom reads in two tongues and some of the Sisters, like Susannah Nitschmann, can read huge, hard books with gold color on the edge. Not one of them can bake the way I do. I have been baking and cooking for so long. They always tell me how good my food is and how I should marry a baker so we can bake two times as much. When I think of marriage, *ach du lieber*. I feel a chill on my shoulders. It goes down my arms. I used to feel this way when I was a little girl, but no one knew. When I was lonely I felt tears, but I did not let them spill.

Now there are so many Sisters around me. The Count has decided that we group into what we now call Choirs. My Choir, called the Single Sisters, has only unmarried women. Later, if we marry, we belong to the Married Persons' Choir and there are even Choirs for the widows and widowers. I think this is a plan that is *sehr gut*. We can learn about our Lamb this way, all of us together. The Single Sisters tell me about themselves and about how to love our Saviour. I never knew anything about our Saviour until Herr and Frau Vogt came to my village. They told me God loved me. I felt so special. I wanted to believe them. Now that I live here at Herrnhaag, I think I do. It is as though I have a whole, big family. I have not spoken to the Brothers much. I hope they are kind men. I will pray very hard to my suffering Lamb to make all of them kind. Then if I must marry to get to the New World with my new family all around me, it will be *sehr gut*.

Susannah Nitschmann has stirred the fire and calls my name. The large pot I scrubbed clean needs water for cooking. It is time for me to fill the bucket at the well, and get food ready to feed my hungry Sisters.

CHAPTER THREE

Christina Barbara Krause

The days had passed very quickly since I arrived at Herrnhaag in that spring of 1743. I measured their passing by the rain which seemed less sharp and cold; by the greening of the grass and the tiny seedlings that had begun to peer up through the black dirt. I felt myself to be one of those fragile plants—eager to grow, pushed forward by an inner force, yet not sturdy or strong enough to withstand the lashing storm of questions that assailed me. Oh, I was sure of Him; of Him I had no doubts, for the whole world must have been fashioned by His hand, the order of sun and stars and the changing seasons I so loved. No, it was I. How could I be part of any eternal plan? Whatever could He see in me that would cause His beloved hand to touch my heart? I sat in contemplation in our *Saal* in the Sisters' House and tried to pray.

"O, my Saviour. O, my dearest friend . . . " I had to stop, for I could not keep my mind in one place. Often I found it impossible to pray. I might try to concentrate on one thought, yet even that ran from me like a difficult child. I will think very hard about asking for an understanding heart, one that feels and believes in your love for me. I will ask only for that gift. But as soon as the words formed in my head,

I imagined myself searching through the corridors of a heavenly house for His dwelling place. Pulling my thoughts back to the *Saal* where I sat on the hard wooden bench, my hands clasped in my lap, I was very aware of the sun shining through the tall, many-paned windows. One bright shaft pooled on the wide, knotted floorboards. Obeying a sudden impulse, I walked to the center of the light and stood in the aisle to look up at the brightness of the western window. I stared hard, though I knew when I looked away I would be blinded, but I was certain that I was somehow required to look directly into that sun-filled window and to repeat my fervent desire for a believing heart. In my bright blindness I saw the sunken face of my mother, the empty road that had held my father's final leave-taking, the silent cold of the unlit forge. I had no tears, but felt instead a bitter knot gathering in my chest. I stared hard and willed my eyes not to blink.

I could then see the bright shards of sunlight on the brook behind our house and hear its gurgle. I felt its clean cold in my hands as I bathed my mother's yellowed face and then, days later, washed each of her blue, icy fingers. I was only a child. How did I bear this? Had I been alone or was there some loving presence that sang me into sleep; that helped me to kneel and to pray again, though I had lost everyone? Could I have believed in His grace enough then to sense His presence though I had no signs? I blinked and turned away from the light. Though I peered hard at the benches on each side of where I stood, I could see nothing. All light was gone. I heard myself speak aloud, "Dear Saviour, open my heart." I was spineless, light-headed, weightless.

I wept, and as the tears brimmed and spilled, my sight returned. Slowly, out of darkness, I saw the outline of the benches, the height and depth of the large room, the windows reaching high to the ceiling, and through the western panes, the setting sunlight, now orange, gently touching the deep window well.

My heart, a rich, red blossom, unfolded its petals one by one. I inhaled the fragrance of clustered flowers though none yet bloomed in that early spring as my own heart waited, open at last, to receive my Saviour's gift of faith.

I was ready then to join the Brethren and Sisters the next day in holy praise. I was ready to pull the white festival petticoat over my head and smooth its folds over my hips. And at last, I was to tie the wide ribbon under my chin.

BROTHER LUDWIG STOOD BEFORE US to receive us into the Congregation. I could smell a smoky odor, for the farmers nearby were burning last year's bracken, and I thought of the incense burning in the church of my childhood. Here, no wooden statues looked down on us from dark corners; no colored light from the square window set in a stone wall. The organ behind me began to breathe as a Brother pumped the pedals. Softly, he played a hymn and the strains of harmony seemed blended together as I felt all of us to be.

"Do you believe in Jesus Christ, His only son our Lord, who loves you and gives Himself for you?"

"Yes, oh yes. I know that I believe." I looked at the Count's face as I said this.

"Is it your desire to walk steadfastly in the teaching and fellowship of this church?"

Oh yes, oh yes. I will go wherever I am sent I will go . . . I stole a glance across the room and saw one man, taller than the others. The plane of his high cheekbones darkened the hollows of his deep-set eyes. His hair was dark. I willed him to look at me. I squinted my eyes so hard that orange and pink lights danced before me. I opened my eyes very wide to look again at him and, although his face was expressionless, I felt his eyes meet mine. My folded hands flew to my breast.

"Lord, hear us," Brother Ludwig's voice filled the *Saal*, filled my heart.

How we all sang! We women called forth in clear soprano and were answered antiphonally by the male voices on the opposite side of the room. Their voices touched me, resonated deep in my breast and, though my body remained with my new Sisters on the white-washed wooden benches, my heart flew from the high-ceilinged room to sway and soar on the wind. Free, unfettered and one with the April morning.

It was in those early days when I become a true member of the Brethren that I felt every task I performed had a special quality. Could it be that sheets billowing against a brilliant sky were luminescent? Could it be that candlelight reached further into the darker corners of the Sisters' dormitory bedroom and flickered more brightly on the white, vaulted ceiling above my bed? Always tender to small creatures, I now dug a place for the wet, wriggling worm that crossed my palm and covered its tiny body with black earth to ease its blind journey. My heart open, my questions of faith abandoned, I could open my arms to embrace the whole world—the gently rising hills, the meadows fertile, seed planted, the wide sky of the Wetterau, the surrounding joy that comes to us, perhaps, when part of a journey is done but what remains lies just beyond and everything is possible.

The sky had been gray for most of the week, but one morning the heavy mist began to burn away as the sun rose further. I was working in the kitchen and stopped to watch Susannah's strong hands as she cut the hairy roots from turnips. She asked me to fetch more water from our well. I reached for the bucket in the corner and went to open the heavy kitchen door. The Brother I had noticed at our service stood there, and in my haste I almost ran straight into him. He was much taller than I, and although the sun was at his back, his face in shadow, I could see that his countenance was serious. His eyes were very blue. It was at that moment that the tearing ache of my past loneliness reached deeper into my heart, kindling my need.

O, MY SAVIOUR, had I pushed past him in that very moment would I know the joy I have known? The loss and sorrow? Would I have felt in my belly that small, special inner life that is me and not me? But I did not move aside. And he looked down at me, to me, in me.

How young I was! How ready for love. No matter the question put to the Lot, the wrapped paper in the metal box that held our fate, I would have found him. Before I felt his hands that would cup my face, before I curled against his length, I knew how it would be.

This stifling heat makes me forget things I must remember. My mouth is very dry. I will rise from this bed and pour the water from the pitcher myself. I must not stay here idle. I must try to place myself in the Wetterau so long ago when I was swift on the stairway, nimble with my needle and filled with a yearning I had not felt before.

HOW FAR WAS IT from Herrnhaag to Marienborn? My memory only allows me to feel the buoyancy of my steps as we walked the short distance; for the smell of grass and the dark, wet earth, the lengthening days and the pale green leaves that feathered the tree branches brought a lightness to my thoughts and to my body. Any journey would be easy. I could skim the surface of the green ocean even as I ran over the greening grass; and Brother Ludwig's noble purpose to work with those who knew not our Saviour, ignited me to carry myself as a living flame to lighten any faraway land, no matter how far. How we laughed as we walked the rough road to Marienborn, my Sisters and I! Sometimes running ahead of the others, and even skipping with Susannah and Sisters Anna Maria or Rosina, I felt that whatever I had anticipated was already here, and my only wait was for the wildflowers to bloom in the long, green grass.

In Marienborn we came upon several large houses. Most were half-timbered and set in a kind of square with a tall gate in a wall where some men and women were awaiting us. They called out in greeting and we hastened to them. I had not known how well-positioned these grounds were, with far more room than we had had at Herrnhaag and this spaciousness was probably the reason we had been sent here. Sister Anna Maria Thom had told me that the Count would take up residence here, and when I saw the house in which he lived I so wanted to peer into one of the windows. But of course I was not that bold. By the time I had snuggled into my quilt that night, I had learned of the nuns who had lived here so many hundreds of years before us and, drowsing into sleep, I wondered if they were as merry as we; if they picked up their Habits to dance for a moment in their own coming spring.

The first few days at Marienborn I found myself rising early— sometimes even before Susannah. Wanting to be busy, I would set out the heavy mugs for morning tea or add wood to the fire. I must confess that as I performed these simple tasks my mind was wandering to where the Single Brothers had come to live. Was the tall stranger I had seen at our festival making fire as I was? Did he leave the house to gather wood and, cradling logs in his arms, did he ever think of me?

With little effort I can recall how easily I became used to the routine we had: the morning worship, the question and answer sessions where I learned about our tasks as helpers to the missionaries who would bring the good news of Jesus to other lands. Not only was I terribly curious about the dear women who were quickly becoming friends, but also I asked as many questions as I dared about the tall young man from Silesia named Matthew Krause. In memory I can see us yet, during that bursting spring. It took me no time to learn his name, and I said it over and over as the fruit trees bloomed white and pink. Had he walked here from there? Had dear Brother Ludwig brought him to Herrnhaag and to me? All these questions and hundreds more whirled in my head. There were very strict rules as to when and where men and women could see one another, and yet I confess that I did speak to my dear Matthew in all too brief moments when our paths crossed by design.

During our worship, even though across the room, I watched his face for each changing expression, hoping to catch his smile, his slight frown that deepened the line between his heavy brows; to etch on my heart the hollow of his cheek, the blue of his deeply-set eyes. Once, only once, we stole away to sit on the rise of a greening hill beyond the gate. Knowing it was against the rules at this time, it seemed our need to know one another was great enough to steal away just before dark. A new moon had already risen and I saw my love in silhouette as he spoke of his deep love of our Saviour. His words carried such fire I wanted to catch the heat to my breast; to feel the flame between us.

Oh, and I remember more. It was several days later, just after the Sabbath. The sun had not set and the sound of our *Singstunde* was still in my ears as I walked alone up the slight hill behind our chapel. I pretended to myself I was alone, but I had seen a tall figure silhouetted against the pink, twilight sky. There was a stillness about him. There remains a stillness. I knew I had to see his eyes. I had to see myself mirrored there; to stand in front of him without touching and to look forever into his eyes until I was lost. Were there words that we spoke? He bent and put his warm mouth on my neck against my pulse. For a long time he paused with his face close to mine, above me, and then he gathered me to him. We dropped slowly to the ground, each of us kneeling. Then, our bodies parted, he took my hands and we looked at one another. I remember the quiet, the sky no longer pink. I remember his mouth, warm and moist as mine and my hands warm and curled in his. In the small space between us a wild poppy had struggled through the grass and, untrampled by our feet and bodies, bloomed alone and red. Matthew's searching fingers found the tiny stem and broke it to bring the blossom to my face. But, even at that first moment of picking, of separation from its source, the petals, paper-thin, withered inward around the dark center.

WHEN I FIRST CAME TO NORTH CAROLINA, this land of red clay and straggly-limbed pines where I now dwell, I had thought memories would sustain me; but perhaps something shrivels and dies within us when we part from the place in which love is born and from which we take its sustenance. Now, I toss in fever and swirl unattached to this world or any other. I cannot see my Saviour's face nor hear His voice, so I must cry out to ask what He wants of me now.

I RECALL HOW AT MARIENBORN in 1743 I pulled the white festival petticoat over my head for the second time. Close by, the hum of my Sisters' voices rose and fell but there was no girlish giggling, for now that we had been received into the Congregation, we realized the great importance of taking the bread and wine together for the first time. This, our Communion day, was one for serious demeanor; excited as most of us felt, we restrained our usual merriment. The month of May had burst into the valley with the smell of lilacs on every breeze, and when I went to the small window in the timbered second story, I felt I could see for miles—perhaps even back to Herrnhaag, if I tried hard enough. Gazing out over the green fields, I was very sure that I was ready to receive the bread and wine on this day with my Brothers and Sisters.

I confess to being somewhat uncertain during the past weeks. It was the Moravian custom for one of the Sisters, usually one who headed a small group we called a Choir, well-versed in the ways of the Brethren, to question those of us who wished to take the holy meal. Because the Choirs were made up of those of us who were either unmarried, married or widowed, I guessed that the leader of our unmarried choir would speak to me before I was allowed to participate in our Communion.

I fretted over being found wanting in faith. Waiting to be questioned, my nights were restless and I tossed and turned in agitation until the pale dawn lightened the window panes. During the day I struggled with my doubting nature, and before I raised the first spoonful of soup or straightened the quilt, or lifted the wooden buckets, I whispered, "O, pray God my whole body and soul be preserved blameless unto the Lord's coming." I said these words very quickly, but while I said them I tried to see each one, a dart piercing my beating heart. The Saviour's light that first came to me in Gelzhausen—oh, and then again here in the *Saal* where it surrounded me so briefly, fled somewhere before me as I searched the dark passages of my mind to see and hold that brightness. Had my Saviour's presence left me when I had walked so far to find Him? I willed myself to see the outline of Jesus' face and dug my fingernails into my palms to feel His final pain. I could hear the echo of Matthew's quiet voice, " He loves us, Christina. By His stripes we are healed." How clearly the face of my beloved appeared, his deep-set eyes. Would that the face of my suffering Lamb was as clear to me.

It was the Single Sister Hoepfner, the Leader of the Single Womens' Choir, who had taken me into a small room overlooking the front courtyard. Some of the Brothers were unloading supplies and I was curious as to who they were. My back was to the window, but within seconds I was no longer distracted by the deep calls of the men to one another. Rather, I found myself looking intently into her face. I noticed the shadows under her brown eyes and the lines on each side of her lips that surely would deepen with age. When she questioned me about my love and loyalty to our Saviour, my words came hesitantly. I feared I had not attained childlike acceptance of my Lord's love, as Brother Ludwig had urged us to do. He had told us to search our hearts, air our doubts, so as to come before our God in each other's presence with purity of intention. Could I utter my doubts to this kindly woman?

She said, "Do you remember our hymn that says, *'Following God demands our stillness/rushing to employ our powers/even with the best intentions/we confuse God's will with ours?'* " She was smiling.

"Yes, our dear Brother Ludwig penned it. I remember it tells us not to trust only in our own strength, but to lean on God's Grace."

"My dear Christina. Today, at this moment, you have taken one step toward understanding. In being here in this room, at this small heartbeat of time, you have moved forward on your pilgrimage. Often it goes slowly, dear child. You cannot leap into faith."

She sat before me, her hands clasped in her lap. I said nothing.

"Do you want to pray with me, and I will recite the last stanza of his hymn?"

"Thank you, Sister Hoepfner. I have felt doubts sometimes; I feel I am sometimes in darkness . . . "

"Hush, my dear. Listen. *'Let us ever in our living/through each fleeting day and night/wait in calm and growing brightness/Lord as you are in the light.'* "

I felt no surge of power, no bright light glistened around our heads, now bowed. But my heartbeat was steady and strong. I knew I could wait in stillness for our dear Saviour to clasp me to Him.

Now that the day of the holy supper had finally come, I stood at the small window and drew one last breath of spring fragrance into my lungs. I felt at the least I was more ready to join my Sisters and Brothers in partaking of the feast of my Saviour than a year ago. Then, in the small stone church in Gelzhausen, the holy bread had stuck in my throat as I took it from the pudgy hands of the young priest. I could not erase the anger I had had when he came to our house to persuade me to join the nuns of our Catholic Church. I knew that his resentment of my refusal had not diminished either, and so the act of participating in the sacrament at that time was neither holy nor pure.

The sound of the trumpets, high and strident, was answered by the deep trombones as though to announce a royal procession. The past fled, the moment filled my soul and heart. I knew with great clarity that I had made the right decision to be there in Marienborn with those I had come to love. I joined my Sisters and entered the *Saal*.

There was the rustle of petticoats as we knelt, the scuffle of feet, the deep voices of the men and the higher ones of the women. My mouth watered. This is my thirsting for the wine, the sweet taste that binds me to my dear Lamb and to my fellow communicants. Let thy wine, thy blood mix with mine. Let it make its way into the beating of my heart, I prayed as the chalice was passed from one to another. As we raised the bread in unison I thought, bread of life, bread of life, feed me. O, Lamb of God that takest away the sins of the world, O Lamb of God.

The Count extended his right hand to lead us in song:

> *Once more we pledge both heart and hand*
> *As in God's presence here we stand*
> *To live to Him and Him alone,*
> *Til we surround his heavenly throne.*

The last musical notes trembled for one moment. The organ no longer breathed and there was silence in the room. Then the Count raised both hands and we stood, all of us together.

I am one with my Brothers and Sisters. We have consecrated ourselves to our Holy Lord, to do His will. At last, I thought, at last I am part of their bright vision while the blood of the Lamb circles in my veins. I could feel this in the tips of my fingers, in my wrists and the pulse of my neck. The trombones burst forth in triumph. A shaft of sunlight struck one gold throat and, blinded, I had to turn away.

A FIRE HAD BEEN LIT in the large tile stove of the common room to take away the morning's chill and Susannah sat opposite me, stitching. I noticed her face was flushed, but with her fair complexion she often had a rosy blush on her cheeks. Several times Susannah began to speak and then, clearing her throat, she said nothing. Finally she paused with her needle in hand and said, "Do you remember how warm the weather was a few days in April?" I gave a nod and she continued.

"I could not stay in bed one morning. I crept out quietly so none of you would hear me—I carried my shoes." She paused then, as though savoring the memory. "The grass was so cool on my bare feet and I could smell the bread baking for our Lovefeast. The smell came to me all the way from the bake-house. It really did. The door of the bake-house was open and the smell just made me walk on in. *Ach*, I could not have stopped." She looked down then, and said very quietly, "I saw the baker George Partsch, but he did not see me already. He was putting the loaves on shelves. His shirt sleeves were rolled back." She looked up then, "Maybe you have seen him, *ja*? He is about my stature, but darker. He is really a weaver but they needed more bakers, so he . . . "

"Oh, I do remember the man," I said. "He does everything quickly. I have noticed when he puts buns on the tray his hands move so fast, they blur." We laughed in agreement.

"Well, when he saw me standing there he looked right at me and he smiled. Not a scowl. I was expecting him to be angry, for I surprised him. Men do not like to be surprised. *Ach nein*, they can be . . . " She paused for several seconds, her face wary and then, as her expression changed and became relaxed, her mouth became less tight. She continued, "But he smiled. Then I remembered my bare feet. I ran."

Susannah put her mending on the table next to her and rose to walk about the room. Turning then to me she said, "I have asked Rosina and Sister Wahnert about him and they say he is a good man. I don't see anger in him. I would know anger, Christina."

How little I knew about this woman. We had planted together, our fingers deep in black dirt; we had boiled clothes in a large pot over a hot fire, each of us pushing down with a wooden pole, a sleeve, a billowing petticoat; and I had watched her face, round and crimson from the steam. I had seen her in repose as we sat in the *Saal* listening to the words of those brave men and women who had been already to worlds across the sea where rythmic drumming called to heathen gods. But I did not know her.

Susannah continued, "I love the smell of baking bread. That yeasty smell. And the way it rises." She smiled to herself. "When I was a little girl I used to pull back a corner of the cloth my mother put on top of the big round bowl. First the bread was just small, but the next time I looked it was really big. *Ach*, I always wondered how that happened." She began to pace back and forth over the wide wooden planks. "The smell of bread makes me feel so safe, and yet . . . "

I said nothing, for I had learned that Susannah would continue if I said nothing.

"When I was a very little girl, I did not know the Saviour. I used to steal pieces of the warm bread . . . " She twisted her hands then brought one finger to dimple her round cheek. "I want to tell you things, Christina, but I . . . I don't know; I just don't know."

She stopped pacing and knelt before me, her hands on my knees, her face gazing up at me seemed that of a young child.

"It would be as though we are old," she said, "and you are my Choir leader, *ja*, and I have to tell you how it was with me so you can help me write my life story."

It was strange to think that one day we would be very old and a Choir Sister or Brother would write about us as we began our journey Home to our Saviour. I looked at my hands. Would there be brown spots on them, wrinkles, knots at my knuckles? It was too hard to imagine being so old.

Susannah began to speak. At first, her words came slowly, as though each one hurt her.

"Remember I told you my mother married a man soon after my father died. I was still in her belly and she married this man. Maybe she was awfully poor. *Ach,* I don't know. What I do remember when I was very little, he was always creeping around after me in our little house. I felt safer outside."

I felt a chill. There were children in Gelzhausen who seemed always at the corners of houses, peering out from the darkest part of our church. There were the stories about them—the kind of stories parents stop telling when children come into the room. In the market-place I saw them dart in and out—even the smallest ones, their skinny little arms reaching so quickly to steal an apple, a small pastry. Was it this way for my new friend? Had she a piece of stolen fruit under her apron? Were her blue eyes quick to look away when greeted by another?

"He was always mad at me—I think he hated me, though nothing I did."

She clutched at my petticoat as she said this, bunching the dark cloth in her hand. "Nothing to make him hate me so."

"Well, this one day I was sent outside with a basket of wet clothes. I was not yet ten years old. Maybe I was about seven years old. I went out with this basket, so I could hang the clothes on bushes for the day was dry. My mother took in washing from two families in Büdingen. I knew she hid a few coppers secretly in her apron when they paid her. She did not know I knew, but I watched and saw. My mother said I could walk to the platz while the clothes dried. I loved to go there so I could look into the candy store window at the sweets. *Ach*, they were so beautiful to me."

I could imagine little Susannah, her fair hair in one braid perhaps, her apron tied, her hands behind her and standing on tiptoe to look into the window.

"The storekeeper's wife always wore a clean apron. She was fat; her arms jiggled below the short puffs of her jacket and she did not have sharp elbows like me. There were dimples there in her arms. The children in our town liked her even though she sometimes swished us away from her door; but some days when she saw me looking in the window, she would say I could go in. *Ach du lieber*, the shop smelled like icing on cakes and sweet pudding and chocolate her husband made to dip the strawberries in the summer. I liked those the best. This one morning—Christina, it seems as though even if we suppose something bad will happen we never think it would be on a day so sunny when the store smells *sehr gut*."

Susannah's eyes filled with tears and when they spilled over she did not dry them. "Well, that day Frau Laubach—that was her name—said I could come into the store. When she smiled at me I knew she would give me a sweet. I could hardly wait to see what she would give me—a little square of sugar with a tiny flower on it? A candied fig? But this time she had something special for me and reached behind the counter to a place I could not see though I was on tiptoe. She held out a piece of marzipan. I had only tasted this once but I could sniff its nutty sweetness even before I popped it in my mouth." She stopped speaking then and, twisting her hands, she looked out into the spring day. "I have never eaten marzipan again." She was quiet for such a long time that I thought she might not continue with her story; but then she began to speak and her voice was soft.

"I had to go back to my house, but I was slow about it. I rolled the sweet around my mouth, first on one side and then the other and when I put it in the middle of my tongue, where it tasted the sweetest, I wished I could walk forever sucking on it and never go home."

Many times I, too, had walked up the main street of my own childhood village, sucking on a sweet. In memory, those days seemed so sunny, so warm. Though death waited for my family, I did not know it. But as I looked into Susannah's face I knew she had always—even as a little girl—always known that behind a door, under a stairway, someone was waiting to terrify her. I was protected, she was not. What are these strange ways of our Lord?

Susannah rose and walked to the window. Looking out she said, "I knew he was there because I saw his heavy rake propped up outside the front door. I walked to the back of our small house because he got very mad if I came in the front door. I heard no voices. Usually he was ordering my mother to do this or that, but this day it was quiet. I pushed open the door into our kitchen and it squeaked the way it always had. He must have been waiting for me. I felt his hand on my arm.

"'Thief.' *Ach*, he said this so quiet. He did not yell. His voice whispered at first. 'Dirty little thief. Did you think you would get away from me? Did you think I would not find the money?' He put his face right next to mine and I could smell his awful breath, like dead flowers. His hand went around my whole arm, Christina. It hurt.

"'I found the money, you wicked wench.' His voice got loud then. I wanted my mother. I did not know where she was. I remember all the words he said that day. 'You thought you could hide the coins in the wardrobe. But I am too smart for you. I am much smarter than a little thief of a girl; a skinny, dirty, ugly little girl.'

"Then he began to hit me. He slapped my face, and I felt as though my head would snap off my neck, and the tiny piece of marzipan almost choked me. It stuck in my throat. I tried to swallow. He hit my ears. His hands were on each side of my head. I felt so dizzy. I bent over and my legs would not hold me, so I fell. I could not even put out my hands. Then he pulled up my petticoats and hit and hit me and yelled. He kept asking, 'Where is your mother? Where did the whore go?'

"'I don't know, I don't know,' I told him. My ear hurt so much. Christina, sometimes I think nothing ever hurt me so much as my ear, that day. I pushed myself up from the floor. I could not stand straight. I could not run straight. But I ran. I ran out the back door. I never looked back to see his face all red with spit in the corners of his mouth. I never looked back at him, but I see him in my head."

She stopped speaking and I knew she would say no more about this now. A wind came in our kitchen door. I held out my arms and she moved close to me, her body sturdy, but somehow smaller in that moment.

"Oh, Christina." She said these words close to my ear. "My mother used to hold me when the red welts puffed and burned. You are my friend, *ja*? Will you be my friend?"

"I am your friend forever, dear Susannah. You are safe here with the Brothers and Sisters. Sister Wahnert says we are safe in the Saviour's arms, Susannah."

"When the Sisters tell me this, I do believe them." Susannah's face was so earnest. Then she drew back and looked directly at me. "Now I have a best friend and we will travel together wherever we are sent. To the New World, maybe?"

Yes, I thought, but I was less sure than my friend. Perhaps, I thought, only perhaps will we travel together.

The voice of our Night Watch called out the hour. After midnight. Susannah slept beside me, barely stirring. I must have been the only Sister awake. Was my dear Matthew awake as I, or was his long frame stretched out, relaxed, asleep? Perhaps he slept on his side. If only I knew. If only I could turn and find him there. I longed to touch his cheek to feel the rough bristles; to run my finger over each eyebrow. Susannah stirred and sighed in her sleep. I thought she would be married to the baker—a kind man I had heard. I remembered the warmth of my father's body, his arms strong, holding me against him. I could almost smell the smoky smell of him. O, my Saviour, I prayed. Let me understand love.

The pace of our days quickened as the weather warmed. Every breath I took seemed to bring me closer to my Saviour, and when I walked out of doors I picked clover to suck the juice from each small purple arrow and pulled pieces of the long grass to chew the tender end as though it were food I needed to live. Since that first pink twilight, when I prayed the Lot would be positive for me and my Matthew, I asked anyone who would tell me about his life. I learned his mother had lost several infants when they were born, but that he had survived. He even told me, "I always wondered why I had lived and they had died. I wondered if there was something I was to do for God." I remember he turned to me with a slow smile. "When the good Count came to our town and I heard him speak to us, I felt I had to follow." He gave a rueful smile. "Christina, it has been so easy to follow . . . maybe I thought I was like one of the fishermen who left their nets where they were and just . . ." A Sister approached us then and he turned from me, but it was as though his words entered my body and wound around my heart. I felt almost sick with love and prayed to my Saviour that the Lot submitted for divine guidance would be positive for our uniting at the end of May. In the evening as I washed my body with the rough cloth and cool water, I could feel the soft firmness of my breasts, the even beat of my heart, and, if my hips did not seem so wide for bearing, still I knew I was ready to consecrate my love of my Saviour in a way I had not known before.

THE TIME WAS SO SHORT, it occurs to me now. I had only arrived in Herrnhaag the end of March when buds had barely appeared; I had been received into the Congregation and experienced blessed Communion with my Brethren and Sisters. Then came the 27th of May, in the year 1743. I knew this date would be written on my heart, for it was the day of our Great Wedding; while a warming sun streamed through the windows of our *Saal*, I would be wedded in love to a quiet man from Silesia. Twenty-seven couples would stand before our blessed Brother Ludwig to hear again of our sacred mission to America across the sea, and then in groups of four we would listen to the words uniting us.

It was early morning yet, and before I slid from under my blanket I lay quietly on my back to stare at the white, curved ceiling of our common bedroom. I wanted to stay for one more moment, nestled and warm as the sound of some Sisters' voices came to us up the stairway. I could not help but wonder what kind of bed I would sleep on as we traveled. Would I feel roots and pine needles under me? Would my ceiling be starlit? There was no room here in Marienborn for Matthew and me to share a bed and I knew I would return to one bed tonight; but I would be different. The marriage vows would be said aloud, and I would become Sister Krause. Words spoken, name changed, and I, too, changed—a wife.

Far off and almost undiscernibly, I could hear Brother Weiss playing his trombone—scales, a few short bars of a hymn. My father used to fix parts of brass instruments though he was not trained to do so. He would twist and shape, narrow his eyes and hold the tiny piece to the light of the window and then, carefully, he would slide the piece into place and hand the instrument to the musician for him to blow. A squeak, an ear-splitting screech and then a few clear notes. Tapping his foot, the musician would begin a merry tune, and if it were one my father knew, he would sing out the words. Once he caught my mother around her waist and twirled her in the tiny room. I held my doll and watched, for only occasionally did I see them touch; but I do recall one day it was very hot and my mother came into our back door with a basket of squash. My father, that robust man whose square hands fashioned magical things, raised one finger to my mother's cheeks and so gently wiped the moisture away. I stood at the edge of their world, and could not take the step to enter. I was lonely. After today would my loneliness vanish? Would Matthew Krause take it away?

It was at that moment between my reverie of the past and anticipation for the future that I heard the sound. It was very soft and I could barely discern its direction. It came like a breeze touching my cheek, and then, as I half-sat, I knew it was music. Not a harpsichord, nor clavichord, not struck, but plucked. A metal string but somehow a gentle sound. I had learned that the Brethren and Sisters followed the good Count's suggestion that music heard on awakening was a beautiful way to greet the new day and I had gotten quite accustomed to hearing the sound of Sisters' voices as I swam from dreams into the day before me. But this gentle plucking was new to me. Whose voice was the sweet soprano that wound its way up the stairway on this early morning in May? I do not remember, but clear to me is my first awareness of the sound of the cittern. This graceful instrument was carried across wide seas to many countries on the globe and came to America to soothe our path several years later, but it was in those moments in Marienborn, when I was but a maiden, that I first heard the steel strings played softly as though by an angel.

I ran the palms of my hands down my thighs and wondered if sometime after today my body would know soreness or whether I would bleed. Our wise Choir leaders had been frank with us in discussion, saying that we should rejoice in our own womanly bodies because our dear Saviour had been born of woman. I well knew how it was between a man and a woman. What I had not been prepared for was this longing, this need to touch the roughness of him. A breeze from the window by my bed brought the scent of newly growing things and I was filled with joy. Would my Sisters say this was a sign—the abundance of life we know when we understand His sacrifice for us? But I could not think of sacrifice at that moment. I was too full of something else.

Gathering in the large *Saal*, we raised our voices together. We sang to those we would wed. But the verse was intended to include much more than that; for those men and women who stood beside Matthew and me were those we had pledged to love and support in Jesus' name as we journeyed on our pilgrimage here on this earth.

> *Join together heart to heart*
> *Grant no woe them e'er shall part;*
> *Knit thou now with thine own hand,*
> *Our dear elders' marriage band.*

Reverend Languth looked at the four of us before he began the words of marriage vows that bound us together. Beside Matthew and me, Johann Hoepfner seemed rooted to the ground while his intended, Maria Magdalena, swayed like a willow. I could hear the soft sounds of the other ministers as they said the sacred words to other couples and the voices became a wave that never crested but rolled on as we stood silent.

Then I heard as from some distance, "Brother Krause, will you love our Sister, Christina Barbara, to thy wedded wife, to live together in holy wedlock?"

Matthew looked down at me and, as on the first day I saw him in the doorway of the Sisters' House, he seemed to look into my eager, beating heart. He said, "I will."

"Sister Böhner, will you love him, honor him, and be subject unto him in the Lord . . . "

Yes, I thought, oh yes anything, anything. But I answered aloud, quietly, "I will."

Brother Languth's words came to a close, but I repeated to myself, "Holy matrimony was instituted by God himself and is therefore an holy estate . . . man and wife shall be one flesh . . . replenish their hearts with love . . . with love . . . with love. Throughout the room I heard the quiet "Amen" of the others. Then it was still, except for Brother Biefel's cough and a quiet sniff from someone across the room. I leaned against Matthew—my husband—and felt the rough cloth of his coat through the thin cloth of my jacket. I looked up at his face in profile as he stared ahead.

Count Zinzendorf walked to the front of the room and began to speak. The sound of his voice on that day echoed in my heart like a mighty organ and a special form of grace when he spoke. "You are His brides-people, souls destined to draw all souls, without distinction, unto Him."

Our group was to be sent across the wide sea to a place in America called Pennsylvania. We had been told that the chosen missionaries would carry the Lord's word to those who would listen, and we, as helpers to those brave men and women, would work also to bring light into the darkness of our own souls. Everything was planned and Matthew and I would be part of this great mission. I knew that the group who had preceded us had already spoken to the natives of that land and that shelters were being built in the vast wilderness. With a shiver of pure joy, I realized I would walk through deep forests, over the hills ahead, and in the cleared meadows sow seed beside this tall man I had married in our Saviour's name. I remember sensations of an almost dizzying kind as I drank the watered wine sprinkled with nutmeg at our Lovefeast. A Married Sister's soft hands gently held my face and kissed each cheek. I do not remember who she was, but I can recall the warmth of her fingers on my face.

THE EARLY SUMMER GRASS had grown very tall by June. The sound of brasses, now mourning, now joyful, filled the valley. Beneath me was warm earth and I smelled the freshness of trampled grass. Lightly, lightly he kissed my eyes, my cheeks, my mouth while his hands pulled me into his arms, close to the full length of his long body. I had loosened the ribbons of my cap and as it fell away, my hair, freed and soft, fell to my shoulders. He buried his face in my hair and said my name aloud in a way that made me press closer to him. His voice was almost a groan, full of pain so that I tore at the lacings at the front of my dress. Is this the way it is? Is this the way love is?

Matthew pulled away from me, holding me still. He was very serious and very quiet. Then he said my name again. "Christina Barbara. Christina Barbara." He said this over and over as he brought his lips to mine and the words caressed my lips. He whispered my name in my ear, his breath warm and sweet, then looking at me again, he said, "Do you want me?" I could not answer; but in a kind of wild agitation, I felt I was not close enough to this man. With the pain of his entry I pushed against his shoulders to move away but his arms held me, vice-like, and I felt pinned to the earth. "Wait, wait," I wanted to tell him, but I could not make the words come. Then he cried out and I thought Adam must have made this sound that first time. Our faces, cheek to cheek, were wet; when he looked at me again, I saw his blue eyes blurred with tears.

"I am sorry," he said. I was filled with a tenderness I had not known.

"Why?" I asked.

"You. You. Oh, my love. I have hurt you."

My breasts were cold with our parting and I pulled him to me for warmth and for our comfort.

"No," I said. "I love you. I feel no pain. I will go with you."

I will go with you. That is what I said, but I knew not what this meant.

I well remember the smell of June grass and wild thyme trampled from our lovemaking; the sound of trombones praising our Lord—a glorious sound in the twilight. Now my poor babe in my womb rolls and turns as if, perhaps, it carries the memories of my journey here to Carolina, though this cannot be true. I was sure then I would accustom myself to the fetid summers. But it is so hot here in the southern part of America and many of us have been sick with fever. We have had no news from Bethlehem or Nazareth for months. I have been wrenched from the places I loved, and my tears flow.

CHAPTER FOUR

I try to remember the days in order, but it is difficult—the memories come into my mind and swirl away like dry leaves. Sometimes I cannot put them in any sequence . . . but I recall that before we left Herrnhaag and Marienborn, we had several weeks of summer weather, little rain and gentle breezes. The wildflowers swayed above the meadow grass and it seemed to me they were asking me to pick them; to stoop and pull at their hardy stems. I think there were daisies left with their bright golden centers and the Queen Anne's lace dusted the green meadow with white. I loved the sounds there with only the wind and the buzzing of insects, a birdsong only occasionally; for early morning had passed and their twitter would not come again until twilight.

Brother Ludwig's words seemed etched in my head. He told us of the ancient Hebrews who stumbled over hot desert sand, bending their heads against the scorching wind. They must have wept for their lost homeland, I thought. But we would be part of a new mission. There would be no desert; but heavy seas, freezing cold and little fire to warm us except our dear Lamb's love. I would not weep for my homeland, I thought, for I was picked by my Saviour's hand, even as I picked these bright flowers.

The bell rang for *Singstunde*. One more flower, one more golden, sunlit center. I bent once again. Was I that last flower? I loosened my fist and placed the daisy in the center of the cluster. There, I thought. There. I am surrounded by the Brethren and ready to move anywhere. I felt the summer breeze on my face and stood to look over the green meadow. I would walk as far as I was called, my head high, my eyes on the banner with the Lamb and the Latin words *Vicit Agnus Noster eum Sequamur*. Indeed, I would follow our Lamb and help to build a new Kingdom in the wilderness. As the bell rang again, I ran toward the large, stone building and entered the *Saal*, breathless, clutching the daisies. A tall older Sister stood in front of the women and raised her hand to stop the whispers.

"It will not be long before we shall leave for Frankfurt, where we will pick up the barges to Heerendijk. The short trip from Heerendijk to Rotterdam will not take long, and it is there we will be met by our Moravian Brother, Captain Garrison, who has sailed from America."

More whispering as women spoke to one another. The Sister raised her hand for quiet. "Our ship, the *Little Strength*, is sturdy and well-built and Captain Garrison has made the journey before. You may remember Brother and Sister Wahnert, who will be among those who are making the return trip to Europe. They will be on board to greet us, and will accompany us to America."

Sister Anna Maria Schropp, who seemed never too shy to ask questions, spoke up. "I have heard that Brother and Sister Bischoff will also accompany us, having also been to America." I knew that Sister Schropp was eager to speak with Sister Bischoff because she and her husband had already begun working with the Indians in America, and Anna Maria did so want to bring the good news to them as well.

The tall Sister answered Sister Schropp in the affirmative and Anna Maria clasped her hands together, her face alive with joy.

The tall Sister continued, "As you know, we shall first prepare for the journey to England to stop for our English Brothers and Sisters." I squeezed Sister Anna Maria's hand. "We have decided it is more efficient —and more comfortable—to travel in small groups."

Whispers became murmurs and the tall Sister raised her hand again.

"Brother John Brandmiller will call out the names of the separate companies—or bands—so that you will know your traveling companions."

O, my Saviour. I had no idea. I thought we would be traveling together. Where will Matthew be? Where Susannah?

Brother Brandmiller had a loud, tenor voice, and with a paper in one hand, he called out, "Sister Partsch, Sister and Brother Nixdorf, Sister Krause . . . " I waited on the edge of my seat, my poor bouquet drooping. He did not say Matthew's name and went on to the second grouping. It was not until the last company was called that I heard Matthew's name and that of George Partsch, Susannah's husband. Why was it decided this way? Did the Elders want to keep some husbands and wives apart? Why did no one question this decision? I looked around the room but saw no expressions of wonder or sadness.

The rustle of our petticoats, a whisper, a cough. We rose to sing in unison:

> *Join we all with one accord*
> *Praise we all our common Lord*
> *For we all have heard his voice*
> *All have made His will our choice.*

Anna Maria Schropp sang her sweet soprano, Brother Sensemann slightly off key.

"No more strangers in the fold."

I looked to my right and then to my left. The women—all of them —were familiar to me now, each face distinct in her white bonnet. No, there were no more strangers here. I have sung the words with my Sisters but can I feel myself joined to them in one accord? I bowed my head to utter quietly, "Please, dear Lamb, give me courage. Keep your shining light before me—let me know Your will is done."

I remember little of the details of our parting except that I had been given new shoes. They were soft brown leather and laced up to my ankles. Good shoes for the journey. But where would this journey lead? I had known only Gelzhausen and Heilbrunn where my life changed though I did not know it then. Now Herrnhaag and its close neighbor Marienborn, but I could hardly imagine the river travel or the buildings of Heerendijk that I heard could be seen across the flat tableland of Holland.

I felt an ache in my belly knowing Matthew and I would be parted— that when the country opened before me, I would not be able to share the wonder of it with him. That night I prayed to be able to keep the image of our holy Lamb before me. Our trombone choir played lustily that fair day of parting, the tone pure and resonating in my breast.

"We will meet in Heerendijk. It will seem a short time, my love." Matthew stood opposite me and placed his hand on my arm.

I could not answer him, but I had no tears at our parting for it seemed my dear Saviour had heard my fervent prayer as I looked to the clouds and seemed to see the image of our holy Lamb before me. I took his hand to press it against my cheek and was the first to turn away to join my own company.

MY SISTERS KEPT A BRISK PACE on our trek to Frankfurt. Susannah remarked that every smoking chimney signaled a goose for dinner and there was teasing about her constant thoughts of food. Dogs wagged their tails and scampered at our feet. At times small children skipped beside us until a mother would call out, often in alarm, for them to return to the doorstep. We saw many wagons on our road, the passengers greeting us in a friendly manner. When the buildings of Frankfurt came into view, I remembered how much I had wanted to see this city only a few months ago. So much had happened since then. I had left my childhood behind in

Gelzhausen, I thought, as I pictured myself a tall girl running to the brook with a swinging pail; kneeling in the chill of the stone church. Once a cart passed close, the driver nodding his broad head in greeting. His heavy shoulders brought Friedrich to my mind, his tears when I told him of my decision to leave. Thank you, my Saviour. Thank you for entering my heart so I could leave my birthplace, so I could know your love. I stroked my own cheek as I recalled Matthew's hands on me. Did the Sisters see my blush as we pushed forward to Frankfurt?

We hastened to the river, making our way on crooked streets past shops and small houses. Frankfurt was a tidy place, doorsteps swept and gardens tended; but it seemed very crowded to me. Carts laden with vegetables from the nearby fields clattered over the uneven roads, and children darted in front of them with no heed to their own safety. One little boy began to rush into the street unaware of a horse that made its way quickly. I grabbed his arm and he looked up at me with a kind of apprehension. "Wait. Look where you are going," I said. But before I got the last word out he shook loose from me and disappeared amongst the wheels and hooves. I wondered if the city of New York would be so crowded and if children ran unattended down twisting streets.

"There it is—there is the water," Susannah called. Indeed, I could see the wide expanse of water between the low warehouses. The river sparkled in the sunlight as we drew near. The barge before us looked heavy and well-made for travel down the Main River and into the Rhein. We walked a narrow plank to the barge, and, once aboard, I felt the sway under my feet for the first time in my life; for I had not grown up near a river of any size. I stood feeling the motion and it was not unpleasant, for the bounce had a certain rhythm. Men were carrying provisions on board in wooden boxes and a few rolled some barrels to the flat deck. I sat on a bench near the side and unlaced my new shoes to rub my weary feet. Breathing deeply, I could smell the river weeds and horse droppings and although it was a warm day, I felt the onset of autumn—its chill on the wind. I could see a long way over the land, flat and marshy and a straight horizon where the land met the sky. Once we began to float down the Main, one of the Brethren said the first one who sighted the entrance to the Rhein would get a fresh apple as a prize. So we began our voyage with anticipation and merriment.

Floating onto the larger river, there were some waves and the men found it difficult to pole and row at times, though we were going down-stream. As we traveled, I could see the landscape change from flat to rather high bluffs on either side, and, thrillingly, the ruins of ancient castle turrets stark against the sky. It was difficult for me to settle into sleep even as darkness came upon us because there was so much to look at—so much was new to me. As we passed from Germany into Holland, the landscape grew flat again, and everywhere was the smell of water and green weeds. Dew settled on my arms lightly, even when the sun was at its height; and when we stopped the barge to jump to the edge of the river, my shoes sank into the grass and mud. Fog came in before nightfall and in the morning it was hard to see ahead as our Brethren poled their way.

We often sang to make our labor seem easier. As our harmony hovered over the river I felt that the music brought our dear Lamb close to our hearts, touching each and every one of us. Late one afternoon we were so filled with love and music we sang on even as the sky darkened. From each side of the river we could see the doors of clustered houses open to our sound as inhabitants of a small village drew close to the shore to hear us. Some, bolder than the rest, joined us and in this unity and I found it hard to sing when unexpected tears filled my eyes. The memory of that night stays with me. The air was soft and smelled of salt, and when I settled down to sleep our music remained in my head. Turning on my narrow pallet, I felt such longing to have my husband beside me.

Our company arrived early in the day at the Brethren's settlement of Heerendijk. During the previous year, men had built a large house under the leadership of the master builder, Christian David, and I could see that outbuildings were still being constructed. We disembarked from the barge to walk toward one three-storied building. Clutching my small bundle of clothing to my breast, I felt for one moment very far away from the small, rustic house in Gelzhausen. But I had not time to think much on this, for there was settling to be done. I wanted to wash and plait my hair, and change my skirt. I so looked forward to seeing my husband, for although we had been parted for a little time, I needed to see him and to hear his deep voice. Matthew was sure to come in the next few days, and the thought came to me that I could climb to the highest floor of our sleeping quarters to be the first to see him when his band arrived. Taking linens to the rooms on the third floor that would house the women, I looked out the windows at every chance to see when the others would come into view. Finally downstairs, I pushed open the door to again look down the road to the water. I heard a shout and saw a grouping of men and women disembarking near the channel some distance away. The figures were too small to distinguish individual characteristics, but one seemed taller than the rest. As the group advanced I saw it was Brother Nitschmann, whose head bobbed above his fellow travelers; I turned away, disappointed.

Our dinner was hasty that night, for we all were tired; and as soon as I settled in my bed I must have fallen into a deep sleep. A sweet sound pulled me into wakefulness. The sound of angel voices, faint but clear: '*Vater unser im Himmelreich . . .*' Who is singing the Lord's Prayer? Where does the song come from? There was a rustle of sheets and I saw Susannah throw back her bed covers and step to the window. She peered out, then turned to the rest of us.

"It is the others! The Choirs—the Companies—you know, our Brethren and Sisters."

I leapt from my bed to join her at the window and peer into the darkness. Someone mumbled that it was the middle of the night and, indeed, there was no sign of dawn. I tried to see who stood singing in the courtyard, their voices full of laughter as well as praise. Wrapping ourselves in blankets, we ran barefoot to the staircase. Sister Anna Sensemann almost tumbled down in her haste to greet the singers. Then she flung herself into the arms of her husband, Joachim. Oh, how I wanted to do the same when I made out Matthew's tall frame in the half-light of the candles! But I did not. I stood, my blanket wrapped around me. I did not hear the rejoicing or the hearty greetings, I only saw him smiling at me across the room.

IT WAS EARLY IN SEPTEMBER, just after our arrival, that we had such a jolly Lovefeast in the garden. The day was warm and dry as we set up the long tables and picked yellow field flowers to place in jars. We were ready for our visitors from Amsterdam and Haarlem for some time before they actually arrived. Susannah kept picking up the flowers and setting them down again in her anticipation until Anna Maria Schropp began to laugh at her. I suspected that the Moravians and other townsfolk from these Dutch towns were as curious about us as we were about them. They knew we were bound for America. I wanted to stand just a little taller as they came into view, for I knew I had been chosen for a very special mission. Our Dutch Sisters were dressed like us, of course, but how different their language. It was not like German and I had to pay close attention to catch the separate words, repeating them quickly to myself. My heart swelled with pride as I carried the large trays of buns from long table to table. We laughed, we sang, we drank the hot coffee, the sugar of the buns sticking to my fingers, tasting sweet and grainy as I licked them one by one.

As the last note of our night music ended, Susannah and I traipsed up the stairway, arm in arm, loathe to settle into sleep, not wanting the day to end.

"Have you seen Brother Bezold?" she asked as we stepped out of our petticoats.

"I know he will give us marriage instruction before we leave. I think we were supposed to speak with him before we even left for Holland, but everything happened so quickly. He has not yet called for either my husband or me."

"Perhaps we will leave before he speaks to all of us. Perhaps there will be no time." Susannah had her back to me but her voice was suddenly serious.

"We will receive our instructions sometime, I suppose." I knew our leaders had wisely arranged especially chosen men and women who were well versed in the joys and trials of marriage to speak to the newly married couples. Most of us had not met our spouses before we arrived at Herrnhaag and it may have been difficult for some who did not really know one another. Of course our dear Lamb speaking through the Lot had approved of the choices, but I did wonder a bit whether all of the Brethren and Sisters were as happy as I was. I shook my hair loose from my cap and, feeling it on my shoulders, I knew the memory of Matthew's hands cradling my head. I had certainly thought much about the instruction and Anna Maria had told me that it would be Brother Bezold alone, without his wife, who would speak to us of marriage. I had not spoken about this even to Susannah, who was fast becoming a dear and close friend. Climbing into my bed, I pulled the light blanket over myself and thought about Brother Bezold. He had kind blue eyes and a smooth, square face. Did he know that dear Matthew and I had known each other's bodies before we spoke to him? I felt my face grow hot. We all knew that Brother George Harten had accused his wife and Brother Pryzelius of being alone together, and that he was sure for a time that they had known one another. But Brother Bezold was a fair judge and listened to Brother Harten's wife as well as to Brother Pryzelius. I suppose he talked to all of them for some time, and Brother Harten realized the foolishness of his accusation. I turned on my back and opened my eyes to the high ceiling. Brother Bezold would see our devotion to each other and to our Lamb. I slept.

My turn to meet with Brother Bezold came sooner than I had expected. We sat alone in a very small room off the main hall that held only a table and two chairs. There was one window—someone had brought a green plant and placed it on the wide stone sill. I could see the wash-house and, beyond that, the flat field and the straight road leading to the river.

"Sister Krause, I am speaking first with you alone, then with Brother Krause, and a third time with both of you."

"Yes," I nodded, "this is what I have been told."

Brother Bezold leaned forward, his long red hair falling into one side of his face. "You also have been told of our firm belief that unification is performed not only for procreation and pleasure, but also as a holy act. Christ so loved the church as a husband loves his wife . . . a liturgical act; for, you see," he smiled a little, "during unification, the Lord blesses us."

I could no longer hear him for I could feel Matthew's rough face, his mouth eager to find mine, his hands seeking . . . Oh God, could Brother Bezold know what I was remembering at that moment?

" . . . the union of wife and husband is the sacramental enactment of the union of the soul with its Saviour, Sister Krause. Unification is sacred, as is the union between Christ and his Church." His blue eyes looked into mine and I did not look away. His smile was warm, so like a good father.

Yes, I thought. This must be a sacred act. My longing for my beloved is so like the longing intensity I felt just short months ago—the need to be part of and joined to the radiance that surrounded everything; the bright flower painted on our best platter, the scarred wood of our common table, even the simple tools that tamed metal were gleaming silver. All these ordinary things had taken on a new radiance when I first knew of my Saviour's love. And now yet again, as I am filled with love for the quiet man from Silesia. My beloved husband. I see his serious face in a shining light, but no, this must be my Saviour's face, my sweet Lamb of God . . .

" . . . And so, Sister Krause, after you and your husband have practiced, you might want to see me again . . . that is, if you have questions?" He pushed his chair back from the table and stood.

My wandering mind came to rest again on his square face. I wanted to ask him when Matthew and I might be together—where, how . . . it was all so crowded here, and I knew that on board ship we would not share a bed. Will we not lie together until we reach America and would my husband hold me close again on the other side of that wide sea? Winter would be raging there by the time we got to Pennsylvania. Was there a small room, a bed, a fire in the hearth? Would sheets tangle around our joined bodies? But I asked none of these things.

As it turned out, Brother Bezold and I did not meet privately again, for we were asked to leave almost immediately for Rotterdam. Carrying our belongings in bundles, some of our number climbed onto a ship that had come in from Germany. Others were to walk to Rotterdam, leaving their heavier personal things on board the ship. The air that September was wet but not cold. The morning we left, a large gaggle of geese flew over us on their way south. They flew close enough for me to hear the heavy flap of their wings and to hear their wild cries. Would that I could join them, I thought. To fly over this flat land, the water-weeds turning from green to brown, the morning mist hanging low. I raised my arms to them and felt strong and brave and sure that my life was now beginning. We worshipped by singing as we floated downriver, drank a measure of beer in the evening and sailed smoothly to the edge of Europe, where another vessel would take us into the North Sea to England.

OUR SHIP WAS SO TALL. I marveled at its size, for I had never imagined that a vessel so large could float. We stood on the dock looking up at its wooden, curved front and tall mast. We had been told many things about sailing and the sea by those who had sailed before. But until I saw the ship bobbing in front of me, until I stood with the others on the wooden dock with the sun warming my back, nothing they had said explained the feeling to me of beginning this adventure. I could not look around fast enough to see the horses and carts on the dock, the men calling to one another and then, my heart in my throat to see a man crawl up the ropes like a careless spider until he reached a cross beam and pulled at the ropes binding a sail. Seamen must be different from landmen, I thought.

I was standing at the rear of our group of about one hundred souls and it was difficult to see either Captain Nicholas Garrison or his assistant, Captain Thomas Gladman. I knew Garrison was an American but because he was a member of the Brethren, I felt calmed and the small darts of doubt I felt when I looked out past the ship to the undulating water that stretched to the horizon seemed to leave me. We all jostled for a better view as Garrison greeted Brother and Sister Spangenberg, who had just arrived on a return trip from England. Sister Spangenberg was in her mid-thirties, a somewhat heavy-set woman, yet graceful in her manner. Brother Spangenberg was, of course, one of the instigators of the missionary endeavor to America and I was eager to press closer to see the expression on his face and to hear the words he would say to us.

It was a warm greeting between the men with Spangenberg pumping the Captain's hand, rapidly speaking in English—such a strange language then to me. A favorable wind blew from the sea: wet, cool, fishy. I could smell the tar on the ropes as the sailors heaved and pulled, their muscles straining with the task. With the Spangenbergs in the fore, the Captains just behind them, we lined up to walk over the gang-plank. It shuddered from our weight and I looked below to see the sea, brown then in the shadow of the ship. We gathered on the upper deck, our voices quieted as Brother Spangenberg asked us to bow our heads in prayer. Did he ask for a safe journey? I cannot remember, but would guess that rather, he thanked our dear Saviour for allowing this chance to do His work.

Reluctantly I left the upper deck to go below, for we had been warned while in Heerendijk to keep out of the sailors' way. We stowed our small quantities of luggage carefully, using ropes to secure it. We had been told it would roll if we had rough seas. Our sleeping arrangements on board ship separated couples, with the men in hammocks on the lower deck while my Sisters and I took the staterooms on the middle deck. I was not surprised at this arrangement and felt the separation was practical; for intimacy between man and wife would have been impossible in the crowded quarters. We arranged benches outside our staterooms in order to be able to sit and chat if we could not sleep throughout the night. The trip was to take only about twenty-four hours to where we would dock at the Isle of Wight, off the coast of England.

It was as late as four o'clock in the autumn afternoon that we set sail. The sea was gray, by that hour with small waves. The start was quite smooth, and most of us, being too excited to sleep, sat up to speak of our coming journey. But after only two or three hours I could feel a change in the movement of our ship. It was then I knew what the Dark Angel could do with the wind. The sea became so rough it dashed up over the stern. We were ordered by Captain Garrison to stay below and those who had remained on deck obeyed, stumbling and sliding down the very narrow steps to safety. At first I was happy to be out of the raging wind, but several of the Sisters had become sick and the smell of their vomit was stifling in that small space. Sister Wahnert began to move amongst those who were most affected, giving tea to one, wrapping yet another in a warm blanket. At first I huddled in the corner of one bench, my feet pushing hard on the floor to keep from sliding as the waves knocked the ship about. I looked up to see Susannah staggering toward me and, had I not been so distressed, I think I might have laughed aloud at her for she walked so like the man we all teased in Gelzhausen when he made his way down the main street from the town tavern. Susannah sat beside me and hugged me to her, the heat of her body warming me.

"Are you sick, Christina?"

"No, I hate not being able to see the sky. I feel so confined here."

"Can you help me mop up?" She stood, legs apart.

I arose unsteadily and followed her to the bow. The odor there was very strong and I felt my stomach heave. But when she handed me two mugs of tea that Sister Wahnert had miraculously brewed in one corner, I bent to Sister Nixdorf and held the hot liquid to her mouth. The other mug warmed my hand and my stomach settled. I watched the young Sisters who were unaffected move swiftly to those sick Sisters and felt their strength. Such brave women, I thought. But we were only girls then and knew nothing of courage, or even of love.

We scrubbed with hard brushes and rags heavy with sea water to wash the places where some had vomited. I was relieved at not being sick, for if I had bent to cough and then taste the bitter liquid as it dribbled on me as some had, I would have felt less strong than my Sisters. It was much better to be the helper than the helped. By late afternoon, with the English coastline in full view, the odor of seawater and our pungent soap permeated the whole of our deck. Below us, the men had been at the same task and I heard their deep voices as they heaved water from the portholes.

We sailed along the coast of England and, as the sea calmed, I could see from the upper deck, green fields above the chalky cliffs. By afternoon I joined a few of my Sisters to drag boxes of potatoes into the corner of the ship's galley, while the men lifted heavy flour bags to one side in order to make room for the provisions that our English congregation was expected to bring on board. When we finally arrived at Cowes on the Isle of Wight at about four o'clock in the afternoon the sun had slipped into the gray sea and only an orange glow was left on the now calm waves. As our ship slowly, it seemed so slowly, moved closer to a pier that jutted out to us, I could see a small band of men and women who waited and, although I could not yet hear what they were saying, as we drew closer I could discern their welcoming faces. Our ship bumped the dock once, twice, and yet again as a sailor threw the heavy rope around a wooden stump I guessed they used for this purpose. I knew little of the landing and leaving of ships, but thought myself to be a seasoned seaman after having spent the night on the Channel waves.

I was eager to look at everything and to hear the strange tongue of the English people as they greeted the Wahnerts and a few others who spoke the language. There was such a commotion and a mingling of people as the sailors directed the oncoming men and women and we waited for our new directions.

The Englishmen carried fresh milk in large tin containers, and I smelled good, aged cheese in the round wheels. Apples were packed in bushels. My mouth watered at the sight of that juicy fruit, for we had had too little fruit on our journey and I longed to taste the sweet juice. I looked behind me when I heard Susannah exclaim. She held a large red apple in her hand and then with a blissful expression, took a bite, the juice trickling down her chin. I laughed aloud. One of the English Sisters who had just walked up the gangplank had apples in a basket whose handle hung over her arm, and when she heard me laugh she made her way to me, an apple in her outstretched hand. She had a round, open face and when she spoke I saw her teeth were small and crowded. I did not need to know the words she spoke, but her gesture was one of love. At that moment, I felt we would somehow all learn to know one another though we came from different places. Not a tower of Babel perhaps, but rather a ship of like souls.

Along with the confusion, the carrying, lifting and hauling, the eagerness to be on our way, we often found ourselves laughing; for the spaces were small and we were constantly bumping into one another, excusing ourselves in several languages. After endless clearing of baggage at the Custom House, it seemed we were almost ready to begin our long journey across a very wide sea. Sister Wahnert called all the Sisters together for a short meeting of our whole company. We stood in the bright sun and I strained forward to hear her soft voice over the creak of the ship and the lapping waves. She was a slight woman and the way she held her narrow shoulders made me feel she was strong though she was almost middle-aged. Her face was long, her mouth narrow, yet her smile came quickly and showed her even teeth. I learned to listen to this woman, not to hear her words, but to watch how she soothed a frightened Sister with a gentle touch, or a quiet word.

Our murmurs quieted as Sister Wahnert turned to Brother Spangenberg. The sun was warming my face and arms and I squinted to see his round face. He said that if anyone had changed her mind for any reason, that person was free to return home. I looked at Susannah and she seemed in a sort of reverie, perhaps remembering her aged mother and the crooked streets of Büdingen, the tower and bridge. She would be free of fear at last, I thought. Brother Spangenberg waited and we were silent. I imagined myself sinking to my knees and patting the green mound of my mother's resting place. Did my father wander with empty eyes or was he, too, beneath the grass? The smell of the fire, the sound of metal on metal seemed to reverberate in my ears and then the loud ring of our ship's bell broke my dreaming. The floor lurched and I grabbed Susannah's arm.

CHAPTER FIVE

It took a very long time, the sea journey that separated the two parts of my life. Eight weeks on land passes quickly, unless one is a child. Then every day holds such wonder, such terror and joy that the moments in themselves seem to be endless. But growing, we find ourselves at nightfall wondering where the day has gone—when we ate, drank or walked the miles before we fell into sleep. Being at sea was almost like being a child again, for some moments were endless, and each day suspended in a strange, slow time where our little ship pushed its way through the water connected neither to the Old World nor the New.

Often on cloudless mornings when the bell rang at 6 o'clock, I darted past my Sisters to the deck to look for the sun. Rising slowly it struck the stern as it had the previous day; as the orange ball rose, monotone gray became shades of blue and green. Sometimes when I peered over the side to look far below at the wake our small ship made, I saw the foam turned pink. But as the day wore on, the sun overtook our small ship, sinking far to the west in front of us, trailing purple clouds as the sea again turned gray as the charcoal under my father's forge. We never catch up with the sun, I thought.

These clear, bright days when the sea was calm and we had plenty of wind for our sails to catch, hold and carry us westward, we women often sat on deck to do needlework or listen to Anna Maria Schropp read to us from the book of our Saviour's life. We sometimes tried haltingly to voice the sounds of a Sister who spoke words different from ours; for when we had stopped at the Isle of Wight, we had taken on English-speaking members as well as those who spoke the dialects of Ireland, Scotland and Wales and the words of the Scandinavian countries far to our north. The sounds of Czech and Swiss-German were more familiar to me since we had spent time with these Sisters at Herrnhaag. Captain Garrison had told us that fourteen languages were represented amongst the one hundred and thirty-three of us on board. I soon came to believe that Brother Spangenberg had told us a great truth when he said we were all related in our hearts and in the spirit of our mission. Although our words were often haltingly spoken, we seemed to understand one another with little difficulty when we sang and worshipped together. Wisely, Captain Garrison had suggested that we perform the tasks of cooking and cleaning with those who spoke our own languages and we often sat in earnest conversation in the evening when it was clear and calm. I learned much at those quiet times on the upper deck, when the sun still gave some warmth before the chill of the evening set in. It was on one such quiet occasion that Susannah began speaking very seriously.

"Christina, did you have a talk with Brother Bezold in Heerendijk before we left for England?" Her countenance was grave, her round blue eyes direct when she asked the first question.

"Yes. He was very sweet. We left so . . . "

"Well," she interrupted, "he spoke to both George and to me separately, but we never . . . that is, he never got to see us together because we all had to leave so quickly." She hesitated and looked away. "I did not really tell him anything."

"What do you mean?"

"I did not tell him I never wanted to be married. What I wanted, you see, was to join the Brethren and come to America."

"Wait, Susannah. You told me once that you thought George Partsch was a good man, that he seemed kind, that . . . "

"Well, he is." She stopped then and looked out to sea for a long time. "He is a good man and if I had to marry someone, I suppose he was the best man for me but . . . but I did not want to marry anyone."

I had seen Susannah stand beside Johann George Partsch as I had stood beside Matthew. She must have answered the questions, promised and made the same vows. Why would she do this if she were not sure in her decision to marry the Baker?

Susannah continued, "I wanted more than anything to come to America. Well, first I wanted more than anything to join with the Brethren—to have a family, Sisters and Brothers who all followed our Lamb."

"But, Susannah, you could have all that and not marry. There are Single Sisters who follow our Saviour."

"No, you do not understand. There are no Single Sisters on this trip—they asked for only those who married and I wanted to come to the New World now." She stamped her foot on the deck. "I wanted to go with you on this Second Sea Congregation—on this ship, the *Little Strength*."

Susannah's chin was firmly set and her full mouth a straight line. The set of her shoulders against the afternoon sky was square and I thought at the time, as rigid as the cross beam of our mainmast. A determined woman was my friend Susannah.

Recalling her story about her stepfather's cruelty, I remembered my own sturdy father tossing me high in the air and catching me with sure and steady hands. For I had learned love early and she, terror.

"Susannah, the Brethren are kind; they follow the Lamb as we do. They are not like your mother's husband."

"I know that, Christina. I know our Brothers are good men and seem kind, but I, but I . . . " She covered her face in her hands. A small wind flapped the sails above us and I shivered.

"You see, before I knew our Saviour, I never prayed. I knew only how to get away; to turn and run—to hide and find little places where that man could not find me."

"But could not your mother help you? Did she not know he was hurting you?"

"My mother finally saved me. It was my poor, scared mother who went to the Büdingen Magistrate, and he handed me over to the Schuberts in Meerholtz. That was after he—my stepfather—had boxed my ears. *Ach*, I was so swollen on one side. But even she did not know about one time . . . one terrible time. I never told her. I never told anyone."

I clutched my cape more tightly and hugged myself but could not get warm. I did not want to hear this. Perhaps some things in our lives are better left unsaid. Susannah seemed not to notice the cold; her cape slipped from her shoulders and she sat with her hands in her lap, looking not at me, but out to sea.

"Last night the sea was calm," she began. "It rolled like a cradle. I sleep all night—I never awaken." She looked at me, her eyes searching my face. "But something woke me up, *ja*? You were all asleep. I listened. The creaking of our ship was as it always is. I lay there in my bunk.

Then I heard the words. I don't know if I really heard them, but they came to me. Does that ever happen to you, Christina?"

Susannah gave me no time to answer but continued in the strange, soft one-note way she had begun.

"The words were those our Lord said—maybe when he carried that heavy cross. He said, 'I suffered.'" She placed her hand on my leg.

"It was not a whisper—it was more like the sound was in my head. It was over and over: 'I suffered.' Then I started to cry. I did not want to wake any of you but I just cried and cried and it felt as if even my heart was filled with tears. I had to answer somehow so I whispered, 'I will be healed.' Is that strange, Christina? Is it strange that I would say that?"

"No. Somehow it must have been our Saviour's message to you."

"I have to tell you this thing. I have to tell you fast and—please, Christina," she leaned close to me. "Please, Christina, do not say anything. The words are so hard for me to say."

She leaned back and sat very straight as though she was reciting a piece for a schoolmaster. Again her voice took on the sameness of tone and her words came quickly, yet they were separate, as if she were piling stones, one on another.

"He was fat. He had a red face and his eyes were close together. He always smelled of dung and he never put his hands in the bowl of water my mother put out for him to wash away the day's dirt. He used to pick up his meat with his knife and when he chewed he swore at my mother if the meat was tough—or even if it was not. Mama and I sat and watched. She never ate. She just watched and waited to see if he wanted anything. When he looked at her and started to yell I stuffed food in my mouth as fast as I could—I even swallowed without chewing. If he caught me stuffing the food he would grab my chin and turn me to look at him. Sometimes my chin was red for a while. It hurt."

She stopped and waited, then continued in the same voice. "But it did not hurt as much as the other. Most of the time when he caught me, he pulled at my ears or put his two dirty fingers on each side of my nose and held them there until I gasped for breath. He called me a fish; then he slapped his leg and the smell was like moldy hay and grease. It made me sick."

I could feel my throat close as I imagined this and turned to take in the sweet smell of salty water that splashed about the bow of our good ship.

"Oh, Christina, once in our attic he even put his slimy tongue in my ear and then he—he put his dirty fingers between my legs. He said I was a bad girl and that is why I was given to him—to train me. I had no breasts but he put his hands all over me and said someday I would grow up and then some man would do this. I promised, Christina. I promised no man would ever touch me."

Susannah's voice had risen. Anna Maria and Rosina looked over to where we were sitting and I put my finger to my lips. Susannah placed her hand over her mouth and then softly, so I could hardly hear, she said, "I remember the sound of his tearing at the flap of his trousers—buttons flew—I watched one go through the air, hit the floor and bounce once, twice. I tried to follow the button with my eyes but I lost it.

"*Mein Gott*," he pushed me down to lie on me and tried—he tried to get next to my private parts. I could not stop my legs from shaking and he began to swear at me. I was afraid he was going to pee in me. He said I was not obeying him. I wanted to scream and cry but I was afraid he would hurt me more."

The ship rocked gently. We should have a storm now—a wind should howl and the sails flap and tear. The sailors should yell into the wind and we should taste the salt of sea and tears. I felt tears on my cheeks then. I could taste them. But Susannah's eyes were dry and like the surface of a mirror, reflecting only me but with no depth, no life surging from inside.

"*Ach*, I was such a little girl, yet. He turned me around—over—and came at me from the back. I had to lean on my knobby elbows and put my knees on the floor. I could feel him between my legs but it did not hurt because he did not try to get in me. He groaned and breathed faster.

"There was one window in that attic and I saw a little spider weaving and weaving its web. It swung on a very thin thread and worked so hard to make its home. It was such a pretty design and a goldy sunray caught one corner of it. I watched and watched the little spider spin her web, her home."

Susannah's voice remained very quiet and her words came more slowly. A small smile would come and go on her lips and she turned her head as though she saw something I could not see—far away and somehow beautiful to her. She stopped speaking. The ship's timbers creaked, one of the Sisters sneezed, a Brother laughed. Usual sounds; sounds that were familiar yet not comforting, for I knew that Susannah's pain was bound up within her.

Susannah began to speak again, still quietly, still more slowly but with a higher tone—more like a child.

"I watched the spider, *ja*? All its little legs moved together and the thin, thin, thread came from its body to make tiny safe spaces, the silk plaited together to make a design.

"He breathed so fast and then he yelled in my ear, swearing about whore and other words I did not know. Then he got off me. But when he started to leave, he kicked me and I felt a terrible hurt on my leg—his shoe buckle opened my skin. Then he left me there."

I wanted to take Susannah in my arms. I wanted to shield her forever from the kind of hurt she had endured, but only took both her hands in mine, and waited.

"My poor bottom was all wet and sticky already, and I thought I was bleeding but when I looked under my dress the only blood I saw was from the buckle wound on my leg. I could not get up. I did not cry. For a long time I watched the spider as it spun and wove until the room grew dark and I could not see it anymore."

How long did it take to tell this story of hurt and terror? Only a few moments. Yet the time of her suffering must have seemed endless. Her hurt, her humiliation and the spinning of the tiny web had slowed time and I could never know how it was for her when the sun no longer shone in that attic window and the shadows gathered to hide her in dark safety.

We sat across from one another silently, for Susannah had asked me not to speak. But I could not longer restrain my feelings and reached to take her arm. "Oh, my dear friend. You were such a little girl and he—oh, my dear Susannah."

We both stood then and I reached out my arms to embrace her. My strong friend seemed almost a child again. As I held her I looked to the darkening sky. "Make her whole, dear Lamb. Make her safe forever—forever." Our bodies parted, but I felt as though I had taken her suffering into me.

Barely discernable, I heard the sound of a low drone. One Brother began the sound and as others joined him the note was not louder, only more full. Then the melody—a sort of chant sung by the women and taken up by the breeze to mix with the wind in our sails.

Jesus bitter torture, Jesus bloody passion
Thou are't our hearts' cure
Ave Christe. Gloria.

As though sleepwalking, Susannah moved from the circle of my arms to step carefully, stiffly like one in pain, to where the small group of women were singing. Anna Maria reached out her hand to take Susannah's and she seemed taken into a holy circle of sound. I saw her raise her head and sing, *"Ave Christe. Gloria."*

The ship rocked. I put my arms around myself to feel some warmth and looked to see Susannah beckon me to join the women. I could not move. The darkening sky was still cloudless, the sun's rays shafts of orange on our bow; the ocean losing color. I looked up to the tangle of ropes on our masts, like Susannah's spider web made heavy and strong.

I wanted to join the circle. I wanted to feel the comfort of the women's bodies next to me and to join with their sweet voices in praise of our dying Christ. The rich, sonorous sound of the men's drone continued, but the women had stopped singing and stood close in their circle, swaying gently. They were very close together and I could not step in the break their rhythm, though I know they would have welcomed me. In my mind I wandered blindly through a chaotic, disordered world where my words of entreaty reached no one and God was too far away. I sat alone until the darkness settled upon us. the *Little Strength* continued west toward the unknown.

I SOON LEARNED that watching the sun overtake our ship was preferable to feeling myself enclosed in gray once we were far, far out to sea. At least the sun had given me a marker. But once the fog settled in I felt no boundaries, nor could I fasten my gaze at the line where sea met sky searching for an irregularity that would mean land though I knew we were still far from America. The wet slithered in through closed doors. The sheets of our beds were damp and our cloaks never really dried so the smell of damp wool permeated our middle deck.

Susannah had not mentioned again her reluctance to be a true wife to George Partsch nor had she approached me to add any details to the tale she had told. In fact, after speaking to me about such a serious subject, she seemed lighter of heart—I could hear her humming from time to time and as usual, first to waken, she went about her work in the galley with vigor. Could it be that telling a friend such a terrible tale could bring relief? Or was it the gathering in song with the other Sisters that brought her peace? Had Susannah's heart been awakened by the

Saviour in some way I did not know? Perhaps His comforting presence brought ease to the sore places of her childhood memories. I prayed she could hold fast to a new-found faith; that it did not vanish into the foam of our ship's wake.

It was the wisdom of those who had traveled the sea before to break up our days as best they could with song fests and weekly parties when we feasted on sweet cakes. I loved the taste of sugar and cinnamon, but more than this I loved the laughter and fellowship though often I had no idea of the meaning of some Sisters' words, foreign to me still. One Irish Brother had brought his tin whistle and his tunes had our feet tapping as we women sat on the benches placed before our staterooms.

There was no seasickness once we were abroad on the sea and the advice to move about in the fresh air to keep us healthy proved true. Even Sister Opitz's face was no longer the green-gray of the seasick. At times it was hard for me to stay awake for the rocking of our ship lulled me into sleep as I sat with my sewing. But it was at night, feeling the rise and fall of the waves, cuddled in my blanket that I longed to feel Matthew's tall, warm frame next to me. I would try to imagine how it would be if we were ever to share a bed all through the night, though I knew full well that even our first months in the New World would be spent separated, for the living quarters were built as they had been in Herrnhaag and Marienborn.

There was little opportunity for time alone with one another on board ship; the men had their hammocks on the lower deck and we slept in our staterooms above. I did so long to watch my husband's face, to see him smile as he looked at me, the frown mark between his heavy brows smoothing as he touched my hand.

I confess to moments made all the more sweet by their stolen pleasure. One time on an empty deck in the rain, cool droplets on my face were made warm by Matthew's quick kisses. For one moment I was pressed in his arms, his cheek rough and wet; and then he was gone. Dizzy, I clung to the rail, shivering with the chilling emptiness that brought an old yearning and all around me the gray swells of the sea.

We had had no rough weather traversing the English Channel, and I think we were all lured by the Fallen Angel into thinking the remainder of our journey would be as smooth. We were wrong. For the fury of Evil must have its day and perhaps we all had to learn again our Saviour's lesson that only in cleaving to Him do we know safety.

It began innocently. I suppose Noah himself did not know the power of water though our Lord had warned him. Whether our brave Captains Garrison and Gladman could foresee the storm I never knew. No matter, the only warning I was aware of—and I did not understand this at the time—was the rain turning colder, more stinging and the wind changing its course. I had the fanciful thought that a giant hand had taken the huge, full bag of the world's wind and had freed a burst that pushed me. My cap shook loose and danced down the deck. My hair blew into my face. I knew I should go below, but the one burst of wind seemed singular, as though it was at play and meant no harm. I felt the sway of our ship to be still regular and I was not unbalanced.

My hair, my dress, my hands were now dripping. Still I stood on deck, fascinated. I looked up at the sky and saw layers of clouds, all in varying shades of gray scudding madly as though they were on some mission of their own, racing to some unseen place outside our world. But my world is very small, I thought. My world is only on this small, regularly bobbing ship.

It began as a roar. From some hidden place the wind first whipped wavelets, tipped with white as far out as I could see, then growing stronger, scooped huge mounds of gray water that rose and fell, in deep valleys and ever-moving mountains. Then waves of water, first on one side of the bow and then on the other, crashed onto the deck; the overwhelming salty odor of the sea itself at that moment enveloped me in green and blue as if we had sunk underwater, gliding through waving weeds where slow-moving creatures stared with dark, protruding eyes and fish flung themselves against our sides as we made our watery way. The sails, wrapped with rope, seemed curled into themselves as if to defend against the wind that pulled at them with unseen fingers, while the mainmast did a strange, stiff dance.

I grabbed at the rail. Then the icy rain stung my face and the ship began to buck like a horse not wanting to be shod. I knew I had to get below but I was a distance from the small cabin that covered the steps. Could I crawl to the double doors and, if I reached them, could I open them? My clothes were plastered to my body but I did not yet feel the cold. A flash of lightning, darkness, then another flash; in that instant I could see one door pushed open against the heavy wind. George Partsch stood there, crouched against the wind.

"Sister Krause, for God's sake. We thought all were below."

I started to let go of the rail to move toward him, but he yelled, "Here, a rope. Take hold of it. Take hold."

Brother Partsch's voice was almost lost in the roar. The rope landed in front of me and I picked it up, knowing where it lay more by its thud than by sight. It was wet and greasy. Hand over hand I pulled myself the short distance to where George Partsch was braced, holding one door with his body. He put both hands around my waist to draw me into the darkness. The door thudded behind us.

The roar of the wind and stinging rain was not as loud inside but our ship swung madly from side to side. Candles had been extinguished and the darkness was so profound I felt myself to be in some underground cave. George held tightly to my hand, creeping before me through the narrow passages. Then I heard the familiar, comforting bass voice of Brother Matthew Weiss. His voice was not louder than the storm but rather riding on it, as though the tempest was a chorus for his song of faith. One by one the others joined him until most on board crowded into the space of the middle deck poured forth their praise.

Now let all the heavens adore thee.
And men and angels sing before thee
We rejoice and sing hymns of joy eternally.

We sang the ancient melody as though to ride the storm. It was counterpoint to the roar of the gale, the creaking boards and the ferocious sound of water.

Was it only a few short months ago that I had stood before my small home in Gelzhausen to bid goodbye to Hans and Greta and their little ones? I had pledged to follow my Saviour though the path be stormy, yet then my feet were on unmoving earth and the wind carrying the smell of spring only gently touched my face. Now only the straining timbers beneath me kept me from the grasping, watery fingers of an angry sea as I waited in dread to hear the crack of a mast. Would the soaked wood hold together? Would our masts bend with the gale? Oh, that our Saviour would see this tossing, windblown, forlorn ship and guide it to safety!

We rejoice, we rejoice, we will sing eternally. We sang on.

The tossing of our ship lessened after what was probably two hours and the wind lost its roar. Someone lit a candle that flickered uncertainly and then grew stronger. In its glow I could see their faces, the men and women I had pledged to join on our uncertain path. The candlelight caught at the hollows of cheeks and eyes; it cast shadows of profiles against the walls. Men and women from middle Europe, from the far north, from England, Ireland and Scotland—we all sang together, a congregation of strong hearts and brave souls. Perhaps, I thought, perhaps surrounded by their faith, I will find faith. My voice blended with the others, and though I had no image of the holy Lamb I could feel the fire of my resolve returning in the burning flame of my beloved Brethren.

I searched to find Matthew's face to see he was looking across at me, and I felt loved. George Partsch's brown hair was slicked to his head, his shirt still sticking to his husky body and when he looked at me, he smiled and I felt warmed.

It was Brother Greening who spoke, first in English and then in German. He was a medical doctor and scholar. He had joined us at Cowes and had already proved adept at bandaging cut fingers and giving advice on all sorts of matters pertaining to our health. His graying hair stuck out on each side of his head, his breathless voice, rapid in both languages.

"Our dear Saviour has been with us," he said, and the sound of assent filled the space. "What proof we have . . . what proof." He made a step to one side as the ship lurched and Matthew Schropp, Anna Maria's husband, reached to catch the English Brother's portly body. Brother Schropp said, "Some of you are wet. I suggest the women try to get to their quarters to find dry clothing and I need a few of you Brothers to assess any damage—to see if we have taken on sea water."

Captain Garrison's voice reached our deck from above. "It is calming now. He has led us through the worst. We will keep our sails furled until the wind dies. Daybreak is almost upon us and, praise to Him, we are not far off course."

"Amen, amen," the high voices of Sisters in answer to his good news.

Dawn broke to a gray day, the sun hidden from our sight. It must have been the close presence of our Saviour who had kept us afloat.

I WAS NEVER WARM on the ocean. Some days we had sun, but most were gray with low flying November clouds and it seemed a miracle that our good Captain stayed his course across that vast expanse. The heavy storm had not damaged sails or masts, and for the most part, we were able to catch and hold the wind. Great care was taken by those like Sister Wahnert, who had sailed before, to see that our spirits were cheered and our minds busy. When the weather was not stormy, we were able to rise early, dress and empty slops before our short prayer meeting and breakfast; although I slept and ate with Sisters who spoke my own native German, I began to feel more and more at ease with those women who did not. Our classes in English and German brought us together.

Brother Dohling was the German teacher. He held a lens to one eye, peering through it when he called on some English-speaking Sister. He was so strict and unsmiling I wriggled in my skin to feel her discomfort and wanted so badly to whisper the answer for her. Brother Greening, who taught English, spoke so rapidly it was difficult to follow what he was saying. But we could not help but laugh as he stood on the stairway between the Brothers' deck and ours, his head bobbing to and fro, his hand waving as we recited the words. Thank goodness, I thought, that Anna Maria and a few others were so quick; because had I been called on alone, I would have been embarrassed by my poor memory and my blushing cheeks.

"And why would I want to read another language when it is hard enough to read my own?" Susannah raised her blond brows while turning down her mouth.

"But Susannah," Anna Maria's heart-shaped face was serious, "It is important to be able to speak and read others' words and in America many speak English."

"Well, I don't have to talk to them. I will bake good bread. That will make them full and happy." Susannah pretended to knead dough and we all laughed. She had such a way of making us laugh and was often so cheerful I began to wonder if her story of terror, once told, failed to bother her. I should have known better.

It was on the day it was discovered that several of our water casks were leaking. Susannah and Brother Reuz had noticed that the floor was wet around the piled casks and reported the worrying news that twenty-three had some defect. Brothers Fisher and Wagner, who were responsible for the ship's stores, called a meeting; my Matthew offered to repair the casks. There was a great deal of talk on the women's deck and many voiced concern, but Susannah seemed more worried than the others.

"Christina, we will have even less to drink."

I knew only too well what she was saying. We used sea water for washing our dishes, our clothing and even the cloths we used for our monthly flow though the salt stiffened materials terribly. I could still taste the acrid salt in my throat and feel the stickiness on my skin since my experience in the storm.

"Susannah, we still have water, and America cannot be more than a few weeks away." I looked closely at my friend as she began to clasp and unclasp her hands. "Is something else worrying you, my Sister?"

Susannah lowered herself onto the bench near our stateroom. "I cannot help but think about drawing nearer and nearer to America, Christina. I want so to be there . . . to land . . . to stand where it does not move. But . . . but . . . "

"And the water casks remind you that we must pray for strong winds to push us westward. But why ever would you not want to land?"

"Oh, yes, I pray that we will land. But then, but then we will settle in a Pennsylvania forest and live together as husband and wife."

Susannah did not need to tell me that she was afraid to live as a wife to George Partsch; that her stepfather's cruelty had placed such fear in her heart. My prayer came so easily, "Help her, dear Lamb. Help my friend." It was as effortless as breathing, as stepping over a rise on the road, as pushing a sharp needle into soft linen cloth. Effortless and without thought.

Captain Garrison's voice swept the ship. "All on deck. All up on deck."

We hurried up the stairs, my petticoats held in one hand, the other pushing my cap more securely on my head, the ribbons streaming and untied. Captain Garrison announced that Matthew and Brother Biefel would fix the casks and I felt the flush of pride as I heard the men say that my husband could "fix anything." But it was George Partsch whose words seemed to catch at my heart and open a door for me when he said, "We should take a moment to thank Him who guides some hands to repair. But more than this . . . more than this." He looked down at his feet and hesitated, as if his idea was beyond his power to express. "Seems to me we should thank Him for showing us the leaking casks. Had we not seen this . . . " He stopped then for we all knew the consequences of such an error.

Yes, I thought. Yes, he is right. Our Saviour must be watching over our little ship. Yet as I gazed out over the gray sea, the ever-moving waves, the vast space between our little world and the land beyond, a dart of fear lodged in my heart. For we had such a long way to go and I knew our continued safety depended on our faith in the One who guides our lives. I prayed for that faith.

I hurried to the upper deck to see if the sunshine had burned through the clouds, but knew the day was wet again and raining, for I could smell it even before I pushed open the heavy doors to the deck.

Yet another day of damp, clinging clothes and slippery flooring. Sister Anna Maria Schropp was leaning over the rail and at my greeting, she said, "Thank our Saviour for more rain. We may yet fill our casks again."

I felt a momentary stab of guilt in the pit of my stomach. I had been so despairing of the rain and yet it was that very gift from Heaven keeping us from parched throats. Taking Anna Maria's arm, we stepped back to the swinging door. Surely this must be a sign. I must pay attention to this, I thought. I continually look to see our dear Lamb, to find reassurance in His face; yet His work is all around me; His love and care. Do my Brothers and Sisters see more than I? Are their hearts more open—their rapture glowing on every upturned face? O my God, I prayed as the rain beat on the decks and swept through the rigging. O, my holy Lamb, I prayed, as our ship made its brave way to the west. Help me to see.

It was November 20, 1743. The deep bass voice of John Christian Ehrhardt called out, "Forty-five fathoms." Such a welcome sound for our floating congregation. Though many of us knew little of the depth of the sea, we knew his call meant land was near. We were prepared to celebrate by having our Lovefeast of hot coffee and sweet cakes on deck; however, by noon a strong wind had risen. The sailors said little but we could tell by their dashing about and their serious faces that all was not well. Captain Gladman announced to us that we were attempting to reach Newport, a settlement on the coast of America, but because the winds had not changed direction, we might try a bit south near the cape of Delaware. Land had never been sighted and it was only soundings and the screech of gulls that would tell us we were closer to America.

I heard a gull's scream one early morning. At first I had to stop to identify the sound, for sea birds were not part of my experience. Perhaps I was too excited to notice their cry when we embarked from England in October. I remembered, though, that their cry meant a meeting of land and sea. On that November day I wanted to rush on deck and fling my arms out to welcome them as they swooped and cried above us. But after three days of our sailors pulling at the rigging and our excellent Captain and his mates using all their skill in sailing into the teeth of the wind, tacking and coming about without losing precious time, the cry of the gulls grated on my nerves, their constant screeching the cruel laughter of some devil who pushed our ship close to land and then, in gleeful pleasure, blew it out again.

It was after midnight on the twenty-sixth when I awoke again—none of us had slept through the night for some time—to feel the movement of the sea different from the past week. I could almost hear a steady swish, a constant forward push.

"Christina, are you awake?" It was Susannah's voice in the darkness of our stateroom.

"How can anyone sleep when you are talking?" Sister Anna Sensemann muttered.

"The sea is different. The wind is different. I can tell." Susannah rose and lit a candle as we all stirred, ready to get out of bed, yet reluctant to face yet another day of rain and fog. But it was not Susannah's words or the feel of the sea that caused us to hurry from our beds, hastily put on our clothes and, without aprons or caps, hurry above. It was the brilliant, cheering sound of a Brother's trumpet that announced land—a voluntary that praised God with thanksgiving. Such a simple array of tones that brought tears of joy.

I could see the rim of dark land out by the horizon as I clung to the rail beside Anna Maria and Susannah, and, turning when I heard my husband's call, I saw his smile, his nod. I caught my breath.

Then the mist descended and land was again lost to us. A groan, a communal sigh rose from all assembled. Would we have to wait still longer?

Anna Maria murmured, "I think the Lamb has given me patience but I fear I am losing it."

"Will my petticoats ever stop clinging to me? I am very tired of being wet," Susannah said.

The thoughts in my head echoed those of my Sisters as I turned from the rail to descend the steps. I was tired of the sea—tired of the constant motion. I longed to stand on dry land that was unmoving beneath me and to warm my hands before a fire that burned within a huge hearth. I knew I would find no green leaves nor blooming flowers in November, but even the brown of the fields would be better than this gray water and incessant movement.

Again it was Brother Ehrhardt who called, his voice heard on all parts of the ship, deep, and as musical as the bassoon our Brothers had played in Herrnhaag.

"Land! Land before us!"

The curtain of mist lifted and the sun's rays broke through, burning, dissolving the fog and we could clearly see the bay, bounded by blessed land.

"New York harbor."

"Blessed land."

CHAPTER SIX

Wwe came in gently. The water changed from gray to green as we floated past flat, marshy islands; odd, spiky sea grass, low, dark-green pine bushes, their twisted roots growing from white sand. I felt no wind but our sails made an irregular, flapping sound in syncopation to the lap, lap of the water. We floated almost soundlessly. I was aware of the chilling air, the mist cool on my face. I remember no words. Perhaps we were silent as we stood on the upper deck on that November day. Quiet after the ordeal of our crossing.

We have come the long way, I thought, our little ship pushed like a stick in a rushing brook. But we have survived. We are on the other side. I have left behind Gelzhausen: the clang of metal on metal, the hiss of water on the curved and burning shoe; Greta calling me to gather her children for our meal at the long wooden table. And my mother's quiet smile. Could I still see them in my dreams now that I have crossed the sea? Would I hear my mother's gentle warning call, "Christina" when I waded in a rushing creek on this, the other side?

"Staaten Eiland in view."

Brother Ehrhardt's deep bass broke my reverie.

"If I had dry clothes, I would walk anywhere," Susannah pulled at her wet petticoat.

"Oh, for land beneath us that doesn't rock. I fear I cannot wait much longer." Anna Maria's heart-shaped face took on exaggerated woe.

"But we are here." I said to myself. "All healthy and with a thousand reasons to be thankful, we are here."

I remember the lapping waves, the chill breeze and my mind wandering. Are "here" and "there" separated by an ocean? Or are "here" and "there" ideas divided by a decision that, once made, changed me forever? Did I think thus and then this? My hands gripped the ship's wooden rail. Strong hands; long-fingered, nails short. I often looked at my hands, watched them pull at a cow's udder, beat batter with a wooden spoon, grasp a quill to write a few words. Once, there were dimples at my knuckles. But as a young woman, I saw the bones, my skin a bit brown from our outdoor life of travel. And my hands have held the face of my beloved—to search his face.

To know his heart and to see myself mirrored in his eyes. Have I become another by the mystery of my love's love or has it been my dear Saviour capturing my heart and changing me so profoundly that I am no longer the tall girl who swung the pail of glistening water?

"Christina, look, look. Can you see the little birds with the thin, long legs? How they peck at the sand?" Susannah leaned over the rail in her excitement.

I had to peer intently to see what she meant, for although we were very near the shore, the little birds were the size of insects. My thoughts flew into the wind as I heard the shouts of the sailors, the murmurs of the Sisters and Brothers. But the refrain, "We are here" repeated itself in my mind.

We entered a smaller channel and pulled yet closer to the low, sandy ground. I could see a few other craft now—rowboats and one or two with small masts and one sail. The men in rowboats waved and shouted as they pulled at their nets, sometimes a glimpse of silver between the heavy netting.

This is very different, I thought. This is very different from the other side. I scanned the land to look for some building, a Custom House perhaps. One that stood at the water's edge. Or busy wharves, the sound of wheels clattering on the wooden slats. I saw no twirls of smoke, not even a stone wall. Only seagrass, sand and twisted pines.

"We have to sail past these islands before we get to a civilized part of America," Anna Maria told us. "But I think Captain Garrison lives right on the large island of Staten."

"But how long will it take?" Susannah flapped her petticoat in an attempt to dry it.

Captain Garrison's voice called from the bow. "Gather here. We will soon see my home, where we will dock for the night."

I wondered if we would leave the ship. I suddenly felt I could no longer bear another rocking movement under my feet; could no longer sleep in the stateroom below. My body felt constricted, as though to protect myself from something I did not know. Our eight-week journey felt like a lifetime. I had such a need to reach my arms to the sky, to run fast, my leg muscles pulling and stretching. I felt at that moment that if I were allowed, I would run all the way to this place, Pennsylvania. I would leap over small trickling waters and finally, panting with exertion, would fling myself onto the ground—the unmoving, solid grass-covered ground. The last evening on board ship passed surprisingly swiftly; once we had docked, I felt our whole group take on a festive air. Brother and Sister Almers, who had come months before us, hurried aboard. Following them, were men carrying crates of apples and loaves of brown, crusty, newly baked bread. Without waiting for the dinner hour we each took a thickly sliced piece. American apples. American bread.

Brother Opitz began to sing *'Jesus, source of our salvation,'* and we joined in with hearty voices. Then, in the silence that followed the last stanza, I could hear the waves lapping at our ship, now at rest. In the deepening darkness, the nimble fingers of an Irish brother played the high, clear sound of his tin whistle, its notes skipping over the now gentle sea. Brother Hoepfner sat crouched against the rail, scribbling in his diary and, as I began to step down the narrow way to our quarters, he looked up and smiled. Was he writing of the tang of American apples or did he note the pitch of a tin whistle that pierced the silence that night?

I slept very soundly; the gentle roll of waves seemed a cradle. The next morning after a very hasty toilet and even quicker cup of tea we all crowded into the packet boat that took us from the large harbor, upriver into the place called New Jersey. The land was still flat that near the sea, and the river meandered through low meadows, brown now in autumn. As we moved on the river, the morning mist dissolved and I could see beyond the low land an outline of gentle hills, darkly forested. Susannah sat before me, turning her head from side to side to take in the newness of the river, the low bank, the few dead branches of small trees that had broken and lay twisted, half in and half out of the muddy water.

Early the next morning I lay on my bed in the windowless room of our first lodging in a small village called New Brunswick. How far I was from Gelzhausen, I thought, and though I should have been comforted by the women awakening near me, I felt lonely, suddenly unsure of myself in a place so new to me.

A bird called. It was not the screaming plea of a gull but the sweet song of a land bird. Not a robin, nor a wren in this chilling month of November but a call, a melody, a chirp so cheering that I forgot the damp cold of the room, the thin not-quite-clean blanket that covered me. It was on that cool morning, on this side of the sea where there seemed so much land un-peopled, where the river wound westward to a place so unknown to me, that distress fell like a wet shift shrugged from my shoulders. How could this happen so quickly? Could the singing of a small bird take my uncertainty from me? Surely not; and yet I recalled it was the call of one dove that signaled the end of Noah's sea journey. I felt the lightness I had known in Marienborn and yes, even in Gelzhausen when I first knew of my Saviour. A sense of calm, my breathing peaceful, even; all was well. This must be the way my beloved knows our dear Lamb. I felt it in the quiet of Matthew—his stillness.

The rustle of bedclothes, the blended murmur of my Sisters' voices brought me back to my surroundings; to walls new, the wood still green, the sticky sap oozing onto the mortar between the logs. Everything would be new here, I thought. I will no longer find shelter within walls that contained the cooking of years; or run my hand over the stone chimneys that have held bright fires and shaped the course of smoke toward the sky for many generations. Nor will I listen for the sound of whispers, long gone but held somehow in the ancient cracks of an old shop or inn that had stooped close to the dirt roads of my girlhood. Only the land untrod would be old, the streams not yet bridged, and the trees where every year songbirds must build their nests. I heard the chirp again, nearer now, and I threw my bedclothes back, ready to step into a new day and a new land.

Once our large group had gathered outside the inn in New Brunswick, Captain Garrison called out the names of small companies who would travel together in much the same manner we had walked from Herrnhaag to Frankfurt. I whispered a hurried thank you to my Saviour, for Matthew and I were to make the trip together. I love to watch him, I thought: not just with my eyes but from my inner self. For it is my need to be part of him, to lodge inside his mind and see with his blue eyes this new world around us. Perhaps if I looked through his eyes I could even begin to see how he holds his faith so close that it seems to flow with his blood.

George Partsch was also to be with us, but Susannah had suggested to Captain Garrison that she would walk with a very small group that included the English Sister Bannister, Brother Payne's mother. Susannah had voiced her concern to me about this Sister; for despite the woman's apparent good health, we knew that she was at least seventy years of age and did not, perhaps, know the rigors that were to come. I see her yet, her determined mouth, her prominent nose, the brown spots on her face that spoke of advancing years. Susannah put her hand on the older woman's shoulder and said in German that they might like to walk together, indicating with her other arm the path before us. Sister Bannister raised her chin and taking Susannah's arm they began to walk. I watched the small band until they were barely visible. My throat dry, I swallowed with difficulty, as I thought about my dear friend who had taken it upon herself to help an older Englishwoman along the path where few had trod. Brother George Partsch stood next to me, his face unreadable as he waved once to the disappearing group.

We had avoided the bustle of a Custom House, for our belongings were transported to New York City by wagon; thus we had only to make ourselves ready for the trek to Bethlehem, which we were told would take several days depending on weather. I was relieved to see that there were wagons to accompany the walkers in case one of us became tired or sick. The men joked amongst one another about who would need to ride, and we women joined in their laughter when George Partsch pretended to limp.

It had snowed slightly some days before our arrival in New Brunswick and the ground was hard. This made it easier for the horse-drawn wagons than if there had there been mud. I felt strong and eager as I took my first steps on this land on the other side. I could feel the stretch and pull of my leg muscles, so long cramped on board ship. Again I wanted to run. I was sure my good shoes would take me across the brown stubble and I could push aside the thin branches as I moved swiftly through this virgin wilderness. But, of course, I stayed with the other Sisters—the men leading the way. Matthew walked with a long stride, not moving his arms much; George Partsch, shorter by several inches, seemed almost to leap over jutting clumps of frozen grass, swinging his ax at small bushes.

The men called out to one another and we women chattered with questions about the size of our new house, the care our Saviour had taken of the men who had some success in hunting this autumn. Anna Maria Schropp wondered how many books had been brought across the sea, and one Sister said that she hoped the next congregation who braved the journey would have a spinet on board. I, too, longed for that sweet sound and tried to imagine how the tinkle of notes would sound in the deep forests of America.

The day was gray and windy. The clouds scudded swiftly across the sky, and I wondered how Susannah was faring with her group; whether Sister Bannister had been imprudent in her decision. Was Susannah worried about the days to come, when she and her husband would share a bed? It seemed as though the excitement and anticipation of our journey had overcome her anxiety. I looked ahead again to see George Partsch throw back his head and laugh with a freedom that made me more than sure he would be the right choice for my friend. "O, God, help dear Susannah. Make her at ease with her husband for he is a good man."

The brisk wind touched my face and I smelled pine. This is the journey I was born to make. This is the place I should be—tramping over the brown stubble, the cracking of twigs under my shoes, my beloved walking before me with sure and steady feet.

CHAPTER SEVEN

Susannah Partsch

The way is hard. And I am hungry. I try not to think about my stomach, but with every step I can hear my rumblings. *Ach*, smells of bread baking and pots of venison and gravy I think about. We take turns riding on the wagon sometimes, but now Sister Bannister walks beside me and does not complain. She is a strong woman and I should take a lesson from her. She is old, but she never speaks of hunger yet. When the end of the day draws near, she puts her hand on my arm and then I know she needs just a small help to keep herself from stumbling on the rough ground.

Sometimes we have to cut our way through the brush—the men go ahead and swing their axes. Most of the time we have an uneven path. It was made by those who have walked before us. The sky is gray but the mist that came in around us the first day is gone. Now it is colder and it may snow. *Ach*, how I loved the snow in Büdingen! When the first flakes flew from the sky I wanted to dance and swirl as they did. I did this once—but only once. My stepfather caught me. He grabbed my arm and swung me hard around and around. I fell to the ground. I was dizzy and hurt. *Mein Gott*, then he laughed.

Brother Greening is laughing now. The sound flies out into the trees and startles the crows. They caw back at us as if they want to join in, too. He laughs often. It is *sehr gut*. I like to hear him. He leans on the stick when he strides uphill but I think he does not need it, for he is a strong man. He has so much in his head already. He speaks German, even though he is an Englishman. He is a doctor, too, and knows what to do when one of our Band is sick or scratched from a briar. Briars are dangerous. The small cut can grow and ooze green pus. It must be washed or maggots put on the wound to eat out the rotten flesh. No one has had this happen—*Gott sei dank*—thank God—but there are times when the older ones are weary. I am tired at the end of a day, but I am stronger than most of them, and used to hard work more.

I think our Band of pilgrims moves more slowly than the other Bands. Sometimes I am impatient and want to run ahead. I could not wait to get to land when we were at sea. I wanted to dive from our ship and swim ashore. I spoke of this to Christina and she smiled in her quiet way. *Ach Gott*—I wonder where she is now. Has she got to the gathering place of Bethlehem? Are they all eating? Carrots. When they are not all cooked, they crunch. Herr Schmidt did not like them that way. But I did. *Nein, nein,* I must not think of food. It is not yet time to stop and make our fires.

I will think about my friend, Christina. I never had a friend before. Not at the Schuberts when I was a little girl; or even at Government Councilor Schmidt's, where I was a cook. *Ach,* what a grand house! Herr Schmidt was good to me, but I knew that I must leave to follow our dear Brother Ludwig. To call this great Count, Brother Ludwig is hard for me. I am just a cook. I can hardly read or write. But Sister Susannah Nitschmann says I should remember I am a child of our dear Saviour who loves us all. I try to remember this.

The sky is so gray. I cannot see where the sun is now, but the day is getting darker so I know that soon we will stop. Brother Nixdorf says since we left the inn in New Brunswick, we have made good time. It will be only a day before we arrive in Bethlehem. I wonder about the large house in Bethlehem. Sister Almers says it is huge and three-storied, made of wood cut by the brothers. It will be warm there with the fires blazing in all the rooms. She says there is a large sleeping room for the women on one side of the attic and one for the men on the other. So we will again sleep as we did at Herrnhaag and Marienborn. My heart beats faster. Is our way more rough? Are we treading uphill? No, I can see where it leads straight and flat through the trees. I know my heart beats faster because I have thought about George Partsch. Now my hands are wet with sweat in my pockets. *Ach du lieber,* I am afraid. No, I am not afraid. I am NOT. I must not worry and try to believe my God will be with me.

Brother Bezold was going to speak to George Partsch and me about married life. And about unification when we were in Holland already. But there was too little time, so only to me he spoke. I could not tell him I did not want to be married. I just wanted so bad to be here. Even in this forest with trees so much taller than I have ever seen. Even with the stony path, the streams that hurry over the jutting rocks, even the dark at night when we cannot see at all; and the cold. Even all this I wanted. I want it still. I want to follow my Lamb and have these people as my family. I have many Sisters now. And I have my best friend Christina. If I had not said I would be the wife of George Partsch, I could not have come with this, our Sea Congregation. I would have had to wait. I do not like to wait!

Brother Brandmiller raises his hand. We will stop for the night. The ground is dry though cold. The trees make a sort of ceiling over us. Again I will wrap my blanket around me against the cold and feel my legs warming. The tea is hot in my stomach. The bread stops the rumbling.

Someone calls. "Sister Partsch, Susannah. Awake."

Was . . . was . . . Who calls to me? I am tightly curled. I taste fear though I do not know who . . . or what . . .

"Sister Partsch. You called out—you cried in the night." It is Sister Nixdorf. She has been a special friend on this journey and understands my life. She too, was taken into service at a young age yet, though not for the same reason I was. I tell her I am alright—that I just had a bad dream. I smile so she thinks I am not afraid.

We walk forward. It is mostly uphill now, but Sister Almers says these hills are the ones that are near Bethlehem, and by nightfall we will arrive. She has made the trip before. We are now feeling eager and hopeful though wet flakes of snow are whirling around us. The cold wind blows at our faces. I am walking with Sister Biefel and between us, Sister Bannister. Rosina Biefel says she is used to walking because she walked all the way from her home in Silesia to Herrnhut. She says she left her parents to join the Brethren. When we traveled to this side of the great ocean, I left my country, but I left my poor mother years before. It was when she went to the Magistrate to tell him about how my stepfather beat me. I carry her face in my heart, but it is a face of sadness. I do not want to think of it often.

There, I see the crest of the hill beyond the valley where we walk. Brother Greening says they have built the large house right there. He says we will build a city on the hill just the way the Bible says. I wonder who will be there to greet us? Will Christina run out of the house without her cloak? And Susannah Nitschmann, will she call out to us? And what about George Partsch? I see trees, bare and tall against the clouds. We walk up a steep rise and I reach out to touch a pine trunk. The sap sticks to my fingers. It smells sharp and sweet. *Ach,* I hope I always remember this odor.

We slip and slide down the slight grade and then tread level ground. I can feel the stones under my shoes, the uneven weeds and grass. I reach out to grab at saplings. I see the river, curving and gray now through the trees. Then I smell the woodsmoke. The frankincense given our dear Lamb could not have smelled this welcoming. *Wie schoen*—how beautiful. My heart lifts. I know I am coming home.

CHAPTER EIGHT

Christina Barbara Krause

It is strange the way in which some details of my life's journey come so easily to me and others have been lost. I seem to recall the small occurrences more clearly now when the fever comes—the heat, then the chill, and the floating sensation in which my body is not a part of me—all this mixes past and present time, and those I have loved and lost appear again to answer my call.

I can recall our day of arrival in Bethlehem; the swish of water as the welcoming Sisters bent to wash our weary feet, the life-giving heat of the crackling fire on my face, and my first taste of clear broth that warmed my whole body. I can hear the racking cough of Brother Hantsch as he entered the door, the whinny of his horse as he let loose the reins and staggered toward us.

Most clear to me is the anxious waiting for Susannah, Brother Payne's old mother, and the others not yet arrived as the weather turned colder and the sleeting rain pelted against the window panes; and the blessed relief of finally hearing the rusty creak of wagon wheels, the horses stomping and sneezing—a familiar and comforting sound to me, for I had often been awakened thus as a child when my father was called early to the forge.

Some days I feel a bit better and can get up to walk but I find that most of the time I have to sit in a chair or lie in my bed. It is this swelling that bothers me. Perhaps I should be bled, perhaps not. Oh, the strange vertigo is coming back. I can sit no longer but must lie down again. I have found that I can ignore the pulse that beats so under the swelling of my neck if I put my mind in the past—to remember the cold and the smell of pine when we first arrived at the *Gemeinhaus* in Bethlehem . . .

THE WIND SEEMS TO BLOW more violently on this side of the ocean and during that December of 1743 it roared amidst the tall, bare trees, making their branches crack and groan as though in pain. Would I ever feel this was my home, I thought? This enormous land, these huge trees, the streams of such force they assault the jagged rocks as though to cover them, then rush on in bubbling haste. Would I ever see trees cleared, the seed sown, the harvest gathered and the children of my own body running through an open field, as I had done? Surely the faith of the Brethren would help to make my home in this wild land.

There had been some snow, and the stubble of grass was stiff with frost. A storm gusted about our *Gemeinhaus* on the night we began our celebration of the Saviour's birth, but during a lull earlier in the day we had gathered boughs from the forest and hung them about the walls. The odor of pine freshened the air, bringing with it the clean smell of the wilderness. We kept the watch all through the night and as we sat and sang in the wooden, backless benches, the men on one side, the women on the other, I remember I was filled with such love for the babe who had been born that night long ago; and I watched Matthew's face as he sang, struck dumb with the strength of him, his faith shining brighter to me than the candles that lit our room, his shoulders solid amid the wavering shadows that seemed to dance with the songs against the log walls. I could feel the warmth from my Sisters' shoulders on each side of me and their blended voices; *In Dulci Jubilo* continued in a steady harmony as I sat in my awe.

When the hour of midnight came, we each lit a small candle and rose to follow Father Nitschmann to the stable area. On this holy night a year ago, the blessed Zinzendorf had himself walked into this little stable, and, reminding the Brethren of our Saviour's humble birth, had begun to sing

> *'O blessed night, without compare on earth;*
> *The night whereon the wonder-child had birth.'*

We, too, joined our voices to sing as he had done. I particularly recall the watch-word for our first Christmas in the New World: *And the name of the city from that day shall be, the Lord is there,* from the Book of Ezekiel. And at that moment, as though some angel had touched her, young Maria, the Leinbach's daughter, raised her sweet voice to begin Adam Druse's ancient hymn.

> *'Jesus call thou me, from the world to thee*
> *Speed me ever, stay me never, Jesus, call thou me.'*

How beautiful it was. The munching sounds of the animals, the strong glow of our candles that gave radiance to each face. In the warmth and love of our little company, my mind wandered outside where I imagined the darkness lit only by the sputtering fires of the ignorant heathen huddling close, as the shepherds had done on that far-away, star-glistened night of our Saviour's birth. And in a manger, just like this one, the girl Mary labored and gave birth. Was she a stranger there in Bethlehem as I was? Was she afraid? She did not know the wrenching sadness she would have to suffer before she finished her journey to the Celestial Kingdom. Not that night. Not that night of quiet sounds and bright stars.

I looked around at my Brothers and Sisters who were sharing this holy night with me: Susannah stood with her hands clasped quietly. As we all joined to sing, Brother Weiss's bass dominated the men's voices; David Bischoff's clear tenor carried the melody and Matthew Schropp's face was gentle in repose.

'*Not Jerusalem, lowly Bethlehem t'was that gave us Christ to save us, not Jerusalem.*'

Anna Maria Schropp, next to me, sang in a sweet soprano; her eyes on the far window lit by a single candle, and next to her, Rosina Biefel, who would walk with me the long miles to Carolina, though as we sang on that December night I had no idea of the autumn journey to come or how my heart would tear in pieces.

WE TOOK A MONTH TO REST before we began our trek to Nazareth. Twenty men left earlier, right after Christmas, to add the finishing work on the large stone house that would shelter those of us couples who would labor there to plant the land and harvest our reward. On the tenth day of January the weather was clear, the men swinging their axes as they walked before the women who carried provisions for the ten-mile trip.

The journey was not difficult although the path was overrun with brambles, and large trees stood tall and close together. Thick brown vines wound around the tree trunks, sometimes dotted with red berries like tiny drops of our Saviour's blood. Blood shed for us, I repeated to myself as I trudged the path. After several hours, I looked up to see that we had walked out of the woods and had come to a clearing. The late afternoon sun slanted across the frozen meadow, turning the ground pale orange. As the sun sank slowly, I thought about how terribly lonely it would be out here if I were alone. I shivered and burrowed my hands more deeply into the folds of my cape. I looked ahead to see Matthew, who was walking rapidly now, his legs taking long strides, the ax swinging easily in his right hand. Then I heard a Sister's voice call out, "Oh look, that must be the house!" The outline of the roof against the twilight sky comforted me and the building seemed solid and part of the slight rise behind it.

The few who inhabited the stone house must have heard our call to them, for they seemed to tumble out the large door, heedless of capes, to greet us. Soon we were sitting together at long tables, our heads bent, to thank our dear Lamb for his care. Then, with lots of chatter and plates heaped with root vegetables and venison we caught up on each other's news. Somehow the ten-mile trek from Bethlehem to Nazareth seemed nothing to me, and once seated with our Brethren and Sisters, the joyful expectation of work to come filled my mind.

We Sisters were shown our sleeping quarters in the large attic, and as I ascended the narrow stairs, I wished Matthew was at my side so I could curl against him in the darkness. I must have sighed aloud, for Rosina, behind me, asked if I were terribly tired. "I am rather weary," I replied, "but it is a good feeling to know we are here at last to begin our Saviour's work." I did not want to share my thoughts of Matthew with anyone.

We each chose beds and undressed. The sound of occasional laughter filled the room; some of us knelt at our beds for nightly prayer and soon we all were settled. I could hear the even breathing of my Sisters and, accustomed to sleeping in their presence, I thought I would sleep immediately. But I was not even drowsy. My thoughts darted, half-formed and unfinished in content. Events had happened at a dizzying rate in the past few months; I could picture our good ship and again feel the sway and hear the creak of its timbers. I could smell the cold, wet leaves of the forest—the woodsmoke, the roasting deer meat on a wooden spit. I curled into my quilt and could imagine Matthew's dear hands touching my body, kissing each of my breasts tenderly. Thank God, oh, thank God we are made this way, I thought as I grew warm. I slept.

The sound of the Brethrens' axes rang in the cold air—more distinct as the weather grew more frigid. With their bare, cold hands they fashioned the wood into shelter for our provisions and our animals. Gradually the shape of Nazareth came into being: one area to hold our cattle, swine and sheep once they were acquired; another, built for the bakery, the curing and storing of flax, weaving looms, and still another which would hold a cider mill and a place for the smithy. Of course, all this building took many months, but my heart leaped when I realized I would soon hear the sound of metal on metal as one of our brethren would work at the forge as once my father had done. Matthew said the buildings were so like his Silesian village that he could close his eyes and find his way blindfolded. Because the Brethren had planned so well, we all worked at the tasks we well knew, weavers, spinners, joiners, metal workers and other work that helped us to survive in this new land. We women sewed, chopped frozen root vegetables, gathered bundles of sticks in the deep woods and milked cows with stiff fingers. The work was terribly hard. We were often hungry. Yet our unspoken fellowship, born of this hard work and hunger, perhaps, kept us singing, sending our prayers to Him whose presence we knew was with us.

In our communal effort I was seldom alone. As I carried and fetched with my Sisters, I was aware of a kind of grace as we passed one another, our petticoats rustling, our shoes stepping on the wooden floor.

"Sometimes when we work together I feel as though we are dancing." Anna Maria bent over a low table, her hands covered with flour.

Susannah patted her lump of dough quickly into a circle and, placing it onto the long-handled baking pan, said, "A strange dance, with no music," and raised her pale eyebrows.

"May I have the honor?" Joanna Sensemann reached for my hand and curtsied, dipping her head to one side. Carrying our wooden bowls of dried herbs in the crook of one arm, we clasped each other's free hands and swung our arms to and fro. Sister Anna Maria Schropp began to sing and, with a nod in her direction, Susannah joined her, for the hymn song was known to us all. We started to place our bowls on the table, but when Susannah and Anna Maria began another verse we swung our arms and sang again. As a child, I had often sung to myself as I watched raindrops slide down our small windows. Skipping down the main street of Gelzhausen, I sang softly in time to my steps. But I had never known the pure joy of singing with others as I did with my Moravian Sisters. As Brother Ludwig had said many times to us, "A song is not ordinary, but it is sublime speech." And somehow I knew this was true, for when we sang together, my heart lifted and I was taken out of myself. I became, for the moment, part of something larger than myself. I knew not what this was. I only knew I felt it, and it made me more at one with my Brethren and Sisters. In my memory the early days were primarily a time of joy; for working with each other and for our Lamb, the days were short.

I am ashamed that my memory also holds to the times of weakness for me. Some days, exhausted, I looked at my broken fingernails as I tried to rub sensation into my weary feet. Darkness overwhelmed me. *"O my God, I cry by day, but thou dost not answer and by night, but find no rest,"* rang in my ears in Matthew's voice, for he often spoke the Psalms.

It was then I would make my way to our *Saal*, and, sitting alone on a wooden bench, I forced my mind to remember the remainder of that Psalm of anguish. All I could recall was his plea for God to come close. I earnestly prayed that God would show Himself to me. I shut my eyes tightly and clenched my hands together. Only darkness. I opened them to see the stone walls, the one candle flickering on the table at the front of the room; the wide floorboards at my feet, the windows dark against the night. On that winter's night of silence and snow I think my Saviour did answer me, but not in any way I could have foretold. His words came to me in the form of some Indian, and brought to us by our missionary Brother Zeisberger, who had learned the Indian tongue. Words I could almost hear in the quiet of the night.

"Sometimes I go about pitying myself, and all along my soul is being blown by great winds across the sky." So those who lived in the forest, who covered themselves with bright blankets and came so quietly into our presence to listen to our words of faith and praise, must have offered their own to give each of us humility.

I rose from my bench. I was still bone-tired. My arms ached from lifting heavy logs for our fires, my legs unsteady; but my heart was strangely calmed. I walked across the threshold to join my Sisters.

CHAPTER NINE

It was very cold that night. The bright moon made black shadows of the tree branches unmoving against the clean snow. And it was so quiet. The western wind that had brought the storm blew itself out in haste over the ocean, and left no snow clinging to the bushes, nor one last wail to signal its leaving. Here, on this side of the great ocean, there was a winter's stillness I had never known in Gelzhausen. For even the bitter cold in Germany carried sounds of life to me: a barking dog, a child's cry, a jolly laugh from the tavern down our road. But here, standing in one ray of moonlight, it seemed the whole world had become silent, as though I had suddenly lost the power to hear, and had only my eyes to tell me where I was. It even smelled cold on this, the other side—so clean, as if the world were new. I wondered if snow fell in Eden, and if that first couple stood in wonder at the cold, the snow and the newness of it all. But no, I thought. It was always a garden, forever green with the Tree and the ripe fruit. Only here, only in this wilderness with the bright moon moving so slowly across the sky, is this kind of quiet.

Wrapped in my woolen cape, I was not cold and I was in no hurry to return to the *Gemeinhaus* where my Sisters would be preparing for bed; shaking their long hair loose from the confines of their caps, loosening the laces of their jackets, teasing, laughing, dipping fingers into the cool water of the china bowl.

Not a twig's snap nor crackle of a dry leaf announced his arrival. I had no warning. There he was before me, his face not visible in the shadows, his large figure so close I could have easily touched him. I did not gasp; I had learned not to, for my intake of breath might either frighten or offend him. I recognized the scent of bear grease he used to tame his long hair, and the wild smell of the tanned animal skin that covered his body. I had never been so close to a native of the woods and I was a woman alone; yet strangely, I was not afraid. We stood in the silence facing each other. How long did we stand there like statues in the moonlight? It was as though we were a part of that night, that stillness, that winter's cold; just shapes rooted to the ground and every bit a part of the landscape. He raised one hand, held it up for a moment and stepped ever so lightly away. I strained my ears to hear his footsteps in the frozen snow, and peered through the darkness to see the place where he had disappeared, but he was gone, and I was left alone again in the silence. I think I did not move for some moments. Had I actually seen one of our heathen brothers, or had the cold and the moonlight confused my mind in some way that a shadow became a man who stood before me? But I could not have imagined the pungent odor of his hair, his clothes. Unwittingly, I had encountered a heathen who knew nothing of our God; a descendant, perhaps, of that ancient lost tribe who wandered through the centuries from Israel's desert sand to this cold, moonlit forest.

I must tell him. I must tell him about the blood of our Lamb, I thought, and recalled the passion I saw on my husband's face when he spoke the Gospel of good news. But I was too late, and I could not follow the Indian into the forest. There was no rustle of dry leaves, not even a breeze as I stood again alone. Perhaps my utter lack of fear was because his appearance was meant as a sign for me; our Saviour's message for me to hold tightly to His robe—to know in my heart that His love would protect me from doubt. But if my encounter contained a message just for me, I would not share our meeting. I would keep it hidden and safe in my breast to remind me why I was here and of the work I had to do.

I felt the cold then. I drew my cape around my body and began to walk to the door of the *Gemeinhaus*. And as my shoes crunched in the icy snow, an even, regular noise in the quiet, I knew I was tied to these strange people. How could this be so? Their language so foreign to my ears, their facial configuration somehow different from ours, yet I was drawn in as though one of their beaded necklaces had encircled my heart.

IT WAS SHORTLY AFTER my moonlight visitor's appearance that we gathered in the *Saal* to sing together, hear from Brother Rauch, who had been laboring among the Indians. He brought a story about Conrad Weiser, who, although not a member of our Brethren was sympathetic to our views and helped to teach our missionaries the native tongues. As a young man Weiser lived near a settlement of Mohawks and became well-versed in their language. Brother Rauch had consecrated himself to work with the Indians, and he and Weiser were often together in the wilderness further north.

Brother Rauch was a good-storyteller. He had our rapt attention as he stood at the front of our *Saal* while he cleared his throat, straightened his waistcoat and rocked back and forth on his heels before beginning to speak.

"Conrad Weiser had been walking through snow twenty inches deep for several days," he began. "The snow in upper New York lasts until mid-April, you know."

I looked at the drifts that had settled in the window wells of our *Gemeinhaus*, and hoped they would be gone by April this year. We had had enough snow.

"Weiser told me he had been journeying among the Cherokee and Iroquois to effect a peace settlement between them. He was completely exhausted, hungry and cold. He called the wilderness 'frightful' and, indeed, it can be." Brother Rauch looked out over our small band of men and women, and I felt a shiver of cold that shrunk my skin so that I drew my cape around me.

Brother Rauch lowered his voice. "Starvation stared him in the face.

He could not go on. He sat down with his back to a tree and resolved not to get up—to die there in the cold. The Indian Shikellimy, whom he had known for some time, was the first person to discover him there. The Indian stood before him in silence for a few moments. Finally he said, 'Why are you here?'

Weiser answered, 'I am here to die.'

'Ah, brother, only lately you entreated us not to despond. Will you now give way to despair?'

'My good Shikellimy, as death is inevitable, I will die on this spot.'

'Ah, brother,' said the Indian, 'it was you who told me we were prone to forget God in bright days, and remember him in dark days. These are dark days. Who knows but He is now near and about to help us? Rise, brother.'

"Conrad told me he was so ashamed at this rebuke he rose and dragged himself through the snow for two more days to Onondaga." Rauch stopped his pacing and looked out at us. "Brothers and Sisters, I believe that it was the Saviour who showed His love through the eyes of the Indian."

AS THE WEEKS PASSED I was to learn how shy these Indians were, how reluctant to enter our stone house and, once inside, how their quick glance seemed to take in the paned windows and large open hearths. The men never spoke to us women, but I had heard stories that they would be either gross in their manner, or somehow like children who perhaps wanted to learn, but did not know how to ask. Neither seemed true. They possessed a kind of courtesy I had not expected, and though they did not look directly at any of the Sisters, they held themselves with grace, their voices grave, serious and direct when they met with our Brothers. Indeed, Count Zinzendorf himself called the six tribes in our area, "Kingdoms" and treated the men with all the respect he would give foreign dignitaries. We, after all, were on their land; not they on ours. In his correspondence, Brother Ludwig wrote that he had told the Iroquois leaders he had a different method of teaching than the missionaries they had met previously. He asked for their patience and for their permission to travel among them so they might all learn of one another's peculiarities.

But, despite the early friendships our people seemed to be making with the American natives, I often felt we were strangers in a strange land. Our relations with the Indians had embittered many of our white neighbors against us. Those who were French said we were in league with the English, and the English said our religious practices were likened to the French. Both French and English accused us of using the Indians to spy on them.

During that first winter in Nazareth, we heard terrifying stories about the brutal treatment our missionaries had suffered in those early years in upper New York. My God, why was this so? And who were those who were so against us? Many of those who called themselves Reformed members had welcomed our men and women into their settlements; yet others of the same denomination had hardened their hearts. I remember it was Anna Maria Schropp who opened herself to me as we sat spinning. Her sweet face was serious and worried; the warmth from the hearth brought small beads of perspiration to her upper lip as we worked, and we spoke quietly to one another of the troubles surrounding our settlement.

"They think we are too friendly with the Indians," she said. "And the Indians have been lied to by many Whites. Why, I even heard a story about the French who swore to some Indians that our Saviour was born in Bethlehem . . . " I interrupted her, saying that indeed this was true, but then she continued, "No, they told the Indians that Bethlehem was in France and that the English crucified Jesus." She shook her head as I stared at her in disbelief.

"How can these rumors be believed? They cause such hatred." We sat without speaking for a moment, the whirr of our wheels the only sound in the room. Anna Maria took her foot from the treadle, and said, "I think the only way to try to stop rumors and to help the heathen to understand the good news our people are bringing is for our missionaries to listen closely to Brother Ludwig's words. As he said, we must understand their peculiarities as they must learn to understand ours. Perhaps that is the only way."

I, too, stopped spinning for a moment to think about her words. "I do know that Zinzendorf has been able to help the Indians to trust us. Had you heard that some Mohawks have often left their children with our people—for days, sometimes, and even for weeks?"

"Yes." She raised her arms above her head and stretched. The Indians are very loving with their children and to leave some with us must mean there is trust. You know, sometimes I think ignorance is the cause of so much trouble. When Brother and Sister Mack learn the Indian tongues in a place like New York, it must help to bring trust and peace between us." She sighed.

"We seem to have problems here even with Whites who do not know the German tongue, and so distrust us. Maybe they are just confused." I was struggling for some answers to persistent questions we were all wondering about as we learned to live in this new country.

"Sister Christina, I think you are perhaps too kind. I don't know that it is confusion. Perhaps it is envy. We are hard working and we accomplish much." She looked into my face with a serious glance and then resumed her spinning. My concern was far from allayed.

We were silent for a while, the whirring of our spinning wheels and the crackling of the fire making the only sounds in the large room. I had had the insistent feeling we were disliked by even some of our white neighbors, and the increasingly frightening messages brought to us from New York caused me to feel I must check behind each tree when I gathered fuel for our fires at eventide. The wild beauty of the winter forest had carried with it a certain excitement for me; raw and new, it was so different from anything I had ever experienced. But now, there was an added sense of a force out of control—something that could not be held back by our small band of believers. O, our blessed Lamb, I prayed silently. Please, if we must suffer in your name, make me brave and sure.

When I heard the clear ring of our axes echoing in the forest, I listened too for the clap of gunfire to break the silence in an uneasy and discordant rhythm. And when water dripped from the icicles on the *Gemeinhaus* roof and the warmer sun began to melt the snow, I grew afraid.

CHAPTER TEN

Wild onions. I could smell their pungent odor before I reached down to grasp a small bunch, pull it from the brown, crumbling earth to see the tiny pearls clustered in my hand. Always after the snowdrops peered over the February melting snow, the wild onions of early March stood bravely amidst the dead brown leaves and twisted vines. Such a time of moods is my birthday month of March, with its sleeting rain followed by the warming sun, its wild winds that swoop into our chimneys to send a gust of smoke, and then, despite it all, the beginnings of green, the soft pussy willows and the smell of wild onions that promise the awakening of spring.

Three of us women were to make the trip to from Nazareth to Bethlehem in the early afternoon. Brother Sensemann accompanied us, walking the first mile or so from Nazareth just so we would not miss one turn on the path that led to Bethlehem. We women knew the way, but I suspected Joachim Sensemann was taking this opportunity to walk a way with his wife, even for so short a way. Anna was a plump young woman who glanced at her stocky husband from time to time, though she did not touch him. The couple had been admonished by Brother Bezold in Holland that in public they had been too *fleischlich*, or physical in their manner toward each other; and although they attempted to keep a decorous distance between them, we all knew they were more than eager to enter the small private room at the top of the *Gemeinhaus* here in Nazareth.

Anna Maria Schropp skipped on the path beside me, partially to keep up, for her stride was less long than mine, but I was sure her skip was due to the smell of spring and the chance to go to Bethlehem. As usual, her dark hair had escaped from her cap and she reminded me of my small niece in Gelzhausen who always skipped to church with me on Sunday.

It was a good day for the trek. The weather was somewhat warmer than it had been, and dry. Even though we had no proper road, months before men had cleared away the small bushes, and our path wound around the thicker stumps of trees. I was happy to be making the trip, for it was always good to see friends in Bethlehem, and I was eager to share news and see for myself the large stone buildings the Brethren had been working on. Our journey began with much animation and joy, for we were discussing the prospect of new life—lambs for our fold. Several of the Sisters were with child and Sister Almers had given birth just after we had arrived from our sea journey.

What will it be like to feel a child move within me, I wondered? Matthew's child. I could almost hear my beloved's quiet voice whispering 'O Lord, thou hast searched me and known me.' The Psalmist was singing of his God and yet—and yet—the thought of my husband's voice, deep and steady as the hum of a cello, seemed to search my own thoughts, and yes, my own body.

I picked my way carefully over the exposed roots, my shoes sinking into the soft, dead leaves. I well remember a hymn tune wove its way through my head; the words from our new Liturgy of Blood and Wounds. '*Beloved cleft where we hide without fear,*' I sang the words to myself. '*Beloved red cleft of Jesus*' side, an entrance to the warmth and safety of His body, the liturgy taught. And then my thought—my beloved has entered me, and I will cradle his seed within my body until with wrenching pain and the stream of blood and water, I will know relief. My Saviour had no relief from his final pain when he cried out. I could feel sudden tears. Better to think of the sheltering wood of his birthplace than the rough wood of His cross.

It was Anna Maria's hand on my shoulder, saying that Brother Sensemann was turning back, and this brought me out of my reverie. I managed to arrange my face in a quick smile. My imaginings were not appropriate to our joyous trek through the woods, the meeting of dear friends, the awakening season.

It is a mere ten miles between Nazareth and Bethlehem, and many of the Brothers and Sisters had made the trip several times since our group had moved to Nazareth.

In fact the two settlements were as one because we were dependent on one another, Nazareth providing the grain and livestock, Bethlehem the crafts both for our own use and for sale, both so essential to our existence in the wilderness. I marveled at the ease of travel this trip, for we were carrying little with us and, of course, there was no snow to contend with. The sky was a deep blue, birds called and I heard the scuffle of small animals as they scurried out of our way.

Anna Sensemann stopped and raised her hand; our chatter quieted. Until this moment I had felt alone except for my companions on the forest path, but with Sister Sensemann's upraised hand I had the sense of being surrounded. As though the dense underbrush hid menacing figures who moved silently, their eyes always on us. I was aware that birds had quieted, and then a flock fled the high branches of one tree near our path, twittering nervously. That single movement changed the merry feeling of the day. Now there seemed a need to listen, to wait.

The birds resumed their chatter, one squirrel sitting on a branch above me twitched his tail and nibbled at the nut he held in his paws. We began to walk again but now there was no conversation, our footsteps careful, our senses alert. Then I heard the sound of footsteps on undergrowth followed by muffled voices. Sister Sensemann moved closer to me, and Anna Maria Schropp said it sounded to her like men laughing.

I was not prepared for the two men who stepped out of the underbrush to block our way. They were white men, dressed in breeches, high boots, wool coats. One wore his pants tied by a rope gathered below his overhanging belly. Another, thin and stooped, wore a black hat. The heavy one stepped close to me. Clearing his throat, he spat on the path, then spoke in the English tongue. His voice was coarse, rusted, full of phlegm

I made no reply and the second man grunted. His face unshaven, his ugly smile showed missing teeth and those remaining were blackened and jagged.   I understood that he said something about our being Germans. He moved toward Anna Maria Schropp, and she shrank back, her shoulder close to mine. His face was cruel, and I could feel my heart pound. Anna Maria shook slightly beside me, but she raised her chin and would not look away from their gaze. I felt myself tremble. I could not understand all their words but their manner was jeering and frightening. What if they had knives? Most everyone carried knives while in the forest, to cut off the thin branches from bushes that leaned into the path. Why had they stopped us? Did they think we had money?

Anna Maria did speak a few words of English and, raising her chin, she looked at the heavy man, saying, "Surely you not us detain." I could see her fingering her scissors that were hidden in her apron pocket.

The thin man leered at her. He moved closer to me and I could smell his foul breath. "Detain?" he mimicked. "Detain? "No, *Nein*, we only want to speak to you little sweeties."

I turned my back on him and began to walk forward. "Come, my Sisters. We must continue our journey."

At that moment, the fat man grabbed Anna Sensemann's arm, pulling her to him while the thin man began to screech and laugh. Anna Maria called, "No, No! Don't you dare touch her," as I stepped back to take Anna's other arm and pull her away. I was no longer really afraid. I was terribly angry and, as heat seemed to fill my body, I screamed as loudly as ever I could. Both men stepped back in some alarm. Then Anna Maria began to scream, followed by Anna Sensemann. Two crows joined us as though their caws would somehow aid our plight. I saw Anna Maria take the scissors from her apron pocket. The sun glinted on the metal, sharp, dangerous. We screamed again and again.

I could see confusion on the attackers' faces. The fat man stepped back from Anna and tripped over a root. He fell to the ground, cursing. Anna Maria spoke, her words coming like another scream. "Our men are near. They will hear us."

The thin man looked around in alarm as we continued our screaming. "Come on." I understood his words as he leapt away from the path and into the bushes. The fat man raised his bulk clumsily, and followed, half-crawling into the bushes. "Indian lovers," he croaked. I could hear twigs crackling as he made his way.

My throat was sore, my voice sounded hoarse in my ears. "Anna Maria, careful, careful. You will cut yourself." But it was too late. She had somehow cut her hand with her scissors and she screamed one last time, almost a howl as she dropped her scissors and made a fist with her hand.

"Are they gone?" Anna said in a low voice.

"I think perhaps we really frightened them," Anna Maria answered, looking at the slash on her hand.

" Here, let me see your hand. I will bind it up with my petticoat," I said as I raised the fabric and tore off a piece with my teeth. I wanted to sit down. I wanted to stop and not move, and perhaps my Sisters felt the same. But we knew we must return to Nazareth which was but a few miles away. I found myself trembling and Sister Anna put her arms around me. We stood thus, alone in the forest while birds twittered as though the danger was over. The crows lifted off from the branches above and flew away.

We did not speak much as we hurried as fast as we could on our return. Often one of us would stumble on the path, another steadying her as we half-ran, half-walked. I felt tears on my cheeks and saw them also on Anna Maria's pretty face. My breath came fast, but I was afraid to stop.

"Why? Why?" I asked of the early sweet spring air. "Why?" I threw out to the not-yet-budding branches. The sun still sent shafts of light between the huge, dark trees and pooled on the ground; the smell of wild onions still tickled the air; but there was blood on the path. I remembered Susannah, those weeks ago—her tear-wet face, her blue eyes, "Oh, Christina, why do such terrible things happen on such a good day?"

Let me hide myself in thee—let me hide myself, drummed in my head. But there was no place the hide. The forest had become a place of danger and the crackle of each small branch brought fear. Is our Saviour here now? With us? Did He hear our screams and cause the horrid men to run away? Or was it the glint of metal scissors? My breath came faster as we stumbled on the narrow path. I fear I will remember this anger, I thought. There was no love or forgiveness in my heart. My legs had begun to ache and, as I reached out to grab a small branch to steady myself, I wondered why I had left the safe town of my birth for this wilderness.

Finally, our painful stumbling brought us back to Nazareth. The afternoon air was cold as we made our way to the *Gemeinhaus*. Empty-handed, bruised and sore, we brought no thread, no flower seeds. We brought only our story. It came out in jagged pieces; first one of us would remember a part and then another, as our Brothers and Sisters murmured, or exclaimed, urging hot tea, giving us their strength. We all realized it was too difficult to trace the two men who had frightened us and, thanks be to Him who watches us, we were not hurt.

Joachim Sensemann was quite angry and blamed himself for leaving us, but Brother Nathan Seidel spoke reassuringly. "Listen, my Brother. We have had no trouble like this here before. Frightening as this terrible incident was, I cannot help but think the trail between Bethlehem and Nazareth is safe." Turning to look at the three of us who had just arrived, he continued. "My Sisters, we will make sure that all women have a Brother to accompany them in the future on any trip."

Brother Schropp spoke then. "It will be crucial that we keep our wits about us, while at the same time we remember that our people are not always looked upon in a friendly way." There was a general muttering as men and women spoke to one another. Brother Schropp continued, "We all remember what happened in Philadelphia."

Terrifying news from the large City of Philadelphia was common knowledge to most of us before we set sail for America; for the Brethren and Sisters had been honest with all of us about the dangers we might face in taking our Lamb's word to faraway places. Count Zinzendorf had been well received by most of those who had begun to make their homes in America, but some others had allowed malicious gossip to disturb their reason, and in one shocking incident, the good man was attacked in a church where he was preaching. Women armed with sticks had tried to push him into the street. In another incident, our Brother Pyrlaeus had been dragged from a pulpit by a crowd of anti-Moravians who screamed, "Kill the dog."

Would the violence escalate with whips, clubs, knives and screaming, enraged voices? With the recent attack so fresh in my mind, I could not help but wonder if Nazareth would be next?

It was time for our evening meal, so we took our places and bowed our heads for grace. Brother Seidel clasped his hands and thanked our Saviour for our safe return. It seemed he was speaking not only to our Lamb but also to all of us who sat quietly.

"We have come to this wilderness to share the joyous news of our Saviour's grace to all who will listen. We have been careful to speak to each heart— to open it so that He might enter. It will be good to remember what Brother Ludwig had said to us that we must trust in

God's grace." I felt Brother Seidel looking at me and I raised my head. "It is very difficult to forgive or to let go of fear, but as our faith grows we will find it easier, perhaps, than we ever thought."

In the night, our watchman called reassurance with the hour. I did not yet feel safe, but I prayed that if I could not be truly reassured, I at least could begin on the path to faith. Those about me believed. I prayed I, too, could place my trust in Him.

HERE IN BETHABARA as I awaken I am not sure where I am. I was dreaming of my husband. He swung his axe and called to the other men as we walked to Nazareth. His voice said the Psalms and we knew that Christ was in the room. He touched me gently and became me and I him and it was right and there was a holiness everywhere. God's love had entered my heart before I took Matthew's face in my thin, young hands. They were not puffed and swollen then, not burning as they now are.

My mind races about in a gray place. I try to snatch at the years of my life so I might put them in order. Then I might take a quill and write how it was when we brought our innocent hearts to this wild place. Was it yesterday I was thinking of winter—our first winter? But I was gathering berries when an Indian startled me. Was it cold? No, it must have been summer, for there are no red berries in the snow, little droplets of blood—our Saviour's blood, shed for us. Was it I who gathered berries then or was it Susannah? I miss her so. When our apple trees bore their first fruits she held out her waiting arms. How long has it been since we have spoken with one another? How long as it been since she took my hand and told me she had begun to trust George Partsch—that she felt she could be a true wife to him; to see her union with him a true sacrament of Christ's love for us humans.

The sweat runs into my eyes and I feel the wet under my arms. That must mean the fever is breaking. Soon, I will rise and not feel the vertigo. Perhaps I shall gather the sage for our meat and pinch the rosemary between my fingers. Then I will put the years in order and recall Susannah's face more clearly when we were eager young girls in the midst of our mission at Nazareth.

CHAPTER ELEVEN

Susannah Eller Partsch: Nazareth, Pennsylvania, 1740s

S o. This is the room. Now I am here, I should let out the breath I have been holding in, but it will make too much noise. I hold my own hands. There is the bed. There is a table on one side and a chair. I have not wanted to be here. Not ever. I knew of this room but I never came to peek inside. Sister Sensemann did. She said she and her Joachim had waited ever so long. She told me not to be afraid; that Brother Ludwig had said unification between a man and a woman was a wonderful act; a holy and beautiful act. She said this is true. I want to believe this, but . . .

George Partsch sits on the bed. He looks out the window. His back is to me. Should I speak? Does he know I am here? *Mein Gott,* he turns to me. He says nothing, but now he smiles just with the edges of his mouth. I have to shiver though it is not really cold. A breeze comes through the window and the candle flickers. I do not want that candle to blow out.

He is getting up. What if he moves next to me? The room is so small. What if he touches me? I am near the door. But it is closed. I try to swallow, but there is no water in my throat. He says, "Sister Partsch." It sounds so strange. I am really Susannah Eller; the little girl who left Büdingen, the girl who runs fast. My back is near the door.

George Partsch is holding out his hand and he speaks again, but this time he says, "Susannah." It sounds like a question. He says my name so soft. I move closer to him. I smell wood fire in his clothes and maybe even yeast—just a little from his hands maybe. My mother had yeast on her hands when she baked our bread. When she held me to her I could smell the baking smells.

George Partsch reaches out and takes my hand. He moves very slowly and leads me the two steps to the bed. I sit beside him. He says nothing for minutes, I think. The curtain blows in. I hear someone practicing on a trombone. The notes come in the window with the breeze. He turns his head and looks at me, but I look at the window. I am holding my breath again.

He says I am his wife. I say nothing. I know we stood in the big room a year ago almost. I remember how the Brother said the marriage words. I smelled the old bracken burning in the farmers' fields and did not look at anybody that day. George Partsch moves my face with his one finger on my chin. Will he twist my skin and hurt me? No, he does not pinch me. *Ach*, I barely feel his finger. It is as light as the breeze from the window. I must look at his face now. I want to. I see my face in his eyes. His eyes are brown and round and his nose is not straight. He smiles now, and I see just a little his crowded teeth. I say I do not want the candle to go out. I say I am afraid of the dark. I am not afraid of the dark.

He puts both his hands in his lap now. He does not look at me all the time but just once and then away and then looks again. He is saying that husbands are to honor their wives. He is saying how he will never touch me except to love me. He stops talking and looks at his feet; but then he takes my hand in his. I can feel the rough places from the hard work he has done. I am no longer holding my breath so much, and it comes out in a sigh. George looks at me, and I see kindness in his face. *Ach*, I remember the kind face of brother Vogt who told me about the Brethren and how they loved God. I believed him then in Büdingen. I trusted him. Now I trust my Brothers and Sisters.

George says let us rest. I lie next to him. I put his hand to my cheek and it grows warm. The bed is soft and I sink closer to him. I think we will sleep now. I think we will sleep like brother and sister, at least for a while.

⚜

CHAPTER TWELVE

Christina Barbara Krause: Nazareth, Pennsylvania, 1740s

Early morning. The scream came once, loud and shrill. I tried to shake myself out of sleep. I must have been dreaming. I was running through the woods toward Brother Sensemann. I think it was Brother Sensemann. He was standing over a human heap, crumpled, still, dead. There was blood. Why didn't it sink between the leaves, stain the remnants of snow? I must be asleep. George Partsch was there also, bending over the body. I forced myself to look, really look, again and saw that the dead man was an Indian warrior. Who had murdered this man? What would be the consequences of having this still body, lying so close to our *Gemeinhaus*? I tried again to push myself from sleep. "Christ save us."

That voice was Brother Sensemann. Thumping at the door. I wanted it to stop. It did not stop. "Open the door!" How could there be a door in the woods? Who was thumping so hard? Was that Susannah's voice?

"Open the door. Hurry. I need your help!"

I must awake. I must push the scene of murder from my mind. Not yet fully awake, I put one foot on the floor and called, "I am coming." I stumbled down the steps and fumbled with the heavy metal lock.

"Hurry. This woman needs help."

Susannah Partsch leaned against the frame, her other arm supporting an Indian woman of great age. The woman was terribly thin, wasted. Her sparse gray hair hung about her wrinkled face, her hooded eyes open but unseeing. We helped her to sit on one of the benches, but she lurched forward. I took hold of one of her arms. No plump flesh gave itself under my hand and I felt only bone.

"We must get her to a bed," Susannah said.

George Partsch came forward and picked up the woman as though she weighed no more than a child and carried her to the women's section of the *Gemeinhaus* and laid her on the nearest bedstead. I bent down to loosen the top of her linen shift which had somehow been twisted and Anna Maria hurried to fetch water.

I had seen dying before. I had washed my mother's wasted arms when I was a child, but the onset of death takes so many forms. The Indian woman's skin was leatherlike, soft and crinkled. It seemed she was the oldest woman I had ever seen. It was as though her body had been long ready for the earth and her spirit already flown. But she blinked her lashless eyes and looked at me. Anna Maria lifted the mug to her withered lips and she sucked in the water. She tried to speak. Her single words seemed to come from her breast and sounded to me like the dying breath of an organ when a hymn is over, the notes no longer struck. I bent close to better hear, but I could not understand her. The sounds she made were words I did not know. She made no movement, but lay like a corpse on the bed. Then she tried to speak again, a rasping sound struggling from her throat, and I felt her panic as though she was caged and screaming but there was no one to hear.

"I will fetch Brother Seidel. He knows." Anna Maria picked up her petticoats and ran from the room. I touched the woman's old, old face and cupped her jaw in my hand. "There," I murmured. "There." She looked from one corner of the room to another, three or four times. Then her eye seemed to catch mine and she said a word. Again I did not understand, but somehow it did not matter. I smoothed her hair and she closed her eyes.

Brother Seidel came into the room with some reluctance, as though uneasy with the place in which the women gathered and slept. He had come early to the wilderness with Brother Ludwig and had managed with diligence to learn some of the Indian tongues. He knelt by the bedside and took the woman's wasted hand in his own. She narrowed her eyes, the tendons on her neck straining, she tried to lift her head to be closer to him. I felt their words hang above my head suspended and full of waiting. Finally he turned to us and said, "The woman has been looking for her grandson. He has been away from their campfires for many months. I believe she wandered further than she had intended. I am not sure."

The woman began to speak again, but her words came more quickly and our Brother placed his ear near her mouth. The heavy lines on either side of his mouth deepened. He nodded. "She says she has had a vision that her grandson has gone from this earth; that his spirit flies . . . "

I could not stop the tears that gathered and felt them spill onto my cheeks. I had seen his wound. It was in my dream. I had seen his blood that drained the life from his body. Was the hand of one who struck him cruelly the same hand who thrust the spear so long ago into the side of Jesus? I rubbed my eyes to erase my terrible images. Surely my dream must have been fashioned from the terrible rumors that circled our small outpost. I knew rumors were dangerous and that somehow I must be strong enough to cause their disappearance by replacing these images with the face of our Lamb. I looked once more at the figure stretched before me.

The woman raised her arm to the sky. I imagined her face to take on a radiance as though lit from within, and then it faded, her arm fell and a sigh escaped her old and wrinkled throat. I knew she was dead.

"We will bury her quickly." Brother Seidel gently let go of her hand and placed it on her breast. We stood quietly; each of us sending our petition to God to bless these people.

THE WEATHER IS COOLING A BIT here in Bethabara and my Sisters are gathering herbs this afternoon. Why at harvest time do I think of death? My mind seems to drift back to some of the fearful days when death was near, so that I must wonder if my time is coming.

Perhaps I should remember the times of birthing, the times when new life burst forth even in autumn, as we gathered what we had sown. Susannah birthed her little Elizabeth and October was warm in Nazareth that year.

CHAPTER THIRTEEN

We all knew of the ancient Indian village called Welagamika, and it was there that Brother Seidel had bent his head, his hands folded in prayer over the gash in the earth. And as my Matthew and Brother Schropp lifted the heavy wet dirt with their shovels, I prayed the god of this heathen to spread His hands over her resting place. The sound of returning geese overhead called a wild benediction. Matthew stopped, his hands resting on the handle of the shovel as he looked to the sky. "Amen," Brother Schropp intoned.

"Amen," we answered.

And then it was planting time again. The men had cleared large fields, hauling huge tree stumps with the pair of oxen we had purchased. We all sowed wheat and flax, and one very early morning one Brother brought his violin to the field. As we grasped the seed and flung out our arms, his tune kept us in time, the rising sun warming us. I was not tired and felt I would never be tired, for my body was part of a great whole, the curve of the furrows, the curve of the sky as it touched the trees at the end of the field, the curve of my back as I bent and straightened, only to bend again.

I remember this time as one of great joy, in planting, in songs of praise and our deep growing love for one another and our dearest Lamb. Although rumors of violence still came to us, the road between Nazareth and Bethlehem appeared safe. I remember feeling we were, for a time, secure under the wings of our Beloved Protector.

The mornings turned cool again, the mist rising from a still-warm ground. The sun rose later in the morning as autumn came upon us, and the sun's rays, more tentative at this season, touched the east windows with a burnished copper. It was in those early years that many of the Sisters were with child. Although they had flung seed, planted the orchard and finally gathered the dry grasses, it seemed some moved to a slower melody, and as they churned the cow's milk to butter, the clump of the paddle became silent in their hands, their eyes seeing inward.

I recall one day watching Susannah as she walked up the path to the barn where I stood, the boards warm against my back. The bulge beneath her petticoat was becoming distinct and round .She told me her time would come in late autumn or early winter and had asked that I be with her when she was brought to bed, for it was our custom to have the husband and friends to assist in a Sister's labor. I had never stood with Dr. Otto to help a babe into the world; nor had I first-hand knowledge of the special weekly services attended by those who were with child. Susannah told me she loved these meetings, for the friendship between the Sisters seemed especially precious to her, and the women who had not yet been through childbirth were heartened by the experiences of those who had. Susannah stretched and rubbed her back, her smile a gift to me, so I would not be afraid when my time came.

I placed my hands on my narrow waist. How will it be, I wondered? Somehow I felt that our Lamb' s presence must attend those women as they felt the first flutters of life; but it was His mother who knew better than He the strain and push that brings a new child into the world. Sweet Mary. I had thought often of her bumpy ride to Bethlehem, the innkeeper who had no place for her and her husband. But the squeeze of her labor pains, borne with only Joseph to help made her so tangible. The wooden, scratched statue of Our Lady in the church of my childhood was devoid of life for me; the painted tears a lie that gave no comfort to my childish prayers for my mother's life. How much closer she seemed here in the wilderness. Her glimmering in a shaft of light through the thick foliage, her quiet spirit unseen but with us as we, too, swelled with new life, as she once had.

The afternoon Susannah was brought to bed was bright and cold. There were still flashes of red and gold in the trees, but I knew it would not be long until the heavy winds would sweep the leaves into piles on the ground where they would turn brown and die. A good time to birth a babe, I thought, as I walked toward the birthing room. A good time to bring new life. I could smell woodsmoke as I opened the heavy door of the *Gemeinhaus* and Sister Mücke hurried toward me, saying that Susannah was about to go into heavy labor after having been up part of the night and all morning, pacing back and forth. She put her hand over her mouth as though telling a secret and said Susannah's husband had not left her side. Our God moves among us, bringing trust between husband and wife when needed, I thought with a smile.

The small room in the *Gemeinhaus* that held a fireplace on one wall had been set aside as a birthing room when not being used for drying apples and berries, the table replaced by a narrow bed. When I entered the room, I saw Sister Susannah Nitschmann standing near the head of the bed and Dr. Otto at the foot. George Partsch held Susannah's hand, his face serious and worried, the bristle of his unshaven beard telling me he had been up for hours.

Susannah looked up as I entered and tried to smile, saying, "*Ach*, Christina. I am afraid this little one is taking its time." At that moment her face changed, a look of surprise, her blue eyes widening.

"Now the little one is ready to come," Dr. Otto said. I moved to the opposite side of the bed from George to take Susannah's other hand, but she cried out and Sister Nitschmann quickly instructed, "Take the twisted sheet, Sister Partsch. Hold it in both hands, and when the pangs come, pull hard."

Dr. Otto's voice, low but insistent, "Push harder, Susannah."

"I AM pushing."

Susannah was covered with one sheet; another was tied to the end of the bedstead and twisted into a fat, white rope. Sweat ran in rivulets from Susannah's tousled hair to make moist paths down her round, young face as her pains came closer and closer. She pulled on the sheet and squinted her eyes in a way that drew her whole face together.

"Sister Partsch, our Saviour watches over you. You are in His hands. Remember His precious blood that saved us all" Sister Nitschmann's voice was soft and sure. I tried to imagine His wounded head, His precious blood, but at that moment, in that room of Susannah's labor, I saw only blood on the sheets—red and spattered. I did not want to see this so I bent close to her. "Susannah, remember walking from Bethlehem? The Brothers needed us to help steady the wagon and to push. Remember how we pushed and laughed."

"*Ja*, I remember," her words were separated by jagged breaths.

"You slipped in the snow." She panted, "You fell. I called you a fallen angel." Her face pleated itself again. "Oh," she said, "oh, oh, oh." Fast, like gun bursts in the forest. "For our Saviour, Susannah Partsch," Brother Biefel spoke. "Push, Susannah. For His laughter," I whispered, my face so close to hers I could smell her sweat. And I could smell her blood, too, a metal taste in my mouth. Susannah cried out, "Now. Now. Now."

The little head. I could see the top of the little head. Fast, fast the child came from between her legs. Slippery, wet, spotted in red and white.

"*Ach gut*—a girl." George's voice was pleased. Relieved. He smoothed back Susannah's hair from her face. Was there a tear in his eye that spilled over onto his rough cheek? Or was it his own sweat that mixed with hers as he bent to kiss her? I knew how precious this little one was to him, a gift from our Lamb, perhaps rarer than anyone in the room knew. For Susannah's fear had been changed into love, and at the sight of the small, blood-spattered girl-child, I felt His presence.

A stir in the room. Movement amongst us as Susannah strained yet again and clean hands ministered to her. I heard shoes shuffle on the wooden floor and the mix of voices, soft but suddenly fearful. As if the world had stopped, we waited for the sound that meant life. The sun must have slipped past the house without my noticing; only faint rays touched the log walls.

"A candle. A candle, NOW! I must see," Dr. Otto's voice commanded.

The scratching of flint. We held our breath. Rosina Biefel moved close to her husband, clutching at his arm. Sister Nitschmann seemed a statue as she stood at the end of the bed, staring. Susannah's face was suddenly older, suddenly gray. She had closed her eyes and with her lower teeth grabbed her lip. I thought she would bite through the skin. I reached out and cupped her strong fingers into a fist and covered them, although my hand was smaller. I held tight to her. We waited.

A slap and then another. Dr. Otto held the small, naked body with her head lower than her feet and slapped her tiny back. Again and again the slap sounded in the quiet of the room. The fire glowed warm and red, licking the logs. I could not look to see if the little girl's face was turning blue. I closed my eyes to better see our Saviour's face, but there was no face. Only blackness. I opened my eyes when I heard the scraping of his boots as George Partsch reached over to put his finger in the tiny mouth. Dr. Otto's hand, large on the little back, slapped again. Then a cry. It started as a bleat—a little lamb bleat and then the babe squinched her eyes tight with effort and cried out once, and again; a steady cry then, and strong.

We all began to speak at once. George did not take his eyes from his wife. I saw awe, gratitude, and great joy pass over his tired face as he stood at first without moving and then, covering his face, he cried.

Susannah reached up to touch him and he sank to the bed, all the while held in her gaze. I could not look away. It was as though something was passing between them that our eyes could not see; and yet it was in that small room as surely as those of us who stood in silent witness.

Sister Nitschmann wrapped the little girl in clean sheets and placed her on Susannah's belly. The door opened. I could feel the cold air. Brother Sensemann put his head through the opening. "Are we ready for me to ring the bell?"

Susannah herself answered in a strong voice. "*Ja*, we have a new lambkin for our Shepherd," and her smile widened. George reached for his small daughter and cradled her, reluctant to pass her into the waiting arms, who in turn passed her around the room. She dropped off to sleep as we gave her the kiss of peace and whispered to her of our Saviour. When she was passed to me, I felt the familiar shape of a newborn in my arms. So small, so curled in the crook of my arm as once Greta's little ones were. What could I say to this small new life that had not already been spoken? Be as strong as your mother, I thought. Had I spoken aloud?

I looked up from the tiny face to see Brother Otto rinsing his hands with water from the pitcher on the tiny table while Sister Nitschmann adjusted her shawl about her shoulders. Still holding the small one in my arms, I looked out the window. I could no longer see the pine branches that scratched against the panes for the sky had darkened; but I could imagine the sharp spines. Courage was a good gift for a girl-child in this wilderness.

MANY OF US BORE BABES in those early years. Later in the decade, the words of the European liturgy of *Blut und Wunden* would reach our shores, telling us that the small souls of those unborn had taken refuge in the Saviour's open wound. And as we strain to bring new life, did the blood and water of His blessed wound flow as does the blood and water that comes with new birth? Is our hunger to return to that Paradise something we know at the end of our pilgrimage? I pondered so many things as a young maiden, but knew so little then.

The wheel of seasons moved quickly, and Time caught in the turning, brought green, tender shoots, a flash of the dying leaf, the howl of winter's wind around our *Gemeinhaus*, and it was winter again. But this year the results of our labor—houses, barns and out-buildings stood solidly in the deep snow. I could remember the soft tinkling of chords and runs when Sister Nitschmann had touched the keys of our spinet. Such a quiet sound, yet it brought a sense of another world, perhaps that of the Old World's gentry where fingers were petal-smooth and hunger merely the wish for more rich pudding filled with juicy fruit and crunchy nuts. And though I could only imagine that world of ease and plenty, I did not envy or really want its richness; for the rough, stone walls of our *Gemeinhaus* echoed the sounds of our laughter and the music of my dear Sisters. We needed no more than the laurel branches we had cut to bring the beauty of the outdoors into our dwelling. And so December melted into January and January into February while the snow clung to the tree branches and crunched beneath my feet.

It was very early in the morning, completely dark, quiet and cold. I had arisen from my bed in the Sisters' sleeping hall to look out the window at the snow. The moon was low in the west and gave little light. My body was warm from my bedclothes, my nightshift folding around me like an embrace. Although Brother Ludwig had encouraged husbands and wives to take their time alone together at least once a week, I had not been with my dear husband for some time, for we worked long hours; and although we had spent our allotted time in the small room at the top of the stairs, our joy of union seemed too short a hymn, too hurried. I hugged myself, then ran my hands over my breasts slowly. If only it were summer, I thought, if only we could lie in the tall grass and I could feel his hands on me, the sun warming my face as he said my name and kissed my mouth.

Then I noticed the flickering of a lantern in one window of the cattle barn. When I saw the glow, I knew it must be Matthew, for it was his turn to see to the cattle. Almost without thinking I put my bare feet into my heavy shoes and threw a wool cape over my shift. I crept down the stairs, very slowly pushed back the iron bolt and opened the door. I hurried down the narrow path to the barn and slid open the massive door for I was young and strong and eager. The smell of hay and wood surrounded me; the cows stomped, their breath moist and heavy. Matthew stood before me holding the lantern in one hand. There was no look of surprise upon his narrow, serious face. He bent to put down the lantern and held out his arms to me. I could feel the thick wool of his coat against my shift, the buttons pressing against my breasts. He let me go then, and taking my hand he led me to the wooden ladder that connected the two floors. I climbed before him, my hands gripping the rough rungs, my heart beating quickly either in fear or excitement; I was not sure. The loft was very dark; the only light the faint glow of the lantern Matthew had placed at the bottom of the ladder. Suddenly, I knew I was afraid. Should I have left my warm bed to join Matthew in the barn? With a questioning sound, I said his name. He answered nothing but took my hand and, moving ahead of me, pulled me down onto an old quilt softened by age and smelling of sweet hay and soap. He kissed my mouth deeply and slowly over and over again. I knew there was no need to hurry; we would take as much time as we wanted to touch, to taste, to know one another's loved self. Matthew's beard was rough in that early morning and I could feel the roughness against my body, for one of us had removed my shift. Under the quilt the hay gave way beneath us and I imagined us in a rounded nest far away from the world. Matthew put his warm mouth on my belly and I held his head in both hands, my fingers twisting in his thick hair. I had never felt his whole naked body against mine, but at that time, so long ago now, in the cattle barn with the sound of creatures pulling at their hay and munching in a kind of rhythmic bass, I could feel his skin, the softness and hardness of it; his muscles moving beneath, the hair on his chest and belly and his hands finding the secret places of me, knowing me.

I WAS NOT SURE I WAS CARRYING a child for some time, but when the melting snow brought the smell of loamy mud I was surprised at the strange desire to bring its black thickness to my face and to breath in the odor of our substance; surprised again that the sound of my Sisters' singing in the early morning brought me to tears and that the sight of wild dogwood, white in the greening forest made me stop to stand in awe of our Saviour's creation.

"And who else is carrying a new life for our fold?" came Anna Maria's voice and merry laughter. And so it was. The pulling together of cloth to fit where it no longer fit; the apron strings that shorten, the overwhelming need to drowse at odd times of the day, and, then, the first tiny rustlings of a new life.

It has been this way for me every time, except now. Perhaps it is the southern heat here in Bethabara; perhaps it is because I am older, now in 1761. But I know in my heart it is neither of these. As I look at my swollen hands and try every morning to force my feet into my shoes I know there is something terribly wrong with me. Matthew kneels before me as I sit and tries to smile and comfort me. I have heard him catch his breath as he takes my puffing fingers in his hands in a vain effort to ease my discomfort, and he cannot look directly at me.

Oh, how he did look at me. Standing in the doorway of the Sisters' House in Herrnhaag; drawing me close with his eyes before he touched me with his strong hands; memorizing my face, my body. And how our eyes locked that long ago late autumn when my pains came over me in waves, closer and closer together. The Sisters counseled me to pant in short breaths and Matthew put his face near to me to whisper his encouragement. It was easier to bear down if I kept my eyes drowned in his, and when at last our little Anna cried her loud entrance, he put his hands on either side of my face and gently, oh so gently, kissed my forehead. Brothers and Sisters pressed my hands. My thin, young hands.

CHAPTER FOURTEEN

Susannah Partsch: Nazareth, Pennsylvania, 1740s

Every year in late summer the Single Sisters walk from Bethlehem to Nazareth to help us with the haying. We always go to the fields early—the sun peeps through the trees, but it has no heat. I first saw the Indian Sister Rebecca one summer when she came with the other Single Sisters to Nazareth. I wondered then if her hair under her cap was shining and black like most of the Indian peoples. Only a crow's wing is so black, I think. I never thought then that I would be able to speak Indian words with Sister Rebecca, but now I know a few already. She did not smile much when I first tried to speak to her. She stared at me. She opened her eyes wide. They are the color of chestnuts in autumn. But later she laid her hand on her left breast and said the word, "Lamb." I think she means she has the Saviour in her heart.

Christina told me that Rebecca had wanted ever so long to join the Single Sisters in Bethlehem. She said Brother Zeisberger went to tell the Indians in their own words about our Saviour and how His blood washed them clean. Rebecca hid behind a tree to listen. She came to Bethlehem with some of the young people of her tribe and begged to be baptized, so she could have a truly contented heart. But the Choir leader in Bethlehem wanted to make sure she was ready to leave her people. Rebecca's mother tried to take her back to their village. Rebecca would not go back. I think she wept many tears. *Ach*, I know how hard it is to leave your mother.

On the very day when Rebecca was finally baptized and became my Indian Sister, I was there in Bethlehem. I think maybe it was in springtime. It had been raining all day, but when Brother Neisser laid his hand on her head, the sun came out. *Ach du lieber*, it was because our dear Lamb was happy to come into her heart.

Rebecca works beside me now, kneading the round loaves of bread. Her brown hands make our flour seem whiter. She nods to me, and says, "Bread rise?" I say, "*Ja*," and pat her arm. She says English and German in a strange way. It makes me smile.

Brother Ludwig told us we must all try to understand the Indian brethren so we can tell them about how much God loves us. This is hard for me to do because the words twist my tongue in a funny way. I wish I could say Rebecca's words right now to tell her how happy I am when I feel His love all around us. Like the smell of a good wood fire when I cook for my Sisters, it warms me. I wish I could tell her how sad I feel when I remember how our poor Lamb bled when they nailed his hands and feet.

When my little Elizabeth was born from me, I saw blood spattered on the sheets. Sister Nitschmann said to think of our Lamb. I tried to remember His blood spilled out on the soldiers who killed Him. But when I held my little one close to me I knew that spilled blood is not always for dying. Sometimes it is for new life, for borning. All women know about this blood.

I cannot say any of this to Rebecca because we do not know enough of each other's words, but we have a feeling between us. It began maybe yet when I was first nursing my little Elizabeth. My breast had a tiny sore that was red and hot. I did not want to bother anyone about it. I thought it would go away. But it did not go away and began to hurt terribly. Rebecca had come to spin with us and, when we sat at our wheels, my milk began to leak through my dress. I left to sit by myself. I cried because of the hurt. I felt hot and dizzy and could not go into the nursery. I could not return to finish my spinning. Rebecca came to find me. She did not speak to me, but she held something warm in her hand. It looked like some sort of grass poultice, and I could see steam coming from it. Then she spoke a few Delaware words and motioned me to open my jacket. When I obeyed her, she placed the poultice on my breast. *Ach Gott*, it hurt so much and I wanted to take it off, but her face told me I should not. She brought me new poultices all day and the sore got smaller. The pain went away.

We sit together now on the long bench to wait for the bread to bake in our large round oven. I reach for her hand. She takes mine and does not pull away.

CHAPTER FIFTEEN

Christina Barbara Krause

I feel different this morning. The swelling that began in my hands and feet seems to have spread to my face for I can barely feel the outlines of my jaw. What does my face look like now? I search the eyes of those who come to care for me for a clue. I ask Sister Ettwein, how do I look? But she smiles and says I am in the care of our Lamb. Perhaps I do not need to know. Perhaps it is better that I cannot see myself.

I never had a looking-glass. As a child I would sometimes catch a reflection of myself in a shop window if the sun was just right. Always I would be surprised. Who was this girl? I would move and the image would disappear, as did my question; for though it was part of my nature to wonder about many things, the question of my looks did not occupy my time then. And yet, I did sometimes trace the outlines of my face with one finger and understand in some way that, although I could feel my nose, the hair of my eyebrows or the rise of my upper lip, I could not see these things.

Then, on that spring day in Herrnhaag when I was caught and

held by the music of the Brethren, by their words that pulled me into the certain warmth and light of my Saviour, I felt the eyes of my beloved Matthew upon me. I had never seen him before, yet his eyes embraced me at that moment and a hunger was born to see and to be seen. Later in our moments together, though sometimes stolen and hurried, I would ask him to tell me what he saw, and he would tell me the green-brown of my eyes, the fullness of my upper lip, the line of my jaw, and trace these with his own finger, as I had before. But it was different. His finger was rough yet tender and warmer than mine, and I would forget his words and only feel his hand cupping my chin and become lost in his eyes.

We had no looking-glasses in Nazareth. If we had, there would not have been time for more than a quick glance, as we hurried to the loom, the business of a store, the gathering of crops or readying missionaries for the journey to more unsettled places. And yet, as a young mother I thought much about seeing in my child's face something of the essence of my own. When I had nursed my little Anna, her blue eyes so like her father's, stared solemnly back at me, as though she saw my face as her own looking-glass and somehow I felt we were bound together as mirror images.

Our little Matthaeus was born two years after Anna. As I held him in the later months, his eyes seemed to memorize my face. He hardly blinked. His eyes traveled slowly from side to side, stopped, stared, and then, as if some humorous thought had just moved him, his mouth would turn up in a smile, his little red tongue still curled around my nipple. What did he see? Was my joy at him, at his sister, at my beloved, so clear that he reflected it?

Our settlement at Nazareth had taken on a shape familiar to many of the inhabitants from Silesia and Moravia. The structures were solidly built of wood and stone, set in a quadrangle with stabling for horses, cattle and sheep and shops built for our weaver, and smithy, as well as buildings for the curing and storing of flax. The sound of our bell that called us all together for meetings and prayer was fast becoming a sound that brought such joy to my heart. Familiar, I felt I could close my eyes and know the location of each shop. And when John Nitschmann sat to write of our days, the work we accomplished and the songs we sang to our dear Lamb, I knew that our days here would not be forgotten by those who would, perhaps, wander here in years to come when the young saplings had become tall trees.

It might have been a Sunday in the springtime. The Brothers' axes were still. Matthew and I walked from Nazareth to find a place away from the others, where we would be alone. Our Anna cared for, we could take our time. The trees were just beginning to bloom, the leaves still small and fragile; as the breeze touched them lightly, they seemed to shiver. I heard the rush of water before we could actually see any, and my heart seemed to sing when I recalled the small stream behind our house in Gelzhausen so long ago. We found a dry, mossy place to sit by the banks of the river and Matthew teased me to take off my shoes and wade in the water as I had loved to do when a girl. The bank was steep there, so I held on to the roots of large trees as I made my way into the water. It was colder than I had thought it would be, but the feel of smooth stones and the rush of water on my legs made me lift my petticoats high and laugh aloud. Matthew put out his hands to help me up the bank, and when we sat, he took my feet, one at a time and kissed them. Our lovemaking was gentle that day. The woods seemed a sacred place—the scent of growing things, sunlight dappled on green, and the sound of water.

It was near there, near the end of the decade and into the 1750s, that the Brethren placed stone on stone for our new mill. Our first, a mill at Christian Spring, was too much of a trek to carry the bulk of our harvest, so the Brethren chose a new site on a charming creek named the Bushkill. Land just east of Nazareth was purchased so we could plant and harvest as well as grind the fruits of our labor. The clearing of the land, logging, burning of grubs and hauling of stones was difficult work. Brother Andrew Schober, our master mason, declared this would be a fine mill; I well remember his wide gestures as he described the early foundations, the brick fireplaces and wooden flooring.

Such merry festivities we had the day we inaugurated the mill and the beginnings of the house where Matthew and I would dwell, along with the other two couples! We sang, we laughed and we shared the wheaten rolls, baked by Sister Antes. I happily anticipated moving from Nazareth; for, although I had loved the companionship of my Sisters, I did long for a smaller community where I could gather my thoughts and tend to my son. I could hardly imagine having a small room to ourselves at the end of the day.

Our new home was built of logs, with two stories and four apartments which would eventually hold more people. A large barn was also built for our cows, sheep and horses. Shortly before we left, at a meeting in Nazareth, it was decided that Rosina and John Wolfgang Michler would be in the farmhouse with us. When Rosina and I heard the news, we clasped each other's hands in friendship, both happy that the other would be so close. Brother Michler was to be our chaplain of the household, which pleased both Matthew and me because he seemed to have a kind of goodness about him. I had seen him often at his loom and felt the Lord was with him as he held the shuttle and hummed a tune, often with a smile on his angular face. Sister Catherine Mücke and her husband John were also to join us. Matthew had gotten to know John when we were in Herrnhaag, both of them coming from Silesia. He was a man of great strength, a cooper by trade, with huge hands. Sister Catherine always had seemed a bit sour to me, although I am sure I must have been mistaken about this. It was just that her mouth turned down in some way. I chastised myself for these thoughts when I remembered that she had lost some of her front teeth and that perhaps that was the reason. The last to join us were Rudolph Crist and his wife Ann Mary. She was a large, jolly woman, fond of baking little cakes; and Rudolph would know how to handle the work of milling, as that was his trade. Indeed, I envied them the sound of running water as they worked, for they would live in the mill.

We named the area Friedensthal—vale of peace. But despite the wild beauty of the place, I must confess that my heart was not always peaceful. Sometimes when our work was done, I would walk to the brook, to watch the rosy sunlight reflected in the thrashing millrace. Sitting close by the rushing water, I sought to draw comfort from the sounds, for I felt a part of me was missing. Our baby, Matthaeus, was the only child to be brought to the farm. His cradle would be the only one near my bed. Our two-year-old Anna stayed in the nursery at the *Gemeinhaus* in Nazareth, as is the custom of our people. Oh God, it was so much harder than I had thought to leave her. I had just weaned her and it seemed too early for her to join the other children in the nursery. Images of her birthing came to me in the night, and I remembered how little I knew about nursing this little mite, though I felt such a surge of love when I first saw her. Susannah was carrying another little one in her belly then, and she sat close to me as I tried to urge Anna to suck. She took Anna's little head in her hands and placed her near my breast. "There," she said, "it will not take too much time for you to grow used to this." She called back over her shoulder as she left me. "Soon enough when her sharp little teeth come, you will be ready to wean her and let the gentle ones at the nursery teach her of our Lamb."

I still remember how I pushed the thought away. Our Choir leaders had taught us that our children would be lovingly taught His ways; that in order to assure their little hearts were turned toward Heaven, they would live night and day with those who could show them. I recalled how I had questioned Matthew about this. He looked at me in a way I had not seen before—his mouth hard and his words short. His hands held my arms too tight as he stood before me. "Christina, we are part of a vision that belongs to this New World. You know what this means. We may need to travel. We do the work of our Saviour." He dropped his hands and turned from me.

"It is just that I did not know . . . I did not know . . . " It seemed so hard to tell him how it was with me. "Matthew, listen. Just listen. When I was a maiden—before I knew you—before I gave birth to Anna, I did not know how I would love her. How could I know? Oh, how could I know?"

He broke into my words. "You must have known she would be raised by others. I told you. Even before we crossed the ocean." He shook me a little, just a little. This had never before happened. His back to me then, he said, "Christina, how could we take children with us into the woods? There is death all around us; bloody conflict. We are instruments of His peace—part of our Saviour's plan." He turned back and reached out to hold me against him. "Oh, my Christina."

I loved him so. My tears soaked into his shirt. How could I make him know what I felt? I did not even know myself. But a darkness was within me. Did I have to keep this black place a secret, even as Adam and Eve hid from God after they had eaten the forbidden fruit?

So while I could, I cuddled my child, and watched her grow, savoring my time with her. As the months passed, and she toddled unsteadily toward me, her arms outstretched, I took her in my arms and wished never to let her go. Matthew told me again that she belonged to our Lamb and that the Sisters who had taken on the task of teaching the children would help her to know Him. I prayed my babe would love with purity and would not ask the questions that I have asked and continue to ask. Perhaps when she began to know the faces of others as well as mine, the pressing on my heart would be less heavy and I could let her go; to leave her with a waiting Sister who would love and teach her. I wanted to believe this, but my ever-present stubborn will cried out in anger and a kind of yearning, too. For my daughter was of my body and tied by an invisible cord to my heart. How far does this cord reach?

IT WAS LATE on a hot summer's day when I heard the ringing of the bell at the Nazareth *Gemeinhaus*. At Friedensthal we could not always hear when Joachim Sensemann rang that bell; but when the wind was in the right direction, the tolling was clear, its heavy note moving from there to here like a mother calling to her child. I began to count the rings, nine, ten, eleven, twelve. Why this constant ringing? It must mean something is terribly wrong, I thought. I was alone in the house with baby Matthaeus, for the others were away in a field. I felt a clutch in my heart—O, my God, let the small ones be safe in the *Gemeinhaus* nursery. Rumors of wild Natives still abounded, and there was always the terrible thought that someone, Indian or white, would be killed in the angry battles of the French and English.

The bell continued. I thought I should run up the hill, but was not sure. I stepped over to pick up my sleeping babe. The bell continued to toll. The sound reverberated in my chest, echoing my fear. I stood in the doorway holding my babe close to me. The day was very hot and perspiration ran from my neck into my bodice, between my heavy breasts already filling again with milk. Bees swarmed around the honeysuckle and the sweet scent of the flowers made me dizzy. I heard the sound of a horse, the hoof beats fast. Then I saw the dust rising as the sound grew louder. Matthew Schropp came into view, his legs curved around his horse, his body slightly bent in the saddle. My babe cried out. Brother Schropp pulled the reins and his dappled horse stopped in the dust before me.

"A child is missing."

"Missing?" I repeated aloud. Whose child? Is it Anna? I said not these words. My shift was drenched. "Missing?" I said again.

"We need a few men to come in from the field to help us hunt for the child. Are they up in the northern part?"

"Yes. They are all up there, and the Sisters with them." One thought pounded in my head—who was the child? I wiped the sweat from my brow with the back of my hand. Little Matthaeus began to whimper. "Who?" I said, "who?"

"I am sorry, Sister Krause. I should have told you. Our Irish neighbor O'Donnell came to us with the news that his little three-year-old daughter was missing from their farm cabin not far from Gnadenthal. The parents think he has been stolen and are wild with grief. I must hurry to alert the men—to see who might be spared to search."

He turned away to cough, spurred his horse and galloped away. Dust swirled and little Matthaeus began to cry in earnest.

"My husband is in the barn," I called after him, but he did not hear me. I opened my shift and jacket to give my babe my breast, fumbling with the laces as his cries grew louder. As the sound of Brother Schropp's horse grew fainter, I sank down to the door stoop weak with relief. My Anna was safe. Matthaeus made a coughing sound and a little frown appeared between his fair brows. Did my face show my fear and my relief?

"Christina? Christina."

Matthew ran toward me, calling my name. I rose to answer him. Perspiration had wet his dark hair, and when he bent to put his head next to mine, I could smell his sweat, salty and male mixed with the sweet odor of heat on hay. He said Brother Schropp had called to him as he rode past the barn and he was going into the woods to try to find the lost child. I wanted to say encouraging words but could not. The woods were not always a safe place; behind any tree could lurk anyone with a rifle and a nervous finger. But then, his long legs covering ground at a great pace, my husband was gone and I was left with my babe and the lingering sound of his voice.

Sitting on the stoop with my babe nestled in my arms, I tried to keep myself calm. I tried to pray, but stories of Indians snatching white children had made their way up the hill to our farm. Many times when I had sat resting my head against the bony rib cage of our cow as I milked, I tried to hear only the drip of milk in the pail; but the rumors of the Indians taking young girls as hostages had made a jagged rhythm of the steady squirt and drip. I was nauseous with fear.

The sun hung like an orange disk in the western sky by the time the women had gathered at our farmhouse. Heavy-set Sister Ann Mary Crist wiped her face with the corner of her apron, saying her husband was at the millrace looking for the child; Sister Catherine Mücke placed her hand over her mouth when she spoke. She said the other men were spreading across the land. Someone brought in water from the well, someone stirred the fire and put the kettle on the hook over the logs, another cut cabbages for slaw. We spoke little and our usual chatter was stilled by wisps of unease that seemed to sweep over the doorsill and cloud our minds. We all knew that when our supper chores were over, the clatter of dishes stilled, we might give in to fear. Sister Rosina Michler put a cup on the table, and said, "We must all pray that this little child be found safe and sound." She already had deep wrinkles in her forehead though she was but my age, and she had a way of raising her voice as if asking a question.

Sister Catherine Mücke spoke without addressing any particular one of us. "The little one is not one of ours. Its mother and father work a small farm on the outskirts of Nazareth and I hear they are not friendly to our ideas."

"They are perhaps of the Catholic or Presbyterian faith," added Sister Ann Mary Crist. "Their people tortured our people in the old country." She rose with some difficulty from her bench.

"Oh, just listen to yourselves!" The words came from me in a rush, staccato and harsh. I had never spoken in this way. There was silence and the heat of the dying day enfolded all of us. It was stifling. Rosina Michler spoke again.

"I will pray to our Lamb."

She bowed her head and, after a moment, the other women clasped their hands and were silent.

"O, dear God, keep this little child safe in your loving care until it is found and returned to its grieving parents.

A loud sniff. Sister Catherine wiped her eyes with the corner of her apron.

Our settlement sat in the midst of a very large forest that extended further than any of us could imagine. Our clearings in the woods, for all the barns, outbuildings, stone walls; for all the abundance of our fields, and our growing herds, was to me at that moment only a small, vulnerable outpost in the vast wilderness of crowded trees and tangled vines.

As we waited on that hot and humid summer evening, I knew that the peace I often felt at the close of day was, in truth, very precarious, and that the Evil One was not far away.

As if reading my thoughts, Sister Catherine said, "Evil was here in this room. I should not have spoken so of our neighbors. I beg forgiveness of you and of Him who loves us all." She did not cover her mouth as she said these words.

Rosina said, "It is so hard to know sometimes when Evil is in our hearts. We must pray for those who might persecute us."

Amen, I thought. Amen again and again. The room darkened a bit, turning the walls gray, the chairs and table black. Little Matthaeus gurgled in his cradle near the open window. Ann Mary Crist took in a breath, and letting it out in a gasp, said, "Listen, listen." We stopped our tasks, still figures standing in the graying gloom. A hot breeze whirled into the room and as one body we stepped toward the open doorway.

"There, there. Do you see? Someone is out there. Look, over to the right by the big tree."

I could not see as well as the others and squinted to better make out the outlines of whatever they saw. But then I did see a movement and could begin to see the shape of a man—at least I thought it was a man. He was carrying a burden of some kind.

"Oh my God, it is an Indian. I can tell. It is an Indian man."
I felt cold. The sweat that had glazed my neck and throat felt like a cold, salty finger of the sea. I shivered. It seemed some moments until the figure moved, a slight motion as he put something over his shoulder.

"He is holding a child," Rosina said.

"No, it could not be," Ann Mary answered.

I still could not see properly, but in the gloom I knew someone was there and moving. I wished that Susannah were here with us, for I imagined she would call out to the stranger. None of us was that brave.

Then the figure drew closer and we could see that he was, indeed, carrying a child. He walked very slowly toward the house. We crowded into the doorway not moving, not even breathing. The child was either asleep or dead, its small body draped over the Indian's shoulder, its legs dangling like a rag doll's as he came closer. I could not seem to stop myself as I moved from the doorway toward the Indian. The dry grass gave under my feet. Catherine cried out in alarm, her voice strident in the growing darkness.

"Christina! No. No."

Then we heard a cry, and the child raised its head from the Indian's shoulder. With one hand she reached out to me as I stumbled toward them. Her other arm was around the Indian's neck. She did not let go. My foot hit a stone, and I lurched forward. The Indian reached out to steady me. His face was very near mine, his deep-set eyes looked directly at me. His face was lined and worn, his mouth caved, where his teeth were missing.

"Jesus child?" he asked with a question.

"Yes," I whispered softly.

The little girl began to whimper, but she did not let go of the Indian's neck when I reached out to take her. I could see that her face was streaked with tears through the grime, her jacket torn, one shoe unbuckled and hanging precariously from her foot.

My Sisters came quietly to where the Indian and I were standing, and waited. No one said anything. Then Rosina spoke to the Indian. "We think this child was lost. Perhaps you found her?"

He turned his gaze from me and moved toward her. He seemed to be trying to find the words, and hesitantly he said. "Yes, in woods." Then, gently taking the child's arm from his neck he handed her to me. The little one looked from her rescuer to me and back again but she stopped whimpering and wiped her nose with her hand. I settled the little girl on my hip. The Indian turned his back on us and began to walk away.

"Wait. Wait a moment," Rosina said.

He turned and waited.

Rosina walked steadily to him. In a sudden gesture, she touched his arm. "We must thank you. We must give you something."

The man did not move, and in the semi-light I could not see any expression on his face.

Her hand over her mouth, Catherine said, "I think we should just let him go. We do not know if he found the child or if he took her away. We do not know anything."

The child in my arms began to cry plaintively again and struggled to get down. I pushed her wet hair out of her eyes and hummed softly to her. I knew no English or Irish words, but it seemed that if I treated her gently and sang to her, she would be less afraid.

Rosina reached in her pocket to withdraw something—I could not see what it was—and held it out to the Indian, saying, "Will you take this? Will you remember we are friends?"

As we waited to see what he would do, I held my breath, hoping he would accept her offer of friendship. Without words in common we were locked in a world where only tangible items could convey our feelings. He did not smile nor did he reach out to take the small object. I felt the moment pass. The heat was not as oppressive as in the daytime, but the air was heavy with moisture. Rosina wrinkled her forehead, saying, "Please? I need to give you something."

The Indian did not change his expression, but he held out his hand—square like my father's—his fingers slightly curled with age. Rosina pressed the object into his hand. Pausing for an instant to look directly into his eyes, she merely uttered, "Yes?" The Indian gazed back at her. Then his voice low, lower than our bass singer's, he said, "Yes."

It felt as though time had stopped. No breeze stirred the leaves that hung heavy with summer, the sky holding no stars seemed to wait in total darkness. The frightened child sat quietly on my hip, her legs curled around my waist. The Indian began to walk away. We stood to watch him as he disappeared into the gloom.

Catherine Mücke spoke. "You gave him something precious. You did not have to."

"Yes, I did," was Rosina's only answer.

Ann Mary said that we must feed the little girl and we went into motion. The child was not heavy, she rested comfortably on my hip, reminding me of Greta's small ones who had so often sat there. My Anna is carried by another, I thought. But not my son, not yet. Rosina Michler reached to take a round loaf of bread and began to slice it while Ann Mary Crist poured milk left in the jug from our supper. The little girl jumped from my arms to the floor, and without waiting to sit, she grabbed the piece of bread and stuffed it in her mouth. Rosina lit the two candles on our table and in the flicker of light I could see the child's face more clearly. She was very fair, with freckles dotting her small nose; her light hair, unbraided and tangled with brush and twigs, hung down her back. Chewing her bread, she looked up at me and said, "Mama?" I so wished I had the words to tell her we would try to find her mother, but at that moment Ann Mary Crist held the cup for her to drink.

"One of us must go to the *Gemeinhaus* at Nazareth to let them know we have found the child," I said.

"We must tell our Brothers that an Indian man returned the child," said Rosina. As she spoke, we all moved closer to ask the same question: What did she give the Indian? She raised her chin and I could see her swallow before she began to speak. "It was a small, square locket," she said. She did not think it was gold and it had no chain or picture within it. She stopped to swallow again, and I knew it was difficult for her to continue. She told us that after she had decided to join the Brethren, her father never spoke to her again, but her mother had embraced her, and with tears on her cheeks had given her the locket. What did this gift cost her, I thought?

She had pressed the symbol of her mother's love into the Native's gnarled hand. She gave freely, without knowing the reward. Would her own hands, then, be filled with the bread of our Saviour's promise, her mouth filled with the wine of His blood? Surely He was already in her heart. "Mama!" The little girl began to cry and Matthaeus, hearing the din, also awoke. We heard a shout coming from the back of our farmhouse and saw Brother Michler pass by the window and then burst into the open front door.

"Oh, Johann, we have the child," Rosina said. We all began speaking at once while Matthaeus wailed from his cradle and the little girl clung to my petticoat. Someone gave the child another piece of bread, and I took my babe, damp with sweat, to feed him. It was arranged that Brother Michler would take the little girl to the Nazareth *Gemeinhaus*, and he hurried to the barn to saddle a horse. It was quite dark when he climbed into the saddle, and the child was handed to him, pieces of dried apple clutched in her hand, her eyes wide and questioning but not afraid. I lit the lantern for him to carry. Brother Michler promised to call in the other men, suggesting with a laugh that they might enjoy some of the beer the Single Brothers had brewed at their farm at Christian Spring nearby. I remember our mood had taken on a gaiety as we assembled the pottery mugs on our common table and went over the whole incident again, and again, wondering what tribe the Indian belonged to and where he had found the child. We spoke of our own childrens' safety in the nursery at the *Gemeinhaus*, and as I put my little one in his cradle again, I had a moment of understanding the wisdom of placing our children together with loving teachers behind sturdy stone walls.

It did not seem long until Brother Crist's great bulk filled the doorway, with Brother Mücke right behind him. They said Brother Michler would soon be on his way and we need not wait to pass the beer. The taste of bitter liquid was cool and refreshing and I felt my body relax. The child had been found, and no doubt Matthew would come walking in the door any moment, bending his height a little under the doorframe. We cleared away the mugs and dipped them, one at a time, in a bucket of clean water.

After some time, Brother Michler called from the yard to say he was putting his horse away. When he came into the room, he wiped the sweat from his square face, and asked with a smile if we had left lager for him. Rosina playfully curtsied before her husband, saying the beer was coming. I felt a welcome breeze from the open door as the wind rose a little. As Brother Michler sat to drink his beer, I looked across the table at him and asked if he had seen my husband on the road. Wiping his mouth, he told me it was too dark to see anyone, but he had not heard Matthew call out. Despite the heat I felt a slight shiver, for the hour was now late and Matthew should be returning from his search of the surrounding woods. Rosina must have noticed the expression on my face, and, ever kind, she murmured that Matthew knew the woods and was probably delayed by darkness. Not wanting to show my concern, I helped place dishes on the shelf. When it came time for bed, I smiled at each of my companions as I placed one precious lantern in the window.

The bedroom was very dark. No breeze stirred the tree outside the window, and it was too hot for covers. I slept in a thin shift and lay stiff on my back, my arms at my sides. I waited for a sound, just a leaf crackle, a door creak, a footstep. There was no moon, so possibly my husband had decided to make his bed in a tree and await the morning light before continuing toward our farm. I tried to think as he would think. He was a careful man and not one who knew panic. I had lain beside him and felt his even heart beat against my own, steady and slow. My own heart fluttered, and I put my hand on my breast for comfort. Little Matthaeus coughed in his cradle but did not wake. I think I slept but awoke with a start as a tohee called by the window. High, sharp, its morning call seemed to me one of alarm. Matthaeus began to whimper. I lifted him from his cradle, his little body wet with urine. Barefoot I carried him from the room and down the narrow stairs quietly, so as not to awaken the others. I stripped his wriggling body and carried him to a bucket at the doorsill to wash him. I sat on the step to nurse him and to smell the summer morning, heavy with honeysuckle and dew-sprinkled grass. Surely my dear husband would soon walk toward us from the dark woods.

The others awoke soon, the women laughing at something as they dressed and the men splashing in the buckets they had filled last night. I had slipped into the house to dress before the men appeared, my shift sticking on my body that was even at that early hour beginning to perspire. It was too hot to wear two petticoats.

The day dragged on. As clouds began to gather, I heard the rumble of distant thunder. I could not concentrate on anything. I spilled milk as I poured and when I sat to knit I tangled the yarn. Catherine Mücke suggested I walk down the stream and with a smile, showing her missing teeth, said she would gladly watch little Matthaeus. I was grateful to this Sister who did try to be kind, although often her first thought was of herself instead of another. Perhaps if I walk a bit, I will be able to pray, I thought.

As I walked down the hill slowly in the gathering heat, all I could repeat was, "O, my suffering Lamb, bring him back. Bring him back." I stopped to close my eyes and think about that wounded head—o, sacred head – but I saw Matthew's clean-shaven face, his blue eyes tortured in pain, the blood from a crown of thorns, red . . . Could it be that he really was lost, or worse, was he lying at the foot of a tree, twisted, pale, still? I opened my eyes and began to run to the stream. There was less water now, I noticed, sharp rocks dry, moss turning yellow already. I bent down to cup water in my hands to cool my face.

"Sister Krause. Sister Krause."

It was the voice of Brother Michler. He was running down the hill toward me. When he was within speaking distance, he said, "I am going with Brother Crist into the woods to greet your husband when he gets to the trail. One of the Brothers will come from Nazareth with his trumpet. It might be easier for your husband to hear the sound." He reached out and took my arm, a smile on his angular face. His smile worried me because I knew he was trying to reassure me and that he, too, was worried. O, my God, bring him back. Bring him back. The thunder seemed a bit closer and a slight breeze touched the very top of the trees. We needed rain, but I wondered if a heavy storm would slow my husband on his way. I could not rid myself of my fear, my stomach felt twisted. Thunder again, and I hastened to our farmhouse.

Large drops hit the ground hard just as I walked over the sill into the farmhouse. Sister Catherine was walking in a circle holding baby Matthaeus, who looked as worried as I felt. But when he saw me, his face wrinkled in pleasure, and he reached out his plump arms. For a moment I felt lightness at the joy of seeing my son and I remembered that, of course, I should have a strong faith in our Saviour's kindness. Has He not shown me this over and over again as we work to do his bidding in this deep forest?

The rain pounded on the roof and ran down the windows, for there was no wind. John Michler flung open the door. Behind him Brother Crist was already removing his hat and shaking the wet onto the floor. I dared not speak. Their search must have been in vain but perhaps, perhaps . . .

"No sign of him right now . . ." Rudolph Crist said. "We could see the rain was coming upon us, and we had blasted the trumpet many times before the noise of the storm took over." Indeed, the sound of rainwater on the leaves did make a din that seemed to block out other sounds; but surely they might have waited out the storm. I felt an angry retort rise in my throat but said nothing. John Michler came nearer and said in a quieter voice,

"Matthew knows the woods. Has he not searched for missing cows when they have wandered off?" He took my hand then and said, "Listen to me, Sister Krause. I think your husband has a reason to have not yet returned. He is not lost. We heard no gunshots or shouts."

I interrupted, "But Johann, you know that I was attacked with Anna Sensemann and Sister Schropp on our way to Bethlehem. You know that knives make no noise in the woods." I felt tears gather, and I could speak no further, but at that moment, I felt I would have opened the heavy wooden door and run out into the rain to find my love. My tears overflowed as I gave in to my fears. Ann Mary Crist gathered me in her arms. I did not say how the pain of losing my father, of knowing that somewhere he might still be wandering the muddy back roads around Gelzhausen, haunted my dreams. Behind my eyes I saw my mother's drawn face, her labored breathing, and her words, coming in gasps. Had she told me my father would leave? Was it my fate to have those I love leave me? I tried to picture the kindness in my Saviour's face. I felt Ann Mary patting me gently as I pulled away and wiped my tears with my knuckles.

The rain pounded late into the day and throughout our dinner. Somehow I put plates on the table, tried to swallow food that stuck in my throat, and fed my little child. Finally I trudged to our small bedroom and lay across my bed without undressing.

Should I have had more faith? It was easy to sing of faith when our hearts were yoked to a noble idea, our steps in time. So often my heart had swelled with love as I looked at the men and women who had come to mean so much to me. I knew that love is what He put in our hearts, and I felt at those times filled with certain faith. I knew our Lamb lived with us as we felled trees, sowed and harvested, even at those times when I could not lift my foot one more time, when I was so hungry there was no saliva to moisten my mouth. When I ached to see Greta and Hans once again, I knew He was with us, hidden deep in my heart to give me strength. But as I lay alone in the place we called The Vale of Peace, I could not believe the psalm words Matthew had so often spoken: *Weeping may tarry for the night but joy comes in the morning.*

Those words tasted bitter in my mouth, as I lay dry-eyed. If my love were dying alone in the cruel wilderness, I felt that faith would flee from me as easily as it came to me in my childish dreaming when I left Gelzhausen. As though this thing we call faith was as a wisp of wind that took a lone, dried leaf from the branch to dance for one moment, then left it to die with no evidence of its coming or its going. And there would be no joy.

CHAPTER SIXTEEN

The rain stopped. I must have slept, although it seemed I had spent the whole storm-swept darkness lying awake on top of my thin quilt, my arms outstretched as though to reach for my husband's body, refusing to know the space was empty. His pillow was dented, the sheet rumpled, but he was not there. I had an ache in my belly that had nothing to do with hunger. How accustomed I had gotten to another body lying close at night; the sound of easy breathing, the small twitches of his leg and those lovely times when I could feel the hand of my beloved touching my hair or running his finger across my mouth even though he slept.

The morning was hot, and through the small window I saw that a mist hung over the dripping trees; the birds, hidden in last night's storm, flew about in a flurry to catch their breakfast. Despite the heat, my arms felt cold. Empty arms, I thought. Perhaps empty forever.

I got up and reached unsteadily for the water pitcher. The water in the bowl was lukewarm and did not seem to wash the sleep from my eyes. Standing barefooted on the floor, I clasped my hands. "Dear God, let this be the day my husband comes home to us. Let me see him again, let him come home to us and somehow I will find a way to keep You in my heart—to carry You in my very self. I will remember to praise You as I wake, and as I go to sleep." The moment I thought these words I knew I was being childish. One cannot speak to God in this way. And yet, I could not help but feel that somehow, in some way, my behavior would change the outcome. My babe snuffled and then laughed. He must not know his father is missing. I knew I must wash and feed him and try to let him know that our Jesus is always with us and that we are safe in His care.

I heard my Sisters and Brothers stirring, and listened for Sister Rosina's light tread on the stairs. She was always the first to rise and start our fire. I peered into the cradle, and when little Matthaeus saw me his face crinkled into a smile. My mind flew to the nursery where, surely, Anna was rising from her bed with the other children. I felt lighter somehow, as I straightened the bedclothes and bent to take my son from his cradle. Surely today would bring good news. When I walked down the stairs, John Mücke put his large hand on my shoulder, saying he was certain the search for my husband would find him alive and well. Although I had awakened with some hope, his words seemed to bring back the emptiness I had felt since Matthew left to search the woods. Alone, this morning I had imagined my life complete again, my hand in his, or his serious, narrow face slowly wrinkling into a smile as I let down my hair. But the sound of another's reassurance brought back a cool void—it seemed a dark pond, its surface smooth. I could not jump into its depths to be pulled into the darkness, though I wished it. I could only stand on the edge to see the reflection of my pale face, my body cold and trembling against the still, smooth surface.

We sat down to eat the last of the wild berries, plump, red and sweet this year. Heavy cream floated on our strong coffee. We ate quietly, speaking only now and then about having to wait yet another day to take in the flax and hay that was ready for harvest; for the rain, though welcome, had held up our work in some of the fields.

Brother Michler rose to dip his cup into the wash water, "We will begin our search for Brother Matthew quite soon now. We only await some more men from Nazareth who will join in the search." Indeed, I heard the sound of horses before he ended his sentence.

Brother Matthew Schropp was the first to come to the door, having given the reins of his horse to Brother Opitz, who held his trumpet in his other hand. His blond hair was covered with a large hat, which he reached up to remove as he spoke to me.

"It will be easier to find your husband today. Without the pounding rain, I am sure he will hear our trumpet blast."

"Oh, yes," Catherine said, with her hand over her mouth, "Remember 'Joy comes in the morning.'"

Those words should have brought comfort to me, but I felt instead the shiver of fear, my hands clenched behind me, clammy with sweat. I stopped the answer I wanted to give her. Who says there is joy in the morning? There is no joy without the tall figure walking toward me in the mist. What had happened to him? Where is he?

Brother Schropp smiled at me, put on his hat and indicated with a gesture of his head that the men should saddle their horses and be off. I stood at the door until I could no longer hear the hoof beats. One note from the trumpet sounded through the early morning.

I cannot remember how I spent that day. We all had tasks, I

alone in our house to sew, the others to weed in our kitchen garden, and the men to repair a wheel and see to the animals. There was no singing; for I believe my Sisters knew that any song, even one meant to praise our Lord, would bring tears for me. Baby Matthaeus began to fret in the late afternoon as the sun again beat down on our farmhouse and the usual comfort of buzzing bees became only an irritation. How long would we have to wait for news? Somehow I would rather know what had happened to him than never to know. To have him disappear would be more than I could bear. To think of him pushing the thick brush aside with arms growing more and more weak. To think of him stuffing leaves into his mouth when there were no berries. He had no rifle, and game was often scarce anyway. God, how I tortured myself as I wandered outside the farmhouse, threaded a needle, or filled pots with water from the well.

The Brothers who had gone to look for Matthew had not returned and could have made the trip all the way to Philadelphia in the time I spent trying to put my thoughts on my work and my God. I cannot recall this emptiness in terms of time, only that I know I clutched an inner loneliness that seemed so much worse because I was in ignorance. If only I could peer into the woods to see what was happening.

My dear companions touched me gently, and their words were meant to be reassuring, but my only real solace was to work my body until I was tired even in my bones. Over and over I bent to gather the drying hay left by those who had used the pitchfork to toss the yellow, fragrant crop to the top of an ever higher pile. Stalks in my clothes, crackling under my feet. Other years I had loved the scent, the bending, the dance of my Brothers and Sisters as they bent and gathered with me. But now my heart was sore, my mind dark and empty.

The days ran together. It could not have been a week. Was that the piercing call of a trumpet—a note high and strident that made me put my babe in his cradle and run to the door? There—it came again. Then I heard the sound of the bell at Nazareth. It was very faint for the wind had changed but I could pick up the clang coming from the hill with its regular song. It must mean the men had found someone, or something. I ran to the road. I could feel the beat of my heart, and put my hand on my breast to still its pounding. It seemed a long moment until I could see Brother Matthew Schropp gallop towards me; a long moment before he bent from his saddle, his dappled horse snorting in the heat.

"He is alive and safe."

I think he told me much more. I only heard those words. I could not speak.

"He has brought with him Indians he found wandering in the deep woods. They are starving—there is a child. The men are bringing some of them up here to Friedensthal." He kicked his horse and turned her around. "God is good, Sister Krause. We have work to do. Gather the others to make food." And he rode away.

How long did I stand, my feet on the dusty path, my hand raised to this most welcome Brother. I knew I had to tell the others. I knew we had to prepare for however many visitors would be coming up the hill, but I stood alone staring at the curve of the road.

My dear husband was coming home. Matthew, I whispered to myself. Oh, Matthew, how could I doubt that you would come home; would find your way through the trees that gave no hint of direction? Did you call aloud to our Lamb? Or was your prayer a steady drone of sound that hummed in your brain? Was it that your prayers were answered or was it your knowing they would be heard that kept you safe? You have always been so sure that He was with us. But images of your pain and death had filled my mind, and kept me from trusting in His care. Yet, despite my doubts, He has brought you home to me. I felt giddy with the sense of gratitude that enveloped me.

I ran down the road and felt I had taken flight, never feeling the rough stones through my shoes. Nearing the open door I heard little Matthaeus' call. Your father is coming home, I said in my heart. He is coming home to us, I whispered, as I bent to pick up my son.

CHAPTER SEVENTEEN

Susannah Partsch: Nazareth, Pennsylvania

I have sharp eyes. I can see far into the woods. Even with the leaves on the trees a hidden deer I can see. And watch as it runs, its white tail an easy mark. When the long beans are ready for picking, I can see them hiding behind the green leaves and pluck them before my Sisters can even see where they are.

Right now as I spin I can feel the rough flax in my hand and do not have to watch as my feet push up and down on the treadle. I want to keep my eyes on the window that looks out to the woods. Maybe I will be the first to see Brother Matthew. In my head I can clearly see him walking fast with long steps, the way he always does. I can almost hear his call. He sings on one note—Hellooo. He sings loud. Not the way he talks.

I have not seen Christina since her husband went in search of the lost child, but she is my dear friend. So I can feel her worry. It moves from her in Friedensthal, a few miles away, to me in Nazareth, just like the first autumn wind rushing down the hill pushes the dry leaves. I can see her face in my head, the way she bends a little to one side when she listens. *Ach ja*, and the way she reaches to touch her husband as though he might just disappear and she would be left standing there alone. Christina does not talk much, so I watch her face to see how she feels. I have told her my secrets, but I am not sure of hers.

The day is so hot again. I think about stopping my wheel to drink cool water from our well and sing a few verses with my Sisters. We do this often in the day to remind ourselves that our Lamb loves us, and I always feel the ache of my shoulders just goes away as I sing.

The forest trees stand quiet now. There is not even a breeze left from last week's storm. Hot as it is, I am happy it is not raining because I can see better. Wait! I see a small child. There are others. They walk slowly and ...

"Susannah, you have dropped your spindle. What do you see?" Sister Anna Maria calls out to me. I run to the door, calling back to her, "It is Brother Matthew Krause. He has a child with him and a woman is leaning on his arm. I think they are Indians."

"Oh, look, the woman stumbles." Anna Maria moves quickly from the window to the door. I pull at the latch, and it opens with a creak. Both Anna Maria and I stand at the threshold looking across the yard cleared by our Brethren. Strange the way they are coming out of the shadows. They do not seem to know where they are, and Brother Matthew, who always stands so tall and straight, is bent as he almost seems to drag the woman on his arm. He is calling out now. "Help, we need help."

Anna Maria and I begin to run toward him. I see now the blood on his head and his eye is blackened and swollen. *Das ist schlimm*. This is bad!

"Brother Matthew, you are hurt," I say, but he looks over his shoulder and, following his look, see a child and behind, a man. The child's arm is wrapped in a rag, the blood oozing through. Anna Maria reaches to take the child. From out of the woods I see two, three, more Indians. Some are limping; some help others who seem wounded in some way. They all look pale and sick.

"They need food and water," Matthew croaks at us. His voice is thick. Just then I hear hoof beats and Brother Matthew Schropp comes up the road with Brothers Opitz and Michler. The dust is terrible. I have to cough as I breathe. Dragging, half carrying these poor people, we make our way across the yard to the open door. One Indian man collapses right there. I have not seen such sick people since we got to this country.

I hear the bell. Brother Sensemann has come from the biggest barn and is pulling at the rope. Maybe Christina can hear this if the wind is right. We all move fast to settle them on the floor, on chairs, and on our beds if they are strong enough to move to another room. We have only a small fire because it has been so hot, but I take two logs and throw them on. Water is poured from buckets into the few mugs we have. I help one man to drink from a gourd. *Ach*, he slurps like a greedy child. I wonder when the last time was he had a drink. I have a chance now to really look at this band. They all are so thin, their hair stringy and dirty as though they were lost in the woods forever. Anna Maria moves to help the Indian woman who has collapsed onto the floor. The little Indian *fraulein* with the hurt arm says nothing, but her black eyes stare at me as I move toward her. The rag around her arm is full of dirt and blood and seeps wetly. I want to take it off, but I do not want to frighten her. Slowly I reach out and pat her small head. Her hair is matted and maybe even crawling with bugs. She does not take her eyes from my face. Gently, so gently, I lift her arm so I can see better. I begin to unwrap the dirty rag so full of blood it does not stick to her arm. She watches me and makes no sound. Then I see a deep wound running from her elbow down into her thin wrist. The blood oozes worst in the fatter part of her arm, and I thank our Lamb because I think we can gather some of her flesh together once I get it clean. Our Dr. Otto has taught us to clean wounds before bandaging. He says this is why we recover so well from accidents that befall us. I take a clean rag from the hook by the fire, and once I have wet it in the bucket, I carefully dab at her arm. It must hurt so, but she makes no sound; only drawing in her breath through her teeth if I wash too deep. Her eyes never leave my face.

All around me there is movement, scuffling, and the clank of pots as water is boiled on the fire. Brother Seidel enters the room. His thin face has worry wrinkles. Thanks be to our Saviour, Brother Seidel can speak the Indian language, and he questions one warrior who sits on the floor chewing the bread given him. I look to find Brother Matthew, but he must have left the room. I wonder if word of his return has reached Friedensthal.

The Indian woman who had clung to Brother Matthew has been laid on a bed and I hear Anna Maria's voice from the other room.

"This woman is with child." There is the quiet murmuring of the Sisters, but I cannot make out their words.

Then I see Brother Matthew enter our common room. I have never seen him look so drawn and pale; he limps over to where one warrior is speaking with Brother Seidel. "These people are starving. I am not sure if they are all one nation, but clearly they have been driven from their homes—either by other Indians or, perhaps, by who knows." He croaks out the words from a closed throat.

We all know the woods contain some who hate the brown men. My mind flies, as I tend this little one. Would angry men be following this lost band? And if they came here, what would happen to us? The child moves in pain as I clean a flap of skin, but she does not cry out.

As though he is reading my mind, Matthew touches Brother Seidel's arm.

"Listen, my Brother. I fear we will have to shelter, and perhaps hide, these people. It might be difficult to find hiding places for all ten of them, but we can dress the little girl as one of ours and take her and the stronger of them to the lower farm."

"Brother Krause, you have to let one of us look to your eye and you need food and drink." Matthew shakes his head as though he is not in need, but Brother Seidel takes him by the arm. "Sit on the bench by the window." Saying this, he moves my wheel. I hear the voice of Brother Greening, a medical man. "Obviously these people have not eaten in some days. Be careful as you give them food. It will come up as quickly as it went down." One young Indian warrior tries to run from the corner of the room where he had eaten too quickly. His retching stops him from getting to the door, and vomit splatters near my foot. I have some sickness myself. *Ach*, it is hard to keep my stomach still, but as I finish cleaning the child's arm, I keep swallowing and calm myself.

There is moaning in the next room where Sister Anna Maria Schropp is attending to the Indian woman. I know the sound as it comes and goes. It is the sound of birthing. I find the basket of clean rags and begin to wrap the little girl's arm. It is such a thin little arm. I can see her elbow clearly and her hands do not look like those of our plump *kinder*. Her nails are broken and filthy. I ask Brother Seidel if I might clean the child now. He nods to me and turns again towards the Indian he is speaking to. I do wish I could say their words, but I do not know what nation they are from, and I have only learned some of my Indian Sister Rebecca's words. From the other room the Indian woman cries out now. Anna Maria says something too quietly for me to hear. I know this child needs food, and I reach for the bowl of dried apples to give her some. Her eyes never leave my face as she stuffs a piece in her mouth. *Gott*, she hardly chews. Slowly, so as not to frighten her, I lift the dirty dress over her head. I can see her ribs through her brown skin, and as I gently wash her, she stands on her small, thin feet and shakes from time to time, her little nipples shriveled as though she is cold, though the day is so hot. Sister Opitz has found a small shift that will fit the child, and when she is as clean as I can get her, I pull it over her head. She needs no cap or apron now. I lead her to a trundle bed in the corner, telling her in my words to lie down to rest. I hear the woman cry out again, this time louder. Sister Opitz brings broth for the child and asks that I go to help Sister Anna Maria. I have never helped the doctor in a birthing, but my three daughters have taught me as they were coming. I think I know what to do.

The woman is lying on the bed, her legs open and bent at the knees. Dr. Greening is pressing on her stomach; Anna Maria stands by her head and speaks softly. There is not much blood. The woman is very lean; her babe only a small swell. I see no movement. A tremor in her body. She bites her hand, and I see blood. It runs down her wrist in a small trickle. This babe is not ready to be born, Dr. Otto tells us; but it is coming into the world anyway. The poor woman cries out again and I can see the pushing begin. Anna Maria wipes her forehead with a wet cloth and I hold her legs to try to stop the trembling. Then I see the tiny head. Dr. Otto reaches to help pull the tiny babe. It does not help itself. It does not breathe. The color of the child is pale and I see its closed eyes with no lashes, its little fingernails blue. It is very small. Free of its mother I see it is a boy child. I wrap it tight. Such a tiny bundle. The mother has stopped her whimpers. When I give the small babe to her, she takes it, though maybe she is too weak to hold the little one. I help to place it on her breast. Already it turns gray, and the wretched mother puts her mouth on its tiny head. I see her tears and cannot stop my own.

"Too early, too early," Dr. Otto mutters as he wipes blood from the mother. Sister Anna Maria also weeps silently as she bends to dry the Indian mother's tears. None of us say a word. Anna Maria gently takes the babe from its mother's arms, and she turns her face away from us. I hope she will sleep.

I can smell meat cooking on the fire, and I know it must be the small rabbits and birds that George caught yesterday. We have not had much game ourselves, but we must feed these starving people. How long had they been wandering before Brother Matthew found them? *Ach*, who knows? But cooking is something I know how to do. So I walk to the fire to take over the kitchen duties. I feel a hand on my shoulder and know without looking that it is my dear George. Once he was a weaver, now he runs our household for our workers and missionaries. Once I was afraid to know him. Now I know his ways, I know his gentleness. Today we work for our Lamb. Our shoulders are touching.

CHAPTER EIGHTEEN

Christina Barbara Krause

I ran down the hill. I had to be the first to see him, to take his hand and to look into his eyes. Let the others take care of the Indians. Feeling short of breath, I slowed my steps. It was very quiet. Usually I could hear some Brother's ax or the creak of wagon wheels on the bumpy road to Friedensthal, or the snort of a horse; but even the birds seemed to be hiding behind still leaves, their usual chatter silenced. Something about the silence of the day made me hesitant, afraid to run as though any headlong movement would bring danger of some kind. Then a small band of people came out of the woods; Brother Schropp first, then three Indian men and, at the rear, a little girl dressed in the garb of the Small Girls' Choir member, with a dark skirt and red ribbons on her jacket. It was Susannah who held the little girl's hand and I squinted to see better; but no tall figure walked with them. Matthew was not there.

These Indians might be some who were made to wander the woods due to the lack of game or the drought that plagued us all. Or they might be those who were fleeing because of the wars of various nations in the area. These men must have lost their weapons or perhaps had fled without them. In any case, without rifles or bows and arrows, hunger could have quickly become their deadly companion.

The small band of natives, two of whom looked young, another old, seemed wary and held back as Brother Schropp wiped the perspiration from his forehead before he spoke.

"We will need to help these men and the child as quickly as possible. There are more Indians in Nazareth with your husband . . . "

I interrupted. "Is he all right? Is Matthew safe?" Brother Schropp nodded in assent. Motioning to the Indians to follow, he began to walk toward the farmhouse.

I clutched Susannah's arm. "Susannah, why didn't Matthew come with them? Why isn't he here?" I could feel moisture under my breasts and my heart beat in an irregular way.

"He must stay there to give his full report to Brother Seidel and the others. He does have a slight wound above his eye, and he was limping a little when he came to us, but he will heal quickly. Come, these people we have to help."

The others must have needed him, but if my wait was to be long I wondered if I could bear it. I had hidden my consternation well in the past few days. Dear Lamb, give me strength, I whispered.

The Indian girl looked to be six or seven years old, and though the red ribbons of her jacket were neatly tied, she did not look like the merry little girls in our Children's Choir and was very thin under the dress that hung unevenly at the hem. Her bony ankles were scabbed and red above her leather moccasins. I smiled into her face and held out my hand. When she did not reach up to take it, I gently took hers. She did not resist as we began to walk to the farmhouse. She seemed unable to keep up, so I slowed my steps. Once, when she stumbled she looked up at me, her black eyes wide, her face mirroring her utter confusion. I felt then as I would for one of my own had they been lost and motherless. Was there an Indian mother searching for her daughter, or did she lie broken on brown pine needles?

At the front door Rosina Michler and Catherine Mücke stood to receive us, one holding a round loaf of bread, the other a pitcher. We took the Indians into the house and motioned for them to sit and eat. They pulled off pieces of the large loaves, washing it down with our currant wine. Brother Schropp spoke softly, "I must hasten back to

Nazareth. Brother Seidel is on his way here to help translate from the Indian languages. Although we have not evidence, I fear these people are not only fleeing hunger but perhaps someone chases them."

I could not help but question who would be enemies of these poor Indians? Again, the rumors of savage Indians plundering settlements came rushing to my mind. Although they may have been fleeing those of another nation, it might also be that white men with a murderous grudge were seeking to harm any brown man they could find. Brother Matthew Schropp interrupted my thoughts.

"We must think of a way to help these people or, perhaps, to disguise them so they will look like the Brethren."

Of this I had grave doubts. Many of the Indians who had come to our settlements wore their hair in braids or loose to their shoulders. These Indian men shaved their heads except for a scalplock that fell down the back, and their haggard faces told me they had had little food for months. Certainly we would have to find trousers and shirts for them, but all three of them would fit into the jacket of Brother Crist. The little girl had been easier to disguise, for several of the children in the nursery were Christian Indians, so it would appear she belonged here if dressed in their uniforms of dark skirts and red-ribboned jackets. The child moved toward Susannah, who patted her gently on the head. "This little one is very brave. I dressed a wound on her arm and she made no sound of pain."

"Is her mother or father with her? Do you know if she belongs to anyone here?"

"I don't know, Christina. We have not had time to figure out whether the little group was related or not. Did you know there was an Indian woman who was brought by Matthew to Nazareth with the men?" Susannah lowered her voice and spoke near my ear. "She has given birth to a dead child. We have wrapped it and it will need to be buried right away." Then she looked away and I knew without her telling me that a corpse in this heat would need to be interred very soon. And where would the little body be placed? Susannah must have seen the look on my face.

"I know. This may have to be a hasty thing done back in the woods. The mother is weak and sick. I felt so for her."

Indeed, before I gave birth it was easy to speak of the life and death of newborn babies. The words did not reach my heart. Once I saw my child and heard the cry of life, I knew I would live in a world that embraced dreams of a new kind. The death of a dream so briefly seen would be the hardest trial to bear. Yet we are taught that death to this life is only the birth of another. That our Saviour will reach out to take any child in His arms, the Indian babe as well as one of ours.

Susannah and I moved quickly, taking trousers and waistcoats from pegs. Brother Crist motioned the Indian men up the stairs, and they followed him, docile and silent. Horse hooves announced the welcome coming of Brother Seidel, who swung his agile self from the saddle and hurried into the farmhouse. The Indians were descending the stairs in the Brethren's clothes. One warrior had buttoned the waistcoat over his shirt unevenly, and another's pants hung on his thin frame like a scarecrow. I noticed that these men, though thin, were well-formed, and I was sure they had run swiftly through their woods and splashed in cool streams with as much strength and grace as our men had. But now the poor heathen huddled together, and I felt my heart go out to them, for there must be such humiliation in having to wear our clothes and beg for food. White settlers speaking in a strange tongue had changed their world, and now they were forced to come to us in their shame.

Brother Seidel was speaking in the Delaware tongue to one of the Indians who responded seriously, nodding his head. Brother Michler reached into his pocket and produced a bag of tobacco. Brother Crist pulled a pipe from his own breeches and, handing it to Brother Michler, he smiled broadly at the Indian standing close by. After pushing tobacco into the bowl, Brother Michler struck the flint. The Indian took the first puff then gave the pipe to Brother Crist. It was as though an age-old ritual was being performed. We all began to speak at once. The fear, the desperation we had all felt, left the room, and although I knew these dark emotions would soon return, the moment was precious.

We spoke quickly in hushed tones about how best to save our guests. The Indian men watched each face silently. Susannah said the Indians left behind in Nazareth could be hidden in the great barn there. Even our root cellars here in Friedensthal were large enough to hide a grown man or woman. I asked Brother Seidel who might be the greatest threat to our native guests. He spoke about men who had no alliances with the British, French or anyone but themselves, though they were usually British subjects and, indeed, rogues with stolen firearms. These men were fearful of the Indians even in our region, because they knew of kidnappings and killings in the northern part of New York and Massachusetts. They hated our people as well, because we had traveled much of that territory, and acted as friends to the Indians. I almost felt again the fetid breath of the man who had grabbed me in the forest, and the fear and loathing of that moment. Men like that would not stop to listen if they found Indians they saw as savage beasts in league with us.

Our earnest talk was interrupted by the sound of hoof beats, and Dr. Adolph Meyer pushed open the door. I had often watched him bandage a wound or place his warm hand on a distended belly; and though his smile was reassuring, his deep-set eyes never seemed to crinkle with joy. I saw a sadness in the way he bent his slight body forward; the way tears were never far from spilling when he lost a Brother or Sister to disease or accident.

Dr. Meyer had come with us on the *Little Strength,* leaving his wife to come on the next ship. That reunion was never to be, for on the way her body was commended to the great waves and she now rests with our loving Saviour. Often he had said to me that he knew she was with our Lamb, but I could see the kind words of others only reached part of him; the other part would remain cold and bare forever.

My own longing for Matthew at that moment overcame any other thought, and it was all I could do to not rush to Dr. Meyer to ask if he had seen to my husband in Nazareth. But I sat on the bench and said nothing because I did not want others to see my doubt and fear when we were facing such urgent concerns.

Dr. Meyer said that the Indian woman who had given birth to the dead child was asleep, and that one of our Sisters was keeping watch near her bed in case she might turn feverish. Whether she was safer in Nazareth or here at the farm was something he wished to discuss with us. We spoke quietly, and I noticed that Dr. Meyer was careful to include our Indian guests in our conversation, though I was not sure of their understanding. We were all surprised when the oldest Indian spoke in a deep halting voice. "We hungry. You feed." Then he turned to Brother Seidel and spoke in his own language. The Brother translated from the Delaware, saying the Indians had no wish to bring us danger; that with some provisions and knives or a rifle his men would try to find others around Nazareth and after gaining their strength, would slip into the forest.

I felt myself relax somewhat. It would not be so difficult to hide just the three here, and it should not take too many days until they could fend for themselves. Brother Crist asked our small group if we all would agree to keep the men for a short time until those in Nazareth could find hiding places. We nodded in the affirmative.

Little Matthaeus had become slippery as he wriggled to be free of me so I sat him in one corner. I handed him a bone to chew, and he laughed, banging it on the floor. My mind flew to the nursery at Nazareth where little Anna played and learned with the other lambs in our fold. I told myself the stone walls must keep her safe and, yet, I felt a shiver of anxiety. I knew that Matthew had done the right thing by bringing these poor refugees into our settlements, despite the danger if they were discovered with us. When, oh when, would Matthew come up to the farm? Could it be, I tortured myself, that he is hurt more badly than they are saying to me?

I stepped closer to Dr. Meyer and spoke quickly, pushing aside my reticence. "Could you give me news of my husband?"

"Christina, I have seen Matthew's wound over his eye, and it will heal. I am sure he is eager to see you and the child. At this moment he is discussing with some of the Brethren the move of the children from the nursery in Nazareth to Bethlehem."

"I thought they were safe in Nazareth . . . "

"They would perhaps be safer in Bethlehem because there are more of us to care for them, and they could be moved into the Sisters' House with some of the older children. The whole arrangement seems a sensible one."

I could no longer hear the doctor, for my mind rushed up our hill to the stone house at the Nazareth farm. We had had some peaceful months here and, innocently, I had thought our enclave would stay safe from harm. The trees so weighted with the green leaves of deep summer, the grain abundant in our fields surrounded me with the same sense of peace and harmony I felt when the Brothers sat to blend their violin and cello strings together. But now, I felt disconnected, a broken string.

"Sister Krause, you look pale."

"Bethlehem is ten miles away. I won't be able to visit Anna so often."

He interrupted me. "My dear Christina. Your daughter is not yours. She belongs to our Lamb. She is always safe with Him."

I felt chastised. I also felt a kind of rebellion. This feeling was not foreign to me. I had tried so hard to put it in some dark closet of my head where I could shut the door. Now anger reddened my face. Oh, I knew my child was to be raised by others; I knew she belonged to our Saviour. I struggled with the words, and looked directly at Dr. Meyer. "But why can't I be her guide, her mother?"

"I know, Christina, I know."

Perhaps he did know. Can we taste the salt of another's tears? I remembered the day on ship when he held his wife in his arms. I remembered the loosening of their hands, slowly, slowly. I turned away.

Susannah walked toward us. "It is time for me to return to the farm at Nazareth. I would rather walk than take the horse, though Brother Seidel has offered it. *Sehr gut,* he is." Her mouth broke into the familiar wide smile, and I knew she would run part of the way, sometimes stopping to see if the birds had left us any remaining berries.

I took her hand. "Be well, my dear friend." Somehow the terrible things that had happened to her had seemed to drift away in the smoke of her cooking fires. Her childlike faith was so close to what I earnestly tried to take into my heart. With a sudden rush I turned to Brother Seidel. "Perhaps you can take a horse from our stable, and my husband could return on it when he comes back to the farm."

"That makes good sense, Sister Krause." He mounted, and pulling on the reins, he began to make his way to our barn.

The small Indian child slept for many hours, and when she finally awoke I watched her slip quietly from her pallet and move silently toward the open door. I moved quickly to touch her arm; she stopped, and looked at me in fear. If only I could speak her language! Then I remembered the Delaware word for water. *"mbey?"* She stood for some seconds, her black eyes on my face, her lips pressed together. Again I said, *"mbey?"* and carried a mug to the large container of water. She stood still, not moving arms or legs nor changing her expression. I held out the mug and she reached up to take it. Then Matthaeus hiccupped and laughed aloud. "Baby," I said and then remembered, *"aminenz."* Her lips relaxed but did not turn up at the corners. I reached down to lift Matthaeus, his legs kicking, his babble loud in the room, and put him on the floor before her. She bent her small frame and, murmuring in her own language, she sat in front of him, sipping her water from time to time and looking intently at his face, which broke into a smile that showed his two white little teeth. He handed her his bone toy. Could it be that these two, one white and the other brown, carried our Lamb in their hearts in a way I had not yet learned to do?

I was so intent in my watching that I did not hear footsteps behind me, but when I felt the familiar, warm hand caress my neck, I turned to see his beloved face, tired now and still bruised above his eye. Without speaking I reached up to touch his bruise and he flinched.

"Oh, my dear, I am so sorry."

"No, Christina, your touch could never hurt me," he smiled. I had to catch my breath. Never, never did his smile fail to bring a weakness to my legs. He enfolded me, and I felt my body next to his in the perfect fit I had come to know so well.

"It took you so long to come up to the farm. Was there much to tell them at Nazareth? Or was it that you were too weak?"

"I never expected to be out in the forest so long. In my haste to look for the child, I didn't think ahead to carry arms for hunting. It did not occur to me that I might be out there for several days. There is not much in the woods to eat now. Even that rain was not enough to help the drought."

"My poor husband."

"I thought I knew the woods well, but the dark confused me, and I must have traveled in circles. I confess I felt frightened, for although I thought I knew this part of the woods, the darkness was so . . . how can I say it?"

"Yes, yes, I think I know."

"Darkness can be a place of fear. I was so caught up in it, so surrounded, and separate from anything that I knew. I could not see my own foot, my own hand. When I stopped to try to get my bearings, the words of Scripture came to me, Christina. *Even the darkness is not dark to thee, and the night as bright as day.*"

The Psalms had always been a part of Matthew, as though written on his heart.

"I felt the bark of a tree and decided to lie down at its base until daybreak. I said those words over and over, and it seemed then the dark was no longer separate and frightening but more like a part of me. I grew unafraid." I looked up at my tall husband, and saw him smile a little. I felt his calm nature, his strong reliance on our Lamb. "The morning fog made my way as difficult as the night's darkness, but I tried to walk in a straight line—from tree to tree. I was making quite a crashing noise, that's why they heard me before I heard them and attacked me by throwing a stone—well placed," he said with a sardonic smile, touching the place over his eye, and continued. "Of course they thought I was a militiaman, but after they came closer, they saw I wore no uniform, and I was unarmed."

"Thank God you are unharmed."

"Our Saviour helps us in many ways, Christina. I do not doubt He was with me in the forest. He always is."

I was quiet, grateful that he was with me no matter how he got here.

He reached down to touch his son's head. Matthaeus rewarded him with a smile and a babble that could have almost been a sound for father, and I wondered how we would ever give him up to the nursery. The time was drawing near for me to wean him. The Indian girl seemed to retreat into herself when Matthew touched his son and sat staring at him.

"Do you remember me, little one?" he asked as he knelt beside her.

Her face searched his for some time, as though each feature—eyes, nose, mouth, needed to be taken into her memory. Then she smiled; her white teeth brilliant. She must have known it was this white man who helped them to safety, although we all must look so alike to her. Matthew touched her cheek with one finger and she giggled. My heart was full. How could I not believe, ever, that our Lamb looked out for us, that He would bring my husband home to me?

WE ALL GREW QUICKLY TO LOVE the Indian girl. Not knowing her Indian name, we called her Esther, for she, too, might help her people when she grew to womanhood. She and Matthaeus babbled happily together each day and she became a great help lifting him from the cradle, mashing vegetables for him to eat, and even feeding him when I was busy at the loom.

It was decided that the three Indians should stay with us until they were stronger. Within the silences of their passing amongst us, I noticed the kind eyes of the older man and that the quick-moving, tall Brave had become more robust even in the short days they were with us. One early morning as I drew the full bucket from the well, the stout Indian looked directly at me and said, "White man, tall man, your man?" And when I nodded in assent, he continued, "Good man, God man." I knew that he understood the bond between a man and a woman was as sacred as the one that held us together close to our God. The faded colors of his ragged blanket seemed to spread like a rainbow around my heart. When Brother Michler took out his violin and played in the evening, the instrument small in his large hands, the three Indians stood by the window, and even the youngest of them, tall as Matthew and of a restless spirit, seemed relaxed and calm.

The three Indians regained their strength quickly, their faces less wan, their eyes brighter. When it was time for the three to walk to Nazareth to join their fellow Indians, we gave one man a knife, and another, an ax.

We had no rifles to spare. The tall man paced outside, eager to join his brothers in Nazareth while the stocky Indian leaned against the outside wall, his face calm and impassive as it always seemed to be. My heart went out to these Indians, and I whispered a prayer for their survival, for I was not the innocent I had been when I stepped off the *Little Strength*, and knew the wilderness could hold terror as well as beauty.

The terrible heat had abated, and for several days full, gray clouds had sat above us with no wind. From far away, I could hear thunder. We stood in a circle, the four couples who worked this farm and mill at Friedensthal and the three Indian men we had befriended. Little Esther stood in the circle with us, her hands clasped in front of her white apron, her hair neatly braided in two thick plaits by Sister Mücke. The older Indian, Brother Michler's hat on his head, moved to the center of the circle and in the Delaware tongue said some words I did not understand, but then he held out his hand to the stocky Indian and was given a string of wampum. It was beaded mostly in white with diagonal strings of blue. He also held a piece of parchment. He handed these to Matthew who held them up for us to see. The parchment had drawn upon it a sun sign and waving lines like water. Matthew smiled and said, "Most of us cannot read your language yet, and you cannot read ours. But someday we will speak good words. We send you to your people knowing your God is with you as ours with us." I was sure they knew what he said to them. Not the words, but whatever flew between them, each to each, I was sure they understood.

The forest was still, as though waiting for the much needed rain to fall. We stood in silence, our small group looking intently at the three Indians who gazed back at us. Then a child's call of pure joy. Matthaeus had crawled to the open door and pulled himself up on the door frame. Standing on short, sturdy legs, he crowed with pleasure. Matthew stepped toward his son and swooping him into his arms, he said, "Little man, you stand!" The Sisters' treble laughter was joined by the lower sound of the men and even our Indian friends smiled. He stands, yes—and I felt great joy that my son had lived to this day, but also a pang of regret for I knew this was the beginning of our parting. He would join the other children in Bethlehem. Women would teach him the ways of our Lamb and then, God willing, if he lived, he would learn the ways of men too.

I could feel the restlessness of the two young warriors, but they looked at their older companion as though for a sign. He moved to where Esther stood and, cupping her face in his hand, he looked at her for a long moment. She stood very straight, not moving, her dark eyes steady. He spoke to her softly. She answered him. He reached into a pocket and brought out a red and white beaded wristband. She held out her thin arm and he tied the bracelet. He placed his right hand on her head and all the while she moved not a muscle, looking at him. He turned, nodded to his Indian companions, and began to walk to Nazareth. I moved to put my arm around her slight shoulders and could feel her trembling now. "Father?" I said.

She buried her head in my petticoat and cried. I would never know what the man was to her, but she must have loved him, felt safe with him. With new resolve I promised myself I would care for her and try to keep her near me. It began to rain.

CHAPTER NINETEEN

I dreamed I was back in Gelzhausen. The road that ran through our small hamlet was dusty, the ruts of wagon wheels deeply indented. There was no sound from my father's forge, yet I knew he was near because the flames crackled as though waiting to melt the iron he would thrust into their hungry blaze. I felt the heat. Watching myself and being myself as we do in dreams or in memory, I walked through the small house of my childhood, picking up a cup, running my hand over a coverlet. It was all very quiet at first, and then I heard the sound of our choir in Nazareth. Somewhere was the sound of an organ breathing, the squeak of air and the voices rising and falling in a hymn of praise. In my waking hours I loved the sound of the choir. But in my dream the notes became discordant, the harmony unlike any I had heard before. I felt a great need to see my father working or hear my mother's voice calling to me. I went to the window to look to the stream, hoping to see my mother walking up the hill, her head high as she whistled to the birds. But I saw no one. An eerie sense permeated the whole small dwelling. I looked out again at the road and saw a figure, small and dark in the distance. As I waited and the figure took on a form, I saw it was the woman who had danced her unhappy way through our town when I was a child. I had wondered then where she was going and why, though her song was merry, her face was so wretched. But in my dream, while I watched her, I became her, and my feet stumbled on the stones of our road. I tried to sing her song, but I did not know the words and their sounds were meaningless.

I awoke slowly, and for a brief moment I did not know where I was. A feeling of isolation and great sadness enveloped me even as I awoke. Then I heard the sound I had heard in my dream. A man's voice, but singing in a queer falsetto.

I slipped out of bed, pulling on my petticoat and jacket with haste, and ran barefooted down the stairs. I could see from the window that a stranger was walking in a circle singing to himself. He held one finger up in the air as he walked and stopping suddenly, said, "I hear the Indian. He is the SIN-dian. He is the SIN-dian."

Catherine Mücke came into the house from the back door with Rosina Michler at her heels. Rosina said, "Don't open the front door yet, Christina. It is Harlow, and we must decide what to do with him."

"I heard him even before I was fully awake. Who on earth is he?" Before she could answer me, the young man sang "The bridegroom comes. He comes with blood He comes in a flood of blood."

I could see more clearly as I rubbed the sleep from my eyes. The man was clean-shaven; his brown hair wild and curly at his neck, and his even features would have seemed almost handsome, had his mouth not been twisted, his teeth chewing on one side of his tongue. His shirt was torn at the shoulder, and he swung the end of a rope he had knotted at his waist.

Rosina whispered, "His name is Harlow. He is one of the Englishman who joined our ship at Cowes. He is a Single Brother."

Surprisingly, I had never noticed this man on the journey over. Perhaps at that time, his antics were less strange.

"Ding, ding, the brown men sing. Bringing death and blood to every living thing," the poor soul repeated.

Brother Michler approached him slowly with his hand extended.

"Now Harlow, come and sit with us. How about some water? You must be very hot."

"Hot, not. Hot, not." The man sang in his falsetto.

I took hold of Rosina Michler's arm, afraid, yet somehow fascinated by the scene before us. From behind the corner of the farmhouse, one of our Indian guests stepped forward, and seeing Harlow, suddenly stopped to stare.

"Blood," Harlow screamed. "You, you, blood man!"

The Indian moved no further. As though to pacify an angry dog, he stretched out his hand toward the strange white man. Harlow recoiled and screamed again his inhuman scream. The young Indian moved backward, very slowly, his back very straight, placing one foot behind the other until he turned the corner of the house, out of sight. Harlow continued to scream, but did not move from where he stood.

Matthaeus called from his small bed and, hurrying to reassure him, I picked up my child and held him close to my breast. The realization that this poor, demented soul could bring us danger came to me with a profound shiver. We all knew that he must not be allowed to wander into the woods where he might encounter any small group seeking revenge based on rumor, and lead them here with his babbling nonsense. Sister Catherine Mücke spoke to me in a whisper. "The Crists are at the mill, and your husband has taken Esther with him to get some flour there. I think the other men are in the barn."

I clutched little Matthaeus more closely, so he pushed against me with his little fists. O, God, help us. What if they found Matthew with the Indian child? I whispered to Catherine and Rosina. "I am going to go out to speak to the man. I think I can keep him here until one of you alerts the men in the barn and the other can run downstream to the mill to find my husband."

Catherine put her hand against her mouth in her familiar gesture. "Open the door slowly."

I did as she bade and walked over the threshold. I held out my hand in friendship. A smile came across Harlow's face. Again I noted what a handsome young man he would be, had he not intermittently twisted one side of his face in that clown-like gesture.

"Brother Harlow, I see you have come to visit us on this warm summer day. You are welcome."

"Oh, I know you. You are my Moravian Sister but I don't know your name. Your name is the same, and the same is your name." He laughed then, and despite the heat, I felt a shiver on my shoulders.

"My name is Sister Christina Krause. I think you are a friend of Dr. Meyer. Perhaps you have been looking for him here, but I believe him to be in Nazareth,"

"Dr. Meyer is a liar. Dr. Meyer is a liar. When I preached the word of the Lord he took my arm and slashed with a sword."

I tried to smile. "The doctor bleeds us all from time to time because we believe that some diseased blood makes us ill."

"There is only the blood of the Lamb. I drink His blood. I swim in the blood."

His words were such a confused version of the new liturgy that had come from Europe to Pennsylvania. Yet it did abound in images of our poor Lamb's blood. Somehow I knew this man had been carried away in his head to some strange place where I could not follow. Music, I thought. Music might help.

"Perhaps you would like to sit here on the bench. Would you like to sing with me?" "I sing unto the Lord." Harlow began to sing in a tenor voice. I realized that his voice was clear and sweet, and there was none of the strange falsetto he had affected earlier. His song was familiar. It was the *Old Hundredth* that Count Zinzendorf had written new words for.

'Lord of the harvest laborers send/ who willing are their lives to spend /in scorching heat and chilling cold/ to bring the heathen to the fold.'

The truth of these words came at this moment from the voice of a madman.

At the end of our hymn he leaned close to me and whispered in my ear, "Our Saviour has told me of evil spoken by the brown man. Because of the lie, Indians must die."

"Mr. Harlow, it is time to ring the bell for our singing service. Perhaps you would do this for me."

Harlow's smile lit his face. "I will knell the bell." And he ran to where our large bell was suspended from its wooden frame. As the clapper hit the metal and the notes pealed, I prayed O, keep us safe, Lord. Brother Johann Michler ran to us from the barn. Seeing Harlow, our Brother slowed his pace and, calmly, as though it was time for our singstunde, he motioned others to gather near. A strange group we must have made; I, shoeless, and my dear friends standing close trying to look as though nothing were amiss. Brother Michler raised his hand and began to say the Psalm.

'Behold how good it is and pleasant it is when brothers dwell in unity . . .' When the psalm was finished he put his hand on Harlow's shoulder, saying, "It is time to return to Nazareth. I will walk with you." "No, No, I will not go!" Harlow wrenched away and stood like a defiant child.

Hearing Matthaeus' call, I went into the farmhouse to gather him from his bed. On the other side of the wall, I could hear my friends earnestly telling Harlow that he needed to get back to Nazareth and that perhaps one of the Brothers would accompany him to Philadelphia in the next few days. Brother Michler's calm voice seemed to help Harlow to be less frantic. I knew he might be constrained in Philadelphia, but the safety of all of us depended on his not being near.

Stepping to the door, I could see Sister and Brother Crist walking swiftly from the woods toward us. Sister Ann Mary's breathing was labored for probably they had run most of the way. Brother Johann Crist began, "There is a dangerous situation." But before he could speak more, I said, "I trust all is well at the mill." And looking pointedly at Harlow, "We have a visitor here."

"I need some advice from you." Brother Crist turned to Brother and Sister Michler and motioned for them to come into the house. I closed the door. His strained face was wet with perspiration. "We got here as fast as we could. There has been a terrible attack. A whole family was murdered up near the swamp." He wiped his face with the back of his hand.

I felt sick and dizzy. I did not want to know how many were murdered. This news would spread though the area like a wild wind, and no matter who committed the terrible act, the Indians would be blamed. I needed no one to tell me that our people would bear the blame, for because we had so often helped our brown friends, it could bring down a wrath of fire and destruction. How I wished Matthew was standing beside me here! To lean against his strength would help me to bear whatever was to happen. As he worked with Esther at the mill, was he even aware of this latest news?

A rifle shot. I saw a man at the edge of the woods coming toward us. He was urging his horse very fast. He was a white man, dressed in breeches, stockings, and with a cocked hat on his head. He carried a rifle. Behind him rode another man on horseback, hatless, but wearing similar clothing. He carried a musket, and as he drew closer, I could see a long knife at his belt. Dismounting at the door, the man in the cocked hat said, "We come from Bucks County Court." He was short and stocky, with reddish hair and poor teeth. "This here's another deputy." Unshaven, filthy, his shoes caked with mud, the second man climbed from his horse and fingered his knife.

The stocky man spoke in accent of an untutored Pennsylvanian, "Justice of the Peace sent me. I am gonna serve you with papers. You got seen takin' in your harvest on the Sabbath. That's against the law."

We had worked on the Sabbath because the rain had prevented our cutting and taking in the wheat for many days. Then early on a

Sabbath morning, I saw a pale sun slanting through the windows of our meeting room. As we sang, water still dripped from the eaves into small puddles with an uneven beat. Matthew repeated the day's Watchword, this day from Jonah: *Do not fear, dear land but be joyful and comforted, for the Lord can also do great things.* With those words ringing in my head, I joined the others to garner our hard-earned treasure, throwing the last of it on our wagon by the light of lanterns. My hands still were sore with blisters and they burned again as I clasped them behind me.

The stocky man threw out his chest like a rooster. "I am a deputy. Name is Craig. I have papers. You come with us to Bucks County—probly, you'll go to jail."

Rudolph Crist towered over the man and, coming close to him, he rumbled, "Henry Antes is the Justice of the Peace—a friend to our people, and I have doubts he sent you. He has given us permission to harvest when the need is great."

I clutched Matthaeus to me. Brother John Michler said, "Any one of us could travel to the Bucks County Court House to straighten out this matter. I suggest we go immediately."

"Not so fast," the man with the knife snarled. "There's been a massacre—whole family—children too. The Injins did it."

At the word 'injin,' Harlow began to sing in a falsetto. "I come for the blood of the Lamb. I come to see the blood from the sword of righteousness."

"Who the hell is he?" Craig turned to look at Harlow who had begun to twirl.

"Stop, you crazy loon," the deputy reached for his knife.

"No need to worry, gentlemen." Brother Crist rumbled, "Mr. Harlow becomes agitated, as you can see.

"The Indian child is not mild," sang Harlow.

Craig moved toward him, "What's that you say about an Injin child?" John Michler spoke directly to Craig.

"Mr. Harlow speaks in nonsense rhyme when he is worried."

Turning to Harlow, Craig barked, "Tell me, mister, have you seen an Injin child?"

"Dressed like a white, she will bite. Her brothers kill. Look in the mill."

My jacket was wet, my bladder so full I was afraid I could not contain my water. Matthaeus squirmed to be free, and when I held him fast, he began to whimper.

"Shut up that brat." The deputy swung his musket in my direction.

Brother Rudolph clenched his large hands into fists but spoke quietly. "This man is deranged. He does not know truth from lies." He swung his arm from one side to another. "Go ahead and search our premises."

"Riddle, riddle, where is a pretty flower not flower?" Harlow began to laugh in his high voice. "In the mill," he screeched then. "In the mill."

Rosina took hold of Harlow's arm, and I stepped forward to do the same. Rosina said, "Mr. Harlow. Let me give you some cider. We have had a delicious crop this year," and she tried to lead him the few feet toward the house.

"Stop, Lady." Craig wrenched Harlow from her grasp and pushed me aside. I stumbled, holding my babe who began to howl.

"Shut him up!" He was so close to me I could smell his unwashed body. He reached up to scratch his head. "Goddamned fleas."

Brother Rudolph said, "This has gone far enough. We will not allow you to hurt our women. Come, let us go to the courthouse."

"We're goin' to the mill. We know where it is." And, grasping me by the arm, "Leave that brat here. You go with us."

Brother Rudolph spoke in a menacing tone as he reached for Craig's arm. "Do not touch her!"

I was shaking, but I handed my screaming babe to Rosina Michler. "I will go to the mill, and my husband will show you he is alone there." I hoped Matthew had received news of the attack from Rudolph Crist and would be ready for the men. I wanted them away from my babe.

"No, Sister Krause, I will go to the mill," Brother Rudolph said. The words were hardly out of his mouth when the man with a knife hit the side of his face. Blood splattered and Rudolph stepped back in shock and pain. Brother Johann moved to the soldier when Craig raised his own rifle and yelled, "I will shoot any one of you who moves." And to Rosina, "Shut that brat up!" Turning to his companion, he said, "We'll walk quieter that way."

I was allowed to go into the farmhouse to get my shoes, and I hastily relieved myself, fearful that the chamberpot would tip under my shaking hands. My babe had calmed down while Rosina amused him and seemed not to notice I was leaving as I followed the two who had tethered their horses near the house. It was a short trek through the woods to the stream and down to the mill. Birds chattered around us, but the familiar path seemed narrower as the men's boots trod the brush behind me. Once I slipped and Craig prodded me with his rifle . . .

The stone mill loomed before us and at the door stood my husband. His body relaxed against the door frame, legs crossed, I would have thought he was waiting for any friendly visitor. "Perhaps you men have come for flour. It is very good this year." Craig aimed his rifle at Matthew. The other man strode quickly up the stone steps.

"My husband, these men mistakenly think we have an Indian child . . . "

"Shut up, woman. I'll do the talking." Craig thrust out his jaw.

"We come to find Injins. We know they massacred another family yesterday." He shoved Matthew aside. The single downstairs room was swept clean, containing only a table and two chairs. The sound of the millrace was thundering past one window and sounded louder than when we were outside, the splash and tumble resounding against the stone walls.

"Move them bags over there in the corner."

Matthew walked to where a large pile of filled flour bags was heaped. Craig's companion sprang forward, slamming his long knife into the bags. If Esther were hidden there, surely she would cry out.

"Just drag them one by one." Then, turning to the soldier, Craig said, "Only place an Injin brat could hide would be behind them bags unless maybe upstairs. He moved toward me. Taking a strand of my hair that had escaped my cap, he snarled, "Don't you move little lady. I'd as soon shoot ya as look at ya." He stank of sweat and horseflesh, his breath of rotten teeth. I turned my head away but he took my jaw in his hand and squeezed. He clumped up the stairs. I could hear him moving around, his boots noisy on the floorboards. Matthew continued moving the heavy bags as though he had all day to do so, and I wondered if he were stalling for time. What if little Esther was hiding somewhere behind them?

"We don't have all day." Craig reached to scratch his head. "Goddamned fleas. Get down here, Hank. Them Injins prob'ly run into the woods."

The man came down the stairs as Matthew moved the last of the bags. I noticed a stone unevenly placed against the wall, but its shape and color were like the others and I looked away, praying neither man would see where my eye had rested.

Matthew had not spoken. He had not flinched when the deputy

threatened me, but I could see he was gritting his teeth by the way his jaw was set. Now he turned. "There is no one you want here."

"Let's get the hell out of here, Craig. We got to take them foreigners in Nazareth to Bucks County, and I need a drink." "He dug his fingernails into his neck, bringing blood, looked at his hand and then wiped it on his filthy pants. "Goddamned fleas."

Both men walked out, saying nothing to us. The door swung on metal hinges in counterpoint to the millwheel while we stood in fear and hope that they had really left us. I could not move and was afraid to call out in case the men had not traveled afar, but Matthew ran to the small, irregular stone and put his hands around the top to pull it toward him. It scratched against the floorboards. I felt a terrible panic rise in me as I made myself look at a small opening onto the millrace. Matthew sank to his knees. "Christina, oh my God. Where is the child?" I moved to him and saw a narrow ledge large enough for a small child to perch over the rushing water. It was empty. We looked out over the water, the wheel tumbled and water spalshed, but there was no little girl in sight.

CHAPTER TWENTY

Susannah Partsch

Way high in the sky I saw the bird. I thought it was a black speck in my eye, but when it dipped down over the apple trees, I saw it was a hawk. It was gliding on the air, its wings outstretched. If I was changed to a bird I would glide on the wind and be a black speck in the blue sky. I would fly over the apple trees already, *Ja?* And watch the trees grow their tiny leaves in the spring and their fruit in the autumn. The green apples hold fast to their stems. By the time the winds blow hard from the west, the fruit will be red and juicy. I will gather it in my apron, my Sisters around me. Here in Nazareth's orchard I can feel my Saviour near, as He guides the birds in the sky and touches the apples to make them grow rosy for us. The Brethren remind me we must be grateful for His bloody wounds, but I am grateful for His love and care of all of us here in America. I sometimes want to bend and curtsy to every apple tree that grows.

I cannot curtsy very low now, for another babe is growing under my heart.

Maybe it will be yet another girl. My Elizabeth and little Anna Benigna are in Bethlehem. I was so proud of Elizabeth when she became part of the Little Girls' Choir. She wanted to smile, but she kept her face very still when Sister Susannah Nitschmann tied the red ribbon of her cap. She looked over at her papa, and he nodded to her. Then she smiled. I was older yet when I was taken from my mother. Before then I was always afraid. I was always ready to run. But now I am blessed because I know my little ones are cared for by the kind Sisters who read and write better than I do. Of course our Anna Benigna is too small yet for the Girls' Choir. *Ach*, she left Nazareth only a week ago. When her papa lifted her up to the wagon bound for Bethlehem and Sister Nitschmann took her on her lap, I waved at the wagon for a long time. Even when I could not see it anymore. At night before I pull up my coverlet, I clasp my hands and pray to my Lamb that He looks out for my daughters. And even though I can't see them very often, I know He is watching them for me.

Last week I walked up the hill to the farm at Friedensthal to help a bit with some sewing. I sat most of the afternoon with Christina. It was very hot, but we drank cool water and laughed a bit. She did not tell me really, but I know she is not ready to send her babe Matthaeus off to the nursery in Bethlehem with his sister. She says she has not yet weaned him. It was hard for her to let her Anna go, and I think she does not want Matthaeus to leave her either. When I was with Christina the Indian child came out to watch us sew in front of the house. She is ever so much better than she was when Brother Matthew first found her. Her little arms are rounded now, and she smiles. They are calling her Esther. Young as she is, she learns our language quickly, and Christina told me she helped with little Mattaeus when the Brothers and Sisters worked so hard on the Sabbath to get in their grain.

Now, out here in the orchard, I think about all the people I have come to love here; my Sisters who teach me about our Lamb, and my George. Every day I walk out to our orchard to see to the fruit, and then I go to look at the herbs. Right now I can see a few seeds left from the elecampane plant. They feel hard as pebbles in my hand. The ground here is still very wet from all the rain we had, and the long root of the plant comes up easily. Sister Susannah Nitschmann ground it up and gave it to the Indian woman when she bore her dead babe and already she has more life. I have seen her walk to the place where we buried her little one, and so still she stands. She does not weep. I cannot speak her language, but I can tell she cannot make up her mind to stay with us in Nazareth. When we sing, she stands at the edge like a tall thin bird that will not yet put its foot in the water. I wish I could tell her how our Lamb loves us all, but it is God who must let her heart know this.

I stand here with the herbs growing all around my feet, and all I can hear is a little wind. But now our bell rings over and over again. The noise sounds loud. I don't like it. It sounds like danger, but I can't think what the danger is. *Ach Gott*, I know I must run to the *Gemeinhaus*, but I cannot run as fast with this new babe in my belly. Now I see Brother John Michler jumping down from his horse and running up the steps of our *Gemeinhaus*. His voice reaches me now I am closer. He is panting and saying very loud, "A whole family has been massacred at a homestead near Friedensthal. Men are out for blood." I hear, "Bucks County . . . the mill . . . Sister Krause . . . " He goes in the house and the door slams.

I am out of breath, and it hurts in my chest. Brother Michler did not tether his horse and it stomps by the front of the house. I slide past it and open the heavy wooden door.

Brother Michler looks very frightened, and I can tell it is hard for him to talk, but he pushes out his words.

"Not sure who killed the family, but we got the news from a fellow named Craig."

"Wait a minute, my brother. Tell us slowly," Brother Schropp says.

"This Craig fellow says he is from Bucks County and rode up to the farm with another fellow. He was in a terrible temper, pointing his rifle and yelling about how we were Indian lovers and must know which Indians killed this family."

Brother Seidel hands Brother Michler a mug of water, and says, "Take it slowly, now."

"This Craig fellow heard we had Indians at the farm." He takes a drink and hangs his head. "Poor Harlow was there and told Craig and his deputy to search the mill for the little Indian girl. Craig says he will find the child and use her for bait to catch more Indians."

He sinks to a bench. "That's how it all got started. Harlow is completely delusional again." And then, as though speaking to himself, said, "I think we will need to take this poor fellow to Philadelphia. He has fits, it seems." Then he looks at Brother Schropp. "This Craig was out for blood."

"So you're saying that these two men are now looking for the Indian child." Brother Schropp's voice was always calm.

"Matthew had taken the child with him to the mill, and Harlow let on so that Craig and the other one have gone to find them. Oh, God." Brother Michler wipes his streaming face again.

I am not afraid most of the time here in Nazareth, but when Brother Michler looks frightened, I am, too. He is a brave man. Now he looks as though he might weep. My babe moves in my belly and I lean against the wall. Did Matthew hide the child? I know the haste of the stream up there. It rushes in such a hurry, pushing the millwheel and moving past the grasses that grow like green hair on the sides of the stream. Where could he hide her? Maybe behind the flour bags or maybe even in one of them. It would be hard for her not to sneeze. *Ach, poor little thing.*

Brother Michler takes a big breath and says, "Now the two have taken Sister Krause to the mill."

"So she was at the farm with you?" Matthew Schropp says.

"Yes, she was with us and Matthew had gone with the child. The damned question is that we don't know if Matthew knows they're coming, and if he doesn't, he and the child are in the worst kind of danger."

Ach mein Gott, I have to grasp the window ledge, and I think I am going to be very sick. I untie the ribbons on my cap and try to take in air slowly, as if I am laboring with a birth. "Where is baby Matthaeus?" I find myself asking.

"Sister Crist and the others have him safely with them."

I try to let my breath out as slowly as I take it in. I know all of us at Nazareth had decided to send our children to Bethlehem where they would be safer. But where is it really safe in this place? We hear the French and English are starting to fire at each other, especially around us in the woods. And there are some men who fight for anyone who pays them. Here in Nazareth we have our stone *Gemeinhaus,* but the forest is so close and so dense. At the farm at Friedensthal there is no protection from wild white men or even savage Indians who do not know of our Saviour. I feel very hot and the room seems to spin. Are my little daughters safer in the stone house in Bethlehem? Do we need to build a high wall around us all?

Matthew Schropp is standing in front of Brother Michler. He puts his hand on Michler's shoulder. "Listen, my brother, now, right now we need to remember why we are here. We must remember that our Saviour has brought us to this place to bring the light of His love. Were we afraid of the storms at sea? Are we afraid in this wilderness? Of course we are. Unless, my Brethren, unless we remember He is here. He is with us. He is with Brother and Sister Krause and with the Indian child."

It is very quiet in the room. I am still trying to breathe in and out slowly but I can feel my heart has stopped its wild beating.

CHAPTER TWENTY-ONE

Christina Barbara Krause

Slippery wet, the stone ledge was empty. The water rushed past and the sound pounded in my head as I stared into the millrace, up to the trees, downstream where the river made a sharp curve. I had stared like this when my father disappeared, but then it was an empty road, dusty and silent, the sun touching the bumps and ruts. Now, all was noise. I drew in my head and placed my hands over my ears. My pulse beat too fast and I felt a scream start in the pit of my belly and rise to my throat like vomit. The stone floor was cold under my knees, the ache of an old wound making me move to rise.

"I am going to walk by the water." Matthew's voice was strangled.

I struggled to my feet and picked up an empty grain sack to hold against my breast. The dry smell seemed devoid of health, an empty pod, the seed flown. I could not bear to think little Esther had been caught in the millrace. That Matthew would find her body with her clothes caught on a jutting rock, her dark hair whipped around her face.

"I see nothing here," he called. No one, nothing. He could not bear the thought of her drowned either. Over the water's roar I barely heard him. "I will walk downstream, along the river's edge. Maybe she could have escaped and run downstream."

What can I do, I thought, when my body will not obey me, will not move toward the door, when my mind will not stop its terrifying visions of water and death? In my mind I heard the Count's voice. "My children, He is with you. He will not leave you." I should feel this now. I should imagine that small seed of faith, but God knows it needs a nurturing heart, and visions of warmth and light. At that moment, I had none.

I walked down the stone steps and moved slowly to the edge of the rushing stream. The sound of water has always been my solace. Now it brought only panic. I sank down into the moist soil and knelt; the wet veil of water from the wheel bathed my face and mixed with my tears. I did so love this Indian child. I could feel her silky, straight hair as I wove it into plaits every morning. Oh, my God, how could you take her from us when we have just saved her?

Somehow I had the strength to rise and walk away from the water. I climbed a slight rise to walk around the mill. Then, circling close to the water again, I looked up to see the opening in the wall and the small stone ledge. There was almost a stairway—an odd stairway, large enough only for the footsteps of a small child. Could a sure-footed child step down those steps? Oh, my Saviour, if you can hear my prayer, bring her back. If we could again see her dark eyes squint when she struggled with our language. If only I could again plait her heavy hair. For that I would wake every morning before the sun, and pray more diligently that I even had before to take this burden of unbelief from me. The image of the sun-filled *Saal* in Herrnhaag came to me then. I did have moments when I was so sure. I did have those times when His presence encircled me in warmth and light. But why were those times so brief? Why did my faith become a wisp that disappeared when I reached out to touch it? Do my dearest Brothers and Sisters ever feel as I do? Does my beloved husband? I squeezed my eyes, as I had when a child, to better form my prayer. Colors danced before me against the darkness. The opening them wide, my glance fell upon the heavy bushes that grew near the water, their branches moving with the flow. One thick branch seemed pulled down and was almost still. I moved carefully toward the bushes, watching the movement as I drew closer. "Esther, are you there?" I did not call loudly, but I needed to be heard over the sound of the water. A thin arm reached up. I bent and grasped it, slippery and wet and so loved, and pulled the child into my arms. Back and forth we rocked at the water's edge as I held her small, wet body close to my jacket.

This is how we were when Matthew came upon us. He knelt and put his arms around us and we began to laugh and cry all at once. Matthew helped me to my feet while Esther clung to me like a burr. Huddled together we walked to the mill, up the stone steps. Again the sound of tumbling water bounced from wall to wall, but now it seemed the sound of joy, and I was filled with grace.

I do not remember walking back to the farm. I cannot remember who peeled off our wet clothes or held mugs for us to drink from, but I understood with clarity the message I had received and the way in which I was to act upon it. In this vast and forested wilderness, Esther had saved herself by holding fast to the hand of the Lamb, and it was she who had shown me His ways. It was not I who protected my children, it was our dear Lamb. The realization overwhelmed me as though I had held my breath until pain had forced me to expel the air in a long sigh. This was a hard lesson for me. I must give them up in faith to the loving teachers in Bethlehem, as I had done with our dear Anna. Safer, yes. Safer than here at our farm outpost. With an ache in my heart I also knew my children should be with teachers whose faith glowed more brightly than mine.

I walked slowly to our herb garden, lush with lavender and fennel. I rubbed a lacy bit of dill between my fingers. If only He was as real to me as these growing things that I know are touched by His hand. If only His face was a steady and unchanging presence in my mind. I touched the sharp edges of rue at my feet and wondered: Must there always be sacrifice to gain faith?

I suppose I was comforted when Matthew reached to hold me. He looked into my eyes and then drew me close against his shirt; the smell of new-mown hay and the odor of his sweat so familiar and loved seemed to give me courage to tell him I knew we had to let our children go. I did not have to tell him the ache I felt in knowing others would hear our babe's merry laughter in the early dawn. I think he knew. Smoothing my hair with his hand, he murmured, "Not so far way. Not so far away for them to be safe and sound in the Sisters' House."

I could feel summer coming to a close when we took Esther and Matthaeus to Nazareth to board the wagon. Susannah stood close to me, smiled and squeezed my hand as Matthew lifted each child tenderly onto the seat next to Brother Opitz. As the wagon moved forward, Matthaeus did not turn around, but we heard his laugh as he bounced up and down on the seat. Esther waved to us until the wagon was taken into the forest. Dry leaves of late summer whispered above our heads. One crimson maple leaf floated to my feet. It hurt my heart, but I bit my lip and did not cry out.

CHAPTER TWENTY-TWO

A thin sheet of ice trapped the water in my bucket. I bent to run one finger over the smooth surface and traced the frost designs, not feeling the cold until with a soft crack the ice broke and water burbled from below. I put my finger in my mouth to warm it and, without warning, tears brimmed in my eyes and ran down my cheeks. I sat then and heard my sobs as though they belonged to another and cried for the broken ice, for my broken heart, for my disappointment. For nothing seemed to be what I had imagined it to be when we were given the chance to build a farm here in the upper places near the rushing stream. Why had I imagined we would have our dear children nestled close to us? I knew I had agreed to let others teach them the ways of our Lamb—from the beginning I knew this was the way of the traveling Moravians, and yet, when I pledged to journey the long miles with Matthew, none of the future was real to me. I was like a blind kitten that sucked only from its mother's teat, too content to open my eyes to the world. Surrounded by Sisters who cared for me and cradled in the arms of my beloved husband, I was so sure that true faith had taken root in my heart, giving me the strength to face the hardships of life in this wilderness and the separation from my children. How well I could see Anna's blue eyes, solemn as she took her leave from me, and just this past autumn Esther's turn of head and wave and little Matthaeus' carefree goodbye. All clear in my mind. And I smiled that day as mothers must learn to do, I suppose.

I stood, lifted the bucket and began to make my way into the farmhouse. No one would know my moment of regret. No one would see a tear on my cheek, for somehow the goodness of the Lord would come back to me, I thought, as the words of the Psalmist comforted my heart 'Be strong and He shall comfort your heart; wait patiently for the Lord.' Indeed I would. I opened the heavy door and walked inside.

The cold weather always seemed to bring with it an eagerness to perform our tasks with renewed vigor, and the work brought a sense of calm to me. The more we women joined the men in heavy labor—often lifting logs into a pile as they swung their axes, my dissonant thoughts had no place. We sang as we worked, stopping to catch our breath and to laugh at one another, the snowflakes swirling around us like smoke. One winter day Anna Maria Schropp came up to our farm from Nazareth to spin with me. As the yarn slid over my hand, she began to sing, *'And I shall clothe my family in scarlet,'* to a tune all her own. The whir of my wheel seemed to join hers as we pedaled in tandem.

Winter was still upon us, but the days had begun to lengthen, and there were great plans to visit Bethlehem to attend the meeting of our Pennsylvania Moravian Indians and those from the far north country of Greenland who had journeyed with our missionaries over the past weeks. All of us at the farm were to join the Nazareth group and, together, we were going to walk on to Bethlehem. There, ovens had been fired for days for newly baked bread while, outdoors, fowl turned on a large spit. Hearing of the planned festivities I could almost smell the yeasty bread and sugary cookies. Susannah told me with sparkling eyes that she was going early to oversee the cooking. I could hardly sleep the few nights before we left, for I knew we would see our children again and, although I said nothing about my excitement, my husband watched me as plans were being made and smiled to see my contained happiness.

A gathering such as this was always merry. No matter that our hands were scratched and dry, our nails broken or cut close to the quick. No matter the pinching shoes still damp from the heavy snow. The heartfelt hugs among the women and the warm greetings full of the excitement of seeing one another permeated the clearing outside the *Gemeinhaus*. I spotted Susannah walking toward me, her arms outstretched. "So, at last here you are." I quickened my step toward her. "I hope you are hungry, *mein freund*," she teased. "I made sure to pull out all the fowl feathers and put in the herbs we grew last summer—*ach*, you can smell it from here." I couldn't help but laugh aloud at her greeting. Susannah's marriage to George and the birth of her girls had filled out her face as well as her figure and I wondered if anything would frighten her again, for she was a different woman from the young girl with haunted eyes I had known when we first made our journey together. And she had let go of her daughters with a grace I dearly wished I could have. Was it only the firm belief that they were safer in the larger settlement of Bethlehem? Or was it that she had felt the hand of Him who knows what is best for us without reaching for it, as I seemed to do? She moved away from me, touching a shoulder, laughing at her own humor, leaving a trail of smiles.

"Love has made her grow and prosper." Anna Maria's heart-shaped face was serious with the thought. "I do not know it, but sometimes I think she has suffered . . . and yet she takes her delight in the things He has made for us. Have you ever watched as she picks apples?"

I said only, "Yes," but my mind raced from picture to picture, each frame with Susannah performing a simple task. Reaching up to a fruited branch and pulling it with her strong right arm while she twisted a stem with her deft left hand and dropped the treasure into her pocket; rolling bread dough, the sleeves of her shift rolled at her elbows, she inhaled the odor of yeast and salt and exhaled with a sound of pure pleasure. I had watched her toss one of her daughters high in the air, the child screeching in delight, knowing her mother would catch her to her breast and twirl around in merriment.

"Yes," I said again to Anna Maria, as we walked to the Women's entrance to the chapel where we could hear the trumpets practicing, their high notes contrasting with the trombones being played from around the corner of the stone building.

Once we were seated, the men on one side and the women on the other, the murmurs abated and the sound of the organ bellows whispered its breath against the stone walls. There was a scuffling at the back of the building, and we turned as one to watch the beginning of the procession. The littlest children came first, the girls dressed in white, their red ribbons tied under their tender chins, the boys with dark breeches, their shirts tucked in and the vests buttoned. I spotted Matthaeus right away because he was not looking straight ahead as were the other boys but craned his neck from side to side looking at the crowd of adults. He saw his father and began to wave until the Schropps' boy in back of him firmly took his hand with a look of warning. Esther walked in front of Anna, her dark eyes darting from face to face, her mouth a straight line until she saw me nod, and then I saw a flash of her white teeth. Anna, a little taller than the other girls, seemed to almost float, and I realized with some surprise that she had reached that lovely stage of life just before the beginning of womanhood. How quickly we change, I thought. One moment a child, then with a rush come the changes and then, a woman. Would her teachers soon tell her to be careful with her desires, to pace her dreams? Would I want them to? Across the aisle, Matthew looked toward the front of the room. I thought to myself how often his face was turned from me, his eyes looking ahead to some distant place. I wished he would turn, but he did not.

Before me were our missionaries, who had gathered here from the far north and south of the globe. Brother Grabenstein had come with Arawaks from South America, and Brother Stach was there, of course, with his Greenlanders; they dressed in their native costumes in order to show their white and brown brethren the beauty of their dress. The Greenlanders were shorter than Europeans and the natives we had befriended here, their stocky bodies made even more so by the layers of polar bear furs and sealskin. When it was time for the service that had been planned, the Greenlanders were the central figures of the group. The Arawaks sat next to them and, in a circle around them, were Delawares, Mohicans, Wampanoags and Negroes. In the outer circle were seated the men, women and children of our congregations here in Bethlehem and Nazareth.

While Brother Anders read our lesson for the day, I found my mind wandering to the far north where our missionaries had taken residence for ten years or more. Their lot in life must have been so difficult compared even with ours here in the New World. They had written of darkness that lasted for months, lashing wind and drifting snow that piled against their meager wooden house. The correspondences from our missionaries that were read to outposts all over the globe told of their failure to bring the good news of our Gospel to the Greenlanders and those of Lapland. How, the Natives asked, could we believe in a God who does not show the ways of survival to those teachers who have come to this harsh place? Then, in a strange way known only by our Saviour, one Native who had been traveling in Denmark brought smallpox into the settlement. Our missionaries, free from the disease by the grace of God, wiped the pus from the wounds on their diseased bodies, gave drink to those who thirsted and held those who were dying their ghastly death. The unfounded anger at our Brethren melted like the snow in fire, and little by little the Natives began to listen to the story of how our Saviour loved them. The flashing aurora, shining and quivering against the northland darkness, must have been a sign of hope to our Brethrens' hearts, I thought.

There was a great deal of curious touching and nodding by our American Indians as they tried to communicate with the Greenlanders; and watching as I did from the sidelines, I was struck at the similarity between our brown brethren here and those from the far north. The copper skin stretched tight over their high cheekbones and the lack of hair on the smooth, flat faces of the men. The women were very diffident, standing together in a circle near the rear of the room. Susannah, carrying a tray of hot coffee, approached them with a smile and in clear sign language urged them to take a mug. Shy smiles then showed small teeth and I felt, more than saw, a sparkle, a glint of friendship in their eyes. Our women began to busy themselves with the serving of the meal outdoors at long tables that had been set up after the service and, despite the winter day, we were warmed with the food and with the fellowship of each other's love.

I felt a touch at my shoulder, and Sister Susannah Nitschmann bent to speak to me. "Sister Krause, you know, of course, of our mission at Gnadenhütten just west of here in the Blue Mountains?" She was smiling as she said this, as though she was about to tell a special secret.

"Yes, I have heard much of the mission and the success of our Brethren there. I hear many brown brothers have come to our Saviour and make their homes in a circle around the wooden *Gemeinhaus*." She smiled more broadly then and indicated I should walk a bit with her. I arose and we made our way past groups of women who had begun to clear the plates or were chatting quietly amongst themselves. "Sister Krause, as you know, we choose certain persons to move about here in America as the need arises to serve our Saviour. Several couples are already at Gnadenhütten in the Blue Mountains. You remember the Sensemanns and the Anders who have just had another baby?"

I knew I should answer right away, for I was very familiar with Johann Sensemann and his dear wife, and of course the Anders had been serving in Nazareth with George and Susannah Partsch. A cold feeling caused me to shiver and to withhold my answer.

Sister Nitschmann continued, "Your good husband is well versed in the word of the Lord, we have noticed, and it may be at some time he might want to act as acolyte to a small group. You, of course, have been such a valuable member of the farm community at Friedensthal." She stopped walking and looked into my eyes. What was she asking?

Was she saying that we might be chosen to join the new settlement at Gnadenhütten?

"Sister Nitschmann, I have heard nothing of this from my husband. Are you considering us to travel and begin a new settlement?"

"No, my dear. Not at the moment." She hesitated then and I was compelled to look into her eyes for a clue, but she said, "I am only asking that you think about this move. Brother Seidel is speaking to your husband about this possibility and it seemed prudent for me to ask how you would feel about traveling the twenty miles west to the settlement."

"I am honored, of course, that you would consider us in such an endeavor. I have become so settled at Friedensthal, and our children are near here in school in Bethlehem…it seems far away." I felt my voice tremble and I wished for strength. I tried to imagine what it would be like to pack our belongings and begin the twenty mile trek to Gnadenhütten but no pictures came to my mind. A sense of emptiness covered me as a shroud, cold and gray. I shivered and could not speak.

Sister Nitschmann broke into my thoughts, "I only ask this to let you know we will need more of our Brethren there. It may not be the right time for you to travel or it may be that other plans are in the making for you and Brother Krause." She looked directly at me, the lines around her mouth deepening as she smiled. "Each of us has a certain talent. We must use these talents to do our Saviour's work, which is to bring the glorious news of His life and resurrection." Suddenly serious, she nodded her head and with a pat on my hand, she left me. There was a burst of laughter from my Brethren nearby, carried on the wind to the surrounding hills. "I look to the hills from whence cometh my help," I said aloud, as I saw the outlines of the earth rising and dipping against the afternoon sky. Could I leave the farm at Friedensthal and make a home once again in deeply forested hills? Land had been cleared here in Bethlehem and in Nazareth.

Acres and acres of wet, black earth were turned ever so slowly by our ploughs, and the sweat of our labor became part of the seed and the harvest. Could I leave this place and start again?

CHAPTER TWENTY-THREE

Susannah Partsch, 1750s

I heard the cry of a jay today already. I know it will soon be spring. The leaves are not yet budding and the cardinals not yet calling their mating song, so it is early yet. I am happy to be here weaving at Nazareth instead of sorting seed with my Sisters. I can sit here on the bench and let my thoughts go wherever they want. I know a new babe has made its way from the warmth of our Saviour's side wound to its new home in my belly even though I cannot yet feel its flutterings. A girl again, I think. When I told George that another babe was coming to our fold, he had a smile in his brown eyes and said, "But I barely looked at you, my wife." And I said, "*Ja*, and I barely looked at you." And we locked our little fingers the way we always do.

I feel a peace in my heart here yet with my family of Brethren and Sisters. The kindness of my husband makes me feel safe and strong. He is a man who does everything so quick. The loaves fly onto the shelves, the meat into the pot. But when he touches me he is slow and gentle. I have not yet learned to use the shuttle as quick as my husband. He was a weaver in Silesia, but when he joined the Brethren, they badly needed a baker and cook so he said he would do that work for the community. He still fills in as weaver when they need him. He taught me because I wanted to learn. The way the fabric grows under my hands, I love. I remember how the bread used to rise and grow when I was a little girl in Büdingen, after my mother and I had kneaded it. *Ach*, the bread had such a good smell, and the flax I work with now has none, but the indigo blue and pale white dance before my eyes and make me happy. With my mother so long ago this happiness sometimes I felt.

When our whole congregation was together just this past winter with our brown Brethren and missionaries from far away, the red and white blankets of our Indian Brethren moved in and around the capes and suits of those of us from the Old World. It made a pattern. I would like to copy it on the loom. It was such a *gut* day cooking for my brothers and sisters. I could hardly keep my happiness from spilling over into the ducks and geese I was serving! The hot currant drink kept us warm even when the wind blew. There was not a scrap of food left over and the birds squawked and beeped to eat what had been spilled. Brother Greening came for third helpings, and the littlest birds followed him as he held his plate walking, talking and greeting everyone.

I sliced bread and spooned pumpkin and watched this gathering of all our Brothers and Sisters. Our Saviour must be so happy to see us together—the sound of the different languages, the tall and short, young and old. I can remember how our brown Brethren stroked the fur on the costumes of those who had come from so far away. I reached out to touch one's coat. The fur was thick. One Indian gave us two pair of boots. I even got to try one on, but the boots were very small, and I could not give my toes even one wiggle. Anna Maria Schropp could put her whole foot in. For a few minutes I was a little angry yet at the size of my feet; but then I remembered how they carried me the many miles back and forth from Bethlehem and Nazareth. Then I thanked My Saviour for giving me feet that were so strong.

My husband and I had not seen our daughters since they left Nazareth for Bethlehem last autumn, and I loved watching them that winter day as they ran and played with the other children. I knew they were happy to be in the nursery and school here. Elizabeth's face was rosy from running, her light hair flew out from her cap and my Anna Benigna's laughter bounced on the tree trunks. Christina's Anna stood and talked with her mother for a long time. I saw she is getting taller and will be thin as a willow like her mother, but her eyes are blue as her father's. She has his way of speaking quietly but you can hear every word. I would not have known Esther, the Indian child, unless I looked closely for she has grown so plump. *Ach*, well, that was a great day.

It will not be long now before the Brothers and Sisters come here to the farms at Nazareth and Friedensthal to help us prune the orchard trees and sow seed. Rebecca, my Indian Sister, throws her seed carefully as though she is thinking about each one and what it will grow. I love to just throw it way in the air. I try to walk the rows next to Sister Susannah Nitschmann to scatter seed, because she laughs when she raises her arm and this makes me laugh too. We always thank Our Saviour for sending the rain for the sun is sure to come soon and the small shoots burst out of the ground. It seems to me that the seeds we plant struggle and wiggle in the earth and reach their little green arms up to touch the sun. Then in the warmth they grow strong to wave in the summer wind. I wonder if Sister Nitschmann thinks of this as I do. Christina has told me that

Sister Nitschmann had spoken to her about going to our Gnadenhütten mission, west of here in the Blue Mountains. I already knew they were having a private talk at our winter celebration because I watched them and wondered. I think this would not be a good move for Christina, for she will feel so much farther from her children. It troubled her to send them even the ten miles from Friedensthal to Bethlehem, though it was for their safety and for them to learn well the ways of our Saviour. *Ach*, sometimes I do not understand the thoughts of my dear friend. She will have to confide in Sister Nitschmann as I did those years ago. For all those years I could tell no one of my stepfather's cruelty and, *mein Gott*, my fear that followed me like silent footsteps behind me in the night. Then, when I found that I could tell Christina, I knew that I must tell Susannah Nitschmann, too. I can't say to myself why I knew this, but I did. She did not hug me to her as Christina did. She just looked right into my eyes. I could see myself there, my face, my cap, my shame. She did not touch me. She said, '*Come to me all ye who are heavy laden and I will give you rest.*' The warm feeling I had felt when Christina hugged me was still in my body, but Sister Nitschmann's words took away the heaviness of shame. Perhaps, I thought, just perhaps, there would be no more dreams in the night when I would cry. Perhaps I could turn round on the path and stop listening for those footsteps of fear that sometimes become like a small, crouching animal ready to spring at my heart.

I must watch the shuttle more closely for it is easy to miss if I do not pay attention. But if I go very slowly I can puzzle in my head at the same time about what has frightened me and what has not. I was not ever afraid to pack my little case and walk from Büdingen to Herrnhaag, and although I was so wet and uncomfortable all those long days on our ship the *Little Strength*, I was never really afraid. I suppose it was that terrible feeling that any man might hurt me, and maybe worse, that my mother could do nothing to help—at least until she finally gave me up. *Ach mein Gott*, I was a lonely girl then and tried not to cry. But now, here I sit at the loom, my fingers busy, the spring wind catching at the corners of our *Gemeinhaus*, and I know I have come to the place my Saviour has chosen for me.

I see outside the little window that the Indian woman who lost her babe is standing alone by the well. She comes to us and yet she does not join us. I wonder about this. What would keep her from living in the Sisters' House with us? It is so much safer than being on the outside. Alone by the grave of her little one she stands, but I have never seen her weep. If I could speak to her I could tell her how our Saviour loves her little child; how He holds it already in His arms. But, *ach*, I cannot say her words. I cannot tell her.

CHAPTER TWENTY-FOUR

Christina Barbara Krause

I wonder if I can rise for a few moments? I might try to walk ever so slowly to the window. It is very quiet. Even the crickets have stopped their incessant singing and the water must have dried in the brook, for I hear no frogs. It is so hot. Yet I cannot seem to perspire, and it is as though all the water in my body is trapped inside my skin that seems swollen to bursting. I know Dr. Jacob Bonn is worried, though he smiles when he gently feels my belly. He wants to know if my babe still moves. It does. It moves with a certain strength, though its mother has none. Life surges despite itself. My God, how I want to join the others. The Sisters come to bathe me, and sometimes they sing, but I know they have work to do, that it is they who must care for my poor little ones now. I do not know where the days go. It is dawn and then it is dusk. But it is always hot. I cannot remember winter, even though it surely comes here and I know we first arrived in the cooler days of autumn. How did my feet, so swollen now, carry me over those long miles? Was it strength of my will or was I filled with His will? Sometimes in the darkness here I wonder if any of my musings make any difference. Will anyone remember what we struggled for? Will it matter?

Our large barn at Friedenstahl became a place for prayer for me in the summer. I would steal away from the others to climb the shaky wooden ladder to the piles of hay and settle there to watch the dust motes swimming in the air. The sun shone through the thin openings between the boards and it seemed that little creatures dove, slid and danced their uneven dance on the beams. To watch them seemed a kind of prayer then, for it was so clear to me that every creature, every tiny bit of life was somehow fashioned by His almighty hand with love and with gentleness. My silly human concerns dissipated. I could imagine them disappearing among the swirling bits of life that swam in the sunshine. Since our conversation last winter, Sister Nitschmann had not again mentioned a possible move to Gnadenhütten. Surely she must have known that others were more suited to travel than I. In the years we have built this haven in the wilderness, I have changed though I can yet see the woman I was all those years ago when I faced Hans to tell him I was leaving Gelzhausen to join the traveling Brethren. How young I was! I had pictured myself running as easily over America's fields as those near my father's forge. Was I brave? I do not know. I only do know that my beloved's voice echoed in my ears and was answered by my heart when he turned to the Psalms and told me to 'sing a new song.' And I did learn a new song. I learned the music at our farm at Friedensthal.

My belief that my children prospered under the kind tutelage of the sisters in Bethlehem and the ache to hold them close seemed lessened by visits now and again to see them playing with others and learning the important ways of Him who loves us. Little Esther wore her cap tied with the red ribbon as do the lighter-skinned children, and when I observed her bent over her paper to write, I thought she might be saved from a life of hiding from the increasing hostility around her. Even before the terrible war between the French and the English broke out in 1755, we had constant news of Indian attacks along the great chain of the Appalachian Mountains. Apparently French emissaries had given the Indians the hope to recover the homes of their forefathers and with this hope came attacks on English whites of the most brutal kind. Surrounded as I was by wise Brethren and Sisters, and our sturdy homes and outlying farms, I tried not to worry, for I knew there was safety in numbers. Our missionaries continued to speak of peace to those tribes they could reach.

We Sisters at the farm often were engaged in serious conversation about the plight of our Indian brethren. Starving people came to us in great numbers and we could not but help them in their plight. Our mission at Gnadenhütten was surrounded by at least 300 Indian brethren's log dwellings, and there were plans to build another settlement near Bethlehem where our Christian Indians might grow and prosper later.

Sister Anna Maria Schropp brought us a story last week. She had walked from Nazareth up to our farm here to help in the herb garden. She particularly likes this task, and she had learned much from the Indian women about medicines for our apothecary. She bent over to pick some lavender to rub between her fingers, and said, "I was just reminded of some very good news I received from my husband when he returned from a trip to Bethlehem. Do you remember the Indian woman who lost her babe?" Of course, I well remembered this tall, thin woman who stayed on off and on at the Sisters' House although she never indicated that she wanted to join our congregation. Susannah had told me that she had so wanted to offer help to this woman since she felt fear in her. I had wondered at times if she mourned the loss of her babe silently within herself because she did not know someday she would see it again in our dear Saviour's arms. Perhaps, I had thought, she was fearful of all white men. Maybe the father of her child was murdered by whites. At any rate, we were all interested in her being with us, but yet not part of us. Anna Maria continued, as she clipped some rue to put in her basket. "Well, you know that several of our Brothers have been studying hard at the Indian language school that Brother Pyrlaeus has begun." She looked down at her feet, suddenly shy, it seemed. "I have asked my husband about the Indian language words he has learned there and I thought—well—I thought, perhaps, I might be able to speak to the woman." Anna Maria smiled; her dark lashes seemed impossibly long when she closed her eyes. "I was able to make my question understood by the poor woman, and in the few words I could make out, she said she had been afraid to join our congregation because . . . can you guess why?"

"Not fair," cried Sister Catherine Mücke.

"You must tell us right now," I said and took Anna Maria's hand to swing it back and forth. "Do not tease."

"Well, she said that she believed that in order to join us, she would have to marry one of our Brethren."

"How could she think that? She certainly has not seen our Brethren marry Indian women that I know of." Sister Catherine frowned a bit before she put her hand over her mouth. "Don't you remember Brother Post married the Indian maiden, Rachel? She was a Wampanoag and Brother Buttner baptized her. Brother Mack had baptized her father." This news had been brought to us from New York, and I must admit I was pleased with myself for recalling this. "But, tell us your story, Sister Anna Maria."

"Well, the rumor in Bethlehem is that 'anything might happen in Nazareth.'" Anna Maria tossed her head with a laugh. Then she said, "The lovely part is the Indian woman wants to join our congregation and that means she will learn of His love for us and will know that her little one rests with Him, and . . . " She broke off as though out of breath, and then she began to laugh. I have always loved her laugh. It reminds me of cool brook water and bells, all at once.

And so that serene summer passed. Our settlement prospered as we busied ourselves with handcrafts that we sold to the increasing population outside Nazareth and from our farm at Friedensthal. By harvest time the crop, watered by gentle rain and given strength by bright sunshine, had turned corn tassels to silky gold and the flax stood ready to be cut down by our sharpened scythes. Animals were becoming plentiful with over two hundred creatures on the farms near Nazareth and, of course, in Bethlehem. We had no sheep at Friedensthal, but we did have cows. We even had acquired twenty pigs. I had always liked pigs, even back in Gelzhausen when the farmer down the road from us had taken me by the hand and into his large barn where a mother pig had just given birth to a new litter. How they tumbled over each other, those little ones. That summer was full of close friendship. As we sowed and reaped, ground our grain and baked our bread, we also took the time to sing together, our melodies weaving the bond between us that would never be broken.

The arrival of Brother August Spangenberg was a more significant event than I knew at the time. Far more significant. Brother Joseph, as we were asked to call him, was the Count's eyes and ears in the New World, and he had proved himself diligent and far-seeing as he advised the heads of our farm as well as our industries. Our spinners, weavers and seamstresses often sold their wares, and our flour was the best in the region. I often thought, that even from far away Europe, his careful advice, though arriving long after he had written it, seemed to fatten our cattle! When the news came to us from Bethlehem that Brother Joseph was to arrive this summer, we were more than pleased: He would certainly greet all of us here in Nazareth, and the surrounding farms. Spangenberg was not a big man but his girth and all-welcoming smile gave the impression of good will; the strained buttons on his waistcoat spoke more of the pleasure he took in living than of one who hoarded for his own gratification. Preparations were made for his coming, and in anticipation of his stay in Nazareth, Susannah had all kitchen hands busy at their tasks of cutting, slicing, kneading while our hunters scoured the woods for game that was often not plentiful in those years. We loved an excuse, though we needed none, to celebrate, to eat, sing and pray together. The advent of so loved a guest propelled us forward to that summer day when he would arrive. Of course, Brother Opitz was ready with his trumpet; its golden notes would echo through the tall trees and bramble bushes from miles in the distance.

We had heard before Brother Joseph's arrival, that many months ago he had been in serious discussion in the Old Country with Count Zinzendorf and the English Earl of Granville about purchasing some 100,000 acres in the Southern Provinces, and with this idea in mind, had journeyed to Philadelphia to ascertain conditions in a dense wilderness named Carolina after the English King, Charles. Anna Maria Schropp, who seemed to find out anything we all wanted to know, told me that at first Brother Joseph was discouraged by some men who said the way there was rough and difficult. But we all knew that rough travel is made so much easier by the blessed hand of Him who guides us. So he was coming to greet us all and to join with some of the Brethren who would accompany him on his journey.

Matthew seemed bursting with excitement when he said that he had spoken to Brother Loesch, who would be traveling with Spangenberg. His vision was to build a settlement in North Carolina as a model of peace and harmony, much as we had done here. Such a place would serve neighboring families and perhaps awaken the hearts of the Indians there, too. I thought to myself that, indeed, that is precisely what we had accomplished here in a small way. For not only in America had we carried our message of joy but also in such far away places as Greenland to the north and the West Indies to the south. My husband was full of news about the journey south, his face so radiant that I reached up to touch his cheek and, taking my hand in his, he put it to his lips with a smile. "This will be a golden opportunity to spread His word, Christina."

In the way of our people, extensive planning was made prior to the journey and the men who were chosen to accompany Brother Joseph were well suited for travel and equipped to provide help for the task before them. On that day, we all gathered to see them off after our communal meal. It was a hot day in August and I must admit that I did not envy the travelers' journey ahead for, if it was hot in Pennsylvania, it surely might be almost unbearable further south. But I knew little of the countryside then. Brother Joseph swung into his saddle with a grace surprising for his rotund body; Brother Merk swung a long, thin leg over the saddle he had fashioned, and Brother Loesch gentled his nervous horse before he, too, joined the others. Brothers Miller and Horsefield were already moving onto the path through the woods as we all joined a hearty chorus to send them on their way.

As this scene filled with anticipation comes to my mind, I also blush to remember as I watched the small company disappear into the woods that I was distracted by a flutter in my womb. When had this small soul made its way from our Saviour's side? It must have been in the springtide when flowers were just beginning to toss their colored faces and the air soft on our cheeks. Was it the time Matthew caught me unaware but desirous as I leaned against the gray boards of the cow barn and, in our eagerness to join, never sank to the ground but tussled as we stood? Or was it yet another time when lashing rain was thrown against the windowpane and my cries were crushed beneath the crash of thunder? I often wondered if a babe somehow grew to echo the circumstances of its earthly creation—would it grow as a child, slow and careful and loving or, perhaps, one filled with fire, seeking to take from this existence the riches of sensation only.

Our dear leader Spangenberg and his fellow travelers explored the land for close to six months. It was February of 1753 when they arrived back to tell of their great adventure. Their return was to Bethlehem rather than to our farms in Nazareth, but the distance between the two settlements was a mere ten miles, and several of our men and women took a cart to the *Gemeinhaus* in Bethlehem to hear the news and to report back to us. I would have wanted to hear the news of the adventures myself, but Dr. Otto was keeping a close watch on me, for our babe was close to its birth; although I was healthy and strong, as always at the time, the thought of travel was unacceptable. Later, we gathered in Nazareth at the large stone house to hear that Brother Joseph had named the area he had surveyed Wachovia, because the landscape had reminded him of the Wachau in Austria.

The details of their trip were lost to me for I went into an easy labor just after their arrival. Susannah had come from Nazareth to Friedensthal to be with me and, of course, Matthew held fast to my hand as our babe pushed his struggling way into this world. As Susannah laid him on my belly he looked so like our Anna that my mind was momentarily confused. I was about to call out her name as I touched his little red face but then a word came to me. It was a name: Samuel. "I want to name him Samuel," I said, and was surprised at the strength of my voice.

"A good name, my dear," Matthew leaned close, "tell us why you thought of this. I can't remember if we . . . "

"A prophet," I said. A sense of great weariness came over me. I could feel myself as though in a dream, and my voice seemed to come from somewhere else. "Samuel because someday he may answer to do the Lord's bidding." As I heard my own voice, I wondered from whence it came and even whether it was my own true voice, for I had never spoken thus. This little red and wiggling body wrapped in swaddling, a prophet?

Matthew spoke then the prayer of Hannah, the mother of Samuel, and his voice seemed to sing to me. "There is none holy like the Lord, there is none beside thee; There is no rock like our God." My body liquid, without form sank into the small bed and I slept. I am sure I must have smiled, but I did not recall the whole story when I gave my babe his name. For Hannah gave little Samuel over to the temple when he was weaned; others raised him. Had I remembered, would I have changed his name?

It was decided that the first group to travel south should be men who could devote their full attention to the building of a settlement. Twelve men from our settlement of Christian Spring, near Friedensthal, began to prepare for the journey. None of these men was married, so there would be no separation between husband and wife, and they could devote their full attention to the task at hand without concern for loved ones in Pennsylvania. Hermann Loesch, who had accompanied Brother Joseph on the first trip, was full of plans when he spoke to Matthew. "We had trouble at first finding contiguous acreage that was good for planting. The ground there is reddish-brown and does not look as though it would take well to seeding, but I think we can make it work."

"And pasture?" Matthew asked.

"Yes, there will be plenty of that. Of course, we will have to clear land." And he clapped his hand on Matthew's shoulder. "That is a task we are well prepared for."

And so the group left: strong men who would bend their backs and wrench stones with a mighty heave to build an oasis of calm in the southern wilderness. As I tied a ribbon under my little Samuel's chin, I imagined those twelve sturdy men who had been part of the group who fashioned the great mill at Christian Spring, moving swiftly southward to begin yet again with the Lord's help to clear new fields, as we had done, and to provide the home for those who would send our message of hope and joy to those who had not yet heard it.

The men worked in Wachovia for a year, and because of the rough roads, we had little news from them. What we did manage to hear from Brother Lischer, who was designated as a messenger between here and there, was that the journey down through the steep hills of Virginia was made more than bearable by the ministrations of one Sister who had provided delicious baked goods to make the journey sweeter, and from strangers who became friends as they made their way through dense brush and crossed raging rivers. The weather was cooling by November when the men drew close to their destination. I could imagine their excitement as they came near to the place Brother Joseph had said would be the beginning of a new settlement. Brother Lischer told us that Brother Konigsdorfer had even written a short hymn that the men sang at their first Lovefeast in the new place. Their hearty voices must have lifted above the green canopy as they gathered in a circle, their arms around each other:

We hold a lovefeast here/in Carolina land/
A company of Brethren true/ a little pilgrim band.
Called by the Lord to be of those/
Who through the whole wide world do go/
To bear Him witness everywhere/
And naught but Jesus know.

How I would have liked to hear them; to see their faces, weary yet shining with the spirit of our dear Saviour as they arranged their bedrolls in the small cabin they had found and settled into sleep while the wind in the pines sang a new song. Lischer told us how the brethren had worked. Fields were staked off to be cleared and planted in winter wheat, a bake-oven built and though none was very adept in hunting, one Brother had managed to shoot a couple of wild turkeys that supplemented their monotonous diet of pumpkins. From the expression on his face as he recalled incidents of his fellow Brethren, I guessed the men quickly had formed a spirit of camaraderie. I also could see from the telling of the messenger that there had been a great deal of laughter and teasing when he told us about the Danish Brother Friis, who though well-educated in Hebrew, did not know much of wilderness living. He was finally awarded the title of "keeper of the fowl" after his unsuccessful attempt to make butter in a teapot and, later, as an unsuccessful cowherd who lost the cattle in the woods!

Brother Nathan Seidel, who had accompanied Brother Lisher down to Wachovia and back to Pennsylvania, could hardly contain his pride in saying, "We have even made a trumpet from a hollow tree branch." Looking out over those of us who had assembled, he declared, "No trumpet in Bethlehem has a better tone!" There was general laughter among the men, and Anna Maria Schropp clapped her hands with pleasure. Indeed, our new southern settlement was not only a place of work but also a place of welcoming and joy that must have cheered a weary traveler passing through. I was sure that soon a number of pilgrims would be asked to help settle in this southern wilderness. Perhaps the newcomers to Pennsylvania would be ready to travel yet again when the time came.

⚜ ✳ ⚜

CHAPTER TWENTY-FIVE

It still hurts. I may not be able to think of this part of my pilgrimage without the longing that accompanies my recollections. How could I not have known that life would not always be as I had dreamed? And as I lie in the southern heat, do I have the courage to look at myself as a young woman or as my body swells, even to imagine our final journey?

I remember that the rain was gentle. Droplets hit the leaves of the tall trees while the mist hovered close to the ground. Some of us women traveled without our husbands to Bethlehem that wet summer day to attend the service of homecoming for our departed Sister Brownfield. I had attended many funerals, or Homegoings as we called them, and each time heard the life stories written by the departed or by a friend, but I particularly mark this day for it was in the weeks following that I experienced such unexpected changes.

As I sat in the small horse-drawn cart, I could recall that the way from Nazareth to Bethlehem was but a narrow trail those past years when we first walked it; the men swinging their axes and we women carrying food in small bundles. We blew on our hands and clapped them together to keep warm. The trail then became wide enough for horses, and then a road where two wagons could meet and stop for the drivers to chat. Even the path from our farm at Friedensthal up to Nazareth widened as we traveled back and forth carrying grain from our mill. Other trails became paths, and then roads that went deep into the forest to the north and west.

Birds flying over might well have seen a criss-cross of ways through the deep woods. Small we must seem from above, I thought; small and vulnerable as we moved on our paths from house to barn, to newly cleared fields carrying our own thoughts and in a moment of remembrance, sending a prayer of petition or praise.

Although we Sisters were uncharacteristically quiet as our cart made its way to say our farewell to Sister Brownfield, the trip took little time. Time usually moved quickly when we made this ten-mile trek because we sang on the way, or spoke of concerns and joys of our day; but, somehow, the nature of our journey that day was more somber. Not sad, for we all knew Sister Brownfield was now in His blessed kingdom, but somber perhaps, because it brought to mind our own pilgrimages here on earth. Knowing that we would someday write of our own pilgrimage may cause us to be in the world differently, I thought; to know before an action that it would be recalled in our words when our body was cold and our essence was at last with Him.

I had known Sister Brownfield in Nazareth for several years, but after the departure of her husband she had been living in the Widows' House in Bethlehem, so it was there that we would bid her goodbye. I knew that many hymns would be sung, and that Brother Anders would be reading the story of her life's pilgrimage, and I was eager to understand this woman who seemed to have such a clear idea of where to find our Saviour and to hold out her hand to grasp His. I felt the moist air on my face, and peered through the trees to see we were approaching Bethlehem. How our settlement had changed in the years I had been in the New World! Bethlehem seemed almost teeming with people; carts carrying long logs for building, and women with baskets on each arm, hurrying to the stone Sisters' House. There were Indians weaving amongst them, dressed now in breeches and shirts, no longer standing apart in colorful blankets as they once had done. A group of young girls walked arm in arm, their teacher speaking earnestly to one student. I peered to see if I could see my Anna but she was not there, and I felt a stab of disappointment.

We disembarked from our carts and hastened to the stone chapel as the rain pattered harder. The men entered by one door and we another, as was our custom. We settled quietly and faced forward where Brother Anders stood to read Sister Brownfield's last words. "I was born on February 4th, 1716 in New York and baptized and raised in the Church of England," Brother Anders began. And then he related our Sister's concern for her salvation and her faith in our good Lord's sacrifice that had caused her to live in a blessed state, she wrote, even from the time she was a very little girl.

I had no such thought when I was younger. Caught up in the life of our small village, I had helped my mother with the washing, listened to the rumble of my brothers' voices, and the sound of metal on metal, a musical clanging every day. My actions were propelled forward as though driven by a force that touched not my thoughts but, rather, was pure feeling fired by pictures that danced in dreams and continued during the daylight hours as I walked the muddy road through Gelzhausen. My joining with Matthew seemed driven also by something I could not understand—a strong feeling that took form in his voice as he spoke the words of ancient Scripture until I, too, so wanted to be a part of some great mission, as well as part of his life.

According to her memoir, Sister Brownfield had a great struggle in leaving her family to join the Brethren because they disapproved of our ways. Some of my Sisters here had experienced this—Anna Maria Schropp had told a similar story of leaving her parents in Switzerland. "I never turned back," she said. Of course, it was different for me. I had no parents to stop me, and Greta's and Hans' pleas were not strong enough to dispel my fancies of being the handmaiden to Count Zinzendorf and his wife. Nor could their words dissuade my dreams of skipping easily over America's fields and through her forests following in the footsteps of my gentle Saviour.

Brother Anders' voice carried to the last bench as he read Sister Brownfield's words.

"Oh, love filled with Jesus, oh my heart day and night, Oh how with waking desire I think of Him both day and night." Dear Sister, I said to myself, though doubt sometimes shrouded me, I have had those precious times when golden warmth filled my body. Filled with my beloved, I thought, as Matthew's face appeared clearly in my mind. Should I not instead be able to see the face of our beloved Saviour? To imagine His face surrounded in light? I felt the warmth of a blush rise from my breast, my unseemly thoughts racing. Clearly there must be some lack in me; some confusion that troubles my heart and casts doubt that rises like weeds in a verdant field. I looked to my feet and counted the scratches in the wooden floor to compose myself.

It was early evening when we arrived back at our farm at Friedensthal, and we hurried to prepare a meal of broth and bread. My Samuel was happily cooing in Rosina's arms as I mixed his cereal. I kissed the top of his head, nuzzling his wispy fair hair. I knew it would not be long before he, too, would join his sister and brother in Bethlehem. I kissed him again with a prayer of thanks that he would be only ten miles from me.

When we all awoke the next day the heavy mist had cleared and I could feel autumn. The leaves were not yet tinged with autumn color, nor had they turned dry, but the air had changed. Cool and moist, it made me think of the sea. We were preparing to gather herbs, when Brother Matthew Schropp arrived from Nazareth with the message that Matthew and I were to make the short trip up the hill with him for a special meeting. As we approached the large stone House in Nazareth, I saw that more couples from our other farms nearby had arrived. I waved to Rosina Biefel, happy to see her after many months. Together we entered the chamber where meetings and services were held. It was colder in the stone *Gemeinhaus* than outside and, as I wrapped my cape around my shoulders, I hoped this meeting would not last too long, for I looked forward to hanging the herbs to dry, their pungent scent remaining on my fingers to inhale again and again.

Bishop David Nitschmann had not yet taken the chair at the front of the room. Brother Herman Loesch, recently returned from the south, conversed softly with him while Brother Nathan Seidel spoke to a few Brothers seated in the front rows. I thought it must be a very important bit of news about to be imparted to us, for Bishop, or as we sometimes called him, Father Nitschmann, was a very revered man among the Brethren. He was a cousin of dear Susannah Nitschmann and it was he who made the decision to acquire the large stone house here in Nazareth and the many acres surrounding it. He bent his tall frame to speak to Brother Loesch, who smiled and moved quickly to the rear of the room.

We settled quickly on our benches, silent in anticipation. Father Nitschmann began to speak. He told us that the land in North Carolina had been prepared by the Single Brothers and that the area was ready for Pilgrims to bring forth the fruits of that land. "Some of you will be chosen to do this noble work." He paused and looked over the assemblage. "And, indeed, noble work it is; for by our example we will show others that living the simplicity of our Saviour's life brings eternal joy."

How brave they will be, I thought. For well I knew the nights that seemed oh-so-short when before daybreak we raised our weary bodies to start yet again to clear a field, to plant and sow in virgin land and gather its harvest; to travel in ice and snow, bringing the good news of salvation to those who know it not. And I also knew that the Indians in that southern place did not know we brought no harm to them. The new settlers would have to gain their good will, our missionaries learning yet another Indian tongue. A sigh escaped me as I thought of those who would be chosen to journey the long miles. I looked across the room at Matthew and saw how he leaned forward on the bench. He was so engaged with Father Nitschmann that he kept the pose for many minutes, neither turning to right or left.

At this moment, Father Nitschmann uttered the words that changed my life. There was a quiet buzz in the room as though bees had left their hive and were circling above our heads, though I knew it was simply the quiet voices of my Brethren. Father Nitschmann had become quiet and, in that space of time, we could not help but touch a Sister on our left or right to express our excitement over the new opportunity to spread the words of our dear Friend whose spirit is always with us.

Father Nitschmann cleared his throat. "I am very gratified to give you the news that our asking of the Lot was positive." The word of our Lord written on paper and contained in the metal holder we often used in those days for decision making. Indeed, had not our Saviour spoken in the positive when asked in this way if Matthew and I should wed? The buzz in the room began again, but this time louder.

There was a great deal of conversation amongst us as we made our way back to the farm at Friedensthal. Who would be chosen to go? How long would it take to prepare for the journey? Were there resting places on the way or would there be camping outdoors, and what were the accommodations once they actually arrived in the new settlement? Rosina Biefel was very eager to go, she said. Of course, I thought there was little chance Matthew and I would be asked because we were so busy here at the farm and Samuel was still a small child. I had only just weaned him and he would be joining his sister and brother in Bethlehem soon enough. I would miss holding his little body as it curved close to mine, but I knew I could see him when we made the trip to the nursery and that he was safe with the kind Sisters who cared for him there. I had become reconciled to the short distance between myself and our children.

Matthew and I did not talk over what we had heard, for he was to ride to Bethlehem to discuss farm matters, and I hurried to the apothecary garden to twist the tops of some chamomile that we would use for tea. There was another reason we did not speak to one another on that day, I am sure. I did not want to feel the intensity of his longing to climb hills he had never climbed, to look beyond for a valley where we would begin again to build for the Lamb of God. Certainly I wanted to shut my ears against the sound of his yearning as he spoke of these things. As a young woman I had looked into his eyes and touched with my fingers the set of his jaw. So many years ago I had reached for him to catch this fire—to let it consume me. O, my God, I had wanted to be so loved by him, to know and share that part of my husband that looked forward to a place we had not yet seen. But it was alien to me; as though I wandered alone in gray fog, my arms outstretched to grasp something I could not see, never to find it, never to feel it. We never do know one another, I thought. And if we cannot know one another, how can we know our Saviour as the Brethren entreat us to do? How can we take His light into ourselves? It is too much, I thought. Too much.

I picked three thin blades of our chive plant, bit and chewed its flavor, recalling that an English Sister had told me this herb kept out evil spirits from the garden. A dainty herb, its odor clung to my fingers. Do we breathe in His essence as we breathe in our herbs, or the honeysuckle in summer, the pine boughs on a winter afternoon? I looked about to see my Sisters bend to snap off the herbs in their quick hands, the breezes of early autumn swirling at our petticoats. O, my God, I do love this land. I love the huge trees surrounding our farms, the swell of the cleared land, the knowledge that this is now my home; while Gelzhausen resides behind my eyes, unmoving, always the same.

It was twilight when Matthew returned to the farm. I heard his boots on the wooden step, and then the clump on the floorboards as he moved swiftly to stand in front of me. Little Samuel sat comfortably on my hip, and when he saw his father, he reached out with a little cry of joy. I was afraid to look directly at his face, for a moment's stab in my breast told me that his expression would convey something I did not want to see; but his excitement, palpable in the small room, drew me so that I could not help but look directly at him. Why did I fear what I saw? He was filled with excitement, his blue eyes wide; His smile always so gradual, almost leisurely before it reached his eyes, now seemed to dominate his thin face. "Oh, Christina. Oh, my wife." He gathered our babe and me in his arms and I could feel his trembling.

"What? What is it, Matthew?" I could only whisper.

"I have spent the afternoon with Brother David Nitschmann. Oh, my dear. He has asked that I consider the position of Acolyte."

I have watched the sun burst from behind a rain cloud to fill a clearing with gold; every blade of grass stretching to be touched and surrounded in light. Suddenly I felt that I, too, wanted to bathe in my husband's delight, his joy, his consummate happiness. So it was only that he had been given an honor. What were my fears? Why had I been so filled with dark thoughts when I heard him close the door behind him?

"My dear husband. You will be an inspiration to others as you always have been. Your words, surely placed by the Saviour . . . "

"That is not all. That is not all! Father Nitschmann has asked that we, Christina, that we travel to begin the new settlement to help spread His glorious word."

I could not take in his words. To travel south? To start yet again? I drew away. I could not speak. I wanted to speak. I wanted to break the thing that had entered into the little room. To cry out against his joy. "No," I whispered. "No. You told father Nitschmann that we would not move; that we could not leave our child, that he is too young . . . "

"Christina Barbara. It has been decided." He took my elbows in his hands, but did not pull me toward him. The babe began to whimper as I turned away, my back to my husband. I could not seem to see, so my eyes darted then from table to window to the dishes stacked in the shelf in some sort of desperate effort to make things right; to center myself in a room that had become foreign as though I had never worked there, sung there, cried there. I placed Samuel on the floor and, taking a wooden horse from the table, I put it in front of him. My movements were deliberate, they were calm. I will not go, I thought. This is some mistake. I will run to Sister Nitschmann and tell her we cannot go.

"My dear, dear, wife. My love. We have traveled so far together. Do you not know we have been given the noblest opportunity I ever dreamed. I never thought, I never thought you..."

"No, you never thought! You never thought of my wishes. But you wanted to go. I know you wanted to go, and now they have given you an honor you could not refuse." I walked to the door and felt the latch cold in my hand. I did not turn to look at Matthew. I could not bear to. I said nothing as I walked out the door. I did not close it behind me.

They never ask more of us that we can do, I thought. My Saviour will help me. He will touch my husband's heart to make him know we must stay and work here. I will talk to Anna Nitschmann. I will walk all the way to Bethlehem and speak to Brother Joseph. He will pat my shoulder and look at me with kindness and say we do not have to go. I walked very fast and when Rosina Michler called my name I did not answer but began to run towards the woods.

I could feel my breath coming in short gasps but I kept on running. The ground was uneven as I approached the trees. "Oh, God, oh, God, I will not leave my children. You cannot ask this of me." The darkness gathered around me, the sky turning from pink to gray and the trees seemed immense as I made my stumbling way among them.

I will go when light breaks, I thought. I will go to beg of Brother Joseph. I will hear his words of reassurance as birdsong in my heart. But I knew this was not true. I put my hands on the tree in front of me. The bark was rough against my hands and tore at my skin as I sank slowly to my knees. I will not go. My Saviour has not asked this of me. I cannot hear his words. I felt the wet leaves beneath my bended knees. "Listen to me, dear Lamb. Listen," I prayed to the darkening sky. The wind rose and fell. A sigh crying through the firs. There was no answer for me. Betrayed, I cried out to dissolve and seep into the earth. I pressed my body against the sharp roots and clawed handfuls of dirt as though to dig a shallow grave. Like some wild thing of the forest I rooted the dank leaves to smell the cursed earth from which we are made, and drew my legs under me as though to ease my pain and I cried out to my Saviour to bear me into darkness. Night came.

When morning light touched the treetops, Matthew stood tall before me, his face was immoveable, mask-like. Scrambling unsteadily to my feet, I heard him say, "It is His will, Christina, not ours." He spoke quietly as he moved to hold me to him. Rigid, I could not move. Then, sinking to my knees at his feet, I bent in two and began to weep. In an instant, Matthew, too, knelt as we had so long ago in Marienborn, but this time we were so much older and filled with sorrow. He reached again to hold me and, knee to knee, I could feel his body shaking even as mine did.

⚜

CHAPTER TWENTY-SIX

I had taken to my bed feigning illness and had not spoken to anyone since we had received the news of our upcoming journey. In fact, I was not entirely well during those days, for I was sick at heart, and although I did not cry out, my tears wet my pillow at night. I could not look directly at my husband. I had held our little Samuel trying to take in the smell of his sweet breath and memorize his little nose, his blue eyes so like his father's, before I relinquished him to Matthew. I could not watch him as he took our babe to the door of the farmhouse, but after the sound of the latch fell into place, I ran to the window to see him walking swiftly toward Nazareth where my little one would be transported by cart with Sister Optiz to the nursery at Bethlehem. I admit now that a coldness enveloped me as though I were encased in gray; my mind unaware of sunlight or dark, the breezes from the window, the voices of my brethren that floated upward to my room. I was neither angry nor sad, but rather felt myself to be a stone statue facing Bethlehem, but seeing nothing. Once, in the night, Matthew had placed his hand on my breast and kissed me tenderly. I was still and would not respond as he gently asked me to love him. Was he trying to bring me to life as he entered me? I did not care. I felt nothing

CELEBRATIONS HAD BEEN PLANNED prior to sending us pilgrims on our journey south. Because of the importance of our new undertaking, a special Communion service had been planned and, of course, there was much talk of the preparation. Our Communion always took place once a month and we prepared for this blessed event at least two days prior to its happening, as each of us took time to examine any emotion that would prevent our communing with our Saviour with purity of spirit. I had always loved thinking about taking the bread and wine with my Sisters and Brothers, and as we passed the chalice from hand to hand, I felt a particular closeness with those of us who labored here as well, of course, to Him whose body and blood we were honoring. Perhaps peculiar to the ways of our people was the sprechen, or speaking, that preceded the actual Communion. This act between a communicant and Choir Sister allowed us to voice our personal concerns about our heart's condition. Although I often found myself reluctant to share my inner thoughts with anyone, I found through the years that a certain intimacy unfolded when I unburdened my heart to another woman in this way. It was as though my voice, speaking aloud, was heard by our dear Lamb and the concerns about my heart's condition were laid to rest in a most beautiful way.

How different it was in this fateful year of 1753! I knew I should be able to simply spill out my anger, my feelings of betrayal and my agony at having to leave my children and everything I had come to love in Friedensthal, but I could not. I could not. Matthew had made a decision for both of us; Certainly I knew I could raise my concerns to my Choir Leader, but I knew also I would feel so different from the others; so deficient in my love for the Lamb. And would I ever leave our community? The very thought caused me nausea for I could not take my children into this wilderness. Somehow I must steel myself. I must not cry out, but try to open my heart; to let Him in to bring healing.

I walked up the hill to the *Gemeinhaus* in Nazareth, the air still warm for the month of October. The leaves had begun to change to red and yellow, and they rustled quietly that morning, a few falling at my feet. My walk slowed, the thud of my heart sounding in my ears for I found myself almost afraid to face this Sister. I should tell her of my anger and despair, but at the same time I knew I had made the promise to follow our Saviour wherever that path might lead. "Too much. Too much," were the words that pounded with the sound of my shoes on the path.

The *Gemeinhaus* rose before me, its sturdy stone walls seeming impregnable, safe from the elements. I pulled at the wooden door and saw Sister Gertrude Graff standing in the hallway. Her rounded cheeks and friendly smile encouraged me. Nodding to the entrance of a small room, she led me inside and quietly closed the door.

"Sister Krause, I am sure you are aware that we will be having a special Communion service prior to your leaving for Wachovia." Sister Graff took my hand and motioned me to sit before her. Then she added, kindly, "I know you have been ill, so I have not taken the opportunity of asking you of your heart's condition." I did not say anything and she continued. "Sister Christina, you might want to speak about your feelings for we believe in going to our Lord's table with a free and open heart."

I felt sick, my mouth dry. My efforts to reconcile my thoughts seemed in vain, but I was determined to express my honest feelings to her before our Communion service. I felt my voice to be rusty and hoarse, unable to begin to tell her the way I felt. Finally, with some effort, I said, "I cannot go to the Lord's table when my heart is in this deplorable condition."

"You have often found it difficult to tell me what you feel. Perhaps I can help. Do you know why you cannot let our dear Lamb into your heart?" I could hear bitter laughter, but it was in my head and never sounded in the little room. Then I looked at her face when she placed her hand on mine for a moment. How could I tell this woman anything when words were frozen? At last I said, "When I think of our Lamb's face, it is sometimes very clear to me, but I struggle to hear His words in answer to my questions."

"But, dear Sister, what questions do you have? Can we not help you to answer these when you ask with such earnestness of purpose?"

Silent as I tried to form the words, I finally whispered, "Does our Saviour ask for sacrifice?"

"He is a living sacrifice. Surely you know this, Christina. He sacrificed Himself, gave of His life's blood, so that we are clean of sin."

Tears began to gather in my throat. I could not speak and tightness gripped my whole chest. I blurted, "I know He was the sacrifice. I know this! But Sister Graff, Gertrude, what is expected of us? What does He ask of us?" By this time tears made my sight blur.

"Oh, my dear friend. He asks nothing except that we love Him." She looked toward the window and then again turning her attention to me, she said, "I believe you may be experiencing the distress that comes to all of us from time to time as we prepare our hearts for the trust and faith that will surely enter." She pursed her mouth in concentration, her blue eyes round. "We know in part now, but later we will understand all. Now we see, as Paul said, through a glass darkly."

What could I say? I heard her speak such kind words. I saw the love and concern in her face. But she had no answer to my question. The band that squeezed my heart remained in place. How could I tell her that relinquishing my children to others seemed a sacrifice to me? Not to see their dear faces, to hear their voices as they grew and matured, was more than I could bear. It was a sacrifice I could not willingly make.

"Sister Graff, I cannot partake of the Lord's supper." I looked into her face, and I think the sweet forgiveness there caused me to cry out loud; to cover my face with my hands.

My tears seemed inexhaustible, yet somehow I found the strength to attend the Lovefeast, and to partake in the absolution given to those of us who would not be taking Communion. But I was absolved of nothing, for I knew thorns as sharp as those that brought His precious blood were wound around my heart to bar His entering. It was Sister Wahnert who spoke after the absolution. "Remember," she said softly. "Remember you must not partake of Communion until you feel ready. Make love your aim."

I knew I was far from ready when I heard the muffled closing of a large wooden door. I knew I was far from ready when rage tightened the binding that compressed my chest, for I could not bring this rage to the table. I could not swallow the Holy bread, for it would not nourish me. I could not taste the wine, for it would turn sour on my lips.

How does one say goodbye? Those words had carried finality for me whether I had spoken them in Gelzhausen or Herrnhaag, but each time they also bore the feeling of excitement and anticipation. As the wind whipped at the autumn leaves in Friedensthal, only a leaden sadness shrouded the words. This was not the sharp pain of grief, but the deadening despondency of words spoken after the shock, after the realization that my life had taken an unalterable turn, and I had no power to change what was going to be. I would never again see the large stone *Gemeinhaus* where Matthew and I began our lives in Nazareth; never again walk over the threshold of our farm house in Friedensthal to set the fire in the hearth, to knead bread, to sit spinning with my Sisters, listening to the whir of the wheels and joining in their laughter. The harvest safe in our barns, I looked out over the cleared fields to see the swell of the land, the woods beyond. I could not feel pride in our work, but the beauty of the place did touch me with an ache that I knew I would carry with me always. I did not let myself think of my children. I could not.

MY BRETHREN AT FRIEDENSTHAL had gathered around Matthew and me, as we prepared to walk to Nazareth to accompany others who would be making the trip. We made a tight little group outside the farmhouse, and as we began our short trek up the hill, Rosina Michler tripped over a jutting stone. Sister Catherine Mücke said, "Oh, that very stone is the one Sister Christina always trips over, but she won't be here . . . " She covered her mouth in a characteristic gesture, afraid she had offended me. I could not pretend to offer a reassuring smile. We continued up the hill.

No work must have been done in the fields that day, for all of our members had gathered from our farms adjacent to Nazareth. Rosina Biefel ran to me, saying that she and her husband Hans would be traveling with us. Her face was animated with a smile, her dark eyes full of anticipation. I knew she was happy to start the new adventure, and I tried to find the strength in myself to be happy for her. My dear friend Susannah walked toward me carrying a plant in one of the bowls she had fashioned from the earth, and glazed in the hearth here in Nazareth. Her round face framed by her white cap was almost that of the young girl I had first met in Herrnhaag. But as she drew closer, I saw that small wrinkles had formed around her blue eyes and deepened on either side of her mouth. We have aged here together, I thought. She did not hesitate as she came near and embraced me, the plant bowl hard between us. "I brought you something to take to Wachovia," she said. "Who knows if they have herbs down there, and I know how you love them." I felt the tears gather but was so determined not to cry before her or anyone there.

"Oh, my friend, I will miss you so." I heard my voice steady and sure.

"But you will have new fields to sow, flax to spin." She broke into her wide smile, "When you pinch this between your fingers, you will remember your friend, Susannah, *ja?*"

I could not speak. She pushed the rosemary plant toward me and I took it, hugging it to my breast. She pinched a sprig and put her fingers under my nose and laughed. "They say George and I may be going to the Indian mission at Gnadenhütten sometime soon. Who knows? We go where the wind blows and help to take care of the dear ones who can teach of our Savior."

"You mean you may not be staying at Nazareth? That you also will be sent away from here?"

"Remember at the gathering with the far-north Indians? Someone spoke to you about going?" She did not wait for me to answer. "I know the missionaries will need someone to run their household and who better than my George and me?" She laughed then and I could not help but smile, for my dear friend always seemed to move easily in any way our Saviour asked. Leaving her daughters in Bethlehem seemed as natural to her as breathing, and for one moment I envied the ease with which she could do this. But how could I envy this friend who had suffered much as a child? Perhaps her heart is more open than mine, I thought. Again I breathed in the pungent odor of rosemary, the herb of remembrance.

Brother Joseph Spangenberg moved to one side of our group and raised his hand for silence. He said we would proceed into the chapel for a short service and then those of us who were to travel would begin our journey, for the sun was well past the tops of the trees. One large wagon that held supplies was already on it way, thoroughly packed with provisions. As we filed into the *Gemeinhaus* and into the *Saal* where we gathered for our meetings, I felt the cold from the thick stone walls. For the first time I noticed how plain our *Saal* was. It looks almost barren, I thought, as I gazed at the crude benches, the unadorned table at the front and the large brown tiled stove that had kept us warm in winter for so many years. It was not until my Brethren's song began to fill the *Saal* with sound that I felt tears again. I swallowed hard to try to stop my lips from quivering. I forced myself to look at those chosen to give the bread and wine. Matthew, serious in his new duty, bent down to place the bread in our Brethren's waiting hands. My hands at my sides, I shivered with cold, but stood in my place and passed the chalice to the Sister next to me, without tasting the wine.

We did not speak much on our way to Bethlehem. The road was worn smooth now, and dry at this autumn time of year. Trees had been cut back, their leaves still clinging, but some turning brown, some still green but dry. The bushes on either side of the road were already dying or at least growing dormant. Like my heart, I thought. But the worst was yet to come, for it would be in Bethlehem that I would, perhaps, glimpse our dear children for the last time.

All the children were there, their teachers standing behind them dressed in their white caps tied with the widows' white ribbons. Anna, head and shoulders taller than her brother Matthaeus, held his plump hand in hers while clasping little Samuel by her other hand. Samuel pulled away from her and toddled unsteadily to me, laughing. Anna and Matthaeus, understanding the solemnity of the occasion, stood their ground. Then, still holding little Samuel, I saw Esther, the Indian child, standing apart from the others, her eyes darting from one face to another until she saw Matthew. Her face was alight with happiness. She moved forward until she stood just behind Matthaeus and placed her hand upon his shoulder. Matthew moved to the children, and holding wide his arms, he gathered them to himself. Sister Maria Shaub from Bethlehem was weeping very quietly, her husband patting her shoulder with a look of discomfort on his long face. I could hear Rosina Biefel quietly explaining to her only child, Johannes, that she and his father would be taking a long journey. Did no one tell the children how far we were to go? How we would be separated to a point where the invisible cord that bound us would cease to exist? Our faces would fade from their minds, our voices only an echo in the night when all was still until an owl screeching in the darkness would be the only sound they heard or remembered. My last glimpse of Anna, the one that stays in my memory, is her hand raised in farewell, and Matthaeus, moving a few steps forward, his stocky body still in motion as we turned our backs. Little Samuel in the arms of Sister Nitschmann, calling for me.

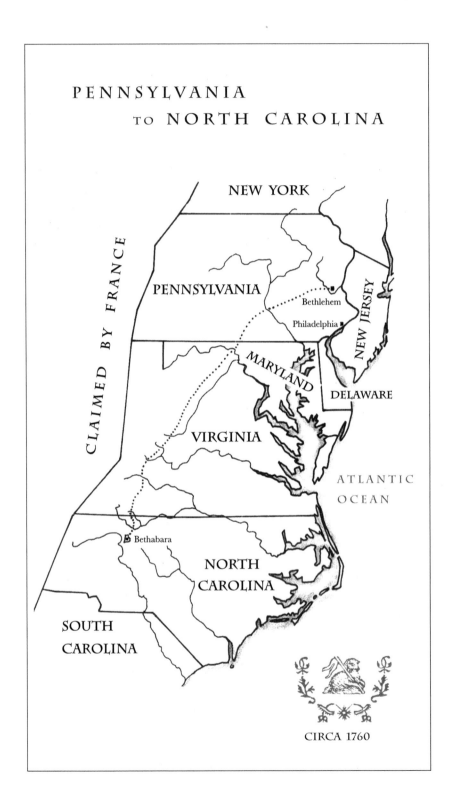

PENNSYLVANIA
TO NORTH CAROLINA

NEW YORK

CLAIMED BY FRANCE

PENNSYLVANIA

Bethlehem

Philadelphia

NEW JERSEY

MARYLAND

DELAWARE

VIRGINIA

ATLANTIC
OCEAN

Bethabara

NORTH
CAROLINA

SOUTH
CAROLINA

CIRCA 1760

CHAPTER TWENTY-SEVEN

Our route was well laid out by the Brethren who had preceded us. The first day we would travel west in Pennsylvania and after a few days we would drop south into Virginia. The Sisters had discussed the route and continued to talk about it as we began the journey, but I was quiet, having nothing to add, my mind numb, my heart cold. No comforting Psalm verses came to me or any words of our Saviour. Only could I recall the cry of poor Rachel with every step I took: *Weeping for her children for they are not.* And Jeremiah's promise that I should not weep, that I would be rewarded, were empty words that I could not believe, as the brush closed in and I stumbled on the road.

"We can call ourselves 'the Little Pilgrim Congregation'." Sister Rosina Biefel's face was joyous as she trudged beside me, her words coming between short breaths for we were walking uphill behind the wagon. "I mean, after all, we really are pilgrims again just like we were when we came over on the boat all those years ago. I was following the Saviour's wishes and remember, oh remember the singing, we . . . "

I could no longer hear what she was saying for the word pilgrim repeated itself in my mind. Yes, I had been a pilgrim, I supposed. I had journeyed to foreign places, had helped with my love and labor to prepare a promised land amid the rushing streams, tangled vines and enormous trees of this wild land. To be a pilgrim is to be a stranger, too, and when this thought came to me, I somehow realized I had been a sort of stranger all my life. In Gelzhausen as a child, perhaps not; but then I recalled my shivering body in the coldness of our little church where I prayed in vain for my parents. Did I feel a stranger then? Apart from those who believed that a tearful petition to the wooden figures would somehow ease the aloneness that followed like a shadow day and night? Perhaps that came later. But the luminous connection I sought was so elusive, fashioned from my own fanciful dreams that at times encircled me in golden light only to turn too quickly to a mere wisp, leaving me alone; a stranger from those who seemed to hold close the rapture of true belief.

The crest of the hill was just beyond us, the sun setting now cast its remaining bright light over the dying leaves that lay in heaps upon the ground and was caught in the drops of rain that remained at the end of bare branches. I stopped for a moment to take in that brightness and prayed for a still-point, just one small still-point in this traveling world where I could remember and hold close the times I had been comforted.

And there were times my Lord had comforted me, I reminded myself. Oh, that He comfort me now. Oh, that he send peace to my tortured heart so that I might look forward instead of back, to the brightness instead of the shadows. I found I was praying all this as we reached the crest of the hill and saw a small settlement below, the smoke rising from a few cabins.

The Saviour had been with us on our journey so far, Brother Schmid reminded us, for throughout Pennsylvania there were helpful Brethren who had made us welcome, supplied us with food for our two wagons. We all wished the remainder of our journey would be as easy. When we reached Yorktown, the inn keeper informed us of the frightening news of Indian outrages where people were killed and property burned. It was not the first time I had heard of problems with Indians or unfriendly English people who maintained distrust of us wherever we traveled. The warring men had made the woods terrifying with gunshot in Pennsylvania, and though we tried to avoid their anger at one another, we could not help but aid those we found who were wounded, or to take in the starving Indians perhaps at our own peril. More and more often they appeared at our settlements, for they were desperate and afraid. I thought of little Esther with a pain in my belly. Thank God we had found her. The poor little one had been so afraid. I pictured her as I last saw her standing straight, the red ribbons on her cap tied perfectly. She did not weep at our leaving. I knew I should not weep in my longing, but the stone in my breast remained heavy, leaden.

OUR FIRST BIG STORM came on us some days later, as we approached the Potomac River. The rain, slight at first, grew in intensity as we slipped and slid on foot down the river bank, our wagons teetering precariously. I held to Matthew's arm, all my anger and sorrow dissipated in the concentrated placing of one foot before the other; the rain soaking my cape, my feet sinking into the mud. He put his arm around my shoulders, and when I glanced from my slipping feet to his face, I saw his resolve and, perhaps, pain as the rain made rivulets like tears down his face. He did so want to take this journey. He believed it had a noble purpose. For that moment, my heart seemed to move in my breast, almost as though it were softening.

The river was before us, gray, surging, small wavelets tipped with white, bushes on either side bowing in the wind. Brother Christian Heinrich, our designated leader for the trip made the decision to stop until the rain abated. Brother Bachhoff, our diarist, leaned against a tree sheltered from the rain; taking a pouch from his coat, he unfolded our map that had been made by Brother Sauter over a year ago when the Single Brothers first took this journey to Wachovia, the place in Carolina to which we were headed.

The rest of us huddled as best we could under trees that hardly shielded us from the downpour, while a few of the Single Brothers went forward to find the ferryman to take us across the river. We did not wait long, and the rain abated to a drizzle. The river current was not as swift as it had looked from the bank, and the crossing was done without incident. We put up the tents, and I slept restlessly, my shift sticking to my body. No one complained, however, and somehow this made it easier for all of us even when we had only dried biscuit and water for our breakfast the next morning.

Matthew and one of the Single Brothers took a small wagon to look for food, and returned in late morning with a butchered cow that a tavern owner had sold them. More than that, the kind man sent a sheep with his Negro servant. Before we began the tasks of baking, roasting, washing and darning, we women made good strong coffee, the first we had had on the trip. We sat then, to sip the steaming liquid from the mugs that warmed our hands, and spoke of our good fortune in crossing the river and the kindness of strangers.

"Do you suppose we will always be so comfortable?" Sister Schaub said as she settled her large bottom on a rock. We all laughed at this, for most of us still had on our damp clothes. Although the clouds were breaking up, a cold wind had begun. The fire spluttered over the wet logs.

"We don't want to be too comfortable." Brother Schmid addressed all of us. "If we sit too long, we will never get to the baking and I, for one, need some of Brother Schaub's johnny cakes." At that, men and women began working side by side. After an hour or so, I stood to stretch, the cornmeal grainy on my fingers. Brother Gottfried Aust, his face half-covered with soap, razor in hand, called out to Brother Bachhof, who sat with his ink well on a rock, his quill in hand, writing in our travel diary. "Say there, Brother B., make sure you write that we men will arrive in Wachovia clean-shaven or those of us with wives will hear no end of it." There was a great deal of good-natured laughter. I saw how quickly we all were becoming close to one another though many of our Band were only acquaintances at the start of the journey. My thoughts wandered back to our dear home in Friedensthal and the fellowship we had created there. Perhaps, I thought, perhaps if we build a school, my dearest children will be brought down to Wachovia. Or, because there are always those who travel back and forth, at some time I might ask to go back to Bethlehem to once more hold them close. I patted the johnny cakes into circles and, hearing strange voices, looked up to see a large group of Negroes who stood watching us, seemingly bewildered by our industry and costume. By hand motions, Brother Opitz welcomed them and soon they were exclaiming in the English language over our horses. Then one large Negro approached Matthew. He was as tall as my husband but very broad of shoulder, his head shaven, his skin very dark. He pointed to the trumpet on a tree stump. Matthew held it up and offered it to the large man who carefully, almost tenderly, took the instrument, put it to his lips, and blew making a loud squeak. Then he threw back his head and laughed and laughed. I had never heard laughter like this. It seemed to come from his belly, including the surrounding trees, and felt to me as though it pushed at the clouds above. It was so infectious that we all joined in. Brother Aust held out his hand to the Negro, and took the trumpet, placing it to his lips and blew a loud blast of notes. The visitors then surrounded him, all asking him to play; and although we knew not their words, we knew their wishes. Brother Opitz also picked up his trumpet and in harmony, the two men played a stirring voluntary. The faces of our visitors were transfixed as the brother then played a hymn familiar to all of us and we joined in the chorus. The crowd listened, rapt in their attention, hardly moving until the last note was played. Suddenly, at an unseen sign, they all began to disperse back to the plantation. I watched the crowd walk slowly away, and my Brothers and Sisters turned again to their tasks. Were they slaves, I wondered, or perhaps freedmen who we heard could travel between plantations? But they were not really free, for the ebony of their skin marked them, and we all knew they had not the same freedom we enjoyed.

O, my Saviour, go with those people, I prayed, as I watched their retreating figures. It was the cruelty with which some slave owners treated their slaves that caused tears to gather in my eyes. I could not stop them from brimming over to run down my face, for I had heard such terrible stories of how often these people were bought and sold like cattle and how their little ones were torn from them. I wanted to weep for their courage in the face of such anguish. Through my blurred sight, I saw Matthew place his arm around the shoulder of Brother Schmid and then hold out his arms to take his load of wood, too heavy for the small Brother. He is a good man, I thought. I must try. I must somehow put one foot before the other though each step takes me farther from those I love.

We retired at about eight o'clock, for darkness had settled over the woods. I slept dreamlessly until I was awakened by the sound of voices. Peering from our tent, Sister Opitz and I watched as a small group of Negroes approached, carrying what we learned later were chickens, beans, chestnuts and apples for sale. The next morning we found that our Night Watch, Brother Meyer, had given them all the change he had, trusting that the bounty came from their own small gardens, and that they could keep it for themselves. Thankfully we had some variety then from our meat and cornmeal johnny cakes.

We started out the next morning at about four o'clock while it was still dark. I could see little in the firelight, but I had grown accustomed to slipping my skirt over my shift that I slept in and unbuckling my boots by feel. Without words, my Sisters and I folded our blankets and the Brothers helped take down the tents. We trudged on. The path was well used and easy walking in this part of Virginia. The birds began to wake as we walked, their singing accompanying the sound of our shoes on the packed dirt and the creak of the wagons. I was walking with Sister Rosina Biefel at the front of our group and, hearing strange voices, I saw two wagons ahead of us. They were progressing slowly. A brown cow was tied to the back of one wagon and a dog trotted alongside, but the only signs of human life were the two drivers, who looked very unfriendly. We tried to speak to them, but they avoided our faces as they plodded ahead. There was nothing to do but pass them though the road was narrow and there were but inches between our wagons. We called out greetings to a thin woman and child driving the next wagon, but they were barely acknowledged and we wondered why they did not give us a sign of friendship as so many travelers had done in the past. Brother Christian Heinrich said he had heard that there was much poverty here, and perhaps the wagon-load of travelers had thought we would take up all the available provisions ahead. As I walked the uneven path some of my Sisters began to sing; however, thoughts of the day seemed to render me silent. Why, I wondered, is there suspicion among some people, yet for others a trusting, open hand ready to share the gifts we have been given? In Friedensthal I would have spoken to my Matthew of such questions but I could not yet take him into my confidence; the hard kernel lodged in my heart still contained anger and resentment. I knew this. I knew that these feelings were those that our Lamb had gently urged us to give up. But I could not. Not yet.

I felt a sudden nausea and slight dizziness and reached out to grab a sapling near the road. "Are you feeling all right?" Sister Shaub placed her arm around my waist. I answered that I was sure I was all right but . . . She interrupted me, saying, "You are pale. I think you had better ride for awhile." Walking with me to one wagon, she asked the Brother to stop so I could ride. I was grateful to her and tried to thank her but she moved forward, her girth not slowing her pace. I smiled, recalling the large figure of Mrs. Schlumberger all those years ago in Gelzhausen, who had taken me to Heilbrunn to see the blessed Count for the first time, and had fed me chocolate and raspberry cakes. My mouth watered. I was suddenly ravenous for a sweet.

WE WERE MAKING very good time, and by October 21st we reached the James River in Virginia. There was a settlement built close to the river. Some of the houses were made of stone, others of wood as were so many of the dwellings here in the New World. There was a rather imposing courthouse on the main road, and as our band of travelers walked in front of the entrance, a man stopped Brother Christian Heinrich, demanding to know who we were and where we were going. He was a well-dressed fellow with a balding head, wearing brown breeches and coat. I was too far away to ascertain his features clearly, but I could hear his tone of voice.

"We stop strangers hereabouts," he said.

Brother Christian Heinrich bowed slightly from the waist, his heels together. "We are traveling Brethren, sir, going to our new settlement in Wachovia." Brother Kremer had a lovely tenor voice. "We have two wagons as you can see, and extra horses. We mean no harm and will be on our way."

The man's voice changed. "I am sorry if I was rude," he said. "We are on the lookout for army deserters, and I am placed here to arrest them." Looking over at the group of us women and then glancing at the two wagons, he addressed Brother Christian Heinrich courteously. "I am assured there are none amongst you." He smiled and bade us farewell.

When we settled for our evening meal that night, we had the most delicious potatoes, baked in embers, the flaky white meat flavorful and better than German potatoes. I should have noticed at the time how good our food tasted and how eager I was to stop for meals, not because I needed to rest, but because smelling the campfires and anticipation of food made my mouth water. I smiled to myself, thinking of Susannah and her preoccupation with food when we traveled our first journey. She seemed to be planning recipes as she trekked along, chattering about herbs and apple jelly and whatever meat we had.

IT WAS CLOSE TO THE END of October when we found a very kind farmer who allowed our husbands to sleep in the corn-crib and us Sisters to sleep in his house. Even though we had no beds, and placed our blankets on the floor, with a ceiling above and walls around us, we felt wonderfully warm, as a wind howled outside. Now that November was almost upon us, the weather had really changed. The trees were speckled with green and yellow leaves and the wind was fierce at times. The sound of it was different here than in Pennsylvania, for firs abounded; as the wind caught in the branches, there was a sighing sound that made me sad. What arms now held my little Samuel and who is running after Matthaeus, I thought, as I drifted off to sleep, too weary to keep awake to mourn?

The next morning we received the news that there were two roads we could take in western Virginia, both rough and almost impassable. We started out blindly, branches whipping across our faces in some places, stumbling into holes in others. The going was terribly slow, and we began to wonder why we had taken this unmarked road until we came upon a farm where the land had been cleared and cattle munched in a roughly built, wood-fenced field. I heard Matthew tell Brother Opitz that the cattle were of good quality. He and Brother Kuhnast, with Brother Christian Heinrich, asked if the farmer would sell meat. The man said he would be happy to butcher a cow if we would but wait. I was feeling the cold as we sat on blankets on the ground which was, thank God, dry. When the meat was packaged and stored in the wagons, Brother Hoffman, one of the Single Brothers, walked quickly to Matthew, who was loading some cornmeal, and motioned him to gather all of us together. Matthew's tall figure was easily seen by all of us as he called us to a circle.

"Brethren, we have been blest today in ways we did not know even as we set out this morning. We took a road, unknown perhaps to us, but of course not unknown to The One who leads us." He stopped and looked into our faces, then continued, his voice deeply resonant. "We do not yet know what pitfalls might beset us tomorrow or in the days that follow, so we must carry Him in our hearts, His love and care always with us."

There was slight movement amongst us, and I took Rosina's hand in mine. "Also, had we taken the marked road, we would not have come upon the farm and gotten ample food." He bowed his dark head. "Let us remember Him who leads us and thank Him for watching over the other traveling wagons on the other road, for our absence left more provisions for them."

How like him to speak of the needs of others! It is always the others, never the one. Never me. With a sharp intake of breath, I suddenly could not stop the voice that said my husband had trampled upon my feelings, had thrown them aside. I wrapped my arms around myself and raised my head to look around me at the bowed capped heads of my Sisters and tried to draw courage from them. O, my dear God, help me to bear this. Help me to walk this path as a pilgrim; a pilgrim-stranger with growing courage, if not constant faith.

That night, wolves howled in the forest. Their eerie calling was so frightening and near that we Sisters huddled close in our blankets against the cold and the wild sound. The moon rose over the tall pines. Finally I slept.

November came with lashing rain. We had settled for sleep in the darkness, our fire sputtering close by. First a wind that came suddenly from the west, bending saplings and tearing at the firs. It made a dreadful sound and Sister Schaub, in an attempt at humor, put her hands over her ears and made a funny face. I wanted to laugh, but then, as though poured from a giant pitcher, the rain came. We huddled in our tent, with no way to distract ourselves from the noise of rain pattering on the top and the wind that whistled at the corners. It felt to me as though the sounds would never stop, but at least we were dry if not warm. Surely, I thought, this would last but a short time, and we could get a few hours sleep before starting out before dawn, as we usually did.

Sister Biefel spoke over the sound of rain saying, "This is the worst storm . . . " She stopped in mid-sentence as the top of our tent bowed with water. I felt panic for we were trapped in the small area, the water above us lowering close to our heads. Then, with a sickening crack, the holding pegs loosened and the tent collapsed enfolding us in heavy, wet canvas. Sister Schaub screamed, "Get me out! Get me out!" as, pushing hard on the canvas, we all crawled from under it onto the soaked earth. The rain plastered my hair in my face, and I could not see who it was that held my upper arm and led me to the still-intact Brothers' tent. Shivering, I cowered next to Sister Rosina. We were packed close although some of the Brothers had departed their tent to try and fix ours. The wind continued to whistle, but the rain seemed to lessen. I wanted so to sleep, my head heavy, nausea rising in my throat. Fitfully, I dozed in and out of sleep until I heard Brother Bachhof call out to us that we had better get ready to travel again. One of the Brothers had somehow started a large crackling fire, and wrapped in a few dry blankets from our wagons, we clustered near, Sisters on one side and Brothers on the other. Brother Aust said we surely looked like Indians. Sister Schaub, her blanket covering her head and slipping down almost over her eyes, began to laugh and her hearty, belly-laugh caused us all to look at one another. The laughter was infectious, as one by one we began to giggle and then to laugh. My stomach was sore with laughing, but I could not stop any more than could my Brethren, until at last, like last night's storm, we stopped and with continued small bursts of sound, made ready for the day's journey.

Starting in this fashion seemed to take away the discomfort of wearing wet clothing with water squishing in our shoes. Also, we knew from our map that we were fast approaching our destination.

CHAPTER TWENTY-EIGHT

I t had been a hard stretch the last few days. The roads were barely passable through the woods, sometimes terribly muddy and always with deep ruts and jutting rocks. Many times I caught myself as I tripped and stumbled, and often found that holding to another's arm was not only the safest way to walk, but the chatter of another kept me from dwelling on the dark, painful thoughts I was trying so hard to hide from myself.

On November 1st, we stopped at a farm we had heard was friendly to our people, but found no one about. The Brothers built a fire and we set up our tents. I found that I was quite adept at hammering in the pegs so that Sister Biefel could slip the rope over them. There was a certain satisfaction for me in doing this small task, but I could not help but wish this journey would soon be over.

It was very dark and almost cold in our tent although our campfire was close by. I could not fall asleep. I buried my head in my arms and begged my Saviour to keep watch over my children. Sometimes, I could call to my mind their darling faces, and this brought some comfort; but that late autumn night, my mind was whirling with longing, and I felt both hungry and nauseous at the same time. Then I heard voices, one raised and rather slurred, the other I recognized as Brother Bachhof who was the watch that night. As I rose on my elbow, the better to hear them both, I thought I saw a dart of light near Sister Helena Schmid's sleeping body. I bent forward to better see and cried out in fear and warning to my Sister, "Fire!"

Sister Schmid scrambled to her knees and, clutching her petticoat which was lying next to her, threw it on the flame to extinguish it. I grabbed my shoes and held them in my hands, stomping on her petticoat. I could smell burning, but a wisp of smoke escaped from the trampled clothing and I knew we had extinguished the small blaze.

"Dear God, what happened?" Sister Opitz exclaimed, while Sister Biefel crawled toward Sister Schmid.

"Not to worry," Sister Schmid assured us all. "The only harm is to my petticoat."

Brother Bachhof must have heard our commotion, for he pulled at the entrance to our tent, his face lined with concern. "What is it? Do I smell burning?"

Sister Schmid hurriedly assured him that we had killed the flame. Perhaps, she said, it was an ember blown over from our large fire outside. At that moment the farmer, a Mr. Drollinger, staggered into my view. He was a corpulent man, his head closely attached to his shoulders and he seemed unable to move his head from side to side. As he spoke, he turned his whole body away so as not to be facing our tent. At the same time, he stumbled, caught himself and mumbled, "I am sorry. I truly am frightfully sorry. I was imbibing a bit, you see . . . "

"Come on, sir, we are grateful to you for allowing us to camp here for the night." And Brother Bachhof took the farmer by the elbow and led him away from our tent. Rosina Biefel pinched my arm, giggling a bit, for the poor fellow did look like a turtle that had crawled onto a strange shore.

I pulled my blanket around my shoulders and settled on my side, drawing my legs near my chest. Quietly, I whispered a prayerful "thank you" for our Saviour's protection. Sleep came as I grew warm and events of the day danced before my eyes. I was startled awake by a sound that was both familiar and at the same time, strange. Sister Opitz groaned, "Oh, no, the wolves are yowling again." One by one they raised their yelping cry to the moon as I shivered with the sound that was impossible to shut out. Why was their calling so frightening to me, I wondered? We were safe, for I knew they would not approach our campsite with a blazing fire. And yet, the wild yearning of their calling was almost malevolent, and seemed to voice the very hunger of the surrounding woods that would devour the clearings, the settlements, and return this land again to its past wilderness. Shivering, I hugged my body and burrowed my head under my blanket.

Then, like a bright arrow in the darkness, the reverberation of Brother Opitz' trumpet blasted into the night. Our small campsite, the surrounding fields, bare and harvested, all seemed to me to resonate with the bright sound of notes that flew into that dark night and rebounded into my heart. The wolves, frightened perhaps, were silenced after the trumpet's call faded and the only sound was the regular, comforting clicking of crickets. I fell into a deep sleep.

The next day was Sunday, and we should have been able to make it to the boundary of Wachovia, but for the English law against travel on the Lord's Day. We were about forty miles from our destination, Matthew told us, but I was happy to have stopped, for the nausea that I felt last night was worse this morning and did not abate until I ate some pork and dried peaches, the taste fresh and good on my tongue. Poor Mr. Drollinger begged to pray with us when we gathered for our short service and Matthew placed his hand on the farmer's shoulder saying he was welcome to join us.

SEVERAL DAYS PASSED and, although we were nearing the end of our long and dangerous journey, I felt no great joy. The last morning on the road was misty and cold; the sun had not yet risen. I was used to early rising but that morning was so dark that we could not make out the road until a young boy who had joined us last night from a neighboring farm said he would show us the way. It occurred to me that there was always someone who showed us the way throughout this journey, in spite of the fact that we had good maps, and a few of the Single Brethren had made the journey previously, the way was rough, the weather often cold and rainy and it was easy to lose our way. Perhaps it was, as Matthew said that the Saviour was walking with us. I so fervently wished I could feel His presence.

It was about noon time when we reached the farm of a Mr. Hannibal Edwards, a Quaker who had been ever so kind to our Single Brethren a year ago. His wife, a pleasant, red-haired woman with a friendly smile, came out to meet us. Clasping Sister Schaub's hand, she asked us in to dinner. Brother Heinrich had mentioned earlier that these folk had little to spare and so politely refused the farmer's kind offer. However, I could see that Mrs. Edwards was so eager for some womanly conversation that I approached Brother Heinrich, whispering that perhaps just the women could join the family, and this was how it all worked out. There was a long table set with crockery, and root vegetables in their juices bubbled in the large hearth. Mrs. Edwards had made cornmeal mush, and though we had had our fill of this staple, it was tasty with the fresh butter she had churned the day before. We sat comfortably on benches at either side of the table, and the two comely daughters served us. I looked closely at the Edwards' daughters, graceful girls who smiled easily as did their mother. Although our language was German and theirs English, we managed to describe parts of our journey to Mr. Edwards and his family. I watched each of the lovely young girls, their facial expressions telling me of their interest in our adventures. Would my Anna grow into early womanhood with such grace? Sister Schaub dipped her spoon and with a great sigh of satisfaction told the girls that not all journeys were easy but that our Saviour had provided us good food and lodging from kind people most of the way. Sister Biefel, who had done much traveling in her life, said that this journey was, perhaps, the most difficult for her, but that she looked forward to settling a new place. Then we recounted the story of the wolves that were afraid of our trumpets, rivers crossed and too much rain. We had many questions for the family about weather and crops in this part of America.

From the open door, I could smell the pleasant odor of tobacco, and the low mumble of men's voices. Mr. Edwards exclaimed with pleasure when Brother Sauter gave him a hat brought from Bethlehem. Brother Foeckel said he would cut out a coat for Mr. Edwards that Mrs. Edwards could sew when she had time. There was much laughter about how little time a wife had on a farm. Sitting at the table, I felt very calm and content. We were almost at our destination, and we were warm and comfortable for the moment. *The day is sufficient unto itself* our Saviour had said, and I understood at that moment just what was meant by these words. Though the past could never return, the heart remembers, and one could welcome joy or, God help us, re-experience pain. These things I knew. And yet I also knew that the days to come were unknown. Of course the Brethren say if we can but believe in His love, we can bear whatever comes. I bent down to stretch my legs under the table, wishing there was time to remove my shoes and perhaps to wade in the small brook that bordered one side of the house. But we had miles to go, so we reluctantly made ready to leave the Edwards' farm, clasping hands and expressing our thanks. Hannibal Edwards placed his new hat on his head and did a small jig, much to our merriment. Mrs. Edwards and her daughters waved to us until we came to the bend of the road, and the farmhouse was lost to view.

I began the morning walking next to the supply wagon, kicking at the fallen leaves that covered our road. Matthew was walking at the front of our group, and when I saw him turn to look at me, I looked away. There would be time enough, I thought, to try to heal the wound I felt in my heart; but I would have to do this in silence and alone for I could feel resentment build in my belly. Maybe it was this that to caused my increasing nausea, I thought.

It was about the middle of the day when we stopped to rest at Lisher's Creek. I did remove my shoes. As the clear water swirled around my hot ankles, very cold and bubbling, our creek at Friedensthal came to my mind. I had so loved to feel the rounded stones, the rush of water. Lisher's Creek was cold enough on that November day to send chills all the way up my legs, but I didn't mind the cold, and when Rosina Biefel called my name, I stood a moment without moving to remember my dear mother and the brook of my childhood.

We continued our journey and, feeling weary, I climbed onto one wagon. The shadows lengthened as afternoon approached; then, barely perceptible, I thought I heard the long awaited sound. The wagon and its wheels on the rough ground made a loud, crunching noise. Added to this was the twittering of birds as they made ready for the long night; so it was not until the sound came again, louder this time that, I recognized the long-awaited notes of a trumpet. I imagined them golden, bright with welcome, as they echoed through the tall pines. Brother Aust, next to me whooped, "Aha, it must be Brother Friis." It was as though our whole troop, quiet, weary, not speaking much, suddenly came alive. We quickened our pace and even our horses snuffled and stamped, swinging their necks as though to rid themselves of bridles and heavily loaded wagons to run free. Brothers Aust and Opitz trotted ahead of us, blowing their trumpets with the verse, "Peace and health and every good be with you." Brother Lisher and Brother Friis rode into view. "Ha! I knew it was you." Brother Aust drew his horse up to Brother Friis' large brown mare. "Your trumpet has a clearer sound than mine."

"Perhaps it is the one who blows, not the instrument that makes the better sound," Brother Friis retorted. Brother Aust called over his shoulder something about how "Those Danes always have to win a contest." Brother Friis raised his instrument to his lips and blasted a loud note.

Our road wound through heavy woods, darkening on that November day. But ahead I could see sunlight. Coming out of the trees, our road passed a meadow, apparently cleared by the Single Brethren last year. There was no evidence of cut grain and the whole area looked as though it had been trampled upon. I called over to Brother Friis from my perch on the wagon, asking him what had happened here. He slowed his horse, that snorted and pranced, eager to get to its barn. "Last summer there were reports of Indian attacks along the Catawba River, so some militiamen were sent up here." He pulled on his reins to slow his frisky mount. "Of course we had planted flax and barley in the spring and had great hopes of a good crop, but the militia decided to hold a muster on that very field." He shook his head, a lock of light hair falling over his forehead. "We had a discussion among ourselves as to why the North Carolina Militia would trample our newly sowed plants and decided they were angry because we refused to fight alongside them." His face took on a serious air and he pulled up his horse again on a short rein.

"We were annoyed to say the least! But as usual, saner heads than mine prevailed." He smiled then.

"But the field lies fallow. You didn't replant. Did you go to the Carolina authorities?"

"No. As I said, more far-sighted men in our group observed that if we said nothing, the militiamen would undoubtedly enter our settlement and see what goods we had to sell." He laughed and slapped the reins.

"At least one of us can usually forget an annoyance and think about what is good for business."

I laughed with this Brother for it was true of the Brethren and Sisters. They did seem to turn anger or disappointing situations into advantages. I knew I had a lesson to learn as the wagon jogged along, but the thought left my mind as I imagined it would not be long before we all sat together for an evening meal. I was very hungry.

The sun was setting quickly, but the day was clear and no clouds obscured the slanting sun's rays which illuminated the small settlement in a clearing, the dark woods on all sides. I was pleasantly surprised at how much work had been accomplished by the Single Brothers in the past year. I saw they had built a shoe-shop and kitchen, and to my delight, also the smithy with its stone forge, the fire still burning, its embers filling the air with an odor so familiar to me. The mill, important to us, had been almost finished and the mill pond dammed.

"There it is. The Brothers' cabin," Rosina Biefel cried out. And, indeed, I could see the small dwelling where the Single Brothers had ate, slept and worshipped. It was well made of logs, but very small. We had been told that the Brothers had taken a sick horse in with them to this small cabin during a few terribly cold days last winter. I did not want to imagine the discomfort of those brethren. Also, they had welcomed many refugees who were fleeing the increasing Indian attacks all around the settlement, sharing their meager food until the worry about attacks had diminished. I knew our people had usually had good relations with the Indians in the north, so if those of us who settled our new land learned the languages of the natives, as we had done before, perhaps there would be no cause to worry.

With one more blast from his trumpet, Brother Aust called out, and about ten Single Brothers came running from the log house that had housed them for the past year. I could feel the anticipation around me, for mail from Pennsylvania was so long in coming between our settlements; however, although I understood their eagerness, my stomach was clutching with hunger. I climbed down from the wagon and approached Sister Maria Schaub. "Do you have any bread or fruit with you? I am so hungry." She reached inside her pocket and gave me some pieces of dried apple, saying, "I always put something there in case we have to wait too long to eat." She leaned close to me and whispered, "I really must get to wherever we are to settle and sleep. My monthly courses have begun and I . . . "

Her words were like needle pricks. Wait, wait, I said to myself. I must stay calm. I tried to count backward, but panic stopped me. I took a very deep breath and started again. It is the first of November . . . when did I last have my monthly time? I felt my breath coming fast, almost a gasp.

"Are you all right, Christina?" Maria Schaub's face was close to mine and wrinkled with worry." She took my arm, and we walked toward the Brothers' House that would serve as our dwelling until the larger building was finished. I placed one foot in front of another and tried to think of months, but still could not seem to put the days in order. Taking Maria's arm, I said, "I am really all right. It is just that I felt so hungry. But your apple helped indeed" It had. The nausea had subsided. Brother Foeckel said that we should all sit down to a meal before we unpacked, and could make ourselves familiar with the place in the morning when it was light. The Single Men served us newcomers as we sat at long tables, the steam of roasted hare, squash, and pumpkin rising from large wooden platters. There was a great deal of talk, Brother Kuhnast telling of the howling wolves and of times when our wagons were pushed up steep hills by the men.

"And by the women!' Sister Maria Schaub reminded them.

My roiling thoughts had subsided as the food warmed me and a strange lassitude came over me. To myself I repeated the words, "I am with child again." But in my heart I did not believe these words. I looked down one long table to see Matthew speaking seriously with Brother Aust. I did not want to catch his eye and rapidly looked down at my plate, now empty. I had no wish to see my husband or to speak with him, and as the memory of our last time alone came to me, I shuddered, recalling his plea for love and my cold acquiescence.

After our brief meal, Brother Friis and Brother Foeckel showed us where we would sleep in the crowded Brothers' House. There were seven couples who had made the journey and ten Single brothers had accompanied us. Of course we had the five Brethren wagon drivers who had to find a place to sleep. The Single Brothers who had been here for a year made our whole group one of sixty souls. The Brothers had made a partition of tent cloth to separate the men from the women and we were told they would put up boards in the next few days. This arrangement, though crowded, would be workable until the larger place was finished for married couples and the various craft houses built, where couples could live together later. Some of the men made their beds in the kitchen and smithy and others decided to sleep outdoors. Though the weather was cooling, it was dry and we had grown accustomed to this arrangement. The women spread blankets on the floor trying to create some distance from one another in the small space, but this was impossible. I felt that if my arm reached out in my sleep I would surely hit Rosina Biefel in the face; So drawing the blanket over my shoulder, I wrapped my arms around me, closed my eyes and tried to calm my whirling thoughts and separate them into some neat pattern. I was going to bear a child. That was the fact I could not seem to truly believe although the signs were evident. How could I have been so blind? I had never experienced nausea of the kind that had plagued many of my Sisters, only feeling it occasionally. Certainly the overriding need to eat often I knew well. But while preparing for the journey, and then finally traveling from Nazareth to Wachovia, I did not observe closely the passing of days and the lack of my monthly cleansings. I took in a deep breath, and knew with certainty it was my overwhelming grief for my children that prevented me from knowing what my body was showing me. This and something more. Anger. My face felt hot, and I clutched my shoulders. Why did my Saviour not let me know of this new babe? Maybe Matthew would not have been so eager to leave our farm at Friedensthal if he had known. Perhaps no one would even have asked us. I could curse my body for its bursting health; for being the expectant receptacle of his seed. I dug my fists into my belly, and vowed not to tell my secret. I did not sleep.

CHAPTER TWENTY-NINE

I could not keep my secret as I had wished, because of what happened. It was not that anyone guessed my condition, for the women who had traveled with me were not as close to me nor as discerning as Susannah had been; nor was it because my husband noticed anything different about my demeanor. In fact, I had been successful in avoiding him even when we passed one another on a path or at meals. I was somewhat surprised that he did not pursue me in some way, but we had known each other's ways well enough through the years, and he must have understood it would be useless to try and reduce my anger before I was ready to give it up. No, my need to hold a secret vanished when we received news that caused overwhelming anguish to our whole community. My selfish anger at my husband and even at my Saviour at causing me to leave my beloved children was replaced with another, larger sensibility that caused me to cling again to those who had been part of our mission here in the wilderness.

We worked very hard those first months here, and my voracious hunger was much the same for my companions. For the women even helped to drag logs for the new dwellings for the craftsmen, set up spinning wheels and took turns cooking large meals that seemed to assuage hunger for short periods of time. The heavy work pulled my muscles and stretched my body and I knew this was good for me, for though I was certainly aware of the little secret I carried within me, the hard work helped me to put aside my anger. I was less liable to spit out the hateful words that rushed so easily to my mind.

The work continued. Brother Feldhausen quickly fashioned a plough so we could till one cleared field, and we burned out hollow logs to make barrels. Deer were scarce, but one Brother managed to kill a large buck to supplement our usual fare of pumpkins and corn. Daylight was with us less every day as winter approached, and we were well aware that cold and snow would hinder us as the Brethren chopped trees, their fingers numb, and we women carried heavy pails of cold water from the well. The rope handle dug into my hand, and the pain of this seemed to please me, as though a physical pain could somehow take the place of that which weighed on my heart night and day.

We had some distressing news in the form of a letter in a newspaper Brother Jacob Loesch had brought with him from New Bern that described us as friends of the French. Of course, this letter echoed the sentiments of those who saw the Indians in pay of the French, and because we had worked among Indians in Pennsylvania, we were implicated as enemies of the English. Brother Christian Heinrich called us together one early morning to advise us to keep quiet about any views we might have if spoken to by a visitor to our settlement here. Despite the cold of that November morning, I could feel the heat of anger rise in my breast as well as a surge of longing for news of our little Indian Esther. Oh, how was she faring in Bethlehem, I wondered? I imagined tucking her shining black hair into her little white bonnet.

The first days of December brought winds and moisture that clung to my clothing as though we were back at sea, and it was during those cold, wet days that Brother Friis made ready to return to Pennsylvania. He was free to go, and I was not. I laced my jacket tight over my swelling breasts and thought wildly for a moment that I would beg him to take me with him. This was demented, I knew. But if only, I thought, if only I could make the journey back. If only I could see the smoke rising from the stone chimney of our farmhouse, see the hill rise behind it, surely covered now in hoar frost, and hear the sweet music of the organ, the toll of the bell. O, my Saviour, if only I could spend just a little time with my Anna, to see how she was growing, to hear Matthaeus' laugh and to hold little Samuel close. We had had no news of those in Pennsylvania, and I so longed to hear.

We had a Lovefeast in the middle of the day to see Brother Friis off. Large cups of steaming coffee were passed in the usual way by some of the Brothers, and I carried baskets of buns to my Brothers and Sisters. For the first time we heard the beautiful, high sound of flutes accompanying the trumpets and trombones in concert. All in all, we now had eight instruments here in these early days and when Brother Meyer raised his violin to play a merry tune, I could almost feel myself back once again up north in the home I had learned so to love. The *Gemeinhaus* so newly built of logs, was warmed by a tile stove as our meeting house had been in Nazareth, and with the smell of coffee and yeasty buns, I felt lulled into a certain contentment. Somehow, I thought, someway, I will find a way back to my children. There was a heavy rain falling as Brother Friis mounted his horse, accompanied by two Single

Brothers who were going part way with him and returning here later in the evening. My heart went with him as I stood in the doorway alone for some minutes until he and the others disappeared from sight, the sound of hoof beats fading against the sound of the rain. That night I retired with my Sisters to our dormitory room. As we prepared for bed, there was much talk about the small houses that had recently been built for the various craftsmen and their wives. Eventually, each couple would have a small dwelling, but at this early time in our settling, the married couples would live in a dormitory as we had done in Germany and Bethlehem. I cannot say I was sorry about this, for I did not want to face my husband alone until I could speak to him with some sense of reason instead of the raging tumult I felt in my breast. I knew I should pray mightily, to share my feelings with my Saviour, and during those cold November days I did try so hard. Even as we washed clothes, gathered corn and salted the beef we had bought from one neighboring farm, I repeated, "Dear Saviour, take this bitter cup from me," as echo of his own prayer at Gethsemane. Some days I found relief. Of course I knew that I could not hold my secret much longer since soon my condition would soon be evident.

The remainder of December passed very quickly, for we all were so busy with our various building tasks that each day seemed to run into the next. The wind caught in the pines with a whistling sound and I could smell snow in the air although it had not yet fallen. The weather grew colder. Most of the leaf-bearing trees were bare.

Often I stood on the road at the end of our clearing, listening for hoof beats, hoping against hope that someone would bring news from Bethlehem and Nazareth. This had become a sort of ritual for me every morning and the gray day that news finally did come was the very day we were to move into the married couples' new dwelling place. Clouds were low in the sky. The tops of the pines were hidden in mist for much of the morning, and I had just taken the last pail of water from the well when I heard the sound of hoof beats. A large dappled horse came into view its rider unfamiliar to me, his legs gripped close to the horse's side, his body bent low in the saddle against the wind. I stood alone at the well, putting the pail down, and waited until the horseman was close to me. He pulled on his reins to stop the beast, its breath vaporizing in the cold air.

"I have some news. Can you tell me where I might find Mr. Christian Heinrich?" He waved his hand over toward the *Gemeinhaus* in back of me.

"Yes, right there."

He threw his leg over his horse and jumped to the road in front of me. His face was red with cold and his countenance very serious. I had the distinct feeling that he wanted to impart his news, yet at the same time seemed hesitant.

"Here, I'll take you into the house," I said, and began to lead the way. It took but a few minutes to walk up the path.When I opened the door, the stranger walked ahead of me into the room.

"I have business with Mr. Christian Heinrich—I think he is the gentleman I need to speak with." His voice was loud in the room; his accent identified him as an Englishman. I was not sure if I was to hear the news this man was to voice, and I moved closer to the door as Brother Christian Heinrich came from another room.

"I have news for your Brethren," he said, and turned to me with a questioning stare. I mumbled a few words and made a hasty retreat, remembering that I had left my pail near the well. I felt discomfort as though my early nausea had returned. Why didn't the stranger speak up in front of me? Perhaps there was news of the conflict between the French and the English and he kindly did not want to alarm me. With that thought, I found myself terribly curious but at the same time felt it prudent to wait. I stood for a moment at the well, noticing that gray clouds were moving swiftly, obscuring the morning sun. As I picked up the pail, I saw Brother Biefel running toward our large bell, which hung from wooden beams outside the *Gemeinhaus*. He began to pull the rope and as the clapper hit the side of the bell, the loud tolling carried its leaden notes over the whole settlement. I ran to him, but before I reached him, he called out that we all needed to gather together; that there was news the messenger had brought from Cape Fear.

It did not take long for all of us to crowd into the large room. The atmosphere was one of cautious anticipation. News from outside our settlement was usually passed around quickly from person to person as we continued our work and it was very unusual for us to be called together in this way. No one said much, and I noticed that Rosina Biefel was frowning and Brother Schmid's forehead was creased with worry. We waited until the last person entered and closed the door against the cold. No one sat, and it seemed to me we huddled together as though our touching would protect us from news that would give us pain. Matthew stood in the front of the room; when there was quiet, he said, "We might well remember our hymn, *As long as Jesus Lord remains/each day new rising glory gains.'"* Then, before turning to Brother Christian Heinrich, "This is a time we must remember that HE is with us."

Then Brother Christian Heinrich stood quietly, as though gathering his thoughts. I knew the news he was to impart was very serious.

"Brothers and Sisters. I will begin with saying to you that a newspaper account—this was not a spoken word—has been brought by our guest, here." He turned to the horseman who cleared his throat and looked at the floor. "While traveling in the section of Carolina, east of Wachovia, our messenger here found a news account of terrifying proportions. This news account said that the residents of Bethlehem had been attacked and that many were killed." He could not continue and turned away to blow his nose. There was silence at first and then Rosina Biefel called out in a strangled voice, "What is the news of Nazareth?"

"None. This concerned only Bethlehem, and we do not know if the report is true." Brother Christian Heinrich turned to Matthew, who said nothing as he stared into space. Men and women put their arms around each other, calling out questions to each other. "Our children, our children, what of them? What of Sister Nitschmann, what of Brother Boehler, what of . . . " The names came from choked throats, from tearful cries. I felt Matthew's arms around me as he had moved to stand behind me, and I leaned into his body. I felt vomit rise in my throat as images, terrible images, came to me. I turned to look into my dear husband's face and saw a kind of anguish I had never seen before. The pain evidenced there made him look years older, his blue eyes, clouded. It was at that instant that I realized I must submit my will to that of Him who knows better than we poor men and women, who have so much to learn. Somehow I had to summon my strength so that we both could go on—to continue the mission we had so eagerly embarked on all those years ago. Calm enveloped me then. Was it My Saviour who put warm arms around me? I took my husband's hand and led him to the door, moving around the bodies of my Brothers and Sisters who stood together in shock, some with tearstained faces, others cautioning restraint. Outside, the cold wind swirled around us as we stood alone on the steps of the *Gemeinhaus.* Matthew looked pale and I took his face in my hands to comfort him.

"Christina, my dearest," he began, "I have taken you from all you have loved because of my own pride. Oh, God, I cannot even protect my children."

"Listen, my husband. We have no proof that our children are in danger for haven't you reminded me that for their protection the children have been moved at times from Bethlehem to Nazareth? Surely, the wise Brothers and Sisters could anticipate an attack."

He began to interrupt me but I put my finger to his lips to silence him. "We do not know if the news story is true. We do know that the Indians have never attacked our settlements. To the contrary, we have made some our brothers and sisters."

Matthew pulled away from me and looked to the sky, "I must remember that if our children have been taken from us, they now are with our Saviour. It is just that I . . . "

We held each other then and both of us wept. We were but two grieving parents without the true human comfort of good news that might or might not come to us. We could only cling to one another then and try to hope. Try to summon the faith that was at that moment so sorely tried. Finally, I drew away and found I could smile into my beloved's face. "My dear, dear, husband, no matter what news comes to us, we have not lost all our children. I have held a secret from you in my anger and sorrow at leaving Pennsylvania. A secret you should know." He said nothing but searched my face as though to somehow know my next words. "Oh, Matthew, I am with child. Our babe will be born in the spring."

Many emotions passed over his face before I reached up to put my cheek next to his. Standing thus, I felt the familiar warmth between us. After we had reluctantly parted that night, each to our own bed, I lay in the darkness, and tried not to hear the occasional sounds of a Sister blowing her nose or stifling her cries. I felt calm and sure that night because I felt His love, His presence in the room. I wished so that others could feel this also, and prayed this would be so. The wind rose and I crept from my bed to look out the window. As I did so, a flutter in my womb came once, and then again. I put my hand on my belly to warm my small babe and looked outside to see it was snowing.

⚜ ✳ ⚜

CHAPTER THIRTY

The falling snow was wet, and when the weather turned colder, the trees and bushes surrounding our clearing were encased in a thin layer of ice. The morning sun rising on that early December day glistened on the branches. I stood by a window gazing at that morning of bright ice. At another time I might have thrilled to its beauty. But my heart was heavy, so even God's gift of beauty could not bring light to the dark sadness that engulfed me. Oh, when, I whispered, when will we have news of our children?

I stood for some time in the silence of the early morning, thinking about this time of year when we eagerly anticipated the anniversary of our dear Lamb's birth. It was a time of waiting, a time of excitement: Usually the weeks before Christmas were filled with plans for celebration. That December of 1755 I wondered how we would have the strength of faith to celebrate if it became known that our children had been hurt or worse. I could not think about this. That day, I did not know that a message of our Saviour's love and care would come to us soon.

The messenger was none other than the Single Brother Meyer, who had been traveling from Bethlehem to Wachovia since the end of November. He arrived here at the beginning of Advent, innocent of the joy he brought. In his unhurried way, Brother Meyer walked to the *Gemeinhaus*, entered and closed the door. Then, from my window, I saw Brother Foeckel run from the Single Brothers' house to the bell outside the *Gemeinhaus*. With great vigor he pulled the rope. The bell resounded in the clear, cold air. Without capes or warm coats, men and women ran from the barn, the forge, the carpentry shop, and I joined them from the married couples' house. Gasping and laughing at once, Brother Foeckel called out, "There was no massacre in Bethlehem. It was all a mistake—a mistake!"

We all spoke at once, crying out to him. "How do you know . . . what really did happen . . . our children are safe, our loved ones . . . " We could not contain our joy, our relief. Brothers and Sisters hugged one another, some wiping tears, some laughing aloud.

My thoughts ran into one another in relief, in joy. My feet slipped on the shimmering snow, and as I hesitated to regain my balance, time seemed to stop. I felt the anguish of the past days when we heard the news of Bethlehem's massacre; the look of pain on Matthew's face and the cries of grief around me as the words spread like a plague. And now, only days later, the world had changed, and our cries were those of joy. I stepped forward, taking the arm of Sister Schaub. As we seated ourselves, I had to ask myself, did our Lamb test our love and faithfulness? To make us feel like God's servant, Job, who stood steady during his ordeal? If I could truly believe that "perfect love casts out fear," my life would be so much easier. But perfect love may not be possible for an ordinary woman. I wondered if our pain is self wrought when we allow doubt to surround us. Or is there some sense to it all that only He can know? I felt so storm-tossed, so unsure. A flutter in my belly as my babe moved. The room swam before me, blurred at first and then increasingly clear, the wooden benches, the warmth from my Brethren as they clustered together. Thank God, how familiar it was, how secure.

There was constant chatter until Brother Christian Heinrich stood before us. His hand rested on Brother Meyer's thin shoulder. "Brother Meyer has been in Bethlehem these past days and has also been in touch with Nazareth and the outlying farms. He knows nothing of any news accounts about a massacre of our Brethren. He told me there have been individual Indian attacks on farms to the west of our communities, but Bethlehem remains safe."

It was the Norwegian, Dr. Kalberlahn, who walked to the front of the room to stand next to Brother Heinrich. He was tall, standing head and shoulders above Brother Christian Henrich. He had thinning blond hair and, usually, a serious mien combined with the calm and confidence of the seasoned physician. However, his touch, always gentle, was often accompanied by a radiant smile as he reassured one patient after another that their bodies would heal. On that December day, he smiled broadly. "Let us bow out heads and consider the Watchword for this day." Of course, we had always a Watchword for each day after our morning meal. But on this early morning, many of us had not yet eaten, and our haste at coming together precluded many of our usual customs. Brother Martin Kalberlahn looked out at us sitting quietly now. "Listen, my Brothers and Sisters." It was very quiet in the room. Even the logs in the tile stove had stopped their hissing as he spoke from Psalms:

"If it had not been our Lord who was on our side, when men
rose up against us, Then they would have swallowed us up alive."

Quietly he walked to the rear of the room. Then Brother Schaub raised his violin to his shoulder and began to play, *"As long as Jesus Lord remains, each day new glory gains."*

The hymn was known to us all, and our voices filled the room with praise and thanksgiving. Strange and wonderful, I thought, that the same Watchword, decided upon for each year at Herrnhut, echoed in all of our communities each day. It was always timely. Surely, this was a message from our Lamb to reassure us that we were safe in His care. My mind flew to the far-flung missions from Greenland to far in the south, from bitter cold to flaming heat. My babe turned within me as though to echo my faith.

ON THE ANNIVERSARY of our Lord's birth, we were awakened by trumpets. Our breakfast was jolly, the buns soft and warm, filled with precious sugar, and we drank our strong coffee from the new mugs fashioned by Brother Aust. When we gathered in the *Gemeinhaus*, the smell of fresh boughs brought in from the forest yesterday to decorate the main room added to the festivities. Brother Christian Heinrich read Count Zinzendorf's Christmas sermon from Europe that he had based on Paul's letter to the Corinthians. His strong bass voice filled the room. "For by one spirit, we are all baptized into one body—Jews or Greeks, slaves or free—and all were made to drink of one spirit."

How difficult it was to reconcile Paul's words to the world we lived in! When strangers arrived in our settlement, they so often brought news of the hatred of one group toward another. I could feel their fear as well as hear their anger. The occasional reports we received from travelers said the war was causing great consternation in the north. Often since we arrived here, I found myself stopping as I sat at my spinning wheel, the flaxen thread loose on my palm. For that moment, the cold sense of terror would overcome me, for I was so fearful for my children far away. I closed my eyes and prayed to keep them safe, whispering only, "Oh, God, oh, God." No other words would come to me. I pushed the treadle to start the wheel spinning yet again, and sighed, thinking of the trouble and strife in this world.

There was a light frost on the bushes the day I saw strangers on our path from the woods. I could make out a man, woman and three children. One little one was carried by the father, and the mother, holding the other children by hand, stumbled as she followed the man to the door of the *Gemeinhaus*. Brother Christian Heinrich opened the door and

hastened to welcome them. Later, Sister Schaub told me the family had
heard Cherokee Indians had declared war. Fearing for their lives, they
hurried through the woods to us with only the clothes on their backs. At
one congregational meeting, we spoke openly to one another about the
difficulty of feeding and housing refugees. But no one was ever turned
away. Leaning over the table at the front of our meeting room, Brother
Christian Heinrich spoke eloquently about maintaining a friendly attitude
to both whites and Indians who might come our way. "For after all," he
said, "we are all children of God and should remember that when rumors
of war put fear in our hearts. We must remember that God loves us and
will protect us." His face was earnest as he held out his hands in an
imploring gesture. I tried so hard to hold to these words, for I knew that in
a few months I would bear yet another child. I hugged my arms around
my body and prayed for courage.

THE YEAR 1756 COMMENCED with many accomplishments in our
young community. Brother Aust continued turning out more pottery
from his kiln, and we were able to get a good price for it from those
who came to buy. More land was cleared, and the men finished the grist
and saw mills. Brothers and Sisters had, since we arrived, shared the
arduous job of washing clothes outdoors each week. But when the wash
house was finished, we Sisters took over the task. I found this work to be
to my liking that winter, because we often sang as we washed; the steam
of heated water and the smell of our newly made soap pleasantly filled
the small house.

The most satisfying hour for all of us was during the impromptu
concerts our musicians gave on several evenings a week. Especially when
the weather was wet and cold, and we had worked hard all day, it was
with pleasure that we gathered together in the evening after supper to
hear our musicians play. Whenever possible, those who had been back
and forth from the Old World, brought copies of the latest music to
Bethlehem and Nazareth and eventually, the copies—sometimes torn at
the edges, I admit—arrived here. How diligently our musicians practiced.
In Nazareth, those Sisters who played an instrument or had sweet voices
often got together to make music. Here, because of our small numbers,
we Sisters had not yet formed a singing choir, and of course it was only
proper for women to play a violin or spinet. Brother Aust was adamant
that Brothers who brought instruments join him when he got out his

252 BARBARA DOWD WRIGHT

trumpet, and gladly they complied. He said that his trumpet was ever so much better and easier to play than the one fashioned from wood that one Single Brother made when he first came to Wachovia. The singing of the wolves in the forest, no longer frightening to me, seemed almost an accompaniment to the strains of our flute, violin and horns!

We had arranged very carefully to have certain Brothers designated as messengers between Pennsylvania and Wachovia. Letters and gossip from Bethlehem and Nazareth were important to all of us. Brother Jacob Loesch, who spoke English and German, was usually the person to bring news. He was an ordained minister, but because of his skill in business, he was made manager of our small settlement and also traveled north and south to deal with various government leaders.

This Brother, with his sense of humor, often caused laughter among us. What I was so grateful to him for was that he never failed to let us know how our children were in school and nursery. The last time he was here, he told us that our mission in Gnadenhütten was flourishing and that several Single Brothers had made the trip from Nazareth to the mission to help the Indians there with our language as well as to learn theirs. The Anders were there with their small daughter, as were Susannah Nitschmann and her husband, Martin. Of great interest to Matthew and me was that Susannah and George Partsch had gone lately to be the housekeepers for the missionaries. I was certain that Susannah would be happy to go because she always looked forward to new work. I could clearly imagine her tramping over the wet leaves on the path to the mission, her mind full of what she would bake when she lit the fire in the hearth. Smiling to myself, I also imagined Susannah briskly giving orders to those Sisters less sure of themselves in the kitchen. She would have the place the way she wanted it in short order! Perhaps the road was safer between Bethlehem and Gnadenhütten than it was here.

Those of us who had made the journey south, knew the roads through Virginia were particularly rough and there was no little danger from highwaymen. Brother Loesch told us that on one occasion he was surprised and somewhat frightened by a horseman who had come toward him at a great speed on a narrow road through the woods in Northern Virginia. Brother Loesch's horse reared as the man came into view, and he was almost thrown from his saddle. The horseman drew his steed to a full stop, removed his hat and greeted Brother Loesch in English. When Brother Loesch answered the man in English, and told him briefly of his task as a messenger between Pennsylvania and the Carolinas for his fellow Moravians, the man calmed his stomping horse and took out his canteen and offered water. He told Brother Loesch that his haste was because he was carrying important papers to Pennsylvania. He apparently had been a surveyor but had recently been chosen for other tasks that he did not divulge at the time. Jacob Loesch was well aware of the conflicts between the French and the English and told us that something about the young man's quiet bearing caused him to wonder if he might have been carrying important but secret papers on this lonely road. Brother Loesch was clear with the stranger that he was a Moravian and took no sides in American conflicts, but he wished the horseman Godspeed on his journey. The stranger said he had heard of the Moravians and of their successful work among the Indians, and introduced himself as George Washington. Brother Loesch saluted the tall, young man as they parted, one going north, the other, south. Such stories of friendly encounters on the road were welcome, for sometimes we all felt bound by the surrounding woods and anxious during the intervals between visitors who would bring us news of other parts of America as well as letters from the Old Country.

It had been some months since we had last heard news from Pennsylvania, except for the joyful report from Brother Meyer who had been on the road to Eastern Carolina and knew only that Bethlehem and Nazareth had not been attacked. Of course, he had told us that there was trouble west of our settlements, but the nature of that trouble was unknown to him. War and rumors of war abounded as always, but here deep in the Carolina woods, the reports of Cherokee attacks worried us most, and even those often turned out to be more the hysteria of families living unprotected and on their own, than the reality of anything murderous. I suppose I was becoming complacent as I spun flax, and dreamed of safe roads that would someday take me back to visit our children, if even for a short time.

It was two traders from Virginia who arrived here and asked for a night's lodging that again brought some fearful news. Matthew had taken their horses to the stable. Speaking to the trader who accompanied him, we learned that the man had read in a Pennsylvania paper that several Brethren had been killed in Bethlehem. Matthew told the man that we had heard such rumors, but that Brother Loesch had confirmed that the news was untrue. As we were gathering for our evening meal, Matthew told me the rumor. "We will see. God loves us. That we still believe, and it will yet prove." His face was calm and serious. I touched his cheek. As he smiled his quiet smile, I had to believe what he said that God's love would protect us here on our earthly pilgrimage. Or, if we were called to Him, we would reside close to His side. My prayers that night for my children were not those of fear but, rather, of hope.

A week later, Brother Loesch, having been to Salisbury to pay our taxes, returned to us. We had had new snow and it was bitterly cold which surprised me for I thought that this southern clime would be warmer in the winter than it had proved to be that year. Our tile stove, newly installed in the *Gemeinhaus* made me grateful for its warmth when we assembled to hear Brother Christian Heinrich. We settled on the backless benches, whispering to each other. Rosina Biefel sat next to me with a quick greeting, and turned toward the rear of the room, her dark eyes seeming to search for someone. She said how cold she had been while gathering firewood this early morning. Indeed, I had noted that my hands were cold and dry when I tried to fix the spindle on my wheel. I was ready for spring!

Brother Christian Heinrich stood before us quietly waiting for us all to come into the room. On our journey from Nazareth, Brother Heinrich had been a steady presence. Now, his sturdy body in an attitude of patient waiting, his face looking out over us, asked that we all bow our heads in prayer. I bowed mine and prayed that I would be able to feel our Saviour's presence whatever tidings were imparted.

Brother Loesch walked to the front and stood before us, the dust of the road still evident on his coat, his boots muddy. He held his hat in his hand.

"Brothers and Sisters," he began, "the Sheriff in Salisbury has it on good authority that there has, indeed, been some sort of attack west of Bethlehem and Nazareth." I could feel an intake of breath as we leaned forward to listen.

"We do not know exactly where the attacks were or who perpetrated them. Nor do we know if any of our Brethren have been killed. I am afraid we will have to wait and pray and trust in His will."

I could feel my face flush, and I clenched my fists in my lap. It took so terribly long to receive news, and even as we received it, we had no idea if it were true. Oh, that there was some way news could travel on angel wings back and forth so that we were not in this constant state of either terror or euphoria.

Two days later a stranger stopped his horse by the well. I was carrying two buckets and put them on the ground when he dismounted and came toward me. The ground was muddy, the snow having all but melted, and I did not want to stand there feeling the wet creep into my shoes. He was a rough-looking fellow, young and unshaven. But he spoke a decent tongue and seemed to know much of the news of the surrounding territory here in Wachovia. He said his name was Dobson and he owed us money. He brought several dozen wooden plates and other dishes which he hoped we would accept on account.

I pointed him to the *Gemeinhaus* and said he could unload his baggage from his horse. My feet were increasingly damp and I wanted to fill my buckets and go back to the kitchen, but the young man was talkative and seemed eager to share any news he had with me. I was half-listening as I drew water, the young man at my elbow. But when he told me he had heard rumors of attacks in Pennsylvania, I looked into his face to ask if he knew the name of the town or place in Pennsylvania. He could not remember the name but thought it was German. I knew this might be important news. I could feel a sense of fear, colder than my now damp feet. I walked with the young man to the *Gemeinhaus*.

When I opened the wooden door, I saw Brother Loesch standing in the center of the main room in deep conversation with Matthew and two strangers. One was an older man, the other, clearly, his son for they shared the same large nose and russet hair.

Apprehension made me quite bold. I spoke in a voice louder than I had meant. "Matthew, Brother Loesch, this young man has just told me some news that you should hear."

Jacob Loesch was clearly a bit distraught. He held a newspaper in one hand and with the other scratched his cheek with a nervous gesture. "Sister Krause, I am afraid this news report is disquieting. It says that Gnadenhütten has been attacked."

"When, when was this? Is the report verified? Have any been killed?"

I could feel my heart beat and without thinking, I took the paper from his hand. The article said that some months ago the mission had been attacked by unfriendly Indians and that six persons had been killed. It gave no names. "Oh, my God!" was all I could utter. My thoughts flew to the mission in the Blue Mountains. Surely our Indian Brethren had not turned against us. I clenched the younger trader's sleeve. "Do you have any more news? Do you know where we can find out?" At his shrug, I turned to Brother Loesch. "We must tell the others."

Matthew put his hand on my shoulder to hold me back, and said to the elder trader. "Have you heard this news while you were on the road?"

The man looked distinctly uncomfortable and spoke so quietly, that his voice was almost indistinguishable. "I have heard that there was trouble in the woods west of your settlements, but I have not yet found out the name of the place."

His son broke in, "I think it was that German name, Pa." Turning to Brother Loesch, he explained, "You know, the name you said."

"Gnadenhütten," Matthew and I said at once.

Matthew leaned close to me and scanned the page. "I see the date on this paper is January, 1756 which makes it rather recent, only two months old. In fact, it is a newer report than that one you brought to us, Herman. I think we have to assume the news here is true."

At that moment young Dobson spoke up. "I was in a tavern just east of here and there was talk of a massacre northwest of Nazareth in Pennsylvania." Turning to Matthew, "I am quite sure the name of the place was Gnadenhütten." He looked at the floor, then in some confusion, and said, "I'm sorry."

Thoughts rushed through my mind, tumbling over one another like waves on a small lake. The one word that seemed to repeat silently until I spoke aloud was, "Who?"

Brother Loesch moved toward the door. "I will ring the bell and call the others from their work. We need to let them know this news."

"We need to be together to pray," Matthew said in a quiet voice.

I wanted so desperately to be calm. To feel the certainty I could see in my husband's face. But I felt my gut clench as did my fingers, as unwelcome images of Susannah running through the woods assailed me. Oh, my God! What has happened at Gnadenhütten? Who has been murdered there?

CHAPTER THIRTY-ONE

Susannah Partsch: Bethlehem, 1760s

Even with the passing time, the horrors of that night of 1755 will never fully leave me. I remember it as clearly as I did when I first told it to my Brothers and Sisters at Nazareth.

Brother Martin Mack wants me to say what happened. What happened at Gnadenhütten, that is. He and Sister Martha Spangenberg tell me that if I say it all out loud, I will feel better and it will open my heart so our Lamb can enter in and heal my sickness. *Ach*, I am not really sick. I am not coughing or hot and cold by turn, but I am sick in some other way that is hard to tell anyone. If Christina sat here beside me, maybe I could tell her. Sister Boehler gave me a pen and paper and told me that I should write down what happened. But the quill sits on the little table in my room and the paper has fallen to the floor. It must have blown off in the night. I don't want to pick it up. I don't want to do anything.

One very young girl told me she has heard me walking back and forth at night. I did not tell her I do not want to sleep. I remember too much. *Gott*, I smell the burning, and I awake and cry. I am afraid of the dreams—of fire and of the screaming. One night in a dream, I called out to Susannah Nitschmann.

Sometimes I feel a bit better. Then I put on my cloak and walk outside. It's cold. The wind whistles in the trees and bushes. Even a little wind frightens me. I think they are coming again, so I have to run to the house, even though no one is chasing me. I have been sleeping in the sickroom and there is no one else here. By myself I want to be. I hope I can stay here until I am ready to join the Married Sisters again. Yesterday afternoon, I heard someone outside my door.

"Susannah. It is I, Anna Maria Schropp," she said. "I brought you some laurel from the woods and a branch of fir. It smells wonderful."

I was happy to see Anna Maria because her laughter makes me laugh. I have not laughed since it all happened. When she came in the room, I could smell the pine branches. She put them in a wooden vase that one of the Brothers had made, and said, "Susannah, I have to tell you something. The terrible night when . . . when it all . . . when you . . ." She took my hand. Her hand was warm.

She began again. "That night when you got away and ran through the woods, we heard you call us." She looked at me, her gray eyes wide and her heart-shaped face close to mine.

I wanted to hear her story but, *ach Gott*, I was a little afraid.

"What I am going to tell you shows that we—all of us here—are bound together. Neither space nor time divides us. Do you know what I mean?"

I was not sure what she meant, but I just waited to see what she would tell me.

"The night when Gnadenhütten was attacked, we had no idea. We had all gone to sleep—the men in their quarters and us in ours. In the middle of the night, I was awakened by Sister Wahnert moving around. She wakes up a lot anyway, so I didn't pay much attention. She whispered to me that a sound had awakened her. I sat up and listened; then I heard someone crying. Oh, Susannah, it was such a piteous sound." She stopped speaking for a moment, twisted a piece of her dark hair with one finger and then went on.

"I got out of bed to see if I could hear where that anguished sound was coming from. My feet were cold on the floorboards when I walked over to the window."

She shivered, but went on. "A few of us were awake by then but we said nothing to one another. I suppose we were afraid to speak. A wind came up and blew around. I think it was somewhere around midnight." She stopped and put her hand to her mouth. Then she went on so quiet I could hardly hear her.

"The crying had stopped, but I heard another sound that was even worse. It was a groan that began, stopped, and then began again. It seemed in the walls or maybe outside. I don't know. Oh, Susannah, it was so frightening."

"It's all right, I want to hear."

"This was not any voice I have heard before." She continued, "I don't even know if it was a man or a woman. It was so terribly sad and so lost. I wanted to cry."

I wanted to cry, too.

"The wind no longer blew the trees. It got very quiet. The moaning stopped suddenly. Sister Kremser stood next to me in the dark and we held on to one another waiting and fearful. It was dark, dark, and I couldn't see anything, really. But I could smell dead leaves and smoke, probably from our hearth, I thought. My husband called out to us Sisters saying he and Brother Wahnert had checked all around and found nothing. I crawled back into bed, and after a while, I guess, I went to sleep."

"Was that all? Just the moaning?" I asked her. Anna Maria stood in front of me.

"No. That was not all. Sometime toward morning, I know it was almost morning because it was a bit light outdoors; the sky was gray and I could see the bare tree branches." She put her arm around my shoulders and I leaned against her.

"Susannah, just before full light, I was awakened by the most horrible, heart-wrenching scream. Then it was so still. It was so still as though nothing were alive in the world." She held me tight against her. She was quiet for a long time, and then said, "We did not know about Gnadenhütten that night, but I am sure our Saviour was letting us hear you so we would be prepared to comfort you. You see, dear Sister. We all heard your pain. We all knew that a terrible thing had happened somewhere and that we should be ready to help."

I did not know what to say. Her words sounded frightening, but in some way I felt better than I did before. It was as though I was not alone when I ran through the woods. As though in some way, my Sisters and Brothers were waiting for me here. To comfort, to help. I told her I am happy she came and told me. When she bent down, I kissed her cheek. After she left my room, I sat for a long time to ponder what she had said. How strange are the ways of God, I thought. There are so many things I do not know. I cannot know. Perhaps Brother Mack is right. Perhaps, I thought, I will be able to tell my story and it will help me.

Today Sister Boehler comes into the room with a pot of very hot tea. I do not know Sister Boehler very well, but I have watched her for many years. Her face is long and narrow, and her eyes are deep-set and dark. I love the way her mouth turns up at the corners. When her portrait was painted, the artist even showed this. I am glad he did. She puts the tea down on the little table and begins to speak in a quiet voice.

"Sister Partsch, you know we usually write about our life's pilgrimage when we feel we are about to go Home to Him who loves us. But perhaps you can start your story now."

"Am I going Home now?" The words are easy to say because I don't care what the answer is.

She sits in front of me and takes my hand. "Susannah," she says, and her mouth turns up at the corners but she does not laugh. She just smiles at me.

"No, my dear. You are not going Home now. I thought that perhaps if you begin to tell me a little bit about yourself, it would ease your heart."

I like the way she talks. I can hear every word, just the way I always could hear Matthew Krause when he spoke the Psalms.

Sister Boehler pours hot tea into a large mug and gives it to me.

"Perhaps you can tell me where you were born. It was in Büdingen, was it not?"

"Yes, I was born in Büdingen in Wetteravia . . . "

I tell her about how my father died before I was born, and how my mother married a very bad man. I think I will have trouble saying the words about when he hurt me, but I can hear my voice, and it says, "My mother raised me until I was seven." She writes this down and the quill makes a scratchy sound. Then I say, "Since I had meanwhile acquired a harsh stepfather, I was given to the Burgermeister Schubert by the Büdingen rulers at Meerholtz and stayed there until 1740 . . . " I am not saying anything more about that part. Ach, I don't need to talk about it. It doesn't hurt so much now. I have my new family of Brethren— my husband, George, my children and my dear Sisters. When I think of George, I have to stop talking for a minute. The burning I think I can smell. "I smell smoke," I say to Sister Boehler. She says they are building fire for the ovens. My hands feel cold, so I hold the hot mug in both for a while to warm them. Then I go on to tell her how I walked to Herrnhaag and joined the Unitas and how George and I were married in the Great Wedding, and came to America.

"We have four daughters now and I thank our Saviour and His mercy they are safe in Bethlehem"

The mug cools in my hand. Before I can put it back on the table, Sister Boehler takes it from me and fills it again. The tea is sweetened with honey and I can feel the sweetness as it goes down my throat.

"Do you want to continue now, or are you tired? Would you like me to come again tomorrow?" Her face is full of concern for me. The small wrinkles between her brows tell me this.

"No, I want to tell you how it was for us. When Brother Mack asked us to travel to Gnadenhütten, I was not sure I wanted to go. You remember how Bethlehem and Nazareth had changed? There were all those militiamen men marching up and down our roads, shooting off their guns. They said they were going into the woods to shoot Indians." I didn't tell Sister Boehler that I was fearful of their faces. They were angry and laughing at the same time. One or two looked like my stepfather. When they came toward me on the road, I went to the other side.

Sister Boehler takes a small handkerchief from her pocket and wipes her nose. "Do you remember when Brother Zeisberger went into the forest to warn the Indian Brethren at Gnadenhütten to stay indoors and not go out into the woods?" she says.

"Yes, I remember," I say quietly. "Our brown Brethren had come from Shekomeko in New York territory because their white neighbors were cruel to them.

They built their little houses around the mission house at Gnadenhütten. Brother Martin Mack said it was a very pretty setting in the woods near a rushing river, and the Blue Mountains were all around." I take a sip of the hot, sweet tea and tell Sister Boehler that George and I walked the twenty miles west from Nazareth to Gnadenhütten when we were asked to do it. I do not tell her I felt some strange feelings when we were asked to go. I remember before we left, I was walking in the woods to the stone *Gemeinhaus* in Nazareth. I had gathered some small pieces of firewood. It was raining. I thought I heard my stepfather's voice in my ear saying, "Where is that little slut?" I stopped to listen. My heart beat fast. The voice didn't come again and I only heard the water dripping from the eaves of the house. I said, "I got away from him. I got away." When I said those words out loud, some of the fear left me. I thought about going to Gnadenhütten and said to myself "*Ja*, my Saviour is with me." Then I knew I would be safe. I trusted in His care.

I tell Sister Boehler again that I was happy our daughters were in Bethlehem. My tiny Anna Rosina was just weaned, and when I gave her to the widowed Sister in the nursery, I knew she would be safe and George and I could go to do our work. We were told that Gnadenhütten would be a busy place where we could run all the housekeeping for the missionaries. I knew the Indians were kind and friendly. I have thoughts in my head now, but I do not say them to Sister Boehler. I felt a shiver of cold though there was no wind.

"It did not take us long to settle in. Brother and Sister Sensemann had arrived before we did and of course, Sturgis you know, the Single Brother? Well, he was dashing in and out of doors asking what he could do to help." I feel a catch in my throat as I say, "Sister Susannah Nitschmann and I found our beds . . . I, I have always loved her. She was so good to me."

"Dear Susannah, I think you have told me quite enough for today." Sister Boehler puts her hand upon my shoulder and pats me a little. Then she gathers her paper and quill and sets them on the small tray with the tea things. "Remember, my dear, we pray that Susannah Nitschmann can find her way back to us, or . . . " I see her mouth quiver a little, "that she is in His arms now." She carries the small tea-tray to the door. I try to rise to help her but she says no, so I sit back down.

The sun starts to sink, and the room is darkening. I am not sure I want to be alone for fear of what thoughts would come to me, but I nod goodbye to the good Sister as she leaves. We have had no news about Susannah Nitschmann. No one found her body. This means she was taken by the warriors. *Ach*, if only she could find her way back to us. If only she is safe.

I wash my hands from water in the pitcher, and as I walk down the stairs, I need to cling to the railing like an old woman. I wonder if I will ever feel strong again? The cooks have prepared some toast, honey and hot milk. I do not want to talk as I eat, but I try to smile before I take my mug and plate to be washed and walk up the stairs again to the room they have let me use. I carry my candle to the bedside table. I wonder if I should open the window? It is cold outside and a wind has come up. I cannot hear it, but I can see the trees swaying back and forth. Someone has left warm water for me in the pitcher and I wash slowly. *Ach*, so slowly I do everything now.

I pray the same prayer, "O my Saviour, help me." I have said this for days now, maybe even weeks. I cannot seem to understand how time passes ever since it happened. I will sleep in my shift and pull the blanket up to my eyes. I can feel my hot breath under the covers. I wonder if I can tell Sister Boehler about what happened. If I put the pictures in my head in order now, maybe it will not be hard for me. Maybe it will be as she said, that I will feel better. O, my Lamb, please make me forget what I have seen. Let the smell of wood fire mean baking my good bread instead of . . . .

I will put it all in order and practice what to say when Sister Boehler comes tomorrow. The first thing I remember after we arrived at Gnadenhütten was that I went into the kitchen and arranged the pots and pans the way I wanted them. George looked over the store of food and said we had enough for a few weeks if some of the men could add to our meat supply by shooting game. The kitchen had a huge hearth and a stone floor and enough room for us to share our meals at the long table. The Indian Brethren lived and ate in their small houses that surrounded the clearing. The Brethren and Indians had built a large barn, a wash house and several craft houses that I did not have time to explore because George and I were responsible for supplies, laundry and all the housekeeping. I liked to organize the kitchen. The Indian women helped me to see how much food we had in the store houses. Joachim and Johanna Sensemann had gotten there before us. So had Brother Gottlieb Anders and his wife, Johanna, and their babe. The child was soon going back to the nursery in Bethlehem, but she must have been slow to wean. Johanna and Gottlieb had two other children in school back in Bethlehem. Martin Presser, a carpenter, was supposed to return to Christian Spring, but he wanted to stay on at the Gnadenhütten mission with his friend, George Schweigert. These two men told George much about the mission and the good work that had been done with our Indian Brethren. *Ach mein Gott*, rest them in our Saviour's arms.

There were several other Single Brothers who traveled with us. John Lesley was born in America. He walked some of the way with George, and said he was eager to return to Gnadenhütten so he could learn more Indian languages. He had been sick with chills and fever in Bethlehem and my husband told him he should ride in the wagon. They all seemed eager to get to Gnadenhütten and our Indian Brethren there.

I was so happy that Susannah Nitschmann and her husband Martin were traveling with us. This dear woman had become a friend. I remember well that she held my hand when our first daughter came. She and Christina, and George . . .

I have to stop now and walk around my little room. The floorboards are very cold on my bare feet, but the cold is *gut*. It takes my mind away from the bad thoughts, the horrible pictures.

The part that I need to practice remembering is what happened that night. That is what they want me to talk about. I remember we were all sitting at the dinner table except Brother Worbas, who was ill with fever and was in his bed in the Smithy where the Single Brothers slept. We heard the dogs barking. That was odd, because they had been fed and we did not expect any strangers at this late hour. Sister Anders hugged her little one close and said, "We are very unprotected here." Then Sister Susannah Nitschmann looked across the table at her and replied, "No, Johanna Christina, not unprotected." I knew what Sister Nitschmann meant, of course, because our Saviour is always with us. Perhaps Sister Anders was trying to look brave then, because she bounced her little one up and down and tried to smile.

George and I had made a good meal that night. Young Sturgis had bagged some fat hares and George had put them on a spit over the fire. I basted them with herbs and the whole small house smelled good. The brothers here had harvested many squash also and I put big pieces of butter on each portion. We drank our currant drink that we had learned to make years ago in Nazareth. We had stored it in the cold cellar and brought it to this mission on the wagons. I remember it was very good to drink with the roasted hare.

Brother Gattermeyer, our Smithy, told us he felt his knowledge of the Indian languages grew better every day. He looked almost like a boy when he waved his fork in his large hand. I felt warm with fellowship and good food. Clattering cutlery and laughter always makes me feel safe. Little Johanna Anders opened her little mouth wide when her mother fed her pieces of squash. We all laughed with her as she clapped her hands and gummed the food. This reminded me of my girls in Bethlehem. I saw George smile at me across the table.

Well, the dogs kept up their loud barking, so Brother Sensemann got up and said he would go to make sure the barn door was locked. He closed the door behind him. Anna Catherine called out to him, "Joachim, Joachim" and it seemed to me she sounded frightened. None of us spoke then. Maybe we were waiting for something. The dogs were quiet. Then one howled. The sound seemed close as though the poor wretched animal had been hurt and perhaps had limped toward us, crying. Brother Fabricius whispered softly and leaned down to pet his little brown dog that sat near his knee. All of us looked toward the door where Brother Sensemann had just left us. It opened very slowly and I remember holding my breath when I heard the creaking. I saw one hand holding a tomahawk in the space the opening door made, and then I saw a face. It was an Indian. He was painted with red and white streaks. Anna Sensemann screamed, "Joachim." Some of us stood, others were frozen in our chairs. I heard a loud BANG! Martin Nitschmann, next to me, half stood, then sank to his knees. I had the strange idea he was praying. I saw John Gattermeyer fall over, bending from the waist and clutching his stomach though blood spurted from his mouth. Presser fell, and then Lesley. I could not see. I could not see George. Then Susannah Nitschmann cried out, "O Brethren, help me." I pushed my chair over backward to get to her. I thought I saw her sink down, but it was so smoky and there was so much blood. Blood on the floor, red blood splattered onto the walls.

Where was George? I could not see. I think I called out his name as I put my hand on the wall so I could stand. I remember my hand was wet. It was sticky. My fingers were red. Although we all must have been moving quickly, I felt that everyone in the room was moving slowly in some kind of horrible dance. Raised arms, bent necks, twisted shapes on the floor. The smell of gunpowder, the clatter of metal plates, savage grunts and cries. *Ach mein Gott!*

I saw Gottlieb Anders take his wife's arm. She grasped their little daughter to her breast. He pulled her up the ladder to the garret room. The child's mouth made a round O, but I heard no sound from her. I knew I had to get to the garret, too, but I had to step over Brother Lesley. In my haste I did not look down to see if he had a face. Hands pulled me through the trapdoor and into the darkness of the garret. The savages had set a fire outside and the light of it came through the window. Sister Anders, on her knees, was rocking her little one back and forth. I think the babe was too terrified to make a sound. In the flickering light I saw that Brothers Fabricius and George Schweigert had also made it to the little room and were standing on the trapdoor. The Indians were shooting at our floor boards, but the bullets did not come through. Sister Anders cried out, "Dear Saviour, this is what I expected." And then her babe started to wail in terror. I was very afraid. I could feel my heart beat in the hollow of my neck. I ran to the window and stood with Brother Sturgis. The gunshots did not follow one another so rapidly, but I could hear the horrible yelling. Worse than that, were the piteous screams of the victims.

Sturgis and I leaned out the window together when the sound of guns almost stopped. But then we heard a sound most terrible of all. It popped and crackled. I saw flames. They ate at the wood of our house and I knew the smoky hiss would kill us.

"Sturgis, could we jump out this window?"

He looked at me but said nothing. Climbing to the ledge, he turned for a moment and, nodding his head, he jumped. I had to set my feet on the window ledge. I crouched there and looked around outside. The warriors were running everywhere hooting, kicking open the doors of storehouses and pulling out bags of flour and fruit drying for the winter. They slashed and tore at the bags. Gunshots again. They fired into doors, into windows, and into the air.

A voice came to me. "Jump, Susannah." Was it a voice of one of my Brothers or Sisters? Or did it come from somewhere else? I do not know. I bent my knees, brought my arms forward and jumped. The ground was wet and my hands and knees sunk into the mud. I stayed there in this way and looked around me. My God, I didn't know where I was. We had only been at the mission for a week and I had yet to get my bearings outdoors. Beyond our clearing were the woods. Somewhere was the river. Which way to go? In my heart I called out, "O, *mein Heiland*, my Saviour, tell me where to go."

By the light of the terrible blaze I could see a bit. There was a path into the woods. I picked myself up and ran to the nearest tree. When I crouched behind it, I could see the window where Sturgis and I had jumped. Someone was on the window ledge and as he jumped to the ground, an Indian bullet caught him. He landed in a crumpled heap. I turned my face away to the woods. I did not look back again, but ran. My feet were sure on the ground. I did not stop even to catch a breath. It was very dark but my eyes got used to it. I could hear water so I ran toward the sound. The gurgle of water got louder but I couldn't yet see the river. The ground was muddy, so I knew the river edge was very near. A great hump blocked the path. I saw it was a fallen tree.

I put my hands on the tree and felt the rough bark. Then I thought perhaps I could slip under the tree to hide, so I crawled down under. I dug with my fingers into the damp. *Gott, Gott,* it was cold! I shivered so hard and I had to clench my teeth. I hugged myself and crouched down. That is how I hid so long ago in my mother's wardrobe. I heard gun shots less often, but I could still hear those wild ones as they sat on the ground and feasted. I knew these were not the Indians I had come to trust. Not those who loved our Brethren. They were drunken warriors. I tried to block their whoops and yells from my ears. I said to myself, "I got away." But then I thought about George. I had to keep from thinking about him when I ran through the forest, but now I wondered if he was lying with Brother Martin Nitschmann and John Gattermeyer? What happened to my husband when I climbed up the ladder to the garret? Did he get outside? I could not think of him burning. I squeezed my eyes shut. I tried not to cry.

It does not seem that I slept, but the rest of the night is lost to me. I know I saw the sky grow lighter and then the outline of the trees became clear. Finally, I could make out the bank across the river. It was still very early morning when I heard voices. I dared not move but I was stiff with cold. I strained to listen and inched myself out of that damp mud. Dirty as they were, I brought my fingers one by one to my mouth and sucked them to make them warm. I listened. I heard a word. It was

"Nein." Then a gruff, *"was ist?"* German words!

I crawled further out from beneath the tree on my hands and knees like an animal. I looked to where I heard the voices. I could see three men as they came across the river toward me. One was on horseback. The other two looked like soldiers, on foot. I thought I could see horses on the other side of the river. I made a sound. It was not very loud. I was afraid they would hear me and afraid if they did not. One of them stopped and held up his hand as though he was listening. He motioned to the other two; then they all came toward me. One soldier carried a rifle.

The man on horseback leaped down and knelt by me. "God, woman, what happened to you?" His voice was kind. One of the others said in English, "It's the same here as before. Fighting, shooting."

"Can you stand? Are you wounded?" The man who spoke German took my arm, as I tried to struggle to my feet. I saw blood making a pattern with mud on my petticoat. I could not see the blood around my mouth where I had sucked my fingers to make them warm. The German gave me his canteen, *"Wasser?"* He said. Then he gave me a rag to wipe my face. I was surprised at the blood and dirt. I put my teeth together so they would stop rattling and told them, "A terrible thing, a terrible thing . . . " I could not say anything more.

"It must have been that mission place they hit. The one at the fork of the rivers." The man spoke English, but I knew the few words that made sense to me.

"Yes, Gnadenhütten. It is Gnadenhütten." I felt the tears come then. I made wrenching sounds and my stomach heaved with them. I could not stand. The German put his arm around my waist and held me to him. As I sobbed and sobbed, it came to me that I must go back there. I knew I had to find George and the others.

"I have to go back." I turned to look into the man's eyes. "I must go back to see if anyone is alive." I began to cry again because I remembered Susannah Nitschmann and how she had cried out. Did she run to the door? Did one of the savages take her?

The German spoke to the other two men. He took off his heavy coat and wrapped it around me. I felt the heaviness on my shoulders. "Here, put your arms in the sleeves. It will warm you better." He began to button at my neck. The other two men hurried across the shallow part of the river where the two horses were tethered. It did not take long for the men to bring them close. The third horse had been standing patiently in the mud near the German and me. I was grateful when one man helped me mount his horse and the German climbed up behind me.

I do not remember how far we went. Not far because we did not stop to eat or rest. Suddenly I was jerked from my half-sleep. A shout! I opened my eyes in terror. *O, mein Gott!* What more could happen in these woods? The shout came again. Hoarse with tears, hoarse with relief. And I knew it. I knew who it was.

"Susannah! Susannah! You got away. I told Sturgis. I told him you were safe."

I slipped from the saddle. I felt his arms around me and I put mine around him. The dirt and blood on his face mixed with the dirt and blood on mine. Our tears came together. We talked at once.

"They were burned, George. They were all burned up."

"I wanted to try and help. I could not save anyone."

"I jumped out the window, George."

"I climbed out the window downstairs"

"I stayed all night under a fallen tree. It was cold."

"I saw Sturgis in the woods. He didn't know if you had jumped to safety. Oh, Susannah." He let me go and looked at my face. "I wanted to go back and save you. I wanted to try and help. I could not save anyone." And his sobs came again.

"I am afraid they were all burned. All burned up."

George told the men that we had to go back to what was left of Gnadenhütten. I did not want to go. To enter that place of horror again made my stomach heave. I walked off a few paces and empty as I was, I brought up bitter, yellow bile. Then I said to myself, "The bodies are nothing. Anna, Martin, Little Johanna. If they were killed, they have all gone Home."

"Come, Susannah. We must go back." His voice was sure. I kept saying to myself that my dear Sisters and Brothers had been taken to Himself. I had to trust this. Then I told the men I was ready to go back.

AT FIRST IT WAS THE SMELL. At another time in another place, this smoky smell meant warming cold hands and cooking for hungry stomachs. But not then. Only one night ago our mission village stood. But I saw only two chimneys and ashy rubble. I could not take a breath. The sharp smoke hurt my lungs. I coughed into my hands. I knew I would have to look into the ruins of what was left of the two-story building. The two soldiers went forward before us, carefully looking from side to side. The horses kicked small piles of ashes and I could see flames dart up and then die. George got off our horse and reached up his hand to help me down. I knew I had to get off, but I sat there. George said, "Do you want to wait? Why don't you wait there?" I knew I must get off.

I made myself look to find the charred bodies. I had to know who they were. It felt very quiet to me. A bird sang a waking song. One scorched beam leaning on another crashed to the ground. The first body I saw. It was on its stomach. One leg bent forward while another straight as though it was still running. It was not running. It was still. I think it was Martin Presser. He must have been hit but pulled himself outside trying to get away. I began to bend closer to see his face.

"Nein. Nein." The German took my arm I turned away but not before I saw the top of his head was cracked open.

"Seems like you oughten' to be here," one soldier said.

I turned to walk away, trying not to look at the corpse of one Indian lying face up, hands open. He had been shot in the neck. Something on the ground caught my eye. It sparkled in the morning sun. I bent to pick it up. It was a square locket, its cover open, the inside empty. I turned it over in my hand. George put his arm around my shoulders. "We don't know, Susannah. We don't know. Maybe it was his." He pointed to the still figure of the old Indian. I dropped the locket near his open hand and stumbled on. There, in front of me on the ground were two bodies. One was very small. The other curved around it. They were burned to charcoal. Their skin was black and I could not see who they were. But I knew. *Mein Gott*, they were so burned. I wept.

I fainted then. From a whirling blackness, it seemed a voice was calling. It told me to awake. It said this over and over, "Wake up wake up" I wanted to stay where I was. I did not want to know anything. I could feel strong hands on my shoulders. My husband was shaking me. I heard his voice again telling me to wake up. Then my own voice from far off. It said, *"Mein Heiland.* I will think of you."

"She is coming around. What is she saying?"

George said, "She is saying, *Heiland.* That's how some of us say Jesus."

I felt the shaking stop as one man pushed me to sit up. I saw the faces, then. All were close to mine and worried.

"Please take me home," I asked. Take me home to Nazareth." I felt tears on my face and they were warm on my cold cheeks.

We left the clearing. We did not touch anything there. I sat on the horse in front of George. The German said he knew the way to Nazareth. The horse moved under me, and the clop, clop of the hooves made a sleepy sound. My eyes felt heavy. I gripped the saddle. I was numb. I could not think.

We came to the edge of the clearing, but just before we entered the woods, George cried out. My eyes flew open as George slipped from the saddle. He walked a few steps to a crumpled figure on the ground. Sitting close, was Fabricius' little brown dog. His nose was near his master's head, his long ears drooping. He did not move when George got near. My husband covered his mouth with his hands. One of the soldiers came to the spot, "My God. My God. He's been scalped and . . . " George put his hand on the man's arm warning him to not say anything more. But I knew. I knew. I had heard the stories about what warriors did. Then I looked a few feet from that place and saw a blanket and a hat with a knife stuck through them on a stump.

"A warning," said the soldier, and turned away.

We continued our sorrowful journey home. The little brown dog did not follow.

SLOWLY WE MADE OUR WAY through the woods. It took us two days but I do not remember any of this. When the familiar stone house in Nazareth came into view, I began to weep, but I don't know why. I cannot remember who saw us first; who helped me down from the horse. I was so weak. I have never been weak before, or felt so stiff and strange. I remember happy sounds when our Brethren helped us into the *Gemeinhaus*. The Sisters washed the blood and dirt from my body. I gave myself over to them. They poured warm water over my head. I smelled the soap and felt their gentle hands on my hair. I felt baptized in a new and different way.

Dr. Otto said I had a great illness and that I suffered. *Ach nein*, I do not want to remember those first days. Tomorrow, Sister Boehler will come to my little room and ask me to tell her how it was. That is so she can write it all down. Dr. Otto says I should tell her as many times as I want. That is what George and I do now. We tell each other about Gnadenhütten. Maybe the place is not there anymore, but we say we can still see it. I guess I will always see it, but maybe not burned. Maybe I will remember the two storied house, and the kitchen and the hearth. That is what I will remember.

CHAPTER THIRTY - TWO

Christina Barbara Krause

I tried so hard to see in my mind a picture of Susannah carrying buckets of water from the well, to hear her laughter when she told us a story about under-cooked chicken or some other mishap in the kitchen. But I could not stop seeing her being dragged, bloody and bruised, into the woods; to become a slave, beaten and abused again. She had suffered as a child. Did she need to suffer still? Was her pilgrimage to be so difficult before she reached her heavenly Home? If we heard that she and George had been called by our Saviour, I knew I would miss them although we already were separated by earthly miles. If they had been called out of time, I should be able to rejoice, for we were admonished to remember that death is only the end of this life's journey. I struggled so with this.

Oh, my God, how difficult it was to be patient as I awaited news of Pennsylvania, and especially of Gnadenhütten! Every night when I put down my head, I prayed for our children, calling each dear face to my mind. Those March nights I also prayed mightily for Susannah and George. Were all the Brethren murdered at Gnadenhütten? Did some escape, and who, dear God, were they? Our Brethren's fate shrouded our whole community, and every hour held a question.

The news came on a day of bright sun. The air was still cold that March of 1756, but wisps of clouds seemed to hurry overhead as though they had finished with their work of holding heavy snow. I stopped on the path to the herb garden when I saw a horse and cart that were unfamiliar to me. Crowded in the small cart pulled by a sorry-looking horse was a worried, weary woman who held a child to her breast. The father, stopping his horse, called out to me asking for our doctor, so I directed them to the door of Brother Kalberlahn. Their little one looked very pale and feverish, and when I inquired of them how far they had traveled, they said they had come from one hundred miles to the north. I asked if they had heard any news of Bethlehem or Nazareth, but their answer was no. Dr. Kalberlahn greeted them warmly, his tall figure filling the doorway. I quietly closed his door to return to the herb garden where I hoped to spade up some earth in preparation for planting. The birds, especially the little finches and sparrows, were singing their spring song, and the rattle of woodpeckers sounded from the woods surrounding our garden. But then I heard another sound, far away but distinct, and knew a horse was approaching. An unfamiliar man was in the saddle. As he drew very near, sweat was apparent on his horse, and it was evident the poor creature had been driven hard. The man stopped his horse directly in front of me, asking which building was the *Gemeinhaus*. I pointed, and he bent in the saddle to again drive his horse on.

I called to him, "Have you news?" He called back over his shoulder, "Yes, I have news of your settlement in the Blue Mountains." Gnadenhütten, I thought. O, my God, it is news of our Brethren. I picked up my petticoat to run to the *Gemeinhaus*, and as I ran I could see Brother Heinrich Biefel reach to pull the bell rope. The sound echoed throughout our community. By the time I reached the *Gemeinhaus*, out of breath and terrified at what we would hear, others had also gathered. We crowded into the main room. The stranger was speaking to Brother Christian Henrich, who raised his arms to quiet the assemblage.

"Brothers and Sisters. There has been an attack by the Cherokee just west of us and we must prepare ourselves to take in the refugees." There were murmurs throughout the room. I pulled at one ribbon of my cap, the bow unraveling though I hardly noticed.

"The news of Gnadenhütten is now known. Those who escaped have told their story and know who still lives and who were plucked by our Saviour." He turned to the stranger who was pulling papers from his bag. He was a fellow of short stature, balding and with a ruddy face. His voice was soft, and we all strained to hear. The room was very quiet.

"I have a list from Bishop Spangenberg," the messenger said. "I think you know him as Brother Joseph. He has written about those of your white Brethren who have lost their lives, but I do not know if any Indians were also murdered." He did not look at any of us, but rather held the paper close to his face and read slowly, narrowing his eyes as he pronounced the names.

"Martin Nitschmann, Anna Catherine Sensemann, Gottlieb Anders and his wife, Johanna as well as their baby, Johanna." He took a short breath and continued with a catch in his throat. "Single Brothers were Johann Gattermeyer, Martin Presser and John Lesley. Also lost were George Fabricius and George Schweigert." He stopped then and looked to the floor. The room was no longer quiet, for some were weeping and others asking each other about those not mentioned.

Brother Christian Heinrich raised his arm again, saying, "Our messenger told me no one yet knows the fate of Sister Susannah Nitschmann. It was thought she was burned with others, but perhaps she was taken captive by a warrior."

"Oh my God." Sister Schaub sank to her knees, her hands on her breast. Matthew called out in his deep voice, "Can you tell us of those who survived?"

"Yes." The man looked down at his paper. "Young Sturgis ran into the woods and Brother Worbas was not in the main building when the attack took place, so he got away also. Joachim Sensemann had gone to check the large barn before the attack, so he also escaped."

I felt faint as I remembered the loving way Brother Joachim had looked at his wife, and how she so often stood close to him, touching his arm, his hand, his jacket. How would he fare now? I waited, not wanting to breathe until I heard about George and Susannah.

"Brother George Partsch climbed out one of the lower windows, and Sister Susannah Partsch jumped from the second story window following Sturgis. She remains in the sickroom in Nazareth but will recover."

I put my hand over my mouth for I had begun to laugh. I didn't want to laugh. I found nothing amusing, but tears wet my cheeks, and I gasped as for air. "She survived. She got away." And then I found myself weeping for those who had had to take such a terrible path to our Heavenly Home. The Single Brothers were so young, and had expressed such joy in learning the Indian tongues. I could yet hear their laughter and see their eager faces. My God, what sort of a place is this New World? I did not dare to ask myself what kind of a God might ask for such sacrifice.

I think we all wanted to stay together in one room, to touch, to look into one another's eyes for comfort and solace. But there was work to be done. We had no idea how many here might need our care as they straggled in from their farms.

OUR WHOLE COMMUNITY had become very adept in arranging room and food for the refugees from our area here who came to us. When we first arrived, just last autumn, there was not much talk about Indian raids, but as time went on, we heard more and more tales of fear and murder. The first little group on that late March day came out from the woods by the small stream. I saw a tall man I presumed was the father, with two sons almost as tall as he, and a woman carrying a little girl. Their faces were streaked with dirt. The woman stumbled as she crossed the wooden bridge over the water. Sister Rosina Biefel and I walked quickly to them, offering food and lodging. In fact, we had not much of either for the strangers. The Single Brothers had just completed a house for themselves, but willingly shared their quarters, using sheets to provide some privacy. As more refugees arrived, we put them in the large barn and even found room in the wash house for one young woman who said she would sleep anywhere. She was lovely, barely twenty years of age with long, brown hair that had escaped its net and streamed down her shoulders. She told me in broken German that she had been born in England and had stolen away on a ship to the New World. I gave her a blanket, and straw bundled in cotton cloth for a mattress, but she was grateful. She reminded me of myself when I, too, came to this wilderness, for I could see, despite her weariness, innocence and an eagerness to experience a new kind of life. I felt a tug in my chest: longing perhaps, for those lost days when we were strong and sure of our mission. I looked at her face, young and fresh, and I felt so much older. My babe turned over within me. I was getting a bit clumsy now that my time was only two months away, and I almost tripped on the door still; but I straightened my back, smiled reassurance, and breathed in the sweet air. I would bear the first little one in Wachovia when spring burst into full bloom.

Suddenly, then, as though a prayer had been answered, I recalled my first experience with birthing when I held Susannah's hand as little Elizabeth made her way into this world. At that moment, I prayed Susannah would not suffer long; that she would soon be directing the kitchen work with her usual direct words. Of course, I had no proof that all was well in Pennsylvania because we had no new reports, but I had to trust that the few survivors from Gnadenhütten were gaining in health and strength. I earnestly hoped Susannah was strong in her faith, as I thought her to be. She had always seemed to draw strength from those surrounding her, as well as being able to impart her strength to them. Had I spoken of this to her, she would have tossed her wheaten braid, and dismissed me with a merry laugh. Perhaps after Easter we would have more news from all our Brethren. In the meantime, we worked and waited.

All of these refugees coming from separate farms here and thus vulnerable to attack, had fled in great fear, some with no warm coats, two even with no shoes. It was decided that we would give what building materials we could spare to those families so they could build small dwellings near us. So again the crash of falling trees and the calls of men to each other resounded and brought back to me the daytime sounds at Friedensthal after we had arrived. Through our efforts there, we had worked to create a place of industry and peace. But, of course, it was an oasis in the great wilderness where too often the rage of the militia or French or English shattered the sweet silences at twilight. Would the dreams of our ancestors, their villages torn by war, ever be realized by those of us now? Perhaps, I thought, perhaps we could set an example, a new place of peace here in this southern part of the New World. But calls of struggle and fight assailed us that year, and we bent our backs to work and our heads to prayer.

After the solemnity of the Friday preceding our Lord's resurrection, there was an air of quiet contemplation amongst us, as we ministered to the refugees who had come to us for help. Frost had covered the ground the first of April, much to our surprise. Our diarist said he would write that the oak trees looked as though they were cooked. Of course this weather ruined the nuts on those trees that we had counted on for our hogs. But despite the cold, I knew spring would come. The season of awakening comes with great haste to this southern part of America. I was surprised at how the weather turned warm so quickly. Only recently we had been hurrying about from house to barn, from field to forest because of the cold, and then one day, all the birds were singing and we shed our cloaks. Tiny lady slipper buds peered from the earth, and my mind turned to planting and to new life.

Easter has always been very special for our people. Our celebration that April 18th was especially moving for me. Trumpets awakened us before dawn, their golden notes shaking me from sleep to hastily dress and gather with the others to sing in joy and thanksgiving to our God. It was cool that morning in the *Gemeinhaus*. Until the tile stove warmed the room, I shivered, standing between Rosina Biefel and Helena Schmid.

Sister Schmid looked at my belly and then gave me a questioning glance. I whispered, "In May" and she nodded with a smile. Our trombones sounded a low note, the trumpets high and clear echoed back. We sang with joy, with reverence and with great hope. I felt part of a noble mission that day, sure that we would succeed in our efforts to form a community of peace; one that might be a model for others to follow if our Lamb awaked their hearts.

After our service, my heart filled with the joy and hope our singing had brought to me, I walked to the top of a hill behind our apothecary garden, the path through the woods narrow and twisting. Tiny leaves peeped from tree branches as if they knew the early spring cold would not last. I smelled the lovely odor of fresh, new growth. Out of breath from the walk up the hill, I stood in the clearing, as yet not consecrated, that would house the bodies of those souls who had flown to our Father. Alone, but for the songbirds' chorus, I raised my arms in exhilaration. May was a wonderful time to birth a babe.

ROSINA BIEFEL KNELT next to me as we dug small holes for our new plants. Her dark brown eyes were darting from my face to the edge of the field as she said, "Sister Christina, I worry so much more here than I did in Bethlehem and Nazareth. The refugees come to us in greater and greater numbers. How ever will we feed them?"

I was looking across the garden and up the path when Rosina grasped my arm. "Christina, look! Two, four, no, eight Indians are coming out of the woods—look there."

I could see them clearly, walking single file toward us. Rosina and I arose together, clasping each other's arms. I was frightened, not knowing to which tribe these men belonged, but I knew I must not show fear. The Cherokee people were the most numerous Indians in our area and, although I had heard rumors of their raids on whites, we had experienced no trouble from them. One Indian, a handsome fellow with plaited hair and several beaded necklaces held up his hand. "White man make pipe."

I was not sure this was a question but I sensed he was friendly, and was perhaps asking about Brother Aust's pipes. I don't know why, but I felt the need to make a gesture of good will, so I smiled, and made a quick curtsy. "Brother Aust has a shop close by. May we show you the way?"

Rosina arranged her mouth in a smile, but seemed unable to speak.

She held tightly to my hand as I led the way to Brother Aust's shop. Brother Aust was not in the small room but we saw several clay pipes on his table, and I picked one up and held it out to the Indian nearest to me. He was about my height, his skin the color of a copper coin, his hair long and bound at the back of his head. He was not a young man. I could see wrinkles around his mouth and eyes, and when I handed him one pipe, he nodded gravely to me. He held the pipe with a kind of gentleness, and ran his fingers down the long stem, then raised the bowl and smelled it. I had the strong feeling that I should say something; that there was a silence in the air that needed to be filled. Feeling rather foolish, I made the hand motion of eating and the old Indian smiled, deepening the wrinkles around his mouth. I turned then, and began to walk to our kitchen. It felt very odd to me walking along the path single file with Rosina and eight Indians behind us. I was conscious of my rounded belly and my ungainly gait, and for at least one moment, afraid for myself and my babe. I felt vulnerable. I needn't have felt so. At the kitchen, our miller, Brother Schaub, greeted the Cherokees with some familiarity and uttered a few words. He explained to us, he had met at least four of the men previously at the militia fort not far from here. We offered them bread which was graciously accepted, and the eight left as quietly as they had come.

That evening, Rosina and I were asked if we had been afraid. I said I had not felt fear but I thought there was much wisdom in living together in a communal way. There was comfort in knowing my Brothers and Sisters were near.

By May, all the oaks had green leaves, and the poplars put forth a beautiful blossom that I had never seen in Europe or Pennsylvania. Along the bottom land the willow's branches were swaying in full leaf, and hickory trees, the most abundant of all, smelled like our walnut trees in Gelzhausen. Of course it was too early for our small apple trees to bear or berries to appear in great profusion in the woods, but my mouth watered for these fruits.

I was brought to bed the night of the 11th of May and our little girl came into this world easily. I labored only a few hours. When Brother Kalberlahn laid the small bundle in my arms, I told Matthew her name would be Anna Johanna. His look of surprise was not unexpected to me, but I had thought long and hard about this decision. Our Anna Christina, so beloved of us, was the first child of our union. But she was far away in Bethlehem, and I had been wrenched from her before she grew to womanhood. So, this babe, the first born in Wachovia, would be called by the same name as our daughter in Pennsylvania. Born of my stubborn resolve never to be snatched away from my children again, this naming felt to me like a bridge between north and south. As my husband bent to kiss my forehead, I looked into his blue eyes for a long time, and thought perhaps my love for him would erase the last traces of longing for my children. How I prayed then that this little mite in my arms, conceived in wretched anger, might never know my bitter taste of loss.

I was awakened by the mewling sound of little Anna as she moved in her cradle by my bed. Then, a quiet knock on the door and Sister Optiz entered bringing with her a soft, warm breeze. She came close to my bed, saying, "It is a lovely day for your little Anna's baptism." She smoothed my babe's head with one finger. Indeed, it was a perfect day for this important ceremony, for our Anna Johanna would be consecrated to Him in His perfect love for us.

In the late morning I arose without much difficulty and, accompanied by Sister Schmidt, I walked with my new babe to the *Gemeinhaus*. Dear Matthew was at the door, his face radiant with happiness when he took my arm. The friends we had named as godparents stood around us as Brother Christian Henrich spoke the words over our little one. When the good brother began his discourse with the words, "I have planted you as a fruitful seed, that you shall remain," Anna made a small sound and I was so filled with our Savior's love. It was a though a golden glow surrounded all of us on the spring day, while our small daughter received the first baptism in Wachovia. Those we had come to love held each other's arms in a nurturing circle, and I looked at each face, my heart awakening to the true hope that I could be at peace in this new wilderness.

CHAPTER THIRTY-THREE

Susannah Partsch

Talk, talk. That is what I am hearing. Many of the Brothers and Sisters sit here in the large room of our stone *Gemeinhaus* in Nazareth and talk about what we should do about those savages who attacked us at Gnadenhütten. Brother Nixton has asked George over and over again. They ask me now what I think. I cannot decide. I have tried to say it is hard to know what happened. That is because I was there. I only remember what happened to me. Burning everywhere. Running and George getting away, too. But I have told Sister Boehler all that. I don't want to talk about the Indians who attacked us. I don't want to remember the screams and the burning.

The wind whistles around the corners. It is raining and the drops make the glass windows look wavy. Father David Nitschmann is trying to quiet those Brothers who talk loud and do not wait for others. He looks tired. Poor man lost his cousin, Martin, and none of us are yet sure about dear Susannah Nitschmann. If she has gone to our Saviour, that would be better than being captured. When I think about her, I become frightened all over again, so I try to look hard at a candle on the front table. Then my heart beats slower.

The Single Brother John Nixton lives at our settlement at Christian Spring. He came with us on the *Little Strength* from Europe. He seems very young to me, for I can see his beard is not yet grown like a man's. His voice cracks. "We have to find those savages. We have to avenge our Brothers and Sisters." He has risen from his seat and his dark hair falls in his face.

Bishop Nitschmann waves his hand for the Brother to sit. He says, "We will give everyone a chance to voice an opinion, my dear Brother. All will be heard." Father Nitschmann is very tall and speaks so all of us can hear. I see his hair has more white in it since we came across the sea to Nazareth together. Sister Martha Spangenberg is getting to her feet. The room grows quiet, and I hear only the rain as it hits the windowpanes. "Dear ones," she says. "Our Brethren have been cruelly attacked. We all feel a terrible anger as we sit here; but I beseech you to stop and think for a moment. Let us take time with our decision." She sits then and no one speaks.

Brother David Zeisberger stands now. We all wait to hear what he will say. He went out to Gnadenhütten after the terrible attack. I lean forward to see because this Brother is quite short and, even though he is standing, it is hard to see him. "As you all know by now, I was traveling with our Brother the Indians call Shebosh. It had been our intention before the attack to warn the Indians in the area that they might be in danger." He stops and puts his two fingers in the frown space between his eyes. I think he might not continue, for I know he is very upset. But then he says, "Of course, when I ran into Sturgis and Joachim Sensemann, and you also, Brother Partsch," he nodded at George, "I learned what happened and headed back here to let you all know."

He stops speaking again and we wait for him to continue. Then he coughs and says, "When I arrived here to tell you of the massacre, Brother Spangenberg opened the Watchword text for the day. Remember, it was the Bible story of Joseph dressed in disguise, and how he spoke roughly to his Brethren. Brother Spangenberg then said that our Lord, who makes himself strange to us sometimes, also had spoken roughly to us. Dear Brothers and Sisters, how do we come to comprehend this?"

I still do not understand about this story, but Brother Zeisberger is telling it again.

"Brethren, the Lord has spoken roughly to us. We have lost those who are dear to our hearts." He sat down. I think he cannot say any more words. They stick in his throat.

"Our Brethren must be avenged. We must find the murderers!" Brother Nixton is leaving his seat and stomping up to the front of the room. Now there is a lot of noise. I want to put my fingers over my ears. I don't want to hear what they all are saying.

"Stop. Stop!" David Zeisberger has gotten up, too, and stands beside Brother Nixton. He is holding on to his arm. There is something about Zeisberger that makes people listen. For years now the Indians were happy to hear the good news of our Saviour from this Brother. He holds up both arms. "Those slain on the Mahoning River were verily martyrs, destined in the mysterious ways of God who 'spoke roughly to them.' Don't you see, my Brothers and Sisters? Their blood was vicarious blood. It has washed out the cruel calumny that has excited so much prejudice about us."

I am not sure what he means. I saw the blood, I heard the screams.

How can anything good come from this terrible massacre that took my dear Brethren Home? I feel tears on my cheeks. I think I cannot stay in this room. But I am afraid to leave. I stand up and from some place—it is as though my voice is not my own, - I say, "How can the death of all our Brothers—our innocent Brothers and Sisters - wash away anything? How can all that blood spilled..." I cannot go on. I sit down and bend my head. I feel Sister Anna Maria Schropp next to me. She puts her arms around my shoulder.

Then Brother Zeisberger comes over to where I am sitting. He takes my arm and pulls me up next to him. I am taller than he is. He is looking right at me and I cannot look away. "Sister Susannah Partsch. You have suffered much, but our Saviour has spared you." His eyes are very kind, and I feel he is talking just to me and no one else is in the room. "Susannah, you remember the cruel words that have been used against us. The words that say we were lovers of Indians and haters of others; that we were in league with the French? Don't you see that it was the very blood of our loved ones that stopped the slander perpetrated by those who are incapable of understanding our mission here in the New World?"

His arm holding me is very strong. I can feel that strength. The rain hits the windows, and the candle on the table flickers. I don't know what he means. I want to know, but I cannot think.

"Sister Susannah. All of you. We have been hated, thwarted in the work here because of the unreasonable belief that because of our love and aid to our Indian Brethren, we were scheming with them against those of our own race. This terrible attack, this blood, shed for us, shows them in their blindness that they were wrong."

Now there are voices in the room. Everyone seems to talk at once. Brother Zeisberger lets go of my arm and helps me to sit again. I almost feel faint. Brother Dolberg calls out over the voices. "I understand, Brother Zeisberger. I understand your point. But we must rid ourselves of those savage warriors who killed our people and will kill again. If we don't go into the woods to rout them out, they will attack our village here. Nazareth is in danger." All the young men sitting with Brother Dolberg stand and talk at once.

Brother Martin Mack then stands up from his seat. Gnadenhütten had been dear to his heart. I know the massacre hurt him. He looks as though he has not slept for days. Before he speaks, he pulls at the cuffs of his shirt. He looks out at Brother Nixton and the other men.

"Remember, my friends, we shelter seventy Indians at this moment. They found their way to us after the attack, trusting that we would care for them. These wretched men, women and children are the remaining fruit of our labor amongst them. After Gnadenhütten they had no place to go." His voice drops, and he slips into his seat as though he can not stand a minute longer.

Brother Spangenberg raps his hand on the table, and the candlestick wobbles. "I want you all to remember what happened at Gethsemane. It was there that Jesus was taken by the soldiers after Judas had betrayed him. As they bound Jesus' hands, Simon Peter gave way to his anger. He drew his sword and cut the ear of one of the high priest's slaves. Do you remember that Jesus rebuked him, saying, 'Put your sword back in its place; for whoever takes the sword will perish by the sword.'" Brother Spangenberg looks to the floor. No one speaks. "Now I say to all of you." His voice is loud in the room. "Do not give way to your anger. The blood is shed. The martyrs have gone Home. There will be no more killing!"

Anna Maria grasps my shoulder very tightly and I put my hand over hers. I am not sure what Brother Spangenberg is saying about Jesus, but I am sure that if some of our Brothers go into the woods to kill Indians, we will never be safe in the forest. Killing makes more killing. My heart is beating as though I am afraid. But I am not really afraid.

CHAPTER THIRTY-FOUR

Christina Barbara Krause

Anna Johanna began her life as a sickly babe. I listened for each breath as she tossed in her cradle. Did my Sisters close by hear her, or perhaps feel my intake of breath that I held until I could discern my babe snuffling contentedly in her sleep? We had continued to have separate quarters for men and women until houses could be built for each couple. For privacy, dividers had been erected between the beds in the women's side of the large building and because my Anna was the only infant in our settlement, it was easy and convenient to keep her close to my bed. This arrangement eased my anxiety about her somewhat. I knew our communal living was more practical at the time, and that it would change in the future. But I often dreamed of when my husband and I might fold our bodies together for warmth at night, to listen together to the sound of waking birds in the morning. But it was not yet to be.

Six weeks after Anna's birth, as was our custom, I was treated to a small celebration with our Choir of Married People. We were thankful together that this little mite had been preserved and wished her a happy pilgrimage, full of blessings. The hymns rang in my head long after they were sung, my heart somehow eased as I rocked her cradle that evening.

As the months passed, our little girl seemed to gain in strength, but she continued to suffer from nosebleeds. Her blood spattered her shift and stained her small hands. Although I could see his concern each time this happened, Matthew seemed not to feel my torment. He reminded me that it was the Lamb's blood that saved us all. How I tried to keep this lesson in my mind, but images of my little one stretched out in a small coffin assailed me, and though I sang the Liturgy of the Wounds with my Brethren, I felt no comfort. I tried to remember how moved I had been in Nazareth when we sang 'O Haupt voll Blut und Wunden' and how this chorus brought my unshed tears when I saw the image of His tortured body. For those moments, I could believe the symbol of our Lamb's blood did preserve the believer from despair; that His blood was a life force that poured into our very souls. But when Anna's nose bled again my panic returned as I held her close. When the bleeding finally stopped, my prayers of thanks were to Mary who knew the anguish of seeing her son suffer. Though the wooden statue in my childhood church had brought only tears, I felt a closeness now to the mother of our Jesus, who lived and bore a child in her own time. It was to her I sent my whispered prayers as I placed the blanket around Anna's small form.

Snow in Wachovia did not last the way it did in Pennsylvania, but rather melted into the roots of the pines, disappearing under their soft piles of brown needles. Still, it got very cold here, and as I watched each season pass around me, I remembered the times my father would take me in his lap and ask me to name them. It was a special game, and if I said them out of order, he would laugh and ask that I start again. How I loved to hear him laugh. As I grew older, we often spoke of how there are really many more seasons than four, and I would describe different smells of each; spring that began with the melting of snow, next the dank, dark earth-smell when the farmers ploughed their furrows and then the scent of lilacs, giving way to the lily-of-the-valley in the woods where the trees tossed their new leaves as though they were proud to wear them again. I treasured these memories and wished I could have shared them with my growing children in Pennsylvania. But I told myself the dear Lamb had given me another chance, and even when Anna Johanna was too young to understand, I would tell her the dry leaves of autumn that crackled under my feet were telling us that soon we would have snow.

WITH THE ONSET OF COLDER WEATHER, we were grateful for our new tile stove. Sister Elizabeth Schaub asked me to help her put up the new, green curtain we had made for the *Gemeinhaus* meeting room, and by the time Brother Christian Seidel came down from Bethlehem to replace Brother Christian Heinrich as Pastor, I had begun to feel that we were not a mere outpost in the wilderness but, rather, a place of comfort and help for ourselves and our neighbors.

A most wonderful addition to our *Gemeinhaus* came in the form of a small clock, and I watched Brother Foeckel reach just above his head to place it on a wall in our meeting room. The room was quiet. I could hear its tick and tock; its steady, even beats. It will tick away time, I thought, through the hours when sunlight touched the wall, and dark night when not even a candle flickered on the table, and all were asleep but the night watch. It would tick away time through winter's ice storms and the new blossoms of spring, and would continue when our time here has stopped.

Ever since we arrived in the south, there was much concern among our neighbors about possible attacks from the Cherokee. One family of refugees who had left their farm stayed for some days with us, hoping for protection. We had allowed others to build small shacks, and had erected a wooden wall of sorts for their protection. In all fairness, I remember that these refugees helped us with our farm work and were always grateful for our generosity.

"How long can we keep these people?" Sister Schaub was working beside me, pouring water from a large bucket into the pot steaming over a fire in the wash house. "We can't keep them forever, and God knows, although we have saved much, we can't feed the countryside."

I could well understand the feeling of my friend, for we had much, but we had gained our harvest through rising before the sun, only stopping at those blessed times for rest and singing a few times each day until the sun hid behind the now bare trees, and I could begin to think about the luxury of sleep. I looked at my hands, red from the cold outdoors and, I must admit, not the hands I had been rather vain about as a very young girl. I sighed without answering my friend; I, too, wondered sometimes about how much we should give, how much we should work for others. And yet, when I heard the pleading in a young mother's voice or saw the fear in the eyes of an ancient Indian who limped painfully into our clearing, I knew I must help. Suddenly I was aware Sister Schaub was talking to me. "I have such trouble, Christina. I can't always tell if an Indian has come to harm us or ask for food. We don't know much of the Cherokee language . . . " She ceased speaking as she lifted yet another heavy bucket, the steam rising from the washing kettle obscuring her face. It was true. We were told, and I wanted desperately to believe, that we are all one in God's eyes. But when I walked alone from the large barn to the Married People's House, and the sky darkened above me, I wished I had eyes to see behind me.

Weary though I often was, I looked forward to our gathering at the end of the day after we had eaten and cleaned our dishes; to sit and hear news from near and far. Isolated as we were in one sense, the whole world was brought to us by the correspondence among our Brethren. As always, we met together in the *Gemeinhaus* to hear the news from the surrounding territory as well as to hear letters from our far-flung missions. I had just fed Anna and she was not yet ready for her cradle so I brought her with me. Indeed, she fell asleep in my arms after I had settled on one of the benches at the rear of the room. Reports from Europe said that, thanks be to God, our congregations had not been harmed although again terrible war raged, and that the English now reigned in India after the battle of Plessey. Every time news such as this arrived, I was astounded that reports from so far away could come to us in our small Wachovian clearing. And not only stories came across the sea. Manuscripts written by European composers also made their way here sometimes faded, sometimes torn, but our musicians managed to play the music which brightened our evenings and made me forget how tired I felt. I settled my child, heavy with sleep in my lap, and leaned forward to hear Brother Seidel.

"The news close to home seems to indicate that hostile Indians have threatened the frontier of South Carolina and that two thirds of the lower North Carolina militia are ready to assist."

Brother Schmidt stood. "But I have heard that Indians who are friendly to whites have helped that militia."

There was a murmur in the congregation and I, for one, was heartened by this for there was some continuing uncertainty about the Cherokees who lived near us. Brother Seidel had urged us to try to put ourselves in the shoes of our Indian neighbors. But it was difficult. Could they not feed themselves, some asked? And what of those who had murdered families in the farms around us? Were we feeding those who wished to kill us? These questions assailed me like darts in my heart.

AS THE DISCUSSION WHIRLED AROUND ME, my mind fled to one recent autumn day when I had left little Anna with Sister Biefel. I had walked alone in the very early morning. Mist rose from the earth and it was difficult to see well, but a north wind had brought the smell of early winter and the mist seemed scented with snow. I walked slowly, trying to clear my mind as I picked my way over fallen branches and pushed the brittle arms of bushes from my way. It was as though I could hear opposing voices in my mind—one who resented those who asked so much of us, another that wanted to follow the dictum of our Saviour to render to those in need. We, too, have been in need, one voice said. It is only because of our sacrifice that we have filled our barns. But is not sacrifice one way to an awakened heart, another voice intoned? For when we give, we can feel hunger, and it is in that emptiness we can know the need of another. My questions that day were unanswered, and back in the room, with my brethren, my mind still unsure.

"I want you to know that we have decided that the sixty pounds of meat we now have is not nearly enough. We need to slaughter more cattle and pigs if we are going to continue feeding refugees from the farms as well as the Cherokee." Matthew spoke louder than usual.

"Yes," Brother Schaub answered. "Giving food to the Cherokee keeps them happy, and us safe."

Brother Foeckel spoke, "Are we giving to our Indian Brethren out of fear, my Brothers and Sisters? I hardly think this is the case. Rather," nodding to Brother Schaub, "it is because they are in need."

I knew these were important decisions my Brethren were making regarding our harvested goods—how much we could give or sell and how much we should keep for the winter months. We all knew that heavy snow was perhaps unusual here, but nevertheless dangerous in that our livestock could not graze and must be fed from our saved provisions. We must keep our barns full.

Brother Foeckel walked to the front of the room, holding a paper in his hand. Speaking as he walked, he said, "I think it is appropriate to read Brother Spangenberg's message from Bethlehem." He bent close to the page, reading, 'how good it is that you are taking pity on the refugees and their children according to your means. Don't begrudge anything, even if according to appearances you seem to have little profit from it. Deeds of love of this kind will not destroy you, but will much rather bring you greater blessings.'" Foeckel stood quietly for a moment. Then, looking out over our gathering, he said, "I know we are gratified that we have put away much in our storehouses; for there may be times of scarcity to come, and we must be ready to feed ourselves. But we all know the right course of action is to give what we can."

There was silence in the room. I had a momentary feeling of guilt, thinking about how tired I had become of eating pumpkin. Anna stirred again and I loosened the ribbons of her cap.

Brother Rudolph Bachhof stood with both hands flat on the table before him. "We now have serious business to discuss regarding protection of our community here. The news from Bethlehem reports that they have built a palisade surrounding the main buildings. Perhaps we should do the same. I open the floor to all of you who might want to speak."

Brother Loesch rose stiffly. He had been on the road, traveling to Eastern Carolina and although he was used to such journeys, he said his knee was feeling poorly. He bent down to rub his leg and, straightening, said: "The stockade they have built in Bethlehem seems the best I have seen. It is easily made of long, sharpened branches, and doesn't take long to put in the ground."

Brother Foeckel turned his thin face, raising one eyebrow. "While we are digging the holes, you will no doubt be sitting in a tavern in New Bern." I felt a relaxing of the tensions in the room.

"Now just a moment, sir," Brother Loesch rose and limped to Brother Foeckel's side. "I'll have you know that I have been made a Captain in the militia. And furthermore, I may require you to salute on approaching me."

Brother Seidel began to laugh but did not rise from his seat when he said, "Yes, we have all heard about your illustrious time with the Governor. Word for word you have told us all of your explanation regarding our position on bearing arms."

"And a very extraordinary argument, indeed, it was; for we all have agreed that rather than bear arms, we will protect ourselves by organizing a "watch" in case of attack." He then turned from Brother Seidel to address all of us, saying, "I, of course, will be most happy to direct the building of any sort of a barrier or palisade we might construct." He was shouted down by the men, the women joining in the laughter. Brother Foeckel quieted our group by raising his hands and one by one we began to share ideas about building a high fence around our community.

Anna stirred, and I changed her position. While the discussion went on around me, I wondered whether a palisade would make better neighbors; whether a wall would separate us from those who came to us for comfort. Then I heard my husband's voice. He had a thoughtful tone. "I wonder now as I sit here if the building of this stockade will seem a barrier to those who come to us for help." Of course. I might have known he and I would think similarly. But the thought was not put to a vote. We were tired. We were sometimes fearful. It was probably prudent to protect ourselves, and without words we agreed to a consensus.

The night was very quiet as I walked back to the Married Choir's dwelling. There was no moon. I put Anna in her cradle, feeling, rather than seeing, for I had lit only one candle for a moment, and then blew it out before I climbed into my own bed. I knew the morrow would bring much activity, for young saplings would be felled. What lead we had would be melted into musket balls. Just in case, the Brethren said. Just in case.

⚔✳⚔

CHAPTER THIRTY-FIVE

Everyone was very busy that year of 1758. Brother Aust had made and supervised the making of pottery and clay pipes two years before, and this year he was able to produce more roof tiles. At last we had a uniform set of cups for our Lovefeasts, and I was beginning to feel we had begun a more comfortable life here. By the end of the year, we sang with eight musicians who played their separate instruments, their feet tapping the floor, all faces beaming with good will and joy. Already our mill was serving the whole countryside, and as we gathered for a meeting, there was much earnest conversation about the pricing of our grain. There was no doubt that our grain was the best in the area, and some of the Brothers felt we should charge more than others did. "After all," Brother Pfeil stood as he began speaking, "it is well known we mill the finest grain for miles around. I think we should charge quite a bit more than the customary rate." He sat down while the murmur of voices in the room became louder.

Brother Foeckel's tenor voice rose above the others. "Remember, my friends, we are not here to make a profit. We are here to set an example of fairness and . . . "

His voice was drowned out. Even some of the Sisters began to turn to one another, their faces serious, and some looked quite angry. It was at this point that Brother Christian Seidel, who had arrived in Wachovia just after our Anna's birth, rapped on the table in the front of the room, calling for order. He did not speak loudly; in fact, his voice was rather the sound of a bass viol that brings rhythm and pace to a piece of music. I was not surprised when our voices stilled.

"You may all remember," he began, "that I had written to Brother Spangenberg in Bethlehem with questions regarding the pricing of our grain." Brother Spangenberg's rotund form appeared before my mind. His sensible practicality combined with a loving heart had advised us so well through the years.

Brother Seidel continued. "Listen to this and think about it to yourselves for a moment. Spangenberg answered my question with regard to the pricing of our grain thus: "We should be aware of the local pricing, of course. But we could certainly afford to return the charge of grinding to those who were poor, for it would not make us any poorer." A sudden wind blew open the back door and it banged loudly against the wall. I was startled and took Rosina Biefel's hand, but said nothing to her. No one spoke for a moment. Matthew rose to close the door. Brother Loesch, who had arrived several moments before our discussion, spoke from the back of the room, "Since you all know I am but a poor messenger," at this point he put his hand to his brow and limped a bit; "you don't need to charge me anything."

The atmosphere became merry as several of the men turned to this Brother at the back of the room, and laughed. How quickly we all seem to change from the beginnings of anger to moments of hilarity, I thought. Surely our Lamb must be smiling on our *Gemeinhaus* meeting. Then, from the women's side, Sister Schaub called out a loud "Amen" as we rose to leave the building, our arms entwined.

IT HAS BEEN PLEASANT to recall the events that ended in laughter. Some others were more difficult. It was in that year that death came to our settlement for the first time, taking little Anna Maria Opitz who was only a week old. Matthew and I had known Carl and Anna Maria Opitz since we traveled together to the New World on the *Little Strength*. This child was the second babe born here, and Sister Anna Maria and I had often spoken about how our children might be friends as they grew together. Anna Maria must have dreamed the same dreams I did about watching her little girl grow. But she was taken. I could not help but wonder why He had plucked this babe instead of mine. This thought truly bothered me when, anxious, I awakened at night to lean over to hear my little one's even breathing. I did not want to think about my own selfish fears, and shook them from me as we walked slowly up the curved path, through the leafless trees, to the top of the hill to God's Acre. Brother Carl and Henrich Biefel carried the little box on their shoulders. Too light, I thought, too soon had she fled. The gash in the red earth looked very small. Clouds had gathered, perhaps ready for snow, and our group of men and women huddled close against a north wind that pulled at my cape, and disturbed the small bushes nearby. Brother Seidel stood at the edge of the open grave, his coat making flapping sounds around his thighs. Matthew and Brother Henrich Biefel lowered the small box gently, back to the earth, while her soul flew heavenward. We sang then, as trombone notes filled the empty space of sorrow. Hard, hard, it was to lose a little child. Could I bear this loss, I thought? Could I summon the faith I should have that assures me our Lamb takes us to himself? Death brings with it many questions. Perhaps it is more difficult to face the passing of one we love than our own.

SLOWLY, TWO BY TWO, we walked back down the hill. I thought about the child's passage; of passages from the place we find ourselves on earth, to that land to which we go. Bethabara, I thought. Bethabara, which was to be the name of our settlement here in Wachovia, meant House of Passage. How quickly it all happens, I thought, as we reached our clearing at the bottom of the hill. Perhaps "House of Passage" is exactly the right name for this small clearing in the pines and woodlands; for it may exist for a moment in time, and disappear as surely we will.

Much later that evening, Matthew held me close. "Remember, my love, "A generation goes and a generation comes, but the earth remains forever."

My husband was whispering Ecclesiastes in my ear, whispering softly and his voice was a balm to me. He turned me to him. "For everything there is a season, and a time for every matter under heaven; a time to be born, and a time to . . . " He never finished his words for my lips stopped him, and I was filled with life and new strength.

By the close of 1759, our church diarist put his notes together to write of a year filled with joy and progress, but also with great sorrow and trial. We were all gratified to hear news from around the globe, for copies of the diaries of other congregations came regularly to us by messengers. Usually Brother Seidel read the latest reports to us in the evening when we gathered at the end of the day's work, but he had traveled to Bethlehem to return with a bride. We all rejoiced at his news and I, for one, couldn't wait to meet the young woman who would join us. Brother Foeckel, who had taken more and more responsibility in Bethabara, stood before us, papers in hand, his narrow face registering the happy news with a smile, and a slight cough. He read that Count Zinzendorf's son-in- law, Johannes von Watteville, sent word from England that he had organized congregations in Ireland and Wales, and our Unity Press had published our second edition of hymns in Estonian, Lettish, and Esquimaux. I was always interested to hear of our far north brethren and my thoughts traveled back to our meeting with those natives of the north when they had come to Bethlehem. As I sat close to Sister Schaub, I looked at my hands. My fingers seemed to remember the texture of the Greenlanders' fur coats and I smiled to myself when recalling the disappointment Susannah had shown when the women's boots were too small for her.

I LOOKED AROUND ME and saw my Sisters' faces, rapt with interest as Brother Foeckel read. Such a gift from our Saviour it was, to have words on a paper that could bring news to us. As a child, when those strange shapes began to make meaning for me on my slate, I felt I could toss the words in the air, and they would float down around me like ripe blossoms on a shaken bush. I felt myself blush at that childish memory. Yet, as I sat in Bethabara listening to those words of war and progress, of hatreds and love, I was taken away to faraway lands where our Brethren labored, knowing now only too well the difficulties they encountered as well as imagining their gratification in telling of our Saviour's love. Brother Foeckel put his papers down on the table and cleared his throat.

"There are reports of more Indian attacks close by, which means we shall continue to have refugees here. We have all become adept at caring for our neighbors. We all know what to do."

Matthew stood. "Our cattle are very healthy and we have a large supply of grain in our storehouses. We have more than enough to share, thanks be to Him."

FAMILIES KEPT COMING, some from as far as sixty miles away. The wooden gate of our palisade creaked throughout the day and night. Not only did we continue to care for our white neighbors; many Indians of the Cherokee tribe also came to us for food. I became very used to seeing Indians walking our paths. Indians sometimes walked along with friendly militiamen. At other times, families came, carrying young children. They did not usually speak to us women, but once a young Indian woman took my sleeve and spoke seriously. "I thank you," she said in German so I could understand her. Her little one smiled shyly, as I was compelled to touch her smooth cheek with my finger. My heart seemed almost to cease for a moment when I felt her warm skin, and the memory of Esther was clear in my mind. O, God, I thought. Thank you for bringing Esther into my life if even for a short while.

It was a warm spring that year, and we had successfully sowed our grain. I sat in the grass while Anna ran and played, and Anna Maria Optiz held her new babe in her lap. She and her husband had named their daughter Anna Maria, as they had the first who was plucked so soon by our Saviour. She seemed a fat, healthy babe and perhaps would live.

"Christina, I am often very frightened when I hear reports of Indian murder." Sister Opitz said, "Do you think they are true?"

"There is danger all around us, I suppose. But it seems that many times, the reports are exaggerated, and our worry is for naught." She placed her babe on a blanket. "I feel safer now that we have the palisade."

"Well," I said, "I sometimes wonder if it is the palisade that keeps us safe."

"Oh, I know it is our Saviour . . . , I only meant . . . I put my hand on her arm to reassure her. "Dear friend. What I meant was that I think our feeding so many Indians is probably what keeps us safe. I think most know we bear no ill will and do not want to hurt them in any way, but rather to just let them know the good news." Then I began to laugh, "It could be that our tolling bell or trombones have frightened some." We gathered our blankets, and I called to Anna. I could see Matthew as he led a graceful new mare into the stable. She was sleek and beautiful and nuzzled his neck as he reached up to pat her.

As it happened, we were not attacked. Not that year, or any year. The Indians who came to us, sometimes in distress, other times in friendship, complimented us by saying our men rode their horses like the devil. More importantly, we often heard they had said, " 'The Dutch fort' had good bread." No, it was not Indian war that came to us, but something perhaps more devastating.

Summer came quickly. The heat was stifling. I was lifting my hoe to loosen the earth around our poppies in the apothecary garden when the single notes of a trombone interrupted the twittering of forest birds. I knew the tune. It told us of a death in our community. Then a second tune alerted me to the death of a married Sister. O, God, it is Sister Rogers, I thought, for she had been suffering from fever. How does this disease come to us, I wondered again, as I had when my brothers and then my mother succumbed in Gelzhausen? As a child I thought a barely formed cloud-like evil entered a throat, an ear. Now, as a grown woman, I wondered again how this fever came. First the heat, then the rash, then the struggle to breathe and, finally, the silence as our Lamb takes the soul to Himself.

We were terribly overcrowded with those families who had fled to us in fear, and I knew there had been sickness among the refugees. But how, I thought, how could such a frightening thief that lurked around them, rob one of us of life as we bathed the heated bodies and bound the sores? Did the evil humor jump from body to body? Too many had been taken to the corpse house and I knew Sister Roger's earthly remains would be taken also. Then we would carry her to God's Acre, singing the hymns of resurrection and comfort. Though I walk through the valley of death, I will fear no evil. I whispered this to myself, as the funeral tune echoed more often. Could these words protect? Could they be as a prayer, I wondered? For my heart beat in time with my steps as I joined in the small processions up the hill, each word a talisman against fear. But I was afraid.

Sister Seidel was the next to take flight. Her husband, who had been her help-meet for such a short time, was broken-hearted. Cruel, it was. So cruel to have a loved wife taken so quickly; the words of the psalm lost their power when I awoke in the night, hot and afraid what the next day might bring. We all watched Brother Seidel, his back somehow bent now like an old man, as he diligently continued to plan for a new settlement here in Wachovia. Then, he too laid down his head. Matthew said that Brother Christian Seidel uttered his last words in a voice barely audible. "It is the end of life. Lonely without my Catherine . . . I have prayed my God to take me to Himself." And he followed her up the hill.

Brother Martin Kalberlahn worked tirelessly among his patients, and I could see the toll it was taking on his health. Dragging himself from one sick Brother or Sister to another, he barely slept. His new wife begged him to take rest, but this dear man could not sleep when those in his care needed him. One hot afternoon as the sun blazed, and our cows seemed too tired to twitch when flies settled on their ears and eyes, I approached the barn. Hearing an anguished cry, I peeked into the door and saw Brother Kalberlahn on his knees, his head upturned. He sobbed. I knew he was praying for strength and knowledge. O, God, how horrible for him to be helpless as he saw his patients die of this malady. I crept away. He never saw me.

Then he, too, was stricken. His wife said a strange calm came over him as he arranged his earthly affairs. She told us he committed those he loved to his Saviour's care, and passed gently out of our time.

The sickness had left us short of workers, but again, the refugees who were living in their makeshift shacks near Bethabara had offered their help. Side by side, our men and those who were no longer strangers, cut hay, raised more small buildings for the men and women engaged in crafts, and some even joined in our *Singstunde*, bringing moments of peace to us all. The sun set in a huge, orange ball after another day of heat and damp that sapped our strength and even seemed to make the plants cry for mercy. Brother Reuter wrote words of comfort for us all.

"A hundred thousand acre field, now sanctified by tears where reapers passing to and fro, seeking souls ripe for heavenly garner, and bearing them up to present before the throne the first fruits of Wachovia."

A farmer's song that held hope, I thought; for indeed they were the first fruits of those who had praised Him in words and song and the labor of their work. What would be the written words of our diarist for that year? Daily he wrote, but when the year came at last to an end, he would have to tell of struggle, of death. But would he would write how we had been blessed by knowing we loved one another and were loved in our time of trial?

At last, at last, the wind came from the north, bringing blessed relief. First a little breeze that barely moved the tree tops; then, growing stronger, it swept into our clearing, whirling the ashes from the Smithy's forge, and even making tiny whitecaps on the surface of the millrace. God, I wanted to dance; to lift my arms so the wind would take me. I threw my small daughter up into the air to hear her shriek with laughter, and it seemed the very sound lifted the dropping blossoms of late-summer flowers. We gave praise for the cooling weather, because it meant an end to the scourge that had taken so many souls from us. I knew that very soon I would see the yellowing of leaves, and smell autumn apples ripening in the afternoon sun. Reports of Indian attacks nearby continued, but we stood fast in our belief that we should not ever be the first to attack, and all agreed in the wisdom of watchful waiting.

Matthew had been assigned to stand night-watch in the month of December. The weather was not terribly cold, so his duty was not onerous. As dawn approached one morning, I awoke to see if I could catch the glimmer of pink when it blushed the eastern sky over the canopy of bare branches. I saw my husband walking to the barn and on an impulse I had not followed for many years, I hastily took a warm cape, ran down the steps and out of the door to hurry to the barn. I was barefoot and the brown grass was sharp and cold under my feet. Breathless, I opened the large barn door, and pushed it closed again. The few high windows near the roof shone pink and purple and I stopped to gaze up at them in awe. Matthew stood behind me. In my moment of gazing, I had not heard him, but then I felt his arms around me. He bent to kiss my neck and, suddenly, I was very young again, eager for his embrace and warm with desire.

Was it our love-making that morning that brought us our new little son in the following months? Or was it the times we turned to each other in our new little house near the barn that had been built in the early spring? As I heard his first cry, I wanted to believe our new babe had been sent to us when we lay together in that early dawn, with thanksgiving for our lives, and our desire for one another. Such a very little child was this son, but his grasp of his father's finger was strong.

"Perhaps these fingers will make beautiful things," I told my husband. He smiled his slow smile and pushed my hair from my forehead. "And what name should we give this little fellow?"

"Oh, Matthew, I do feel so grateful." At that moment I clearly remember the joy that filled my heart. My cup overflows, I wanted to say, but Sister Ettwein and Sister Optiz were busy with sheets and the babe was being passed so others could give him the kiss of peace and a blessing. I kept my words in my heart. Matthew leaned close then, and said, "I want to praise God. How about giving the child the name Gottlob?"

Brother Gotlieb Foeckel put his arm around Matthew, "Say, how about Got LIEB?"

"We already have you, my friend, loving God. I think my son can have a name that praises God."

So Gottlob it was. This very small boy, red-faced and wrinkled, waved his tiny fists and howled at the world he had entered.

CHAPTER THIRTY-SIX

Susannah Partsch: Bethlehem, 1761

At last I am away from that place! *Ach*, I wonder if I will ever feel cool again. The heat crept into my clothes, even under my skin like one of those loathsome insects that crawl around everywhere. When I first saw the Island of St. Thomas I thought it looked like Heaven. The sea air was warm in June and the breeze blew all day. The voyage only was fifteen days and there was so much to see. There were fish that flew. *Ja*, they flew through the air next to our ship, and other fish swam alongside us. Sister Mack said they were called Dolphins. It felt like a very special journey we were taking to a beautiful land. But all that was before I saw what life was like there.

It was just over a year ago—May, 1760. Brother Martin Mack came into the kitchen as we were finishing the baking for the week. *Mein Gott*, he looked so thin that day. His dark brown hair was blown about in the spring wind, and he stopped to stamp the mud from his feet before he told us what he had come for. I have been grateful to Brother Martin

Mack because he was the person who kept telling me I should say out loud what happened at Gnadenhütten. He was right. Better I felt when I told my Brothers and Sisters. Of course we gave him buns and hot coffee when he sat down on the bench.

"Anna and I have been called to the island of St. Thomas in the Caribbean Sea." He said this quietly and then took a sip of coffee. "Our people have purchased a plantation there, as you probably know. Did you also know that our Saviour has awakened more than one thousand hearts?"

Hard for me it was to think about one thousand people on one island. I think it is way out in the sea. Brother Mack smiled and told me no one made buns as well as me. *Ach*, he was being silly. But I think I was a little pleased. Then George asked him if we could help him gather supplies, and what Brother Mack answered really surprised me. He said that he wanted us to go to St. Thomas, too—to run the plantation there. I think I stopped listening to him. How could he ask us to travel so far after what had happened in Gnadenhütten? George brought his hand to his cheek, rubbing it the way he always does when he is thinking. Then he turned to me, but he was talking to Brother Mack. "Yes, yes, I am prepared to do this."

Not say a word I could say.

My husband did not look away from me. "Dear wife. We have traveled far together. If the Saviour asks us to go, we must listen."

I have learned to know my dear husband. I knew by the look in his brown eyes that he thought this request was very important. But I still could not speak already.

Then Brother Mack said that he badly needed experienced workers. He needed us. I think that is when I knew we would go. The Saviour had always protected us. We do not always know His plans for us, but I have learned to trust whatever comes. I took George's hand. To myself I thought, "We will be cheerful and take the long trip!"

We had one whole month to get ready in that spring—just over a year ago now. *Ach*, so sorry I was to leave our sweet daughters. All six in school learning, our little Louise safe in the good Sisters' nursery. But there is always that hard time when a mother has to say good bye. I trusted our Lamb would bring us safely back here when our work was done in that Island. And he did bring us safely home. But I cannot help but remember our time there; to think over and over again about that place with a beautiful sea around it, and good plants so new to me. How could it have some people who were so cruel? *Ach mein Gott,* I think of our Negro Sister, Rebecca, who spread the gospel. And all the others who were been beaten if they were caught going to the Brethrens' school. So brave, they were; so brave!

Now we are back in Bethlehem. No more scorpions, I tell Sister Wahnert! Now, right now, I hear the sound of hoof beats. From the window I see Brother Matthew Schropp riding toward the *Gemeinhaus.* His saddlebags look very full. I hope there is mail from Bethabara. I run out to meet him and shout, "Brother Schropp. If you give me letters from Bethabara first, I'll give you the biggest bun from the oven." He laughs at me as he swings down off his dappled horse.

He comes into the *Gemeinhaus* and opens the saddle bags as a few of us gather to see what he had brought. There is news of Bethabara. They have had bad fever there. *Ach Gott,* dear Dr. Kalberlahn has been taken Home. Christina is again with child and news is she has fever. I walk outside now to think of my dear friend. I try to remember she is strong. I look up to the trees. They are green again now it is June, and our herbs grow in the garden. Christina and I used to plant herbs all those years ago. *Ach,* we were so young. I pray we will gather herbs together again some day.

CHAPTER THIRTY-SEVEN

Christina Barbara Krause

There is no rain, but the air is heavy with moisture. Our herbs grow like weeds. Who gathers them while I lie here in the room that sways with no rhythm? I feel as though I have been bled; weak, unsure of my step, fearful of leaving my bed. From my window I see the palisade, each pointed stake of wood a spear in the sky. It is cruel looking to me, as though to catch a passing cloud and tear it to wisps. Does it keep the Cherokee from us, or the militia? Or can it stay my death for yet a little while?

The world beyond persists in war and suffers pestilence. There is no safety anywhere. Matthew says we are safe in our Saviour's love if we can but let Him into our hearts. But a palisade surrounds mine, for I cannot let Him in to take me Home.

Perhaps I shall fly from my narrow bed, for I cannot walk. My feet are heavy as though held with ballast. Perhaps I could fly over the spears to see the blue hills beyond. Or farther yet to old Gelzhausen to see the main street and hear again the sound of metal on metal. Suspended as though in a dream, I wish I could trace the path of my journey here one more time, to put it at last on paper. But it is too late. I am too weak to take up the quill.

"We have come to pray with you, Sister."

It is Sister Ettwein. Someone accompanies her. I can tell the one voice though I cannot open my eyes for they are too heavy.

"She swells so. Can Dr. Bonn do nothing?"

I hear the voice. There is concern. I know they are fearful for my condition, but I cannot care. Their voices are moths beating on a lantern.

"Sister Krause—Christina Barbara. We have good news. There soon will be real peace with the Cherokee and we shall be allowed to preach among them."

"We have had a good harvest and more money now that our pottery sold so well. Do you remember the sale?"

Their voices are becoming a drone. They run together. I am hot. I am so heavy.

"Let us help you, dear Sister. We will wash you." They take turns now to put wet cloths on my head and to bathe my arms. I feel cool water on my feet. We used to wash each other's feet in the ancient ritual. The dust of Jerusalem. The dust of America. All the dust. "Will I be dust, my Sisters?"

"Christina, we are all from dust, but our souls rise to meet our Saviour. You must think of this."

"I cannot think of anything."

"Oh, see how the blue veins pulse in her breasts. Is it the gathering milk?"

"It is just the swelling. All her pulses beat. Her blood must be heavy."

I had milk for my Samuel. I thought I would never wean him. That forever he would stay with me, this little mite with his father's blue eyes and a fuzz of brown hair. Was it a short time ago we came here? I must ask my Sisters.

"When was it we came to this place?"

You and Brother Matthew have been here in Bethabara for six years."

She says it is six years. How did I pass that time? I have felt the change of seasons as I walked through them to plant and gather herbs for the sick. What is a year? What are six? I must remember how we got here, Matthew and me. It was autumn. The road was not even a road. I did not weep then, for all my tears were used. There were no more. The deep well was full in Nazareth and I drained it in my sorrow.

"Sister Krause, can you open your eyes?"

I have no reason to open my eyes. They are heavy, heavy. My head throbs in time with the beat of my pulses now. I want to call out to the Holy Spirit who cares for us as a mother to her children. Is this path my way Home? Am I to go there soon? I try to look at my Sisters, but I cannot see well, and the outline of blue hills blurs before me as though my eyes are filled with tears, but there are no tears. Not now. Not then. I did not cry aloud when I took each sweet face in my hands and kissed each tenderly. We made our way slowly, the baggage wagons creaking behind. I turned once, only once.

I feel my poor babe turn from side to side as if my consternation lives within. I stretch to make room. We are together yet. Did you stir, my little one? I will carry you Home with me. It is dark now. Or are my eyes so swollen shut I cannot see the light? Little babe—are you sleeping or awake? Ah, yes, I feel you move. You are still with me, but I cannot keep you. I must not carry you Home. I must push and strain as I have done before. I kick the coverlet. I strain. I will free you so you might hear as I have the calling of an oboe in this southern wilderness.

Someone tucks the coverlet around my body. The Sisters take turns to put cool, wet cloths on my head, and to bathe my arms. I am drifting again into sleep. I feel the cool of the water. I see my friend, Susannah. "Susannah, the days are gray. Do you see land yet? Can you see through the mist?" And you—is it you, Susannah, give an answering whisper. "Sleep now, Christina. The water we bathe you with is cool. There is no mist."

"Matthew. I must see my beloved. Do you remember how you took my hands in yours? Put my hands on each side of your face- You are so young. The lines on your face are gone now, so why do you weep? Here, lie close to me and let me comfort you as you have comforted me. I have seen Anna today and Esther too. Matthaeus and Samuel are coming tomorrow. They will all take hands with Anna and Gottlob to make a circle in our meadow. Feel, feel. Put your hands upon my belly. Can you feel the life still there? There. The babe still moves. What joy.

It remains, nestled, curved, asleep. No one will take it tonight."

"Christina. Can you hear us? We will sing to you."

Yes, they will sing to me. We have always sung, my Sisters and I. Their faces framed in white caps; some barely out of girlhood, some wrinkled softly. Oh, how we sang! Sometimes a note, high and clear, would follow that of a small bird perched on the sill of the open window and heads up, our hands still for that moment, we began. I sang with such joy. Such freedom to open my heart. No house then, no windows, no doors, no stone, cobbled streets or rough, uneven paths through the dark woods. There was only sound. We sang of revelation and sacrifice. We sang of offerings as we offered ourselves and praise as we rejoiced. I am filled yet again with the celebration of living and float above myself, light as air.

"Christina Barbara, you are going Home, my dear."

I hear a voice from far, far. What was it she said? Where is Matthew? Where are my children? I am terribly warm and the swelling is in me. I squint to see. Two children stand by my bedside. 'Oh, little ones, you look so solemn. No, I cannot take your hands. I cannot bend mine.

"Listen, Sister Christina. Can you hear? It is little Anna and Gottlob come to say good bye to you. They know you are going Home."

What is it she says? Listen, my children. Do not be sad. We will travel together the rough road north to see your brothers and sister. It may take time, but the trumpet will blow, and they will know we are coming. I have heard it in the darkness. We will run so fast. We will run and run . . .

"She twists and thrashes about. There, there."

My sweet Sisters. I can see them now. They bend their heads to me, and I feel their hands. The deep voice of a Brother. Is it Matthew? Oh, it must be Dr. Bonn or Dr. Kalberlahn. But no, that good man went Home. We took him up the hill and the trombones played. His wife, Catherina, tried so hard not to weep. What is this they give me? I taste a bitterness. I will not let the bitterness get to my little babe.

Where is my husband, my only love? Ah, I cannot see, but you are here. Do you remember how we loved? Do you know though I followed you, doubt often shrouded my heart? Doubt and bitterness. Now there is heat. I am pierced with the fiery dart, and oh, my love, my Saviour, the center of me is filled with your heat and burning. I am burning with heat, but what a clean burning it is that consumes me. The watery swelling is turning to fire and I burn. The fire turns to liquid gold as it courses throughout my body. What is being burned away in this rush? What is being purified—for I know with certainty I am being purified. Bitterness is burned. Fear is burned. Longing is burned away. But love remains. I see without eyes and I hear without ears. Without feeling, I feel. And love remains.

Oh, my love, gather me in your arms.

EPILOGUE

Susannah Partsch: Bethlehem, 1794

My old ears cannot hear the trombones, even though the three musicians stand under my open window. I think I feel the sound in my breast. Now they walk away down the street. The sun is bright on their instruments. *Ach*, there is my grandson, Johann. He tags along behind. He is only thirteen—a good boy. He shows me how to put my hands on our organ when Brother Pieter plays, so that I can feel the notes. My daughter, Anna Benigna, worries about him. She says he does not pay attention. But I know better. I watch his face when he listens to music, and already he plays well the trumpet. He has clever hands like his grandfather, Matthew Krause. When Matthaeus and Anna Benigna stood together to marry, they were in their thirties already. I knew he would be a kind husband to our daughter. On that spring day, I felt as though maybe Christina was standing next to me when our children were joined together. Can those who have gone Home know how it is for us here? I wonder. There he runs to follow the musicians, my Johann. He waves to me. Such joy I get from my Saviour.

A few weeks ago, Anna Benigna came here to the Widow's House to stitch with me. She said I could not hear as well as I used to. *Ach*, I know this. I do not need her to tell me. I have missed for years already the sound of waking birds and of rain dropping from the eaves. I still spin, and when I look at the young Sisters' faces, I can tell from their lips what they say. Sometimes I turn away. My Sisters who traveled with me are gone. And I am left.

So, I sit. But in my quiet I can hear the sounds of other days. Especially at night, when the wind rises a little, I feel it on my face. I hear in my head the call of the trombones that sent us on our great mission. I remember the trumpets that tell of birth, and welcome our people after they have been far away. I feel in my heart the sound of the chapel bell rung so long ago by Joachim Sensemann. My ears cannot hear it. But it orders my days yet. The cough comes more often now. My body has lasted, but it wears down. I am not surprised. I have traveled here longer than most of them.

My door moves. I see Dr. John Freitag. He pokes his head through the opening. I start to walk over to him but he waves his hand for me to sit again in my wooden rocking chair. His little round eyeglasses sit down on his nose. He smoothes a little wisp of hair over his bald head. Now he sits opposite me, and takes my hand in his. I look at his lips. He says I should write my memoir now. To myself, I have to smile. I am a simple woman and have worked for my Saviour without reading or writing much. I cannot write my life-story. He sees me look out the window after he asks, so now he presses my hand. *Ach*, what could I say? What is there to tell? Myself in Büdingen—what a skinny little one. And scared. I did not know I would grow big and strong; that I would braid my hair in one thick braid; that I would wind it under the little cap. And do I tell what happened before I grew—the terrible things? The wars I have seen; the places I have been? I would like to tell about my Sisters; dear Susannah Nitschmann who listened to my story. To me she was kind. *Mein Gott*, I wept when she was captured by the outlaw Indians. She died far away in the snow.

So long ago now, Christina journeyed south. She took my hands in her smaller ones; my quiet friend who left me so soon. It was thirty years ago Brother Loesch came here from Bethabara with the news. He said Christina went Home. Her babe was still with her. He said Matthew began his journey to our heavenly Home only nine months after Christina. Brother Loesch said he had a fever. *Ach*, he had no fever. He had a broken heart.

I want to tell about my dear George and how I grew to care about him. How hard it was to lose him. And of my eight daughters who love the Saviour. What does he say, Dr. Freitag? He puts his hand on my shoulder and I look again at his face. He wants me to tell how our dear Lamb has watched over me. *Ja*. I can say that. And to tell, too, of the fire and burning again. I was strong with my Saviour to hold my hand. I did not fall.

He takes out his quill and the paper is spread on a book. How to do it? I begin, "I was born 4th December, 1722 in Büdingen on the Wetterau. My father was Johann Justin Eller of Hoch Schieserdenber, who died before I was born. My mother raised me until I was seven . . ." I can tell him of the attack. How I jumped to the ground, but I begged the Saviour to tell me what to do . . .

I feel the cough again in my chest. I want the Doctor to go. I will not look at his face, so then he will leave. More blood this time—maybe this is a wound in my chest, as His sacred Head was wounded. His side torn.

I am alone again. I pour water from the pitcher and wash. I will kneel, but my legs are so stiff and bend slowly. I need to hold on to something to rise. Soon the apple trees will be heavy with white blossoms. Later, after the heat of summer, I pray the Saviour will still let my old hands gather the fruit into my apron. *Ach mein Gott*, I have worked and now I wait.

Tomorrow I will wake early again to smell the bread baking in the kitchen. I will see the crocus blooming purple by the door. One morning, I will put my hand in His for my last journey to see my dear ones again. A good *Schwester* will play the cittern as I start on the path.

I will be ready to go Home.

ACKNOWLEDGMENTS

I have spent several years thinking about how best to tell the little-known Moravian story. Close friends urged me to get busy with this work, although I was often detoured onto other paths. Knowing that the Moravians kept voluminous records did help in my decision to write about these interesting Protestants; also, my travels to other parts of the world gave me a sense of how my ancestors and their fellow Moravians lived, creating settlements of peace and harmony. As far away as South Africa, my husband and I heard a Moravian church bell toll over flat fields where ostriches raised their heads to listen; and on the lovely island of St. Thomas, another bell called the Congregation to come and sing. In earlier times there, a conch shell summoned the slaves to worship although their gathering often incurred their masters' wrath. In Prague, the immense statue of Jan Hus seemed to reach out to me; and the friendly people in Herrnhut and Herrnhaag, Germany eagerly showed me the buildings my ancestors had helped to build, and the gardens they tended with such care.

In Bethabara, North Carolina, we hiked the forest path to Christina's and Matthew's graves, flat stones in the red earth. The welcoming staff in Bethabara told us of those Moravians who walked from Pennsylvania to settle the North Carolina wilderness, and even allowed me to play (with one finger) the organ in the chapel! Richard Starbuck, assistant archivist of the Moravian Historical Society of the Southern Province, showed me the beautifully drawn maps of the Old Salem area. He and archivist Daniel Crews were always prompt in sending me any needed information, however arcane.

I sat many hours in the stone Whitefield house in Nazareth, Pennsylvania with Susan Dreydoppel, former executive director of the Moravian Historical Society in Nazareth. She and Mark A. Turdo, former curator of the Moravian Historical Society, showed me diaries, letters, and pictures of 18th-century American Moravian life on the frontier. I am grateful to them for their expertise in teasing out fact from fiction—not an easy job! And I must admit, I have spent quite some time walking the paths in Bethlehem's God's Acre having imaginary conversations with those long gone who have become like silent friends. I hoped they were listening. Peggy Jarrett and Joe Morris, cousins, invited me to stay in the "Krause House" on Bethlehem's Market Street, and it was there that the Moravian scholar,

Beverly Smaby, gave me much information I needed for my work.

The Moravian Archives in Bethlehem are a quiet place that hold the life-stories, (Lebenslaufe), of thousands of Moravians. Paul Peucker, archivist, has always been more than helpful to me as he carries on the work of the formidable Lothar Madeheim who translated many yellowing sheets of paper written in old German script as we studied the lives of Moravian women. Suggestions of books to read, manuscripts to pore over, all are freely given by those who work there. But now, there is a sadness when I think about the Bethlehem Archives, for Reverend Vernon Nelson is no longer there, having "been plucked into eternity" too early. From the start of my work, he encouraged and helped me. His careful reading of my manuscript for historical accuracy has been invaluable. I must now add him to my silent friends who rest in God's Acre and Nisky Hill.

Moravian music lightens my day. I have held the sheets of music, handwritten by my great-great-grandmother, marveling at her neat hand. I listen often to the recorded sacred and secular music that came from the pens of the early Moravians, and thank Doctors Paul and Jan Larson for their information on my cousin, J. Fred Wolle, and the Bach Choir.

So many friends and colleagues have helped to make this book come to fruition. Sid and Pat Moody read early drafts, and I crown Sid the "comma king!" Bob and Connie Gates offered expert suggestions which I eagerly accepted. Dorothy Clair, friend and editor, added her expertise to the Foreword. I thank Professor Janet Loengard who was the first person to introduce me to the Archives in Bethlehem. I so appreciate the fact that Professor Marvin Bressler, who has inspired many scholars through the years at Princeton University and elsewhere, has listened to my Moravian raving with great patience. Finally, my dear friends, authors Mira Stillman, Ph.D. and Joan Weimer, Ph.D. professor emeritus, Drew University, have shepherded me through the long process of writing a book. I treasure their love and help.

It was on the steps of the Central Moravian Church in Bethlehem that I first met Patricia N. McAndrew, of Moon Trail Books. I felt an instant kinship! The team of McAndrew, publisher, and Kenneth F. Raniere, author and designer, have produced a more beautiful book than I ever dreamed. I thank them for listening, for editing, for knowing their craft and becoming my friends.

And a special thanks to Mary Dowd Washburn, direct descendant of Christina Barbara Krause and Susannah Eller Partsch, for lending her likeness for use to the cover.

ABOUT THE AUTHOR

Barbara Dowd Wright is a native of Illinois, but has lived in New Jersey for many years, where she practiced psychotherapy. She obtained her Ph.D. in psychology and religion from Drew University. Dr. Wright lectured on the Moravians during Bethlehem, Pennsylvania's 250th anniversary celebration in 1992, and has spoken at Lehigh University, as well as other venues in Pennsylvania and New Jersey.

Her first book, *Jewish Renewal in America*, was published in 2005. *An Awakening Heart* is her first novel.

Barbara Wright is married, the mother of two sons, two daughters, and grandmother of six.